MANIFEST DESTINY

AN UNHOLY ALLIANCE

JAIDEN BAYNES

BAVIAAR PUBLISHING

Manifest Destiny: An Unholy Alliance

Published in Canada by BayMar Publishing 2022
www.baymarpublishing.com

For questions and comments about this book, please contact us at info@baymarpublishing.com

ISBN 978-1-7780887-6-6 (paperback)
ISBN 978-1-998753-00-0 (hardcover)
ISBN 978-1-998753-01-7 (electronic book)

CONTENTS

FOREWORD

"I am writing this book so that the true past of the Empire may be disseminated among the masses. Many know our great nation's past only through snippets and rumors so it is his Majesty's greatest hope that this shall settle the matter. After all, history ought to be written by the victors. This is not a story, or a romanticized fairy tale, simply an empirical retelling of all my experiences in serving. I would not lie to you. Follow these easy steps of advice and lessons contained in these events and you too can be a successful citizen of the Empire."

Norne von Arcosia

If any of this were true, the book might
have been something like this…

INTRODUCTION

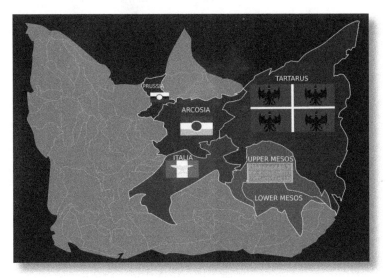

The Star Map of Eurasia

T he borders of nations in the stars are drawn by connecting their furthest most planetary holdings to give the nation its shape. This does not mean that they fully control territory within those borders but rather that no other state is allowed to vie for territory within those lines. Any violations of this gentleman's agreement can lead to war…

Countries

Tartarus: The largest Empire in the known Universe. Formerly a loose collection of tribes called Caucasia that were conquered by the ancient Remans and renamed Tartarus. In the wake of Reme's collapse Tartarus became an expansive imperial force in its own right.

Arcosia: Tartarus' old rival and sometimes ally. Another group of "barbarians" that rose up with their own empire after the collapse of the Remans. It is a hyper-religious theocracy where the church and state are one and Arcosianism dominates the country from the shadows.

Prussia: A hyper militaristic daughter nation of Arcosia that seceded from the Kingdom during a time of decline.

Italia: A powerful, militant and protofascist nation built on the ruins of the old Reman Empire that is seeking to reclaim the former glory of its progenitor civilization.

Mesos: The oldest Empire in the known Universe and the former heartland of a much larger Empire that once controlled all of Middle-Asia. The current nation is divided into Upper Mesos (old lands of the Lugal that survived the collapse) and Lower Mesos (territories that were reclaimed after the collapse and are run by the warrior prince who is in charge of reconquest).

POWER

*"The strong do what they can and the
weak suffer what they must."*

—*Thucydides*

Power is the most important thing in existence, but what is Power? Power is understood to be universal and can be found all around this fantastical realm, having been present since the inception of the Universe. Power grants humans complete domination of the laws of the Universe so that their will is manifested in reality. It can grant people strength beyond imagining, speed beyond comprehension, and to some, even eternal life. Power lets them break rules they didn't even know existed—the cosmic speed limit of light, the law of conservation of energy, and the Schwarzschild radius are all meaningless to its casual subverters.

Power is energy, that can be perceived and manipulated by certain humans who possess it, giving them the ability to enforce their will and manifest whatever they desire. Power is beyond reproach, beyond critique. The naked eye cannot perceive it and powerless people cannot act upon it, instead, they can only wait to be acted upon by it. A million people without Power would be helpless against one with it. It is a miracle to those who wield it and a curse to those whom it is wielded against.

Power exists in units of reality-warping energy that are each responsible for bending reality a little bit. The more of this Power one has, the more one can defy the limits of reality and the greater the supernatural phenomena they can generate. The measurable units of Power that allow for these unnatural phenomena are like photons, yet they are decoupled from many of the third dimension's restrictions. It can take on the properties of any force or phenomenon in the Universe and mimic all its properties without any of its restrictions. However, in its default natural state, it behaves a lot like light.

The general abilities afforded to anyone with Power are:

- Enhanced strength and speed to unreasonable levels, comparable to gods when seen by powerless humans. This is achieved by manipulating the mass and acceleration of their bodies to output unbelievable amounts of force.
- Firing raw Power as beams, bolts, or blasts that can destroy targets at the atomic level.
- A shield of raw Power is able to nullify the above-said attacks, high energy, or extreme temperature to keep the shielded user safe (it is not always active, though, and without it, they are as vulnerable as a regular human).
- Control of the size and scale of not only the attacks but also the damage they do. The "density" of Power controls how much damage it does or how much is required to bring about the desired effect.
- A "Mind" that manages anything done with Power similar to the brain's control of the physical body. Needed for processing high-speed movements and thoughts.
- Telekinesis, including flight capabilities and telepathy with others who possess Power.
- Control over and emulation of the many forms of energy in the Universe, including most commonly kinetic and thermal energy.

- An alternative source of energy from the body. Anyone who possesses Power can survive without air, food, or water as long as their bodies have Power.
- A limited supply of Power that is exhausted with and distinct from their maximum Power output (though often a large supply and a large output capability go hand in hand).
- The ability to detect other sources of Power be it people or natural collections of it. Similar to a human ability to feel heat and ascertain the source's location.
- The ability to gain further Power, by exercising the Power they have. Use increases both their reserves and output (strength) but the most effective way to grow in Power is to put it to the test against a powerful foe—the more it is used, the more it increases.

The higher one's level of Power, the more of those abilities listed previously, and the greater potency of each is available to them. The greater the amount of Power, the rarer the group. The rarest are those born with enough Power to enable them to move or crush planets and race faster than the speed of light. The overwhelming, excessive, physics-breaking gap is incomprehensible for the average human. Power is unfairly distributed. Power is inherited. Power is EVERYTHING.

Power is manifested in two ways by users—Type A manifestation and Type B manifestation. The two types have different uses and simultaneously pull from the total Power amount that one can utilize.

Type A (often called something roughly translating to strength) is a form of Power which interacts with physical matter in the third dimension similarly to kinetic energy. Type A Power is used to enable the user to utilize telekinesis, flight, otherworldly strength, and high-speed movement, as it controls both strength and speed.

Type B (often called something roughly translating to energy) is Power in its rawest form and exists in a state unlike anything else in the third dimension. Being most similar to light-like bosons, it is typically used to fire as projectiles or create energy shields with.

Neither Type A nor Type B Power is one-hundred percent efficient in its manifestation, so efficiency for each type must be trained separately. The result is that people often only specialize in one type or the other.

People born with Power are born with random amounts of each type of Power. They often display an affinity for one type over the other, however. People naturally born with more affinity for Type A Power are more likely to specialize in Type A usage and vice versa. These starting amounts have strong correlative influences from parental affinities. If a parent uses primarily Type A, for example, it is likely that their child will as well.

Adamant is matter that contains Power within its molecules; often maintaining a field of Power around it, it is changed by the Power. Adamant's most common attribute is ludicrous durability; if the quality is high enough, it can even survive a nuclear explosion or supernova. It can be found in naturally occurring deposits around planets or asteroids, metallic ore, or simple crystalline molecules.

IMMORTALS

"Death may be the greatest of all human blessings."

—*Socrates*

Humans are unique in the Universe as the only things that can control Power; animals cannot use it and as such cannot even detect its existence. Most people, through hard work and determination can control Power even if they are just regular matter as well. Power normally cannot interact with biological matter or other overly complex molecules; however, people can be born as pure Adamant. People born as Adamant are called Immortals. Those who are not can be called mortals, peasants, Untermensch, or any other derogatory minimizer of their value.

As the name implies, as long as they have Power, Immortals cannot die from old age. In fact, their bodies cease aging entirely once they enter their primes (about the age of 25). They look just like a regular human, feel the same and breathe the same, (though they do not need to breathe and can survive on Power alone) but their bodies can activate certain abilities. Immortals can regenerate from any non-Adamant inflicted injury. Damage received from Adamant will also heal once the Power lingering in the wound dissipates, assuming it is not critical. Regeneration normally requires minimal energy and most Power lost from taking damage is lost when the hit causes them to leak large amounts of Power. In essence, regeneration will occur as long as an Immortal has the Power required.

When an Immortal's Power reserves are low, all of the privileges it grants are weakened and when they run out of Power, they are just as weak as a normal human.

Immortals can be killed, only by doing critical damage to their brains or completely depleting their massive reserve of Power. However, Adamant makes them mortal, so Adamant weapons can kill Immortals like a regular weapon could kill a normal human. Again, the effectiveness of the weapon and the regeneration vary by the Power of the attack and the victim. Death by a thousand cuts is technically possible with a high enough quality Adamant weapon, so even with their regeneration, Immortals tend to still block and dodge attacks using Power.

Adamant poisons exist but are hard to produce en masse and so remain rare and expensive (a luxury for the nobility to use). A less consistently effective, but equally viable strategy would be to administer regular poison at the same time as Adamant so that the target is made vulnerable, and the regular poison can affect them.

Less than 0.001% of people are Immortals yet the nobility is almost completely comprised of them. The rest are normal mortals, a great majority of whom are as weak and powerless as the humans of earth.

Immortals tend to keep each other's company and detest mortals as inferior. When Immortals die, they become Monsters—terrifying manifestations of the Power they wielded in life.

After all, the impacts of great men do not simply vanish upon their deaths. The consequences of their actions will reverberate through the world long after. Immortals are superior and more powerful than normal humans in every way, but does that justify their tyranny over them?

HISTORY

Humans existed on many planets with surprisingly habitable earth-like ecosystems. Identical in intellect, physiology, and diversity of peoples to the humans of earth, these populations each embarked on their own paths to make history. But lurking among them all, were a select few of great Power and ambition.

With more Power than any one person should ever have, they conquered their homeworlds and from there, they looked up. The Power of these godlike superhumans could not be contained by mere planetary conquest—they needed more.

With Power, even traveling across the vastness of space was trivial. With Power, they could fly anywhere and bring their ambition and tyranny with them. No planet or star system or even galaxy was safe from their ambitions any longer. A nation was no longer restricted to a plot of land on a single rock, but instead could now span planets and even galaxies.

These were the first Empires—great states that grew like cancers all over the cosmos as they drained their fellow humans of everything, simply to enrich and empower themselves. Resources drove several key players to emerge and swallow each other whole in the chaotic era of mass nation formation.

In this chaotic time, the Italic Empire of Europa struggled for dominance with the Mesos Empire of Asia. They alone weathered the collapse of the age of gods with enough strength to absorb their neighbors and survive.

The Italic Empire believed that the Universe existed in several ages:

The Golden Age where godlike men lived in abundance and the strong served as guardians of humankind to protect the weak and the needy.

The Silver Age of stupid humans whose hubris brought about their own destruction.

The Bronze Age of warlike people who killed one another so that the species' number nearly reached extinction.

The Heroic Age of noble god-like heroes whose piety and strength brought back some of the lustre of the ideal golden age. This is the age of myth that many cultures look back to fondly.

And finally, the Iron Age—the final age. A cruel age where warlike men returned and existed in strife and toil as they were abused by their leaders. It was a wicked age that would grow ever worse while awaiting divine retribution from the Olympian gods when humankind reached ultimate baseness.

But in reality, there is no final age. Time marches on and Empires are vile in any age.

Italia and its old rival, Mesos, both collapsed as Empires are known to do (though notably centuries off schedule from the incessantly dour bronze age eschatology). Thus, the entirety of this region in space was thrust into a dark age.

After wasting centuries on squabbling for the leftover Power, their descendant states coalesced around old centers of Power from their parent empires. So many new empires were born. These sick fools naïvely longed for the days long past—the iron age, an era despised by its own inhabitants. Idolizing this imagined past, they refused to learn anything new and instead built their own societies to emulate the failed past ones.

The Italic successor states, beyond the new Italic Empire that lives in the ashen shadow of the two old great powers, have emerged to contend for the throne of the imperialists that spawned them. The Holy Arcosian Empire dominates the Europan region economically and culturally, but military power has long rested with the Tartarian Empire which spans across both Europan and Asian space.

Greatly accelerating the advancements of Tartarus and Arcosia were the inventions of Codices or 'books' as methods of keeping information for future generations and users. History, technology, and religion, all were sustained and propagated by books. Slaves and clergy would spend their days mass producing them from master copies onto the animal skin pages bound within the front and back covers. There were no cover pictures or illustrations—books were not for children. The covers were only adorned with the title and author, identifying what collection of text was being observed. Within them were quotes and ideas—some good, some bad, but all useful.

Technology wise, Tartarus was respectably advanced in regaining the lost technologies of the old Italic Empire. From insulated housing using layers of stone walls, to indoor plumbing using sewage canals not unlike the ancient Minoans, they have done everything they can to revive the failed past within their own borders.

However, after centuries of fighting for supremacy, a brief upset in Tartarus came in the form of a mysterious crisis. The strange event led to a civil war and coup which shifted the balance of power. The King of Tartarus only barely retained Power and found himself ruling over a weakened and declining state. An unofficial shared hegemony of Arcosia and the recovering Tartarus, bound the other kingdoms in a shaky alliance—the Imperial Core of Eurasia. Rather than battling fellow nations of the Imperial Core, they would divert their attention to exploiting the weaker, less developed nations in the Imperial Periphery.

Once they have plundered all they can and restored their strength, the superpowers can settle their score—the new stars Tartarus, Arcosia and the old generation Mesos and Italia—only one can rule overall, and their eternal deadlock can only hold for so long.

Nature abhors stagnation; all it ever seems to produce is repetition. No stage of humanity's violent, bloody past is any more desirable than the last. In them there are no ideals, only potential lessons.

JAIDEN BAYNES

STEP 1

FIND YOUR FIGUREHEAD

"But now, instead of discussion and argument, brute force rises up to the rescue of discomfited error, and crushes truth and right into the dust. 'Might makes right,' and hoary folly totters on in her mad career escorted by armies and navies."
—*Adin Ballou*

CHAPTER 1

The nation of Tartarus was a massive, militant, but still unstable kingdom that, come hell or high water was intent on one thing—expanding.

It had at its heart a capital planet also named Tartarus on which the capital city and origin of the Empire stood. This planet, like its kingdom, was horrendously unstable with the northern half being engulfed in an eternal ice age, and its southern half being so bombarded by meteors that it resembled the magma-filled hellish world of the ancient Hadean earth. Save for a few military outposts, volcanic fruit farms, and mines in the southern half, inhabitants of the planet resided primarily on the northern half where the massive capital city of Eizberg served as the heart of the Empire.

Ever covered by snow, the meltwater of a lake by the same name flowing from the volcanic hemisphere, ensured the temperature of Eizberg was at least tolerable in the summer months, boasting a modest ten degrees below freezing at its warmest. The concept of an exact temperature measurement, however, was beyond the scope of a Tartarian. Their primitive thermometers worked on levels of freezing and melting. The alcohol-filled tube that indicated the bone-chilling cold had been frozen over for some time, which was not a good sign.

This mountainous home world of theirs was once called Caucasia by its native inhabitants. However, when it was conquered and colonized by the Reman Empire, its hostile environment earned it the name Tartarus after the gloomy underworld of the Italic peoples. Even after Italia lost control of Tartarus the name stuck since they now fashioned themselves a successor of Reme.

The proud purple, dragon covered flag once hung on every building, but times were tough and for both economic and morale reasons, the people had long since ceased this very expensive show of support for the monarchy. Purple dyed flags weren't cheap and the nobility's expectation that they be purchased anyways paired with them being curiously unaffected by the nation's nearly two-decade slump inspired something else much more strongly than nationalism.

Despite the biting cold, the capital saw its residents bustling through the streets, shopping from the smuggled goods of spoils retrieved from previous outward conquests. The guards on duty nearby, looked the other way while the black marketeers sold the stolen goods right off the docks for anyone passing through. They had bigger problems to deal with than petty theft.

Near the market, on a small hill on which grew the only tree in the area, a young woman with hair as white as snow, watched the people passing by with contempt. She reclined comfortably in her beautiful princess gown and cape adorned with cute fuzzy fur trimmings, the purpose of which was to keep her warm in the tough Tartarus climate.

Begrudgingly used to the cold, she remained pale and unaffected in the Tartarus winter looking almost like a picturesque princess doll. Most people passing by would adore her as a beautiful foreigner as she sat there exuding the elegance, accompanying royalty, that the people had come to expect from the residents of their sister country, Arcosia. The snowy-haired people famous for cold and doll-like appearances, were rare in Tartarus, giving the uncommon trait an exotic air. In her homeland, brilliant hair and light complexions were signifiers of the master race that sat atop the hierarchy of the swarthy mortal thralls, the mixed commoner Karls, and noble white Jarls.

As she reclined on the hill, the girl read through a blood-red book with a matching set of ominously red eyes, a famous attribute among Arcosian nobility. The unusual shade of eyes confirmed the status bestowed upon her from birth, which was the pride of any Arcosian fortunate enough to sit that high on the proverbial totem pole.

Many admired the presence of such an exotic sight gracing their lowly commoner streets. However, that sentiment was quickly supplanted by another. People who walked by would stop to admire her but suddenly hurry away after being disturbed by the eerie laughter emanating from the otherwise normal-looking girl. As she read through the book titled, *Military campaigns and conquests of King Drakon I*, the girl could not help but snicker at every page turn. Each new horror and atrocity found between the covers of the book would turn most readers' stomachs in disgust. This girl, however, consumed them with delight.

"Wonderful. If I must be married off to his halfwit of a son, at least I know that in my father-in-law I would have a fellow admirer of my more select interests. I guess there *are* upsides to this union besides not being cousins," the girl thought to herself.

She was currently avoiding meeting with the Prince of Tartarus, her betrothed, to instead read her history of Tartarus book and laugh at the list of horrific atrocities committed during the consolidation of its modern territories and expansion of its borders.

"Perhaps this place will be a nice change of pace from home after all." she thought to herself while looking around. Suddenly, she saw an Arcosian religious temple opening with the holy women and soothsayers known as the Nornes exiting the temple to perform their daily ritual to "glimpse the future".

The girl scoffed at the women's ritual. She scowled since, after all, she herself was named Norne. It was almost like a condemnation from birth to be relegated to Arcosia's priesthood in light of being the second-born Princess. She had no chance of succeeding the Arcosian throne. Her fate was to be sold to another country for political gain the instant she came of age. But, for Norne, being married off in a country she hated was preferable to being an Arcosian priestess.

The Norne women went about the ritual. Their snowy white hair, matching her own, identified them as either Arcosian immigrants from a noble class, or "filthy half-breeds" who retained that ever so important white hair. After all, while they received converts from any race or creed, Arcosian temples could only accept servants and officials from the master race to serve their god. Even abroad, communing with the Arcosian deity was a matter of utmost importance for any self-respecting Arcosian. But all of that seemed silly to her.

Going back to reading her book, she turned to the page detailing when Arcosia and Tartarus were once at war. An ancient tapestry depicted the Tartarian soldiers razing an Arcosian temple to the ground with all its inhabitants being put to death by the sword. A mere dispute over mining access in the region had gotten badly out of hand during that conflict.

The Arcosian religion had only recently been permitted in Tartarus as part of the peace treaty that ended the conflict. Seizing the opportunity, the head of Arcosia's religion was pushing for converts, especially among the veterans who were used and discarded by Tartarus. She had already begun this campaign by sending evangelists among the POWs and soldiers in hospitals during the conflict. A stark contrast to the persecution and near eradication of Tartarian king worshipping zealots who nearly wiped out Tartarian converts during the war and wreaked havoc throughout Arcosia, pillaging churches and slaughtering clergy. Norne preferred that violent time to her own more peaceful one.

"Ah…the good old days. A shame that being a mere breeding tool for these mongrels means I can't just finish the job." Norne laughed sadistically. People passing by were weirded out by her sinister laughter which clashed with her otherwise innocent appearance. Taking notice of the onlookers, Norne snarled at them and pulled her book up to cover her face.

"Nosy plebeians. I take it back. I hate this planet. The lower half is a magma-fest and this half is tormented by snowfall ten months of the year and hail the other two. It would take a real fixer upper to make this useless dump worth anything." She huffed as she turned to the next page of her book.

With judging eyes, she observed the town below. As she did so, she criticized everyone, commenting to herself about the gross mismanagement she beheld. "Food lines?" she scoffed.

"What a shock. Honestly, arctic planets are obviously not good at produce production, which is why they need to line up like animals to get tiny scraps of food. Idiots. And selling that many wisent pelts? I understand supply and demand, but they could raise their prices higher if they didn't worry about providing for *every* loser on the planet. Hel, if they keep going like this, they are going to run out of wisent pelts entirely. What a joke. I could run this place better myself."

She continued to scan the marketplace below. "Ooh," she cried, her eyes landing on a particular spot. "The kvass stands are still in stock. That pastry is their only valuable export in my eyes. I guess there is always a diamond in the rough no matter where you go, and kvass certainly is the diamond here."

Suddenly, something moving through the town, caught her eye. "Is that…a flasher?" She let out a laugh as she saw a giant naked man walking about in a confused daze below. The bewildered giant looked around as the townsfolk drew away from him, nervously avoiding eye contact and covering the eyes of any unfortunate children in the area.

"Hey, big guy," Norne called, waving at him.

The man turned to see her holding out her oversized cloak. Smiling, he walked over and took the piece of clothing offered to him as Norne looked away, waiting for him to cover himself up with it. When she turned back to check on his progress, she watched in horror as the giant began chomping on her beautiful royal cloak like it was food.

Shocked, she pulled it away crying, "WHAT IS WRONG WITH YOU!"

In response to this sudden outburst, the tall man standing before her, simply tilted his head like a confused animal.

Annoyed by the lack of a more dramatic response, Norne took a moment to study the man's appearance. She noticed that whilst the gorgeous nine-foot-tall Italic sculpture of a man had the famous Arcosian white hair, his blood red eyes were unlike those associated with common Arcosians who, once stripped of their social status and reverence, had red eyes that could more accurately be described as bright brown.

She had heard that there were people in Italia who possessed their own distinct form of red eyes. There were also other noble Immortal lineages, she knew, that each had their own unique optic tints. Wherever those eyes were from, however, Norne knew for a fact, that they were *not* Arcosian. It occurred to her that the fiery demonic glare she was intently studying might not even be human.

"Some kind of half-breed?" Norne wondered aloud.

The man just blinked at her like an undomesticated creature encountered somewhere in the wild.

"Can you understand me?" she asked him in her native language. Deciding he couldn't, she continued, "if you can't speak Arcosian—" she switched to the local language, "can you speak Tartarian?"

The tall man just scratched his head in confusion before grunting like a caveman.

"A mute?" she wondered. "No. He was able to grunt," she argued. "He couldn't grunt if he were mute. He seems to be some kind of savage. As a last-ditch effort, I might be able to get him to leave me alone if I can communicate with him telepathically. Of course, that's assuming he has the Power to send and receive mental messages without worrying about language barriers," Norne planned.

"Hey, can you not speak or something?" she asked him mentally. She sent the message for him to compute as raw data, not unlike machine learning wherein streams of data can be understood and "translated" into things the receiver can understand, which is, of course, the core idea of communication.

"Oh!" the giant mentally cried out. "That wasn't my thought! Is someone else speaking in my mind again? *Father?* How are you back?" He looked worriedly around in a growing panic.

"No. It isn't your father, it's me," Norne explained, "the girl in front of you."

He looked down at her, "the little one who looks like a woodland creature and yet wears the skin of such a creature herself?" he asked.

"Little one?!" she cried indignantly. Then in reply to the snide comment made about her clothing, she continued, "I'm sorry I cannot walk around in the state of nature like you can, meathead. If you are able to understand the concept of *wearing clothing*, then please, follow suit! Now, wear the cloak, idiot, and do *not* eat it," Norne instructed forcefully, then sighed.

"Thank you," said the man, taking the cloak and donning it this time. The size difference between the two of them was so remarkably great, that Norne's full-sized cape could only serve as an after-shower towel for him, so he wore it around his waist like a loincloth. "I'd hate to hit myself on something by mistake fully exposed." He laughed as he sat next to Norne.

She looked up from the book she had continued reading again and looked him over. "You're big, she remarked. "Even compared to Tartarians. Didn't they have any clothes that would fit you?"

"Oh. I had a loincloth at one point." He smiled. "But it was destroyed when some guards blasted me."

"Yeah. But that's why you always make sure your shield or Power surrounds yourself *and* your clothes." Norne sighed.

"Ooh. Yeah, I'm not that used to clothes in general, so it's all sort of new for me." He smirked.

"I cannot believe you." Norne rolled her eyes. "First, I'm stuck in this dump and now I have a gorilla as my only acquaintance," she whined to herself.

"Little one…what are you doing?" the man asked.

"I'm not called *little one*," she communicated. "I am Norne von Arcosia, second princess of the Arcosians. Who are you?"

"I am me," he replied. "Why did you call yourself that other thing? Aren't you—*you*?" the man asked.

"You—do you not even have a name?" Norne asked, interrupting herself. "Were you raised by wolves?"

"My father did not teach me to think aloud with my mouth. He never gave me a name either. the man replied.

"Well, that is annoying," Norne complained. "How about this—for ease of communication, I will call you by the name of the place you are from. Where are you from? Tartarus?" she asked.

"I do not know… What is Tartarus?" he asked.

"You're no help. Are you seriously from nowhere?" Norne thought. "You don't seem like a very civilized person, that's for certain."

"I grew up far away from here," the man said. "Somewhere very lonely and much colder than this place."

"Fine, you're from nowhere—nowhere, just like the primordial chaos. How about this," Norne suggested, in reference to the theological concept and noticeable commonality in creation myths around the Universe. "You are Chaos—coming *from* nowhere and going *to* nowhere. That's easy enough."

"Chaos?" he asked mentally.

"Yes. Chaos," Norne responded verbally.

"Kay_os," the caveman repeated the word slowly, saying it audibly for the first time.

"Great. That name is suitably weird. Now if you don't mind, *shoo*," Norne said dismissively before cracking her book back open. Chaos stayed by her side, just sitting there. Even sitting, he towered over the girl reclining under the tree. With the addition of the nine-foot-tall giant, even more of the local people gathered to stare and whisper about her.

Norne noticed the nosy townsfolk and grew more and more frustrated, while Chaos just sat there quietly, seemingly oblivious.

"What are you doing?" Norne asked.

"What are *you* doing?" Chaos answered her question with a question.

"I am the daughter of the man who rules Arcosia, and I was sent here to marry the son of the man who rules Tartarus," she replied. "While that is better than having to marry a member of my own family, I still do not want to marry the King's son, so I'm blowing the meeting off. Not that you'd understand any of that." Norne sighed.

"What does "marry" mean?" Chaos asked. "That whole thought made no sense."

"In my case at least—*marry* means that I am being gifted to the Kingdom of Tartarus so that our countries can be better friends," she explained. "Is that simple enough for you?" A sudden hatred came over her face as she continued her dialogue. "At first, the prince wanted to marry my sister—another girl who has the same parents as me—but of course, she said no, and now I have to suffer the consequences." Her lips curled in anger.

"Why not marry? Did sister say no for a good reason?" Chaos inquired.

"Simple," Norne snarled. "The little prick they call Prince around here is a total pain. The kingdom has been on a decline ever since the incident twenty years ago, but he is still so spoiled he's unbearable, even by royal standards. I swear this whole insufferable planet isn't worth my time!" Norne muttered under her breath while staring down at a group of little kids who were acting friendly and waving at her from the market.

"If Tartarus is not good, why is your country trying to be closer friends?" Chaos asked, struggling to understand.

"I dunno. We both stubbornly continue to live in inhospitable climates. Literally no one wants to live on an oversized snowball, which I guess is why we need so many different colonies to import from." Norne sighed which made Chaos laugh.

"I agree. Even I wanted to leave my birth planet." Chaos laughed. "The people here must be dumb."

Smiling at his response, she continued, "I guess there's also an old pact we made when the two nations were in their heyday, but they both suck now, so it's more staying afloat than anything else. Hel, you would probably do a better job than the current king. And you're an idiot." Norne laughed.

Chaos burst out laughing at her joke which caught everyone's attention. His violent, thunderous laughter was reminiscent of a beast's roar. Norne started to blush at his response and watched as he wiped tears of laugher out of his eyes.

"You are funny, little one," he said.

"For the last time, it's Norne. Say, wanna help me play hooky from my wedding interview?" she excitedly asked her apparent new friend.

"I will go with you because I have no idea where I am," he admitted frankly.

"Well, where are you going?" Norne asked.

"To meet the ruler of this planet. That is what *hooky* means right?" Chaos asked.

"Sure, that's what hooky means," Norne lied, closing her book. "My father dropped me off and left me alone here, so I do not know this area that well myself. Let's take a look around."

When Norne stood up, Chaos stood up as well. At that moment, a gust of wind parted the cloak he was wearing as a loin-cloth, putting his entire body on display for all to see again.

"Alright! First things first, we need to get you some pants!" Norne panicked, covering him up again quickly.

In the local clothing store, Chaos got changed while Norne tossed her cloak-turned-loincloth into the store's fireplace. After buying a far less fancy, but tolerably suitable cloak, Norne returned to Chaos' change room. She watched the shirtless, barefooted Chaos walk out sporting shiny purple pants. Norne playfully gave a cat call whistle which made Chaos look down in confusion. "What?" he asked.

"You really aren't from around here," she said. "Purple is pretty pricy. Princesses love to wear it." She laughed at him.

"... yeah. It's a cool color that I've never seen out in nature. Of course, people like it," Chaos said, cluelessly.

"Aw, you're too much. C'mon try on some more, we're meeting royalty and it's about five hundred years too late for that to be fashionable on a man." Norne smirked.

"You're just stalling, aren't you?" Chaos pointed and laughed as it suddenly hit him.

"Maybe. But unless you want to walk around in princess pants, I suggest you get changed." Norne laughed while reclining in a chair, her hand waving him away.

"Well, I like these princess pants very much," he insisted. "Now c'mon no more stalling. I want to meet the king," he said before sitting down next to Norne.

"Ugh, fine. You can have the princess pants. Let's make it quick." Norne sighed before standing up.

"Yes!" Chaos cheered.

"But are you sure a single pair of pants is all the clothing you'll need?" Norne asked. "This place is freezing. Shouldn't you put on more?"

"Norne. Until today I didn't even know what pants were. I do not want too many of these 'clothes'. They feel very restricting," Chaos explained.

"Yeah. Well, we have other stops to make before—" Norne began.

"No! The king's house! We go to the king's house next!" Chaos stamped his feet and threw a tantrum like a child, which made the nervous merchant walk over.

"Is something the problem?" he asked, unable to hear Chaos' thoughts, instead only seeing his sudden violent actions.

"No! It is alright," Norne said out loud.

"Quiet down! You're embarrassing me!" Norne told Chaos mentally.

They quickly exited the merchant's clothing store. Norne then took Chaos to buy a kvass pastry to calm him down.

"I swear," Norne grumbled, "who's the child between us?"

"Tasty," Chaos excitedly devoured the children's treat. "Like a type of berry that I used to eat, but even sweeter."

"They are the one thing of value this planet has to offer. The rare berries used to make them can only be grown in the climate near the magma half of this planet because the ash from the volcanoes there make the land so fertile," Norne explained despite not getting one herself.

"I don't fully get everything you just said, but you sure are smart, Norne. How do you know so much?" Chaos asked while licking the last bits of pastry off his fingers.

"As the leftover, backup daughter, I had nothing but alone time back home. I spent that time reading and studying—among other things." Norne smiled malevolently, betraying that those "other things" may not have exactly been on the up and up.

"Plus," Norne continued, "when there was nothing more to learn from others, I started exploring things further on my own. The witches of Arcosia—the 'Nornes' use spotty magic. My method of magic produced more consistent results than theirs. Most refer to it with disdain as 'science', but my method has produced stronger medicines, tougher metals, and more dangerous weapons than any simple magic could accomplish," Norne boasted.

"Wow," Chaos said in genuine amazement.

"In fact, on me right now—well never mind." Norne cut herself off which confused Chaos.

"What?" Chaos asked. "You started saying something."

"Nothing." Norne quickly changed the subject. "We really need to teach you some kind of language. It's much easier to lie in a verbal conversation than a telepathic connection." Norne sighed.

"Why do you have to lie?" Chaos inquired. "You don't have to lie to me." He smiled. Norne didn't know what to say to that. Thankfully, the awkward moment was cut short when in the next moment, Chaos suddenly got a face full of snow. The kid who had thrown it, stood nearby snickering.

"Haha! You're wearing girl pants." The kid laughed at him.

The snow fell off Chaos' face as he looked around confused.

"Oh yeah," Norne laughed, "this is an open park, so that sort of thing is to be expected."

"That small person just attacked me! Should I kill him?" Chaos asked as he pointed at the child.

"Nah, it's just a game that poor children play to distract themselves from meaninglessness and the futility of existence. It's not a big deal. Besides if you did kill him, I doubt they'd let you see the king," Norne explained.

"Oh." Chaos sighed in disappointment.

"It's actually pretty fun. Look," Norne said before bending down, making a large snowball, and throwing it at the kid's head so hard that he fell over. At that all the children in the area panicked and ran away in fear, while Norne pointed at them and laughed. Chaos clapped at her in amazement.

"Oh, come on. You said you were from a snow planet too and you never thought to do that?" Norne asked.

"My father tended to throw rocks at me instead," Chaos responded bluntly.

"Oh." Norne didn't know how to react to that.

"Hm…how did you do that?" Chaos asked as he bent down and scooped up a snowball which he threw at Norne.

The snow hit Norne right in the face. She was not amused, especially when Chaos began laughing at her so loudly that snow fell out of the tree above her.

"Fine. But I hope you know this means war," Norne said before swiftly swiping up a handful of snow and throwing it straight into Chaos' mouth. Chaos fell over, coughing up the frozen water.

"I win," she said smugly, looking down at him.

"The snow is nice and cold," Chaos said randomly, looking up.

"Oh yeah?" Norne asked before lying down, placing her head right next to his so they could both look up at the wintry sky.

"You're a weird guy, Chaos," Norne said.

"You're a weird guy as well," Chaos said. "Like my father, but nicer."

"I find you very amusing, is all," Norne admitted. "I'm sure I'm having a lot more fun here with you than I would be having with that halfwit, Prince Drakon. But it isn't hard to accomplish that."

"Is that why you don't want to marry him?" Chaos asked.

"Pfft. We would need another hour at least for me describe all the reasons why I don't want to marry him. Besides I am easily a once-in-a-generation talent. I don't have time to settle down. I'm a witch on the rise, man." Norne rotated her hand in a congratulatory way, giving a slight bow.

"Well then, what kind of guy would you be interested in the future? Would you marry a man-witch on the rise?" Chaos asked genuinely.

"Those don't exist," she replied curtly.

They continued to lay there looking up at the sky for several minutes before Norne stood up.

"Well, let's keep moving. There are other sights to see and—" Norne began but Chaos stood up from the snow pile and dominantly stood over her.

"What?" Norne turned around, seeing Chaos annoyed.

"I am growing very impatient," he barked. "Take me to the king now. Or I will kill you." His gaze suddenly became terrifying. Norne paused before bursting out laughing. Chaos was confused and raised an eyebrow.

"You're lucky that you're such an interesting guy," she said. "So, because I so enjoy watching your antics… I won't kill *you*." Norne went from laughing to giving Chaos a murderous glower right back.

Chaos smiled at their mutual psychopathic glares and noticed Norne letting go of a concealed knife which she had hidden in the back of her skirt.

"Fine—way to ruin the mood just when I might have been starting to have fun. Just so that you'll shut up about it, we can go to the castle now. Come on." Norne led the way and Chaos walked after her.

At the foot of the tallest mountain on the continent, they came to a massive staircase that was carved into the very mountain itself. Together they began to scale the many flights of rocky stairs leading to the massive castle that loomed above them. The castle at the top of the mountain was the rich abode of the Tartarian royals. It boasted a hill and a large field of snow, kept well beyond the reach of the peasants below. In the middle of the aforesaid field, at the precipice where the top half of the mountain once was, stood the castle. The majority of the castle had been made of stone which had been smashed to bits from the solid mountain that Tartarian cavemen had flocked to in years passed.

It was a massive, fortified building, owing to its military history. The kings of Tartarus had advanced from living in caves to dominating their own world. They had set out to spread their influence further, continuing their never-ending quest for more power and territory. To match this ambition, the castle saw endless expansions and further fortifications, spreading like a patchwork quilt, with each king trying to leave their own distinct impression on it.

The stone blocks were not even uniform from end to end, as more advanced construction techniques had been implemented over the ages—a testament to the lavish expenditure of Tartarus' nobles. It was a mismanaged sinkhole of extravagant indulgence.

Like the nation of Tartarus itself, the castle's technology was far too sophisticated for the primitive Tartarians. Despite this inconvenience, the construction of the building was accomplished using the brute strength of conscripted laborers and slaves. At first, the rough stone blocks had been piled together in a fashion resembling a child building with toy blocks. The poorly built building would frequently collapse, more often as a result of its primitive and naïve design than from a military bombardment.

Collapsing and being rebuilt with successively superior intent, through much trial and error, eventually, one building was built well enough to stand firm and continued to do so for centuries. The giant stone building towered over the town that Chaos and Norne had just left below. It was a wonder that Chaos hadn't been able to see it from the start.

"I should have figured—the most important man gets the biggest house to live in." Chaos excitedly grinned at the building. Norne saw a disturbing kind of eagerness in the excitement that she could not quite put her finger on.

At the palace gates, Norne passed through after showing her invitation, but the guards stopped Chaos.

"Hold on. He's with me." Norne motioned. "He comes too."

The guards immediately stood down and let Chaos go through.

While they walked to the throne room, Norne turned to him.

"By the way, how does a nobody like you have business with the king?" she asked.

"My father told me about him. From the sounds of it, he owes me something I need, and I have waited long enough," Chaos explained.

"Well then, I can put a good word in for you if you behave," Norne said, as they reached the door to the throne room.

"Sure," Chaos said before immediately stealing an apple from a fruit basket on the table outside.

"Alright, game face on." Norne patted her face before forcing a cutesy, happy-go-lucky, princess smile as was expected from those who didn't know her.

"Why are you smiling? I thought you were just complaining about them. If you dislike them so much, why not just kill them?" Chaos asked.

"You're new to this royal stuff, but I advise you to act as nice as you can even if you hate them. You need to put on an act to keep your true intents hidden." Norne smiled at Chaos like a naïve princess, which greatly weirded him out.

The massive doors before them opened, revealing the king of Tartarus sitting on a throne with his wife standing by his side. The royal throne room was by far the most extravagant of all the rooms in the castle. The king vowed that if he had to spend time there, it would have to be comfortable. As such, it was better heated than all the other rooms in the castle, with a great fireplace lining the floors and forming a path to the royal thrones.

Animal pelts and the bones of great monsters (made of crystalized Adamant) decorated the ground and walls of the rooms. To the right of the King were five great windows which used the revolutionary new technology of glass—their dual-purpose to let in sunlight if there was any on that particular day and to keep out the cold and snow.

The throne room walls were made of the most recent type of stone used in construction, updated, and insulated. A far improvement from this king's predecessors. The boring gray stones were decorated with banners of the Tartarus flag. Further decorations were suits of armor from Tartarus' past and present, increasing in recency as they got closer to the king.

A matching set of suits of armor were placed on either side along the wall. The closest set was a suit of armor that was in truth, a purple, white, and black recolor of an Arcosian knight's armor, due to the fact that the two nations shared the same weapon and armor development.

Compared to the bland outside, Norne could appreciate the majesty of this internal room. And to boot, the king and queen themselves were nothing to sneeze at. Norne, who had never met the king and queen before was taken aback.

King Drakon I of Tartarus had a silent intimidation to his calm and regal presence. Seemingly distant, mysterious, and detached, the impression of silent wisdom came from his prepared royal appearance that matched even the most flattering of personas he had. Always at the ready, wearing a slightly dressed-down version of the Tartarian knight armor, he looked the part of the warrior king he tried to portray. His brown hair and purple eyes were the perfect complement to the national colors and a sign of his noble heritage. At least in appearance, he was an ideal ruler, as if every day were the day of his royal portrait's painting.

Queen Korova of Tartarus for her part was just as gorgeous as she was renowned to be. Her fair skin and snowy white hair were dead giveaways of her Arcosian origin, as the favorite daughter of the house of Ard. Peculiarly, she had stunning blue eyes, a very uncommon feature for Arcosians. Adding to her unusual eyes, the queen was also unnaturally tall. She stood head and shoulders above her husband, almost reaching Chaos' full height. It was clear that she descended from the exotic Jotun clans of Arcosia, but instead of making her a freak, this fact only made her seem more exotic to anyone who laid eyes on her.

Her outfit of the royal purple, white, and black was set apart from the other such colored robes by the adornment of unique jewelry. The strange glassy, obsidian jewels she wore were an oddity for Tartarian culture, not surprisingly, for Norne had heard she was an odd woman. This was exemplified by her obsidian decorated headband which simply sat on her head like a tiara, instead of doing its job of holding her hair out of her face. She just wore it like that because she thought it looked nice.

Norne studied the regal figures before her closely, in surprise at the strong first impression they gave. She noted all the features of appearance and heritage that she could detect on them at first glance, as was customary in Arcosia when meeting new people. To her surprise, she was thoroughly impressed.

"He looks just like he does in the books, a strong king. Certainly, more intimidating than my father at least. And Queen Korova…she is even more beautiful than all the rumors I've heard. Finally, someone who could get my sister Heidi to shut up about how good she thinks she looks. And a giant too. I had hardly believed the rumors about her height, given the stereotype of Arcosian women, but she really *is* twice the size of a normal person," Norne thought while observing the two royals.

After noting every detail of their appearances, Norne was finally able to pay attention to what they were discussing. To her surprise, despite their pristine and noble looks, the two royals were bickering with each other like commoners.

"I can't keep doing this Drak! You say you're 'not in the mood' every time. But whenever Vlatka is over, I catch you being *definitely* in the mood," the Queen accused. "What's wrong? You requested me to sit here and look pretty, but people are starting to talk. All this time and only one child? What is it? Are we not related enough for you!" the exasperated Queen Korova was at her wit's end.

"It is King Drakon to you, you damned woman!" he retorted. "And under the consent of the *king*, I may lay with whomever I desire! Besides, *one* child? Given the beast we threw out before, can I even be sure_NO. No more of this. I told you there would be no more discussion of this!" he yelled back defensively with a sharp tone.

"NO! You also said you would stop seeing her! When I had the pool boy, he was put to death for dishonoring the crown, but *you* get to run around with your *sister*?" the Queen towered over him.

Perhaps the King's appearance of a "distant wisdom" was just absent-mindedness and disinterest. Queen Korova would definitely think so. The two continued arguing as Chaos got bored and turned to Norne.

"Hey, what are they talking about?" Chaos asked Norne mentally, as he took another bite out of the apple.

"Don't ask." Norne sighed.

She had put up with enough nonsense for the day and resolved to try and help hurry things along.

"Ahem…" Norne loudly pretended to cough to alert the King and Queen of her presence. Upon noticing her, they suddenly froze, almost instantly reset themselves and quickly made themselves presentable, putting on an air of intimidation as if they were perfect and holier than all the monarchs portrayed in their portraits.

There was a long and awkward silence. The King looked down on her, impatiently awaiting her formal and professional greeting. Remembering the procedure, Norne neatly curtsied before the king.

"Hello your majesty. I beg your forgiveness for my lateness," Norne pretentiously bowed.

"I accept your apology but do hasten in the future. You reflect Otto by being a lollygagger. Do try to act more professionally in the future," King Drakon I said condescendingly.

"And you should try to act more like a king instead of an out-of-control frat boy!" Norne thought, but outwardly kept her warm and happy smile.

"Of course, your majesty. I am humbled by your sage advice," she said out loud.

"Wow, you are *really* good at that," Chaos complimented mentally, nodding to acknowledge her pretentiousness, then took another bite out of his apple. The noise of Chaos' rather loud munching suddenly drew King Drakon and Queen Korova's attention. Upon seeing him, they both froze in panic.

"Oh gods!" the king yelled and stood up as he immediately recognized Chaos.

"S'up?" Chaos waved.

"Princess Norne, stay back! The demon Typhon! He's back!" King Drakon shouted in terror. Queen Korova screamed and hid behind her husband, despite being so tall she had to bend down to fit behind him.

Guards flooded into the room and pointed their weapons at Chaos who just picked bits of apple skin out of his teeth, while looking around obliviously.

"Who's Typhon?" Norne asked and pointed at him in confusion.

"Who's this guy?" Chaos asked and pointed at the king.

"He's the king of Tartarus!" Norne replied. "Remember, the guy you wanted to meet? Now, who's Typhon?" she asked.

"Oh, Typhon? That's my dad. I think that's what he said they used to call him," Chaos explained before taking another bite of his apple, sinking his teeth into the core.

"Oh. No worries your majesty, he is just the son of Typhon." Norne bowed as she turned back to Drakon.

After her attempt to defuse the situation though, Drakon remained in a panic. Queen Korova was also still frozen in terror, sweating intensely.

Chaos turned his attention to the Queen. "The white-haired one by the king's side," he addressed her. "Hello mother," he communicated to Queen Korova smiling evilly after noticing the queen fit the description his father had given.

"Hold on?! *Mother?*" Norne asked in shock.

The Queen averted her eyes unable to even look at him. King Drakon furiously gestured towards all the guards who had entered the room, pointing at Chaos. "Attack! Kill him at once!" he ordered.

In the next instant, before anyone could move, Chaos flew up to the throne, cackling as he towered over the king!

"You sent me away and thought I'd just disappear? Fool, you should've killed me back when you had the chance." Chaos laughed.

"Please!" was all the king could say in his panic before Chaos used his Power and obliterated his entire body with one punch. His thoughts echoed through everyone else's mind through his final, ghastly death throes.

Chaos licked the blood off his hand before cringing and flicking it away, "Ew, gross!" he spat it out. The Queen, horrified, backed away.

"Wait, don't look at me like that mom." Chaos smirked as he saw her fear.

"You're a monster! You are no son of mine!" she screamed in panic. In an instant, Chaos turned her into a red mist as well with the flick of a finger. "Aw, stop. You're gonna hurt my feelings." Chaos laughed.

The whole time, Norne just stood in silence and watched. The soldiers, equally flabbergasted didn't even move from their stunned positions.

"Listen here! I am Chaos, son of Typhon! I am back from my banishment to take the throne that is rightfully mine! I am the ruler now!!!" he yelled like a gorilla, while telepathically communicating with everyone in the room to impart the messages he could not speak. Broadcasting universally what his tongue could not confess, Chaos made his thoughts abundantly clear to all around him as if he spoke Arcosian, Tartarian, or any other language of man.

Everyone remained frozen as Chaos sat down on the throne. "Any problems with that?" he asked, continuing his grunts paired with telepathy. The silence continued. Just then, the doors opened and Drakon II, Norne's would-be suitor came dancing in completely oblivious to what was happening.

"Heya, Heidi baby!" He shouted while cringingly dancing down the room before bumping into Norne. "Glad you accepted my… proposal."

"Hey! Where's Heidi?" he asked indignantly, noticing her absence. "Why's the ugly duckling here instead of the hottie I ordered?".

Norne struggled to keep up the façade of friendliness and tried calmly responding. "Oh, I thought you were made aware—our fathers agreed to a compromise in which I would be offered as your bride instead of my sister Heidi, Prince Drakon," Norne explained.

"Ew," the prince said in disgust which just annoyed Norne even more.

"Yes... I understand," Norne said trying desperately to stay in character. "I'm glad I have a fellow objector to getting married so young."

"Pfft. Age is not the problem. You'll never be half the woman that your sister is. What an eyesore." He looked down on Norne with so much disgust that she felt herself losing her cool.

"Also, who's that guy in the—" Drakon II began before Chaos pointed at him and exploded his body from the inside out. The prince's blood and guts gorily sprayed everywhere with Norne putting an energy shield up to keep the nasty splatter from landing on her.

"Nice shot. You beat me to it by one second," Norne smiled creepily, as her pure enjoyment of the carnage came across her face. She relished in it before remembering what she came here to do.

Norne snapped out of her trance and panicked. "Great! Well, what now? The king is dead, and you're supposed to replace him!? That would make you Drakon of Chaos. You come from nowhere. Tartarus is essentially dead. Aw, dad's going to kill me." Norne facepalmed.

"No. We will! Bow to the new king!" an eager Tartarian soldier moved in to prove his strength and loyalty. Norne was furious and gave him a look of death. Chaos sat on the throne and did nothing. Another soldier approached him.

"Long live the king. I come with a toast. Your majesty, please, have a drink." he smiled. Chaos took the wine and immediately began drinking as the soldier smiled. Suddenly Chaos gasped, coughing, and retching violently, dropped the glass.

"Fool. You think with such a golden opportunity, we'd hand the kingdom over to a complete outsider? If he was so stupid to drink poison seconds after ascending the throne, he doesn't deserve to be king." The soldier laughed and took out a poisoned knife, stabbing Chaos through the stomach with it.

The evil soldier laughed and turned to the one holding Norne hostage with his sword. The two nodded, thinking they had successfully seized the throne!

"I can't believe it was this easy! Just wait until everyone else hears what we did. This was way ahead of schedule," one said, laughing. All the other soldiers were shocked, not knowing what to do. Without another word, Norne reached out and touched the soldier's arm. At the same time, Chaos opened his eyes and laughed.

"What a wonderful drink!" he cried. "So, this is the alcohol I have heard of before! Shame it went down the wrong pipe, but I must have more of it!" Chaos laughed. The soldier panicked, taking a step back.

"Hold on...what's this? A weapon? Did you try to kill me just now?" Chaos inquired, before plucking the poison dagger out and tossing it aside as if nothing happened. He then stood up menacingly and towered over his would-be assassin as the wound closed almost instantly.

"Your majesty! Have mercy—I—you said you were the son of Typhon, right? I served him when he usurped the throne—you can trust me—I—" the soldier began to stammer as Chaos raised a hand to strike him.

"Oh no you don't!" the other soldier yelled before trying to turn to help his comrade, but he didn't move.

"I can't move!" he yelled. When he looked down, he saw that his body had been frozen solid!

"Yelling for help is useless," Norne informed him. "Threaten to kill me and there is no escape for you," she said, before pushing harder on him, creating a small crack in his icy body.

"No please!" the soldier screamed, but Norne only smiled at him eerily. At the exact same moment, both Chaos and Norne obliterated their attackers—Norne shattering hers into a pile of frozen shards, and Chaos smashing his into a red mist. Chaos wiped his hand off, and Norne glared at the knights.

"Don't cross me, royal guard dogs," Norne threatened. "Chaos, you're the king now, so call them off. I am in enough trouble already; I don't want a genocide to explain on top of everything. Because..." she said coldly, while walking forward and crushing the shattered soldier's frozen head under her heel, "So help me, I will kill everyone on this planet if I have to!" she shouted.

Chaos was shocked and stunned speechless. "Kill everyone on this planet! You've never killed anyone before. How did it feel?" he smiled.

"How did it feel? It felt...incredible." Norne twistedly smiled before catching herself. She quickly tried to recompose herself returning to her princess persona.

As the other soldiers backed away worriedly, Chaos roared with laughter so loud that it rang through the halls of the castle.

"You heard the woman! No one lays a hand on Norne von Arcosia. She is my special guest and friend. Anyone who even touches a hair on her head must go through me!" Chaos pointed to himself with a thunderous declaration that echoed through their minds.

Stunned, Norne blushed in surprise as the soldiers all saluted, "Yes sir!"

"What are we going to do now?" Chaos asked. "You said I could do a better job of ruling this country than King Drakon, so let's see about that, shall we?" he smiled.

"Yes!" she said, already completely smitten with the psychopath. At once, all the remaining soldiers in the room bowed before Chaos who sat back down on the throne, comfortably.

"All hail to—what did he say his name was?" a soldier asked.

"CHAOS! I am the man from nowhere!" Chaos boldly declared.

"All hail chaos! All hail chaos!" they cheered.

Chaos was ecstatic, smiling from ear to ear at this display.

"Bring in the others so that everyone in this castle can meet their new king," Chaos ordered. The knights immediately ran out to make it so.

In the year 1547 of the Tartarus Imperial Calendar the age of Chaos had begun.

CHAPTER 2

L ater that evening, Chaos was reclining on the throne, stuffing his face with all the food the castle's chefs could bring him. Norne sat on the ground with her back against the side of the throne, reading through a massive stack of books.

"So, find what you're looking for?" Chaos asked while chewing.

"Sure enough, your mother had a secret diary so we can confirm the whole affair," she explained, "placing you at the top of the line of succession. You are definitely Typhon's son by the Queen." She flipped through the pages, scanning them silently.

"So, I'm king?" Chaos asked.

"Well, the only line of attack any competitor might use is—how old are you? The Queen didn't write any dates on her diary entries. Are you of age?" Norne asked.

"Pretty old?" Chaos didn't understand the question.

"Yeah, but what age are you? How many years have you been alive?" Norne asked.

"…what's a year?" Chaos asked in genuine confusion.

"Whatever. You're old enough to go through puberty, right? You aren't actually a literal giant child?"

"Puberty? Oh right! When I got way taller and had hair in weird places. That started happening about the time I killed my father. Then I wandered around for a long time trying to find

Tartarus. Long enough to get this big. Is that 'old enough'?" Chaos asked.

"Sure. If anyone asks, you're eighteen, so that legally we have our pitch to get the nobles to acknowledge you as king. That was easier than I thought." Norne let out a sigh of relief.

"Good. Now I can be king just like I deserved. My father told me that being king was the ultimate way to live, so, it only makes sense for me to feel that myself," Chaos boasted.

"From the diary, Typhon did live large. As short as his reign was, his carelessness and self-indulgence are why the kingdom entered a decline it could not escape. If you want to play hard you must work hard too. Or at least have someone more competent helm the ship. Otherwise, you'll just be dethroned and exiled like he was," Norne joked.

"Well, I guess that's what you're here for. Want some?" Chaos laughed before handing her a massive, well-cooked bison's leg.

"No thanks. To both. Honestly, my father is expecting me home with some kind of news in two days, so I'm just here to ensure I won't get blamed for causing the collapse of Arcosia's biggest ally," Norne admitted.

"Aw. Really?" Chaos asked.

"Yes. But it benefits both of us. I need to make sure you don't screw this up. So, from now on do exactly as I say, got it?" Norne asked.

"Right. You're smart so you'll know what to do." Chaos nodded.

"Great. First order of business is getting the rest of the Tartarian government to work for you. You were on the right track by getting the staff up to speed, but make sure no one leaves the palace. We can't have any rumors getting out. You will have to kill anyone who tries to leave and don't accept any visitors before tomorrow is done," Norne instructed.

"Tomorrow?" Chaos asked.

"Right. We have the castle and everything in it, but we need to get the nobles on our side next. We need them loyal by tomorrow, got it? I'll contact them all and invite them to a banquet where we can break the news to them before any rumors get out. Also, we'll need profiles on who we can trust and who needs to go. Hm...tax and provincial records will probably give a good preliminary idea on which ones I'll have to deal with," Norne planned out loud.

"Great! What do I do?" Chaos asked.

"Simple. Sit there and look pretty. And most of all...PUT ON A SHIRT!" Norne lectured him.

The next morning, Chaos was being fitted for clothes far more royal than the ones worn by the late majesties. Norne sat cross-legged on the dresser reading through files on each of the gathering nobles, making lists on what to look out for from each, while the very groggy Chaos pouted at being forced into numerous fancy outfits that didn't fit him.

"That doesn't match up—every time, *everyone* isn't paying what they owe and are *admitting* it!? They have the nerve to admit how profitable they are in one file, and then blatantly send in less than the fealty tax they owe? Either the King's tax people were idiots and didn't compare the two files for discrepancies or—wait—why the Hel did nobles get to decide how much *they* owe in taxes instead of the amount being sent to them?

The King really had no power to demand a proper percentage based on their earnings? Even from the ones who were so arrogant they didn't even bother covering up the fact that they were skimming money off the top?" Norne thought to herself, distraught at how embarrassingly terribly run things had become under Drakon.

Looking up from her records, Norne was just in time to see the dress suit explode off of Chaos' muscular body. Norne facepalmed. "Nothing short of your mother's clothing is going to fit you." She sighed.

"Not true! I want to wear my princess pants again," Chaos pouted.

"You wouldn't if you heard how ridiculous that sounded. We're trying to blow the nobles away to make them respect you as King, not make you a laughingstock. Unless—hey you—the pants he had on before were dark already. Can we dye them black?" Norne asked.

"Of course, Princess Norne!" The royal dresser bowed. "Shall I dye the remainder of Typhon's wardrobe for his majesty as well?"

"If that is all that will fit him, then—wait—why do you still have Typhon's clothes," Norne asked.

"It shall be done," the dresser announced without answering Nornes question.

"Goodie. You can wear your pants. Now then, we need some kind of top for you," Norne thought out loud.

"King Drakon—I found this." A maid entered the room holding a massive black vest that draped down like a cape. Chaos put it on and posed in front of the mirror. "Father was a bit of a small fry, but I suppose this works," he thought while posing.

"Mm. Already black," Norne said. "Damn, black on black wouldn't look good. Fine, you can keep the purple pants for now," she conceded before becoming disgusted that her fashion talk reminded her of her sister.

"I'm glad you like it, King Drakon. Typhon the Usurper had it custom made when none of the castle's clothing fit him either," the maid explained.

"A bit small, but not too restricting," Chaos said before beating his chest.

"I will begin work on a larger version for greater comfort immediately King Drakon," the maid bowed calmly before taking her leave.

"Make sure it's purple! We're dyeing the pants black!" Norne called after her, getting her last bit of fashion critique out.

"Don't they all seem a bit too calm since we killed their King?" Chaos asked.

"Well, you obviously know that your father overthrew and claimed the throne of Tartarus for a while. I mean for crying out loud, they kept his old clothes probably in preparation for the chance he ever came back.

Additionally, from then on, whenever Drakon was away campaigning, a peasant revolt was bound to take over the castle at least once every few years. Why get attached to anyone master after all that? At this point, the staff is probably just resigned to it. This country has no hope, so it's best to just keep doing their jobs and getting paid by whoever." Norne shrugged.

"Thanks for the vote of confidence," Chaos said, noting her blunt opinion of the sad state of Tartarus.

"Don't sweat it, King Drakon. Now that you can dress yourself, I'm sure you'll be capable of running a country. At least better than these bozos." Norne smirked as she teased Chaos.

"Hey, Norne—why does everyone keep calling me Drakon?" Chaos asked.

"It makes paperwork easier. You can change it after, but for now, it's easier to say that *King Drakon* is doing all the things that King Drakon did. That way, no one will get suspicious. As far as the nobles are concerned the King that they knew is summoning them, not you, so everything is still nice, official, and under control," Norne explained.

"I like it. Drakon of Chaos is my name!" Chaos laughed.

"Well, no. It's just committing identity theft for the next little bit. You don't actually—" Norne began.

"Drakon of Chaos!" He stood up and excitedly said out loud.

"Fine, whatever. I guess then at least they won't need to rename anything for you." Norne sighed. Chaos continued flexing and posing in front of the mirror, like a child.

"I suppose I should get changed as well now," Norne said standing up.

"Why? You looked great in what you were wearing yesterday." Chaos grinned.

"You mean it? Wait—" Norne stopped herself from taking the compliment. "You are basically a caveman. Why would I take fashion advice from you."

"I meant it." Chaos turned around.

"Fine… I'll just wear this. They probably don't have anything in my size anyways," Norne said while holding a book in front of her face to conceal a blush.

"Alright! Let's get the party started!" Chaos excitedly laughed.

That night, the nobles all assembled in the royal banquet hall, eagerly chatting amongst themselves as the King's seat at the head of the long table sat empty. Norne sat on the windowsill, silently reading between constant glancing at the grand door. Suddenly the doors opened dramatically, and the assembled nobles became quiet.

"Hail to King Drakon!" they all chanted in unison.

"Yes. Hail to me," Chaos replied audibly with confidence, smiling as he entered the hall. The nobles were shocked to the core. They didn't know what to do, as they muttered amongst themselves.

"Silence! I am the King, so you must listen to me!" Chaos loudly ordered in shaky Tartarian. The nobles fell silent, as Chaos turned to Norne and winked with both eyes. Norne just rolled her eyes at his poor speech.

In the hours prior, Norne had paced around Chaos as he attempted to recite the script, she had given him.

"And what do you say if they keep talking when you enter?" Norne asked.

"Be quiet, I'm the King, so you must listen to me!" He communicated mentally.

"Yes, that's right," Norne sighed. "But you have to say it *out loud*!"

"Si—lence—I—am—" Chaos struggled with repeating the noises that Norne instructed him to use to communicate.

"Gah! How could I forget that you can't give a great first impression with an ape-man who can't speak! All my plans are going down the toilet." Norne began pulling at her hair in annoyance.

"What's a toilet?" Chaos asked.

"Oh, gods! I need to have you potty trained by tonight too?" Norne growled at Chaos' uncivilized nature. There were only a few hours left before the scheduled dinner. Chaos innocently tilted his head in confusion like an oblivious puppy.

"Why not let me communicate mentally? These old farts can at least use Power, can't they?" Chaos asked.

"Never mind, I forgot you're a barbarian. Actually—it might be for the best that you can't talk. Don't try to communicate mentally either. Everyone heard you earlier. You're inexperienced, unfiltered, and raw since you haven't figured out how to turn the link off when thinking about things that should be kept...private.

We don't want that ape brain of yours embarrassing us. It is probably better for you to keep quiet, than show your complete lack of etiquette to the nobles. Tell you what, we can work with this. After getting them to listen up, I'll do the rest of the talking."

In the present, Norne closed her book and stood up on cue.

"Gentlemen. Thank you for assembling on such short notice." Norne walked over.

"What is the meaning of this! Where is King Drakon?" One nobleman stood up in outrage.

"The Tartarian royal family is dead. This King Drakon here, being the next in line for the throne, has assumed his station," Norne bluntly said, getting a collective gasp from all those assembled.

"I killed them!" Chaos recited his line with an evil smile.

"What trickery is this? Just a few weeks ago I saw King Drakon in person!" the noble said.

"Well, things changed rather suddenly. King Drakon here, just yesterday executed all of them. I'd show you their sad bodies but given the circumstances of their untimely demise—this is all I have to show you." Norne smirked. She reached under the table and picked up three pots containing blood and viscera.

"I think this was all of them, but the rest might need to be scrubbed out of the cracks in the floor." She grinned sadistically while sliding the jars down to several noblemen so they could each take a look and pass the jars along.

The jars were half-filled with a disgusting, thick red fluid as well as shreds of royal garb, and strands of hair from each respective ruler floating in the liquid. Some of the nobles had their jaws hung agape in disgust whilst others had their mouths firmly clasped shut to resist the urge of vomiting. While the nobles remained frozen in disbelief, Chaos turned to Norne with a question.

"Hey Norne, I thought I had vaporized them? Where did the blood and guts come from?" Chaos asked in a mental message the others couldn't hear.

"Good remembering", she said condescendingly. I ran into trouble thinking of a sure-fire way to get the message across to these nobles, since seeing is believing and all that. To solve the problem, let's just say I got creative with some prisoners while you were getting changed." Norne gave him an evil smile while grasping at some of her own white hair which was noticeably shorter than yesterday. Chaos' eyes widened in surprise at her before he burst out laughing maniacally.

"I killed them! I killed them!" He mockingly repeated this last line, turning the stomachs of the now shaking nobles.

"This must be some kind of joke! King Drakon was a powerful warrior. There is no way he could be killed so easily!" A noble stood up in protest.

"Oh, Chaos. This one does not believe you were able to kill the former king." Norne looked at him while communicating mentally. Chaos was irritated and disrespectfully put his feet up on the table as he furrowed his brow. Suddenly, the Power inside of him began bursting forth. An ominous emission of Power that could be sensed by all, was so overpowering and so immense that none of them could even move while in his presence.

Even Norne who had planned for this, gasped in surprise at just how powerful Chaos was. The immense density of sheer energy, warped space time, causing dilation that threatened to collapse the entire castle under its weight.

All the servants inside the castle were frozen where they stood, and within all of Tartarus, every Tartarian looked to the castle as violent shaking emanated from it. Worse for those inside, a giant mass of Power—energy that had infinite potential density—was packed into one place.

Everyone within Chaos' presence knew that if he attacked them, they could do nothing to prevent total annihilation by his Power. No one except Norne could even accurately detect the limit of his strength, just like ants trying to fathom the vastness of a building from the outside, yet only being able to perceive the section of wall just ahead of them.

"Well then. It appears I miscalculated his strength after all," Norne thought while simultaneously nervously sweating and excitedly smiling at the prospects of the potential usefulness of this seemingly unending Power.

Finally, after this impressive demonstration, the pressure of energy and shaking stopped. The nobles began to breathe once again, as Chaos confidently beamed and turned to Norne looking for approval. She nodded to him with a smile, having successfully masked the fear she had felt once finally sensing his Power, and continued with her speech.

"As you just sensed, even the former King Drakon wouldn't be able to survive an attack from the new king. In a single attack, the new King of Tartarus rendered the former royal family unable to recover, even with their Immortal regeneration capabilities. Their brains were destroyed instantly." Norne explained.

One of the nobles violently threw up behind his chair. Somehow Chaos' awesome Power put more fear into the nobles than the blood and guts did. As a matter of fact, Chaos' energy had chemically separated the contents of the jars, which had boiled and separated at an atomic level.

"Apologies," Norne said, before holding her hands out to pull the jars back to her with telekinesis. "I suppose it's a good thing we kept the banquet back for later. Be happy we didn't go with King Drakon's original plan of boiling their remains in the dinner itself." Putting the gory props away back under the table, Norne happily smiled at the now terrified noblemen who fell for the deranged adolescent's ploy—hook, line, and sinker.

They hung on her every word, looking up at the smug princess and the beast sitting next to her casually admitting to regicide. A hush fell over the room which lasted for no less than a solid minute as they took time to process the terrifying events that had just taken place. Finally, one of the nobles had the courage to speak up.

"If what you say is true—" he began.

"It is." Norne quickly cut him off before going back to her cutesy smile.

"If what you say is true—" the nobleman said again, "is this some kind of Arcosian takeover? Have you been hiding this monstrous Power in your ranks until the time was right?" he asked.

"I had nothing to do with the former royal Tartarian deaths," Norne said matter-of-factly.

"His Majesty," she gestured towards Chaos, "is entirely Tartarian, being the child of the rightful Queen Korova and the former Tartarian usurper, Typhon. He has nothing to do with Arcosia, and frankly, the only reason I am here is that I'm just having a bit too much fun following King Drakon's demands in order to stay alive. I suggest you all join me. As you saw, his wrath is not something you can simply walk away from." She smiled to convince them that her lies were all true.

"I killed them." Chaos nodded while repeating the only words he remembered.

"You don't say. But since he has taken the name of the former King, can we trust this new administration to live up to his namesake as Drakon?" the same nobleman asked.

"Drakon the conqueror? Absolutely," Norne promised. "We can all sit here and pretend his Majesty ascended the throne because of some divine decision, or the will of the people, but we all know the real reason why—the only reason any noble lord respects a central government to begin with—because he is powerful. With that Power, everything else is assured. I would argue and I'm sure you would agree with me, that the might he possesses is more than enough to justify his ascension. This Power will also serve you well. Militarily, who would be insane enough to oppose you? In exchange for your loyalty, the King's monstrous strength is at your command. The ultimate sword and shield! Will he live up to the previous king? No. His Majesty will make him pale in comparison." Norne claimed, hyping Chaos up in front of them.

Several nobles breathed a sigh of relief, excited to have him on their side.

"So then...under his watch, the kingdom will be stronger than ever." The reassured nobleman nervously grinned.

"Absolutely not." Norne giggled innocently to confuse them.

"How do you mean?" another noble asked.

"I mean just look at him! In terms of brawn, the beast is unmatched. Without direction or focus, he would destroy everything he touched. This meathead is so stupid he couldn't even dress himself earlier. Why if he was in charge of Tartarus, he'd burn it to the ground in a day." Norne pointed and began laughing out loud in a complete one-eighty. The nobles panicked, desperately motioning for her to stop talking to avoid Chaos' wrath.

"What? Him? Please, he's so stupid he can't understand a word we say. Before this started, he had me teach him how to say some words to get his point across, but it just hit me that it also means I can say whatever the Hel I want to his face." Norne could barely contain the laughter. Chaos looked at her in confusion, not understanding a word.

"Hey biceps for brains, try saying something for yourself." Norne laughed.

"I killed them?" Chaos repeated the only words he knew. The nobles looked at each other and nervously began laughing at the revelation that he really couldn't talk. A confused Chaos tried laughing as well just to fit in, which only made the nobles laugh even harder.

"Stick with me boys, and you not only get the strongest attack dog in the Universe, but also the dumbest puppet possible who will let you get away with anything! I will babysit the oaf-king and you can do whatever you want. As long as I'm here to keep him in check and under control, *nothing* can stop you." Norne rallied them. The excited nobles cheered for Norne.

"Alright! Hey cooks, bring in the feast!" Norne excitedly cheered, waving for the food to be brought in and festive music to start playing.

"Gentlemen eat and enjoy; you all have a golden opportunity. Just like he trusts me to speak for him, he's going to trust you all to run the country. I've seen your taxes, so I know what that means." Norne smirked, getting further laughs from the nobles, who she had dancing at every emotional cue she had set to string them along. Chaos completely left out of the loop looked around in confusion at their laughter.

"Alright guys, eat and be merry. Plus, don't be shy to share tips during this prime time to increase your wealth and influence. As long as the ape is well fed and entertained, he'll literally let you do anything." Norne smirked before taking the jars of viscera and dunking them into a larger vat that a servant took and threw outside. The nobles, with the recent horror scene quickly forgotten, were excitedly discussing how the Kingdom should be run in the future.

After dusting her hands off, Norne sat down in the corner of the banquet hall, cracking open an old favorite, *The Art of Battle by General Szu of Zhou*, translated into Arcosian. Of course, her favorite passage, "The greatest skill is not to control the thinking and movements of your own troops but those of your enemies." had served her well.

The greedy old noblemen sitting around the large table, schemed how best to enrich themselves by seizing power from the state. Just as Norne had planned, they had no intention of letting the nation fall apart, nor did they intend to replace Chaos as King, when they had in him such a perfect puppet.

"Hey, Norne. What happened? Why are they all laughing?" Chaos walked over and asked.

"Don't worry about it," she assured him. "They have agreed to keep the nation up and running so you can just chill. Later we can discuss the next step for you to take, but for now, it is important that you go through the motions as their king. Go enjoy the feast." Norne hand-waved him away.

"Wow! You really are the best, Norne!" Chaos cheered excitedly.

"I know, I really am. Even rulers of nations are no trouble for me to manipulate—all according to plan." Norne vainly patted herself on the back. Chaos held out a large goblet of wine, clearly intended for someone of his size and pushed it up to Norne's face.

"Here! This batch isn't poisoned, so have some." Chaos offered, smiling.

"Um…no thanks. My father told me to be professional on this trip." Norne pushed it back.

"Come on, live a little. Are you letting your father's rules boss you around?" Chaos asked, making Norne perk her head up. She gave Chaos an angry look and taking the alcohol from him.

She looked down into the cup as if it were a bottomless body of water. Immortals were inherently immune to the extreme effects of alcohol. However, like with any other poison, Adamant could be used to fix that. The Italic civilization had invented a lead-Adamant based supplement that could allow Immortal nobles to get the buzz that their mortal subjects loved so much. The powder even supposedly sweetened the drink.

However, Norne knew the other, less known side effects of lead-Adamant as well—poisoning. All the usual side effects of alcohol experienced by humans were now generously granted to Immortals as well; addiction, vomiting, liver damage, brain shrinkage, infertility, and increased risk for cancer.

This sweetener was in fact even more toxic than the poorly processed, highly alcoholic wine and had been known to kill Immortals. Beyond tradition, it was just common sense to keep heirs as far away as possible from the stuff.

But here Norne was, left with no choice. She couldn't look weak in front of the other nobles, and worse, Chaos had already made fun of her daddy issues. So, upon seeing the other nobles pour a packet of the dreaded powder into their drinks, she succumbed to the pressure and dropped a full cube of the stuff into her own drink. Everyone was amazed.

Lifting the cup, she held it up as if to drink from it and they all clapped in surprise. Norne, however, grinned as she set it back down. Her exaggerated drinking posture disguised the fact that she had barely swallowed a thimble full of the stuff. She refused to let herself get drunk before ensuring the other nobles wouldn't try to take advantage of Chaos alone.

So, as they laughed and discussed, Norne would continue to visibly take large swigs while in fact barely lowering the amount of alcohol in the cup each time. She observed the nobles carefully, but as the time passed, she watched them take more and more of their drinks with each swig.

By this point, using her deceptive trickery, Norne, herself had only swallowed a literal thimbleful of the wine. But as no ill intent had presented itself among the nobility, and she *really* liked the taste of the drink, she began swallowing more and more and more of it with each sip.

"This is…pretty good," Norne thought. Then, before she realized what she was doing, she downed the entire goblet of wine for real.

Within seconds of finishing the drink, Norne got up on the table in a drunken frenzy of dancing and singing at the top of her lungs, while the nobles clapped along.

Chaos looked into the amazingly empty goblet and simply said, "whoops." He laughed out loud as Norne went from twirling around to a stereotypical Tartarian Hopak kicking dance, skillfully doing it around the table while chanting the city name, "Eizberg! Eizberg!". The native Tartarian nobles were impressed by the foreigner pulling the dance off so well and began clapping even louder!

"I, Norne von Arcosia, humbly offer you all a toast! This is every corrupt politician's dream! Enjoy your puppeteering!" Norne took Chaos' full goblet of equal size to the one she had already finished off and drank it empty as well.

The rowdy nobles cheered her on, raising their glasses to the toast. Norne gave them a twirl and continued dancing on the table in a drunken state. Chaos laughed at the sight before jumping onto the table and dancing with her. When he landed on the table, however, it collapsed under his great weight, smashing down and creating a big mess.

The next morning, Norne opened her eyes, confused.

"Uh…my head." Norne groaned as she woke up sometime later, in one of the castle beds with a wet cloth on her head.

"Oh! You're up!" Chaos scrambled, moving to replace the cold cloth, only to knock a bucket of water over in his haste.

He scrambled to wipe it up while Norne looked around impressed by his attempts to make her comfortable while she had been hungover.

"It's no problem—as Immortals we can resist any negative substances so long as we don't intentionally let them affect us. The hangover is gone now, don't worry," Norne reassured him.

"Oh good. Last night you collapsed, and I didn't know what to do." Chaos admitted.

"Last night? What happened?" Norne panicked.

"You drank the entire goblet full, three times." Chaos said.

"Three?! At most, I remember drinking two." Norne blushed in embarrassment as flashes of her inebriated partying came back to her.

"After that... somebody... broke the table," Chaos explained, "you just got back up and we moved into the second banquet hall for more partying. We kept it going till the sun came up, but you fell asleep halfway through."

"I didn't accidentally tell them anything did I?" Norne asked.

"Nah. Mostly singing and dancing. You have a very nice voice by the way." Chaos remembered.

"Whatever. In my Norne priestess training back on Arcosia, they forced me to become pitch perfect." Norne looked away in continued embarrassment. Chaos smiled at her, happy to see that she was alright.

"Hm...and just to be sure, you didn't try anything with me when I was asleep, did you? Drinking is one thing, but if you tried anything creepy, I'll kill you." Norne glared at him.

"Tried anything creepy?" Chaos asked in innocent confusion.

"Oh. Of course not. He seems to have the brain of a little kid anyway. When I was out, he came to take care of me himself." Norne smiled, noticing remnants of several clumsy attempts to make her feel more comfortable during her hangover, scattered around the room. The curtains were closed to keep the light out for her headache, the fire burning with the wood still in the container to heat the room, and the towels soaked in cold water for her forehead. Chaos hadn't fully understood what to do, but Norne felt it was the thought that counted.

"Never mind. You're not that type anyways." Norne shrugged.

"Tried anything...tried anything. I don't know what you mean. I just left you here and went back to the party where the old guys brought in the beautiful ladies. They said that's what kings do, and it was actually pretty fun." Chaos laughed said.

"Never mind. He is a boy after all." Norne rolled her eyes in annoyance.

"What's wrong? Did you want one of the girls too?" Chaos asked.

"What! No! There are so many things wrong with the things you say. Besides, you shouldn't get too attached to anyone. Just to be safe, a few phases in the plan for now will have to be purged." Norne explained.

"Phases in the plan? How far into the future have you planned this?" Chaos asked.

"Far enough into the future to a point, where if you screw this up, my father can't blame the collapse of Tartarus on me." Norne sighed.

"Aha! Screw this up! So, you were talking about the women from earlier!" Chaos misunderstood.

"For crying out loud, we need to get a language teacher in here! Mental communications are too simple and informal for the future. I guess I should make a note that the new King needs to at least be able to communicate as well as a five-year-old. More work to do." Norne sighed again.

"Well, that's what you're here for!" Chaos laughed.

"Pfft. You can't rely on me forever. Besides, tomorrow I'm heading back to Arcosia to report to my father. You have domestic support, but I need to ensure you have international recognition as well. So, for the next week or so you'll be on your own." Norne informed him.

"What? But you said yourself that I have no idea what to do as king! I thought you were going to do all the heavy lifting so I could relax." Chaos whined.

"I've taken steps towards that already. Just stay inside and kill anyone suspicious before they become a problem. Most assassinations or depositions occur during a ruler's first few years in charge." Norne warned him.

"Don't worry. When it comes to killing anyone, I'm your guy." Chaos confidently posed.

"Good. I'll draw up a list of everyone on the chopping block. Based on my observations last night, there are definite targets, so make sure none of the nobles leave the castle before I return. I intended to do more recon, but because of a certain *somebody*, I'm still not certain about a few. Included on the list will be features to look out for. If any of the nobles act similarly to any of the warnings, kill them immediately." Norne grinned.

"But Norne… I can't read." Chaos reminded her.

"You really thought I wouldn't have a plan for that? Just let me do the talking." Norne smirked.

A few hours later, a select group of knights assembled in the mess hall, which was notably sans table.

"Felicitations, noble ones. I pray you heed this elective pronouncement. You have been chosen as servants of his Imperial Majesty in abetment for his designated functions and perform select royal undertakings as to abate his imperial tedium. To be designated for such a task is a stupendous honor and a sure-fire stratagem to achieve the apotheosis sought after by all at your station! Truly the most blessed of men you are!" Norne declared.

The assembled knights just stared at her in utter bafflement. Norne paused for a moment. The knights were giving her blank stares as if they hadn't understood a word of her eloquent speech.

"What happened? Why're they staring?" Chaos asked.

"It seems I overestimated the complexity of Tartarian vernacular that this selection of individuals was familiar with. When I wrote the prepared oration, I was hoping to speak with peers at a higher level of articulation, but like you, their methods of communication are lacking, compared to my own. I made an error in judgment when attempting to converse with them." Norne sighed, still in fancy speak mode.

"You talk funny. Those long sounds were so confusing I think they got as much of it as I did. And I can't even speak the language." Chaos noted with a chuckle. Norne sighed.

"I don't know why I expected the Tartarian race to have produced better specimens. They aren't as lowly as our mutual peasantry but given that they are only mere brawn in the hierarchy of
being, it follows that their intelligence is naturally inferior to my
own. This is the curse of knowledge—living in a world full of sub-
servient people." Norne thought to herself as she shook her head,
turning her own bungling into a brag. The soldiers still stared at her
blankly, waiting for any form of clarification. Norne cleared her
throat before she tried again.

"Fine. I'll cut to the chase. You have been chosen for the
special mission of being his Majesty's elite guard. To ensure your
cooperation, your families arrived at the palace earlier today to
'meet the king,' and as such will be obliged to stay. During that
time, you will be performing secret duties for his Majesty exactly
as is written in these orders, or he will paint the castle's walls with
their entrails. Got it?" Norne simplified her message.

The knights immediately erupted in protest at the threat.
Norne then nodded at Chaos. Without a word, Chaos powered up
and flashed his incredible Power. Even though only for an instant,
it shut them all up. Some even wet themselves in fear. They hadn't
missed her meaning this time.

"It seems our message is clear. The castle is on lockdown—
nobody in or out until I return while the Capital is in this state. You
will each have duties that will be specified to you. Chief among
them will be reading for his Majesty. As a foreigner, the Tartarian
language both written and spoken is unknown to him. In addition to guarding that secret from everyone outside this group, you
will read each message the King-Emperor receives, communicate
them to him mentally, and speak for him whenever the need arises.
You will also be checking each other's work to ensure loyalty.
Additionally, kill anyone else who learns of his inability to read,
write, and speak. Just know that you are replaceable and that his
Majesty has already memorized a list of names for your replace-

ments. Fail in any part of this goal, and you and your entire family will die. Understood?" Norne explained.

"Wait…did I memorize any names?" Chaos asked after hearing Norne's speech, as she simultaneously sent it to him while speaking aloud.

"I'm leaving you a list of the next most trustworthy confidants to replace any of them, should any of them fail. The next in lines are the guys in the fanciest armor, but if you need a name, just ask a guard to read the names on the list and remember it. A little bluffing goes a long way to get the point across though." Norne explained to Chaos exclusively.

"Ooh!" Chaos sort of understood.

"My written instructions will be left to each of you. Watch over his Majesty as he learns the necessary communication skills and when I return you will be rewarded. But be careful and remember, his Majesty can kill all of you with a single thought. Fleeing is tantamount to surrendering your lives. So… good luck." Norne said as she tossed out files to the group as they clamored to catch her instructions. As they stared up at their new rulers in shock, Chaos and Norne made their exit.

"Wow! You really do plan for everything." Chaos laughed as they walked out.

"Yeah. It's on short notice, so there are sure to be some holes, but the fear of death should keep everything together for a while. And after killing that guard the other day… I dunno, it opened my eyes to how much easier it is to get things done with murder," Norne said in her disturbed frame of mind.

"I know right!" Chaos agreed.

"Remember. For both of our sakes, you can't be too careful," Norne warned him. "I'll only be gone a week so all you have to do is prevent a complete collapse before then."

"Right." Chaos nodded affirmatively.

"Good…now for my part." Norne said worriedly.

Norne left Chaos her master list, then got onto the Arcosian slave drawn vessel, to be flown back to Arcosia. Chaos waved goodbye, before immediately turning around and giving his waiting harem inside the go-ahead to come out of hiding.

CHAPTER 3

Norne waited outside the throne room for an audience with the king. She'd returned to Arcosia but had been kept waiting a week to meet with him. Norne wasn't very high on his list of priorities.

"Oh. You're back." a woman said, entering the hallway.

"Hello, Heidi. It is good to see you." Norne soullessly responded, without even looking her sister in the eyes. Chaos was right, she was good at this.

Heidi walked over to Norne, towering over her younger sister. The two hardly looked related at all. Their only similar features were their matching eye and hair color, which they had received from their father.

Heidi was much more mature than Norne. She was the picturesque ideal of women at the time, confidently displaying it in the newest and most expensive models of Arcosian fashion.

"Bombed the marriage interview? Not much of a loss, though. Even you deserve better than Prince Dorkon." Heidi haughtily laughed. Norne cringed.

"Anyways, is dad in? I need to talk to him?" she asked before knocking on the massive doors. Only glancing at her sister showing off her gorgeous and revealing red dress made Norne glower.

"There's a death by exposure warning on right now, you think she'd at least stop mocking me now." Norne thought to herself, while jealously comparing herself to her sister.

The comparison between the two was night and day, surely great for any growing girl's sense of self-worth. Not to belabor the point, but it was clear which one of the two was prepared for the ancient world that women existed in.

"Hey, is he in there or not?" Heidi impatiently asked.

"He is. I had an audience scheduled with—" Norne began.

Heidi knocked again. "Dad! It's Heidi, let me in!"

"Hold on, he was very busy. As King, he can't just make special allowances, even for family." Norne began.

In Arcosia, fathers were supposed to be distant guardians. Being too affectionate with their wives or children was seen as womanly and degenerate. Men weren't allowed to show emotion or show favoritism, especially over other duties to their country and their god. This was why Norne tolerated her father's neglect. She justified it to herself in her head. "Being affectionate was a mother's responsibility and he was merely doing his job as king." Norne insisted internally. That was why he *had to* be so distant and cold to his children.

And yet, as soon as Heidi knocked once more, much to Norne's surprise, the doors immediately opened for her, and the king's advisors all stood up, bowing as Heidi entered with an informal wave.

"Heidi, my daughter welcome. You needed me?" King Otto of Arcosia lovingly asked, as she went in for a warm hug from her affectionate father. Watching this display take place, Norne clasped a fist so tight that her palms might have bled. Of course, nothing had changed.

"The new batch of silver jewelry just isn't cutting it," Heidi complained.

"People are going to laugh at me if I show up in this. Can I have some more of the prime cut stuff from the treasury for my next jewels? The last set I got from there turned out really good." Heidi implored while looking disapprovingly at this week's sparkling set of priceless jewelry.

"Of course, I'll set the treasury minister on it right away," the king was quick to respond and motioned to an advisor in the room who promptly nodded.

"Thanks, dad. You're the best." Heidi smiled and gave him a big hug.

"Anything for you, princess." Otto laughed.

"Oh yeah, and the runt is here too." Heidi pointed Norne out after letting go of the hug. Everyone looked at Norne who had silently been standing there for a long time.

"What is it, Norne?" the king impatiently asked.

"I was—intending to speak to you in private," Norne began.

"These are the most trusted men in the kingdom, just get on with it so we can head back to the meeting. Did Drakon take you or has he sent you back?" Otto asked, braced for disappointment.

"The plans have changed. King Dra—" Norne could barely get a word out before everyone collectively groaned, expecting to hear of her rejection.

"Really? What did you do? Why did you ruin this?" her father demanded to know.

"The wedding is not off father. The King of Tartarus merely has a more important thing to discuss in person," Norne finally explained.

"Why didn't he send a messenger?" the king asked.

"This is a secret matter regarding the Alliance. He wanted to keep it between as few people as possible. But I have brought a message from him." Norne bent the truth and held out a proclamation she herself had penned.

Otto motioned for a servant to retrieve it and opened the royal scroll. After quickly reading it, he rolled the scroll back up. "I see," he said. "I fail to see why you should be a chief messenger but go back and tell him I will be in Tartarus in a month. I have some business to attend to before I can meet. And while you're there, try to at least make some progress on the marriage front. If not with the prince, then settle for a duke or noble—someone who would be of use to us." The king dismissed her.

"Of course, father." Norne curtsied before leaving.

Going back to her room, she packed more books to take with her, back to Tartarus in a quiet rage. Just then her mother put her hands over Norne's eyes playfully.

"Guess who?" the woman laughed. Norne immediately removed the hands and turned around to face her, unamused.

Norne's mother Beatrix, strongly resembled Heidi, yet somehow appeared to be the younger, more innocent one of the two. A happy medium between the two daughters, she had a warm and loving feeling about her. At least on the surface.

"I knew I smelled hypocrisy in here. Hello, Head Priestess." Norne sighed.

"Uh oh, *Head Priestess*? What's the matter my little snowflake? Did the marriage interview not go well?" Her mother sat down on her bed next to her.

"It's complicated. Things have changed with Drakon, but I can't discuss it until I get back," Norne evaded.

"Now Norne, an opportunity like this is very rare. The transaction has already been approved and the union would be a great boon for the nation both militarily and economically. Being a woman in court life—this is our calling and ultimate use. You've made your protests clear in the past, but the deal has already been made. Your father will likely just schedule a new interview anyways, so there's no use fighting it. That's just how it is being a royal, my dear. Bear this burden for the good of the country...and I'm sure it will make your father very proud of you," Beatrix began with a deceptively warm and comforting tone.

"That's not it...there are new reasons that my wedding with Drakon will likely be called off." Norne sighed.

"Don't tell me you've found someone else?" her mother asked excitedly.

"Hardly. Unfortunately, it appears that all the Drakons I know posses a similar level of intelligence. It must run in their family." Norne heaved a sigh, betraying a bit of truth.

"So, there's an interesting relative of his? He's still a noble then. Someone only a few spots of removal from the throne is pretty good," her mother observed, switching gears with this new piece in play.

"Mother, stop it!" Norne insisted. "The only other person I met there, was an associate." Norne sighed.

"Aha! So, there is someone! You can't hide it from me. He is at least better looking than Drakon II, isn't he?" Beatrix excitedly asked, whispering the last passing insult.

"Of course—but he's not a romantic interest! Stop this or you're going to make it weird when I see him again." Norne panicked at the thoughts she could feel her mother putting in her head.

"You're going back to Tartarus already?" her mother asked.

"I was ordered to return as quickly as possible." Norne went back to packing, as Beatrix stood up and waited in her doorway.

"I suppose I should pray for your safe journey, but you probably wouldn't like that, would you?" Beatrix asked with a playful laugh.

"Of course not. Father is not here so you don't have to play priestess. It's useless when you're with me," Norne stated.

"Hey! It is Head Norne Priestess of Arcosia to you. And I didn't work so hard to get this title for nothing y'know. Having that on your resume is a real trouser dropper, even with kings. So, it definitely had a use as far as you're concerned." Beatrix winked at her.

"Ew. Gross," Norne said in disgust at her mother's joke.

"Well, I'll leave you to it. But don't forget, either for love or for power, if he's worth killing someone over, don't miss the opportunity. If he could be of use to you, seize him. You are my daughter...don't let my blood, sweat, and tears go to waste. Life is a complicated game, but I've led by example, so do not fail." Queen Beatrix dropped her lovey-dovey façade and showed a crazed smile to her daughter.

"Of course. When father isn't around, I've made it clear that I respect your ability to play the system. Speaking of which, please set flowers by the former Queen's grave on my behalf." Norne nodded, amused at seeing a glimpse of her true mother.

"Of course. Okay, bye." Beatrix went back to her happy-go-lucky façade before waving and leaving. She was weird.

"Mother... I think I may be following your example a bit too closely." Norne sighed reflecting on her mother's lesser-known, machinations in her own youth. But even as her daughter, Norne only knew bits and pieces—the parts she was meant to know. Even to Norne, her mother was a mystery.

"But don't think I've forgotten you weren't there when I needed you," Norne's contempt welled back up as she tied her bag shut. "Never risking the façade that you've spent so long building up for anyone. But I guess that was a useful lesson as well."

Norne remembered any time her father would scream at her—her mother had been conveniently nowhere to be found, always being compliant in Otto's treatment of her younger daughter.

She always waited until Norne was alone to come by and be the good guy, acting as if nothing had happened. Just the two of them alone was how her mother liked it and how Norne was made to like it. Norne knew that her father and sister hated her, and her mother made sure she was warned that everyone else did as well.

Norne's mother was her only friend, and she didn't even completely trust her. As much as she encouraged Norne to find a good husband, whenever Norne had tried to make friends with the other girls in priestess training her mother had advised against it. Girls were no good except for using and then betraying you, she said.

The day Norne graduated from basic Norne training and opted for a solitary private education from then on, was the happiest Norne's mother had ever seemed. And Norne was happy for the privacy as well. Other girls were the worst. Except for her mother of course. She at least would drip-feed her compliments frequently enough to keep her going. It truly was a wonder where Norne's more disturbing quirks came from.

But Norne never considered any of that. All that she knew was that she had a blind spot about her mother. She knew something was off but lacked the introspection to consider what exactly it was. It was just a feeling—but that had never led her wrong before. At least it had made her the woman (girl) she was today.

Norne took her things and returned to the carriage. She looked up at the balcony where the other three members of the royal family all waved at her, though only her mother did it earnestly. Beatrix had big plans for Norne and for the first time in a while, genuinely smiled at the prospects.

Norne waved back before entering the slave-drawn carriage. She rode back to Tartarus, alone with her thoughts, able to ignore the otherwise distracting quirk of Arcosian transport, being the cries of pain and agony of the slaves being whipped to move faster.

Norne had managed to get her hand on Heidi's two prized slaves as a minor attempt to slight her, though surely, they didn't feel appreciated being specially chosen. As top former soldiers from a planet conquered by Arcosia, they were among the fastest transport around. They were top scouts and transports before, flying free through enemy ranks to deliver field updates back to their conquered home. However, their new Arcosia owners never cared about that. They were top-grade merchandise and that was all. Neither Norne nor Heidi even knew their names.

She arrived back in Tartarus within a day. She was curled up on the seat, sleeping peacefully, when the slave driver opened the carriage door and lightly tapped her awake.

"We have arrived on Tartarus," he announced.

"Oh good. Thank you." Norne smiled before sitting up and exiting the carriage. When Norne looked out at Tartarus from the dock, she was horrified by what she saw before her. The town had descended into madness with fires raging all over the lawless town. It looked like a battlefield, complete with giant craters as evidence of careless and offensive Power use, as soldiers and people alike looted and killed in panic and frenzy as the capital imploded.

It was chaos.

"Oh good... I'm still in a nightmare." Norne laughed, not knowing how else to respond.

The carriage driver raised an eyebrow as Norne's insane laughter got even louder and crazier.

Shortly after, the castle gates of the Tartarian Palace were violently thrown open by Norne. Soldiers alarmed by the intrusion charged at her but were all quickly frozen solid by the ice princess. She furiously stomped through the foyer towards the throne room. The two slaves and the driver nervously followed behind her, looking at the destruction and dead soldiers left in her wake.

Even more angrily, Norne slapped the doors to the throne room off their hinges and furiously shouted, "CHAOS!"

Inside, sitting on the throne, wearing nothing but a bath towel, stuffing his face with slabs of meat, holding a beautiful woman on each arm, Chaos smiled at seeing Norne's return.

"Norne! You're back. It's felt like forever." Chaos excitedly stood up and greeted her.

When he descended the stairs to give her a hug though, Norne angrily thrust her hand forward and sent him flying into the throne, killing the two women there, and knocking the chair over.

Chaos felt the expanding frost on his chest from where Norne pushed him and laughed. "Ah, missed you too." He sat back up.

"What is wrong with you?!" she shouted. "I left you alone for a week and everything has gone to Hel! My *father* is coming here to approve of you within the international community. He cannot see the country like this! Where are the nobles who were supposed to run things?" Norne screamed.

"I thought I was supposed to kill them! They already did the law stuff to make me king," Chaos whined.

"But they also knew how to run things!" she yelled. "Fine. Then if they died why wasn't the next person on my list given command? Why didn't you get someone else to run the country?" Norne asked.

"He was—he was gonna tell on me," Chaos muttered.

"What?" Norne's eye twitched in frustration.

"I followed all your instructions, I swear! It was one of the nobles, he brought his daughter in for me!" Chaos cried.

"You let someone into the castle! Word got out didn't it." Norne sighed.

"Maybe…after she talked to someone, I made sure to keep her here," Chaos said.

"And where is our leaker now? To fix this we should find out what she confided," Norne said.

"Well… I think she's already dead." Chaos looked back at one of the women Norne crushed by throwing him into the throne.

"Great. As usual, you ruin everything you touch!" Norne yelled at him.

"How is it my fault, you pushed me!" Chaos yelled back.

"What else did you do? One leak wouldn't start a riot," Norne fumed.

"Well—and don't get mad—" Chaos began, expecting Norne's agreement. Norne only gave him a furious look of death.

"At first—when the first guy was being stingy and not letting me—I mean the nobles, bring women to the castle—to pass the time, I would spar with their strongest soldiers," Chaos began.

"Spar? I've seen you fight; how many men are we down?" Norne interrupted.

"Uh—how many guards do *you* think I killed?" Chaos nervously asked.

Norne's glare only grew colder.

"The number doesn't matter. Just that I think the strongest ones were the only ones worth fighting, and those were the ones you had picked to read and help lead and stuff," Chaos admitted.

"So, I left for a week and the country has had no leader for—" Norne began.

"About a week." Chaos shrugged, admitting how quickly things had fallen apart. Norne growled like a wild animal which made Chaos laugh nervously. After her rage looked like it was about to burst, though, she exhaled to calm down.

"Whatever, I guess I have to try and bail you out again. Otherwise, we'll both be killed, thanks in no part to that "natural genius" of yours. Settle these three in, they can't be allowed to report seeing Tartarus being in this state," Norne sighed.

"Wait what?" The driver asked before two soldiers led him away along with the two Arcosian slaves.

"Now…go sit in a room where you can't screw anything else up! I'll figure something out." Norne sat down and facepalmed.

"I've stomached quite enough of that, little girl," Chaos growled while towering over Norne "I found you interesting, so I tolerated much more than I normally do."

"And? Going to throw a hissy fit, you overgrown gorilla? I was the one tolerating you, but your interest is only matched by your stupidity! Useless Oaf!" an impatient Norne growled back. Chaos grinned sadistically, with a furious gaze down at the girl.

Everyone began to back away nervously. Before anyone else could even sense it, Chaos manifested his Power into a great flame of energy that blazed around him. Concentrating the energy into increased mass, Chaos let loose and, in a flash, swung his arm to rip Norne's head off.

Suddenly, Chaos felt strange and noticed Norne was just fine. Frozen and shattered fragments of his palm and fingers were scattered across the ground, while a bloody stump at the end of his arm was half frozen over. It was ice, but it wasn't frozen water. The temperature of Chaos' hand was lowered so absolutely that the air itself solidified into ice-like crystals on his skin.

Chaos also noticed that his great flame of Power had ebbed and dimmed significantly as if a cold gust had nearly extinguished his candle. To Chaos' shock, he'd lost far more Power than he even used up to increase his strength and attack—it was as if *he* had been hit. Whatever had happened to Chaos was beyond merely depleting the temperature, it was if the temperature of his Power had been lowered just as dramatically.

"What a useless attack." Norne smirked condescendingly up at Chaos.

"Little one—space is cold, but I can live there just fine—how can you be colder?" Chaos demanded.

"It isn't just temperature you fool. But the genius of my unique ability would be lost on you anyway so why bother," Norne scoffed. Chaos looked down at his arm and his hand quickly regenerated as if nothing had happened. Shaking the frost off, Chaos laughed. "Arrogant brat!" he said as he made a fist. This insult infuriated Norne who quickly threw a hidden knife at Chaos' forehead while screaming, "SHUT UP!"

Normally he would've just let it break on him, but suddenly he panicked, blocking the weapon with his forearm. The blade pierced through, spewing blood everywhere as he groaned in pain.

"It—it burns!" he yelled in equal parts of pain and shock.

"Of course, it does. You've never encountered a weapon strong enough to pierce you, so the effects of Adamant would be a new sensation. Naturally, my knife is special." Norne smirked again.

Suddenly frost began appearing around the wound. Chaos gasped and out of desperation tore off his own arm. The severed limb hit the ground as solid ice and shattered.

Norne casually walked past Chaos without any fear and bent down to pick up her knife, enraging the giant.

"Go ahead—strike me again. You know what will happen. You're fast, but I've adjusted. The next time you make contact, your entire body will be frozen solid," Norne warned with demonic fierceness in her glare. Chaos paused in surprise after slowly re-growing his forearm.

"You're going to regret getting on my bad side," Norne warned him with a cold glare.

"But if I just hit you once through that strange Power of yours—you will be the next one to fill a bloody jar!" Chaos yelled.

He dashed in to attack, but Norne ducked past him with surprising speed. Chaos' view followed Norne as she moved past him, but to his astonishment, even though he moved faster than before, Norne suddenly bolted away even more blindingly.

It seemed impossible; Chaos was much stronger than Norne physically, so that should've extended to raw speed as well. However, unfortunately for him, Norne's knowledge of the mechanics of Power afforded her certain abilities that brute strength alone could not accomplish.

Despite being much stronger and faster than Norne, Chaos struggled to keep her in sight as Norne darted all around him at speeds he was almost certain were impossible. This was the blitz technique for high-speed movement. The blitz technique was something completely unlike what the Monsters he was used to fighting were capable of. Using that, this puny, much weaker warrior was moving so quickly that she seemed to be disappearing and reappearing all over.

He caught a glimpse of her in the corner of his field of view and swung his arm to attack her but missed. With his side exposed, Norne moved in and gave him a shallow cut with her knife that immediately began spreading ice through his body.

Chaos growled and did his best to melt it by focussing his raw Power there to cancel it out. While that distracted him though, Norne jumped behind him and sliced his back open. It wasn't deep, more akin to the infuriating sting of a shallow papercut since she didn't want to compromise her speed with a heavy attack.

He growled again, and using his superior natural speed swung his arm to grab her. However, Norne was gone again, and this time sliced his abs. Over and over, Chaos tried in fain to catch Norne as she darted around, giving shallow cuts to spread ice all over his body. If anything, Chaos' grabs were getting less accurate as he felt the ice starting to slow him down. His body was quite literally being frozen over and even worse, his Power itself was being drained by this mysterious effect. With each missed strike and sharp pain, Chaos' anger only grew.

"Stop it!" Chaos screamed as he couldn't help but shiver from the frost that was quickly spreading across his skin. Norne stopped and scoffed at the frustrated giant.

"That ice thing is cheating! It isn't fair!" Chaos yelled.

"Of course not." Norne coldly stared him down. He was stunned by her bloodthirsty look. Norne sighed and figured she had time to chat since he was already on his last leg. As far as she was concerned, she would be the only one to leave this room alive. Norne glared as Chaos felt his Power being drained by this strange ability.

Nothing useful was produced of it. Norne wasn't stealing it for herself. She was just destroying it. If she couldn't have it, then no one could. This was her philosophy made manifest. Instead of powering herself up, Norne was sure to weaken everything she touched. Their strength, their speed, and even the very heat of their molecules was canceled out in a destructive wave of interaction. All was frozen over.

The human mind was capable of many things and this product was horrifying. This was the ultimate power—Norne's power—Fimbulwinter.

"Since you're about to die, be happy it will be by my ability. I have no use for regular Power when I have this power to destroy it. After a cold breeze of my anti-Power—my Vanus will strip you of your strength, of your speed, and even your heat. There can be no power that isn't mine!" Norne monologued.

"That isn't FAIR!" everyone thought in unison, in response to what they heard.

It really wasn't.

In the next moment, Norne darted towards him to attack him while his guard was down. Chaos moved to try and block it, but he was so slowed down by the ice creeping all over him, that he didn't make it in time.

Finally, when Norne went for the eyes, cleanly slicing through both, Chaos furiously screamed. It turned out that fighting wasn't all fun and games when you get hurt too. His wrath boiled over into a massive explosion of Power that shook the palace. The force was so great that it knocked Norne out of her high-speed rush and forced her to land and do her best not to be blown away.

Chaos continued screaming as he forced out a seemingly endless amount of Power that blazed around his body and slowly but surely melted the ice all over him. Forcing more Power out every millisecond than most would use in a lifetime, Chaos' body was fully ice-free and regenerated in no time.

While Chaos was off his guard and Powering up, Norne made her move, and using all her strength, swung her knife into Chaos' side. With his defenses down, Chaos couldn't block or dodge in time and Norne's swing hit its target. To her shock, even though her hand finished swinging as if to slice through him, his skin was so tough the blade was lodged in it and Norne's hand was sore from having the blade torn from her grasp.

The powered-up Chaos smirked. He plucked the small knife from the scratch and tossed it away. Yelling angrily once again, he brought forth a massive amount of Power to bolster his strength and speed. Again, he threw a mighty punch, but this time, Norne was smashed with such force that she stumbled away, almost falling over. Her power shield just barely saved her and worse for her, some had gotten through it to hit her directly.

"Ha! I was worried, but I guess the secret to beating your Power is just punching you harder! Your power never knew someone as strong as *me* existed in this Universe!" Chaos boasted, excited that only a thin layer of frost form on his fist which quickly dissolved in the face of his might, as his knuckles healed from the frostbite. Norne spat out a wad of blood but looked back at him with a grin.

"I expected a lot more from someone as big and strong as you. What a useless attack." Norne smirked.

"Don't get cocky! My next attack will be at full strength, and you won't have a chance of surviving!" Chaos cackled. Chaos moved to attack again but suddenly fell to his knees. Looking down at the tiny flesh wound Norne put in his side, sure enough, ice was spreading from it like wildfire. That entire half of his body fell limp, paralyzed.

"Oh, come on!" Chaos growled; his leg completely frozen causing him to be stuck on his knees.

"Y'know…it's funny, I've never been much of a fighter. I only developed this Power to fend off any Monster attacks, and of course to spite my sister but…it seems to work just fine in a real fight as well. After all, with that insane amount of Power and an empty brainpan, what are you but a big, dumb monster in human form." Norne walked right up to Chaos and stared him down face to face, as ice covered his other leg and both arms.

Chaos was furious and opened his mouth to fire a focused death beam of Power. Norne however, jumped up and grabbed him around the mouth, flash freezing his jaw and stopping any Power from building. Chaos' eyes widened in panic and terror. All those flashy displays earlier made him formidable, but in the face of Norne's ability to drain strength, all it really did was waste his stamina even quicker than Norne could have hoped.

In this weakened state and covered in ice, Chaos was completely at Norne's mercy! For the first time in his life, Chaos wasn't strong enough and it hit him all at once right then.

"I warned you that if you weren't careful, it'd get you killed," Norne coldly said while pulling his head forward and looking him dead in the eyes. His eyes widened but suddenly Norne sighed and let go of him.

"What am I thinking? I let my temper get the best of me and just threw a tantrum like a child." She heaved a sigh and walked over to the steps where she sat down with her head in her hands.

"That won't do anything. Nothing will do anything—it's all useless! No matter what, I'd just be digging myself a bigger grave. Maybe I should spend the month finding a place to lay low," Norne muttered in despair.

The onlookers whispered amongst themselves, not knowing whether or not to move after the awesome display they had just witnessed. Overtaken by doubt, Norne imagined her father seeing this failure and her family's shared scorn.

"As expected, I give you one job and you ruin everything." She could almost feel her father looking down at her. Her family's scathing comments echoed in her mind as she could just imagine what they'd say.

"With a screw up like her, it's to be expected." The image of Heidi in her head laughed.

"I suppose I can try to bail you out with your father. Just thank me that you won't be killed," her mother's wicked side would have condescendingly remarked.

"What was I thinking I was way over my head with this scheme from the start. I'll just be embarrassed again." Norne almost began to cry.

Unbeknownst to her though, while she was preoccupied, Chaos had finally thawed through the ice and stood behind Norne, towering over her menacingly. He smiled from ear to ear as the remaining soldiers worriedly looked on. However, instead of attacking her, Chaos knelt down, sitting next to Norne with a huge grin on his face.

"Norne von Arcosia…you have earned my respect. Before, you impressed me with your knowledge but now…you have matched me in battle, a thing that I thought was impossible." Chaos laughed while sitting next to Norne.

"Aren't you going to kill me?" Norne asked.

"Of course not! I want to fight you again. But not while you're distracted by this," Chaos explained.

"What's the difference. What I'm distracted by is that my plan is ruined. Because of that, I will be dead." Norne buried her head in her hands.

"Sorry for messing up your plan Norne, but if anyone can fix this, I know you can." Chaos put his gigantic hand on her shoulder and smiled.

Norne, shocked to hear that, looked up at him. An otherwise ordinary and mundane phrase of encouragement from Chaos left Norne speechless. She stared at him, completely unable to process genuine positive re-enforcement.

"What? Is there something on my face?" Chaos asked.

"Nothing just—I rarely hear stuff like that," Norne admitted.

"How? You're the smartest person I know! Plus, that awesome Power of yours is so incredible, I've never had so much fun in a challenging fight." Chaos laughed.

"What!" Norne panicked in a compliment overload.

"What? It's true," Chaos said in absolute seriousness.

She covered her face and went beet-red.

"You're so strange, Norne!" Chaos laughed and slapped her on the back. She stopped covering her face but kept blushing.

"Ahem—fine. I guess you are right, sitting here and sulking won't do anything. Let's actually get to work solving the problem."

In the king's office, Norne spread out a page on the desk, while Chaos cluelessly looked over to watch.

"Alright…this kingdom has been on the decline for the last two decades. If you hadn't come along, something else would've destroyed it sooner than later. We need something better," Norne stated.

"Better? I thought the old king was the problem," Chaos said.

"He was. The foundation of the nation is faulty. Agreements with all non-capital worlds vests far too much power in the regions, diminishing the king's own power. It's no wonder they had rebellions and revolts all the time. I admit, the nobles were perfectly justified in capitalizing on this out-of-date disaster.

Look at this—taxes are given in set amounts, calculated two-hundred years ago. In total that amounts to so little silver that the other territories might as well not exist at all! And look at how poor the communication and uniformity are within the army. Tartarus' army is adept at going out and conquering, but domestically they're basically nonexistent. With so little oversight and connection to the monarch, no wonder that the peasants started getting ideas," Norne said in disgust while reviewing ancient Tartarus territorial laws.

"Ooh. Okay—I don't get it," Chaos admitted.

"Basically…the king had the same problem as you. Everyone else was running his country for him. The problem was that after he was temporarily kicked out by your father, he lost the plot of the scheme, and nobody here had much reason to follow him. Tartarus still operates like a collection of tribal states, much weaker than anyone else thought, so it's a miracle it hadn't collapsed before you got here. The only thing it ever had going for it was the military! Like I thought before, it's a real fixer-upper." Norne sighed.

"Well…can you fix it?" Chaos asked.

"Of course. This *is* me that we're talking about." She grinned as she took out a quill and began writing with a look of devious inspiration in her eyes.

STEP 2

SECURE ALLIES

"All the pleasing illusions, which made power gentle, and obedience liberal, which harmonized the different shades of life, and which, by a bland assimilation, incorporated into politics the sentiments which beautify and soften private society, are to be dissolved by this new conquering empire of light and reason."
—Edmund Burke

CHAPTER 4

A month later, Norne's father: King Otto of Arcosia arrived. Even as his royal ship made its descent, he saw the towering keeps of Tartarus' gargantuan royal palace and couldn't help but feel envious of it.

"Hello father, welcome to Tartarus," Norne politely welcomed him as he exited his carriage. "I trust your travel went well."

"It was fine," Otto replied dismissively. "Is Drakon ready? I don't have time to wait."

"Of course. Right this way to the palace." Norne smiled before leading the way. He looked around skeptically while following her.

From the docks, things seemed normal, even better than normal. The open black market was gone. Everything in the market was supervised by the Crown itself. The disorderly crowds properly organized in appealing groups marching from stand to stand. Soldiers everywhere. Crime and poverty were gone from the streets or at least they were no longer seen in the streets. Any who weren't executed were put to work in open air camps for the Empire.

It looked better to Otto who nodded approvingly and thought, "Wow, Drakon has really cleaned up the place." Noticing his approving nodding a big grin spread across Norne's face.

They quickly arrived at the Tartarian palace, a pristine building without a single sign of anything wrong. The doors were opened by the guards who bowed respectfully (but not to him).

"Now then… Drakon what was so important that you needed a meeting on such short notice?" he asked as Norne led him into the Tartarian throne room.

When he looked up though, Chaos stood towering at the top of the stairs. As Norne had instructed, he wore a royal robe dyed a pristine purple with his old pants which had been dyed black to make his outfit match the colors of the Tartarian flag. Otto was baffled at the sight of this stranger.

"What in the blazes! Norne, who is this!? Where is Drakon?" Otto furiously asked.

"He's right there. Now bring in the bricks!" Norne ordered.

Groups of guards in teams of ten brought in five metal bricks of solid Adamant of the highest quality, struggling to carefully place them one on top of the other. Then the captain of the guards drew his sword and using all his power, yelled fiercely as he moved to strike at them. His sword snapped in half and the bricks didn't budge. They were definitely Adamant.

"Now then… presenting His Majesty!" the soldier motioned towards Chaos who flexed pompously.

"Norne, what is the meaning of this, I want an answer not a magic trick!" Otto yelled.

"Just watch. Those bricks are solid Adamant, the strongest raw ore in the entire kingdom. Your majesty, it is ready." Norne grinned and nodded at Chaos.

Chaos confidently put one arm into the air with his finger extended. Then in a flash he brought the finger down, breaking through and obliterating each of the solid metal bricks! The Adamant chunks flew around the room, embedding themselves in the wall and floor! Otto was shocked!

"Drakon did want to speak with you. But the one you knew is dead. This is the new king… no, the Emperor: Drakon of Chaos." Norne dramatically presented Chaos who walked down and shook King Otto's hand.

"Welcome to the Tartarus Empire!" Chaos managed to say in Tartarian just as the new flag depicting a massive, three-headed dragon set on a black and purple color scheme—was unraveled and hung behind the throne

"A pleasure. Emperor Drakon." Otto said with a grin.

"Father, things here have changed considerably under this new management. Would you like a brief tour of your newest ally?" Norne asked.

"Alright? Things have changed a lot here?" he asked.

"Of course. Your Majesty, I think it's time for you to go get ready." Norne nodded to Chaos who left.

King Otto raised an eyebrow as Norne led the way.

Passing by the former audience chamber, she directed her father to see a group of men in robes swearing oaths in front of a large bowl containing fire below the new flag. "We swear allegiance to Drakon, and the eternal Empire of Tartarus which is his dominion. May the Ten Tables be our guide in serving the state: in serving the Emperor. Hail to Chaos!" they recited in unison.

"We're swearing in Senators." Norne explained.

"Senators?" Otto asked.

"A new system to Tartarus. Using noble birth to determine leadership led to too much corruption. Now instead of inheriting it, one must be either confirmed by current Senators or appointed by the Emperor or Super-Delegate by merit. They all still happen to be nobles but oh well. There will still be corruption in this system, but the difference is that now it works for the Empire instead of against it." she explained.

She wondered if her father would recognize the similarities to a series of reforms from a working model, she had researched in ancient Italia, and had advised him to implement for Arcosia.

"Interesting new form of government… and running so soon. All this change in a month is incredible." Otto said, evidently not remembering anything.

"Right. You can sit in on a meeting later. We are reforming taxes." Norne smiled.

"We?" Otto asked.

"Well, it would be hard for the Senate to convene without their leader, the Super Delegate. Whoever holds the position holds complete authority over the Senate." Norne smirked confidently.

"I see. I hope you find him." Otto missed the point much to Norne's annoyance.

"All the unnecessary guest rooms have been repurposed as barracks for the Empire's elite new fighting force." Norne said while walking through the halls, passing a line of soldiers clad in black, white and purple armor.

While many of them stood around the perimeter as security, other soldiers in the center of the atrium stepped up to pedestals with swords stuck in them. Dozens of new recruits seized the swords in the pedestal devices and pulled with all their might, trying to pry the blade from the stone. If they retrieved it, the blade would be theirs ever after as a symbol of their amazing strength.

In Tartarian chivalric culture, this rite of the sword was normally reserved for kings at coronations, however, that cultural significance was now applied to all new defenders of the realm. Beyond the obvious appeal of having the new elite pass a trial of religious significance for the Tartarians it also had the more practical purpose of ranking them in Power.

Each pedestal was actually an elaborate multi-level Adamant lock that held the sword in place with nine layers like the sacred pedestal of the king's blade and the very planet Tartarus supposedly did in myth. Each lock only engaged when the last was destroyed and was even more difficult than its predecessor. Knights were ranked in the new order by how many layers they could pull the sword out of with the average Imperial knight being able to remove seven. Less than a tenth could pull it out of all nine and such a feat was the mark of a true hero in Tartarian culture.

Otto remembered Drakon bragging about how easily he pried the blade out of all nine layers during his coronation and so recognized the significance of all this, as well as the strength of those he saw who could do the same.

"For reference, His Majesty had pulled a sword out of all nine layers one-handed without breaking a sweat." Norne explained.

"I see. Each sword and suit of armor is to the quality of the previous king's... it must cost a fortune to outfit the entire army." Otto said in amazement at the Adamant armor.

"It's a worthy investment. Besides not all soldiers receive them. Only Imperial Knights elite forces loyal to His Majesty the Emperor directly. All the Provinces must send one-tenth of their best warriors to make up the ranks. Provincial armies are being reduced and must now have their budgets approved by the Senate." Norne grinned.

Those who retrieved the sword held it up high victorious and by coursing just a bit of Power through it, the blade would transform into a spear, the actual signature weapon of the Tartarian knight. Transforming Adamant items worked like primitive machines as running Power through their atoms instructed them to move and change shape (not at the atomic level but in sections). In the case of this weapon, the sword's handle was made of thin cylinders that could slide into each other for the short handle of the sword or slide out to extend the blade into a spear.

Though this was based on a new science that caught Norne's interest it was of course still an homage to her favorite Reme Empire. The transforming spear was based on the theoretical Hasta Segmentata: a supposed artifact that some argued was a Reman sword that could extend into a spear. Despite those legends modern Italia claiming that no such weapon was ever used in the Empire. Its existence was hotly debated between scholars, but Norne had just read a book about it recently and so the modern offspring of an artifact that may have never existed was born.

Yet much to Norne's annoyance, Otto didn't even notice or remark on her prized new invention.

Next, they passed into the treasury where the high-quality Adamant was being converted into armor and weapons.

"We have hired the best craftsmen in the Empire to produce that dazzling armor." Norne explained.

"From the treasury!? The Adamant is kept as wealth for a reason!" Otto was baffled.

"True. But there's an interesting complex we found. Within the last month, this Adamant has enabled the soldiers to acquire enough wealth to pay for their own arms. Already we are at a net gain. I think we might be on to something." Norne pointed to that very phenomenon.

Otto turned and gasped when he saw massive bags of Adamant being handed out to each knight.

"Some of the nobles had been hiding considerable wealth from His Majesty." Norne explained. "When we rectified the problem there was more than enough to go around and ensure his royal guard would prove more loyal to the crown."

"Then wait… all the nobles…" Otto began.

"They conspired against His Majesty, so they were executed and replaced with others more suitable to his interests." Norne said bluntly as they continued walking.

"I see." Otto said nervously.

"Some radical changes were in order, but I had to accomplish the mission you assigned, father." Norne grinned.

"You? Who did all this?" Otto asked.

"Me of course. I was the architect of the Tartarus Empire. I have the rough drafts of the Ten Tables; the Empire's founding documents in my room here." Norne explained.

"What!?" Otto demanded.

"You wanted to gain a stronger ally in Tartarus, and I did not fail. Not only are they more agreeable, as a high up in the new government I shall grant access to the country's inner workings for

Arcosia. This does not satisfy the goal of marriage, but I trust this more than makes up for that father." Norne beamed proudly.

Her father was shocked, as he tried to process everything while looking around and seeing Tartarus functioning like a well-oiled machine compared to how he had found it only a little over a month before. While he was lost in thought, annoyed that he couldn't find anything to criticize, Norne interrupted his train of thought.

"And that takes us back to where we started." she said while presenting the front door of the palace.

"I see." Otto said, struggling to find a point of criticism.

Norne smiled at him, waiting for the compliment she had worked unrealistically hard for. Right when he was about to relent though, King Otto remembered something.

"Well, how do you plan to reform the prison problem?" Otto asked instead. "Drakon did nothing but complain about how he was up to his eyes in rebels lately. How does one fix that?" he asked.

"I'm so glad you asked." Norne opened the door to the palace revealing a massive cheering crowd of people.

Chaos confidently walked past them and out the front door as the crowd's cheers roared even louder!

"What is the meaning of this?" King Otto asked in bafflement.

"He is a man of the people. The god comes down from his place on high to honor them with his presence." Norne explained. Chaos mounted a gloriously decorated mobile throne carried by muscular slaves. The beloved Emperor was marched away from the palace with the adoring people following close behind.

"Shall we?" Norne asked while motioning for her father to join. They followed the parade which led them to a crater made in the riots that had been filled in with stone seats and walls.

Chaos descended from his throne and walked to the center of the pit. A man already dressed in the Imperial Knight armor entered the ring with Chaos and loudly proclaimed for all, "HIS MAJESTY DRAKON OF CHAOS WHO BROUGHT ORDER TO THIS

GREAT NATION GRACES US WITH HIS PRESENSE!!!" the knight yelled, and elicited cheers from the crowd.

"HAIL THE EMPEROR!!! GREAT AND MIGHTY IS HE!!!" the crowd chanted.

Emperor... they hadn't called Drakon that in years. In his waning and dying years he was demoted to a mere king in their eyes. Norne had told Chaos the significance of being called emperor and so every time he heard that word he was filled with indescribable ecstasy.

Chaos lived for this praise and spectacle. Tartarian culture convinced the people that the mighty gained their power from the weak they killed. The kings of old grew in might with every successful battle or every great dragon they slew. In reality however, Chaos was energized by those indoctrinated in this cult of personality. As the cries and cheers of the slavishly devoted crowd died down, the announcing knight finally continued.

"Hail the Emperor! He is worthy of praise from us all, but the filthy traitors who sought to undermine the nation still refused the embrace of his Emperorship!!!" the knight yelled. The crowd booed on cue.

"But in his infinite wisdom and mercy, the Emperor has offered full pardons to any warriors among the traitors who can gain his favor and prove that they can be of service to the Empire!" the knight announced to the re-emergence of the same boisterous cheers. The planted chanters Norne had hired were working wonders at controlling the masses as usual.

While the audible jubilations only grew ever louder, an overjoyed Chaos flexed in the ring, showing off. He didn't know any of these faceless thralls or cared if any of them lived or died... but in this moment they were making him happier than he ever had been in his entire life. The validation and love he'd been craving had value even if they came from these nobodies. He was the Emperor! He was the greatest!

Next up for the bread and circuses: massive Adamant cages were opened, and the prisoners of war stumbled out into the make-shift ring.

"What's going on here?" one of them winced at the bright lights outside the metal box, not knowing he had just stumbled into a public execution. Chaos knocked his head off before he finished the breath from his last sentence. The other prisoners, horrified, and naked without their armor, clamored for shotty weapons as they were tossed into the ring by the jeering Imperial Knights.

Some lifted the cruddy weapons to fight while the smarter ones mad dashed to escape. Two of those fleeing who took off to fly away both had their heads grabbed by Chaos who swiftly caught them both out of the air before smashing them down into the stone floor! The people cheered at the gory display. Chaos posed dramatically while other prisoners flew off behind him.

"Come on! The Emperor has given you a chance to redeem yourself, fight like MEN!!!" the Imperial Knight yelled at the fleeing soldiers.

Chaos turned around and saw the fleeing prisoners. Sighing at the pathetic attempt, Chaos's eyes began to glow a flaming red before he fired a massive amount of Power up at them, incinerating them!

Chaos turned around smiling at the rest. Any who considered flying away had second thoughts and ran behind those with weapons. After this display, he turned his attention to the prisoners intent on fighting instead of fleeing. He menacingly approached the soldiers who all now armed themselves with Adamant weapons.

"ALRIGHT!!! Now the fight can begin!" the Imperial Knight announced as Chaos stared down the weeping soldiers.

"COWARDS! Stop your sniveling. You should be happy. Now we have the chance to avenge our king!" a voice called out.

The whimpering soldiers were shocked to find the six royal guards of Drakon I stepped up from among their number. Now fully armed they stared at Chaos with contempt. The crowd booed them which made Chaos laugh.

"Cease your laugh, monster! We will cut you down inch by inch to avenge His Majesty." The leader of the former royal guards pointed his spear at the emperor.

"You're going to try." Chaos laughed.

"OH SNAP!" the crowd reacted as if they'd just heard the best comeback in history.

The former royal guards were furious, and all unleashed their full Power in preparation for battle. They weren't the strongest fighters in the land (since they'd all gotten their jobs due to their noble titles and favor with the royal family), but they were still each a formidable knight in their own right. They stepped up to avenge their fallen king and maintain the influence in the old administration that their family had fought for.

One soldier, renowned for his speed in the group lunged at Chaos! With his weapon drawn he ran right at the giant who glared at him in disgust. As the soldier darted at him with speeds that put the others to shame… the sword snapped upon contact with Chaos. Everyone was stunned.

"Finally… I don't know why I bothered waiting for you to finally hit me. It was really sad watching you run all that way like a damned snail!" Chaos shook his head and laughed. "You're not just weak, wow, you'd never be able to even hit me unless I just stood still and let you!" Right after, five fighters all ganged up and attacked Chaos at once from different directions!

After their brutal fight, Norne had given Chaos some pointers. She pointed out that if he couldn't even use the blitz technique, then he was extremely unprepared for modern battle. He had been going off pure instincts with no training to speak of.

He had been completely lacking in understanding of the basic mechanics and tips for combat. The most essential thing that Norne drilled into him was the 3:2 rule. Power was great at doing many things… but fighting multiple opponents at once was not one of them. The focus required to battle multiple enemies was reserved only for the greatest and most experienced warriors. Even for them, common knowledge dictated that a fighter should **never** fight two enemies at once unless they were at least three times as strong as each enemy. Experts debated as to the ideal multiple for fighting 3 at once, but since it was a death sentence for most fighters anyways ascertaining how to do that wasn't very important.

And yet when the prisoners all converged on Chaos, he just smiled at them.

"Great. More slowpokes." Chaos mocked them.

The five warriors all attacked Chaos at once, flying around and attacking with all their might. However, despite his great size and bulky build, Chaos was able to agilely dodge past each of his five attackers simultaneously. Without even trying he made a mockery of them while laughing the whole time. He didn't even receive a scratch. Even his massive bushy hair wasn't cut even once! The fastest of the soldiers was horrified by what he saw! Even with his maximum Power, he was barely capable of perceiving Chaos at his slowest point.

"Come on guys, you almost hit me that time." Chaos mocked them with a lie.

Without even needing to use the blitz technique that he had seen Norne use, Chaos was moving and dodging so quickly that he appeared vanish and reappear! He snapped from view and reappeared instantly in another location, safely out of harm's way (not that any of those attacks posed a threat to him anyways).

A sword swung for his head, but Chaos just grinned. He saw that all five of his opponents were poised to hit a different vital point at once with their full strength. However, from his perspective, despite their desperate full speed assault, everyone excepting him was frozen in time. It was actively a bore to wait for them to even inch their way close enough to warrant dodging. As he was growing tired of playing with them, Chaos just sighed.

In the next instant, the soldiers were all stunned as they had missed Chaos having been rearranged from where they were a second ago. One was kicking another in the groin as he was being punching the face by a third. The other two were flying face first into each other for a double headbutt!

All five fell to the ground in defeat while Chaos stood behind them having not only moved out of the way but also taken the time to pose them each to hit one another. He couldn't help but laugh at his childish prank. However many times stronger than them he needed to be to fight 6 opponents at once... Chaos was well above that threshold.

The team speedster was the only one left standing of the group and he was stunned silent! He hadn't even seen what had happened. But Otto had. Even if it was a bit difficult to see everything that had happened at times, he had inherited high speed and Power befitting a king, so he saw it all. It was no wonder he killed Drakon.

"Well, that was a letdown. Bye." Chaos waved as he prepared to finish the job.

"No, wait! Your majesty-" the 'speedster' cried out.

But it was too late. Chaos' eyes began to glow with demonic flames and from that inferno came a massive beam of Power that vaporized all of them in an instance. Only a nuclear shadow remained where their bodies once were. The crowd cheered as Chaos went on a flexing fest once again. All that was left in the ring were the weaklings who had been too scared to approach him.

"Well then? Are you just going to stand there and let me kill you?" Chaos looked at them with a sadistic grin. The desperate soldiers all charged at him, and Chaos grinned before violently ripping all but one of them apart while the onlookers cheered. The final soldier fell to his knees, weeping.

"If this is about not falling in line—I swear I'll follow the script! Things happened how you say, I'LL FALL IN LINE! Please, I have a son to..." the soldier began weeping at the Emperor's feet.

Chaos got bored and swiped the soldier's head off with one hand. The crowd erupted into cheers as Chaos threw his hands in the air triumphantly.

"Such brutality…" Otto remarked nervously.

"True, but at least the people calmed down as soon as we began offering them these events along with a bit of cheap bread." Norne said with a grin. "The riotous energy could be directed else-where. As far as they're concerned, they are getting revenge for their families."

"How so?" Otto nervously asked while amazed at his daughter's lack of disturbance at the gore.

"Well, before he died, Drakon set free all the prisoners fearing another uprising. I guess he never really got over that Typhon incident. Anyways, Chaos swooped in and killed all the released prisoners and soldiers who were loyal to Drakon instead of Tartarus. He is their savior." Norne explained.

"Remarkable. Almost too convenient." Otto said while looking at Chaos skeptically.

"Almost. I mean… the Tartarus communication infrastructure was pretty bad. Who is to say a few names or dates didn't get mixed up in the official declaration put out? However, what matters is that now the nation is put back together and stronger than ever." Norne grinned. Otto gasped, finally unable to process everything he had seen and heard that day.

"Norne, my daughter. I'm finally proud of you." Her father smiled, finally giving in to the truth.

Norne's smile grew, and her eyes widened but it was short lived. Slowly her expression became lifeless and emotionless. Norne had heard the words she had always wanted to hear, that she had been trained to always want to hear. But now that she had finally heard them, she still felt empty. Her father's approval didn't make her feel anything at all, just cold.

A few days later, on Arcosia, a massive party was held as a summit for the royal families of all allied kingdoms. The Imperial

Core of Eurasia was an alliance that put an end to the constant warring of powerful nations so that they could focus on conquering weaker neighbours existed in the imperial periphery instead.

"Norne… what do I do? You taught me Tartarian for a month, but I can still barely speak it…" Chaos nervously said while waiting outside the party.

"It's fine. Just smile and look pretty. I'll do the talking. All that's important is that my father gets you international recognition." Norne explained while making final adjustments to his party wear before they entered.

"If you say so… but you said they're big and important! I don't normally care but I need to be cool like they are." Chaos worried.

"Don't worry. Royals are all overhyped. There is the usual holier than thou acting that we all learn and have to use but beneath it, most of the guys are high maintenance, sex-pest imbecilic leeches. In between their many mistresses and lavish parties at home they spend their time fighting wars to sate their midlife crises and relive their long-gone glory days to satiate their egos. They're too stupid to run things themselves so all the work is done by other people. The party is just an excuse to slack off before reading from the script their foreign policy ministers had them memorize as to what 'their plan' for the country is this year. Honestly, having your few weeks of language training means you aren't that far off from most of them. We'll be fine." Norne sighed, ranting about her hatred of these royal get together.

"Wow. Thanks, Norne." Chaos obliviously nodded his head. Then he remembered, "Speaking of which, can I get the hot language teacher back? The old man is boring." Chaos whined.

"No. You are learning from him now because I can trust you'll be learning to speak a different tongue, not kiss with it." Norne glared at him.

"Fine…" Chaos whined.

"Good. You will continue your languages lessons until you are fully fluent. Keep conversation to a minimum in there, 'kay? Let's go." Norne said before leading him into the party.

Everyone was laughing, partying and drinking but when Chaos entered you could hear a fork drop. Chaos was no Drakon, but the nine-foot-tall Reman statue of a man made just as much of an impression. Heidi who was bored of the two simultaneous would-be suitors arguing over her immediately laser focused onto Chaos, the hunk!

"No way." she said after seeing Norne walk in next to him, casually chatting.

"Go mingle." Norne told Chaos, "Just smile and nod. Nothing important is ever said in these cocktail pissing contests so there's no need to try and add anything." she nudged him before ironically walking into a corner and pulling out a book: *A Treatise on Empires and Theocracies by Leol Yoystorre.* Her mother quickly made her way over to her.

"Norne, I take it back. From now on YOU give me tips on picking up boys." Beatrix grinned to annoy her as she walked past.

"Mom!" Norne said in embarrassment.

"I'm just teasing. But more seriously, I heard about what you did in Tartarus. Excellent work. You really are a natural, it almost brought me to tears seeing my little girl take after me so much." Beatrix smiled.

Norne immediately perked up at hearing those words. It was different somehow from before, she didn't know she wanted to hear that but as if she NEEDED to hear that,

"So, I bet it felt pretty good, right? All the power that comes with this new position? Getting the chance to see your will manifested on the grand stage of history—to have power over your own life for a change as well as the lives of others?" Beatrix intentionally spoke in questions.

"Of course, mother. I already knew that." Norne responded as expected.

"It's important to love your work is all. Since we may be lightyears apart but will be working rather closely in the future, I just wanted to be sure you'd be having as much fun as I am." Beatrix grinned.

"It beats being cooped up in my room all day. Don't worry, Tartarus will be aligned with Arcosian interests from now on. There's no need to be on my back all the time." Norne sighed.

"I know I can count on you dear. So, I'll give you some space to grow into your own. I can't wait to see what a great shadow leader you blossom into. Plus, I was being honest, I'd kill to have a puppet as charming as yours." Beatrix giggled with her usual fake warmth.

"What useless formalities. Don't you have guests to attend to?" Norne groaned.

"Of course, my little snowflake. This will probably farewell for a while. Give 'em Hel." Beatrix smiled before taking her leave.

Norne had sent her mother away, but Norne still felt warm and fuzzy inside from that conversation for some strange reason. She was now certain of what she had to do.

As soon as Beatrix left however, Chaos waddled right back over to Norne.

"Norne... I'm bored." he complained.

"Fine... there's food. I know you like that." Norne sighed. Chaos excitedly turned to stuff his face, but Norne grabbed his arm. "But remember... eat professionally like I showed you. This is a summit of world leaders." she reminded him.

"Right." Chaos said before hurrying over to the food.

Heidi stomped over, "You. Hot guy. Explain now!" she demanded of Norne.

"He's a colleague from Tartarus: the Emperor, in fact." Norne said simply.

"Emperor! The king was a crusty old fart, and his son was a toad, how is HE related to them?" Heidi asked.

"It was a larger family than they liked to admit." Norne smirked.

"Must be considering Drakon the second would've already been desperately trying to convince me of his prowess with food all over his face." Heidi sighed.

"I wouldn't be so quick to judge. Also, gravy." Norne pointed at a bit food her sister had on her face from eating.

"NO ONE TOLD ME EARLIER!?" she freaked out and ran away, screaming as if she was being murdered.

Norne watched her run out but then noticed Chaos who greedily tried to fill his plate with food. Seeing him alone some royals excitedly walked over to meet the new kid on the block.

"Hello," greeted a man in silver Centurion armor who was wearing a laurel wreath atop his green hair. Chaos nervously turned around, his already face stuffed full of food. Not knowing what to do, Chaos swallowed quickly and began awkwardly stammering in conversation with them unfortunately unable to remember Norne's script.

"So, you're the new king of Tartarus. How does it feel being on top of the rest of the world? I swear, you kids really are over-achievers," the man, known as Aurelian, dictator of Italia said cheerily. "Have you met my darling Aurelia? You two seem like you would get along."

Chaos looked around nervously, before replying. "Hello, killed them," he said, anxiously nodding his head pretending to understand what Aurelian was saying.

"Ah yes," piped in the Queen of Belgae. "I hear the reforms in the nation mean you are killing it. Where did you get the idea for this *senate* to replace the noble council? It sounds fascinating."

"Hello, them kill?" Chaos tried a different permutation, desperate to get back to the food.

"Oh gods." Norne face palmed. When she looked up, Chaos was walking over to her and waved hastily to her to get away from the small-talking monarchs.

Norne sighed, looking down at her book, but less than a minute later, Chaos came toward her with food.

"I intended to read," Norne said in annoyance at Chaos' loud chewing.

"Sorry. I don't know what to say. You said I was dressed fine but everyone else is so much fancier." Chaos sighed.

"Don't worry, it's better this way. All their outfits are just an extension of their pretentious politics. You don't want any of that," Norne insisted.

"But it's just clothes," Chaos said in confusion.

"No—look over there, just recently we finally convinced Mesos to convert to silver currency like the rest of us for easier trading. Prince Grak always appears in place of his father so as representative of the country he is incorporating silver jewelry into his outfit. It's a status symbol for rulers to literally wear money and the more you wear the more confident you are. It's all superficial power plays," Norne explained.

"Oh! But other than that, everyone is wearing different weird stuff. I'm not complaining but a lot of the ladies are wearing things that certainly don't fit this cold," Chaos noted while checking several of them out.

"Yeah, that's a trend my sister started. It's expensive, but using Power, we can control the climates inside of buildings to be comfortable wearing anything. Fashion doesn't mean anything anymore so the one realization my sister ever had was that she could wear as much or in her case as *little* as she wanted. It is more a message to the peasants than other royals. It is to remind them of how comfortably she can live while they freeze," Norne said with childish spite. Norne was obviously not upset at Heidi's apathy for the suffering poor but instead for her sister's positive body image.

"Yeah, her outfit would only be comfortable if you were standing in fire," Chaos said while eyeing up Beatrix.

"That's my mom. My sister is the one wearing red because she insists on standing out." Norne pointed out her sister who had just returned to the party after wiping her face.

"Y'know, your mom and sister are pretty hot," Chaos said plainly.

"Thanks, I can add that to the million times I've had to hear that before." Norne sighed.

"Makes you wonder what happened with y—" Chaos grinned but cut himself off as Norne started drawing one of the many knives she had concealed in her cape.

"Physical appearances are meaningless. My mind is meant to be hidden, all the better to conceal my wit from the enemy. And Power doesn't care about physical traits either. You could be as small as I am and just as strong. This body is nothing but a tool to carry my intellect and Power, that is all. Caring about anything else is useless," Norne dramatically proclaimed.

"Cool. They're still hot though," Chaos said, not understanding anything she said.

"Oh gods—why do I bother." Norne face palmed again.

As Norne looked around in disgust, many of the other princes and princesses were engaged in the flirting traditions of the upper class. Half business negotiation and half hormonal cringe, the noble youths were expected to spend these social events coordinating alliances and picking their favorite mate for life from the short list of advantageous partners their parents had preselected. There was of course a hierarchy of who was even allowed to flirt with whom, and ultimately the final decision of these arranged marriages was up to the more powerful parents anyways.

Left alone, just as the name implied, Immortals would remain eternally youthful. They would undergo the full experience of human development up until their brains had fully developed at the age of twenty-five. From then on, they would look the same and never suffer the effects of old age or die of natural causes. The pressure for wedding young seemed ridiculous among Immortals, however, there was a reason for it. While Immortals were immortal and can regenerate and recover from almost any injury, there were cases when regeneration ceased working. When they were low on Power even sufficient damage to vital organs could kill them just as easily as it did mortals

In societies where men and women alike threw themselves into the fires of war for their petty ambitions, it made sense their greed and foolishness would thin their ranks down to the last if such precautions were not taken. So, as they sacrificed themselves in pursuit of Power, their children too were sacrificed to perpetuating this system of lightning paced deaths and births for all Immortals. To the cold nobility who were eternally youthful, the sanctity of childhood innocence meant little.

Old and young alike played the political games in the hopes of increasing their nation's Power. As they stood and talked and ate, they displayed their wealth with the exotic dishes they presented their hosts and curried favor with the dominant guests.

After about an hour of the farce, the party calmed down and King Otto clapped to get attention.

"Ladies and gentlemen thank you for your attendance. The meeting of kings and queens will commence now. Accommodations for everyone else present are set up in the secondary banquet hall," he explained. People exited the room leaving Chaos and Norne to look at each other, feeling out of place as they had managed to sit the whole thing out.

"Well great. You missed the chance to mingle," Norne grumbled.

The royal chairs were brought out and the head of each nation took their seat. Chaos sat on the Tartarus throne. Norne approached too but her father aggressively motioned for her to leave with the others. Heidi, on her way out, grinned back. Norne hung her head and began to exit but Chaos loudly said.

"No! Norne von Arcosia is with me," Chaos demanded, through mental projection.

"If you insist," Otto relented. Heidi frowned.

Norne pulled up a much smaller chair next to Chaos' throne. Everyone brought their own ornately decorated throne from home as further parading of wealth and status.

"Alright—down to business." Otto opened the meeting. Prince Grak of Mesos, a tall man with spiked brown hair in traditional green and bronze Iryan royal robe took special note as Norne sat at the table.

The rulers discussed their plans of conquest for the next year as to not conflict with each other's targets. A map was drawn up, tasteless jokes exchanged, and a consensus reached with all senior members: Arcosia, Mesos, Italia and Prussia. Then the lesser powers got leftovers.

Finally, the choice was given to Tartarus who had been demoted to dead last in the rank after Drakon's death. When the turn finally came to Tartarus, Otto asked, "and with the remaining territories up for grabs, what will Tartarus be pursuing for expansion?" he asked.

Norne just grinned. "Everything else."

A few people threw up their eyebrows.

"Let me explain. Tartarus will be pursuing an aggressive expansion policy. Why bother imposing any limits? Respectfully if no one else has it, then we will be pursuing it," Norne said bluntly.

"Lady Norne—I understand that you are still young, but we set a limit to begin with because establishing and assimilating new territory is very time consuming," a king warned.

"True, but that is using old and outdated methods. Tartarus will be pursuing a much newer and efficient method." Norne grinned.

"New and more efficient? We'd love to hear it," another king leaned in.

"We will share our methods after testing their level of success. I'm sure it will mean more to you once its proven to work anyway," Norne deflected.

Grak grinned at her responses. Norne commanded the attention and respect of the rulers as if she was a well-established leader, while Chaos just sat by smiling and nodding.

CHAPTER 5

After the meeting, as was customary in those days, the princes and princesses of the allied nations gathered to go Monster hunting for fun and glory. Chaos and Norne were young enough, so they went along too. Chaos was excited to fight and Norne was eager to size up the competition and make even more allies there.

Of the dozens of noble youths assembled, every single one was an Immortal. They could easily be identified from mortals due to their notable features of taller-than-average height, unrealistic physiques that require little to no maintenance, and finally strange hair and eye colours that were unnatural for most humans.

Not all Immortals had any of these things, but those who did were set apart and revered in establishing the beauty standards of their societies. Immortal features could be disseminated among the masses if they reproduced with mortals. There was not sure-fire way to know whether or not Immortality will be passed on, though most Immortal genes are dominant, especially hair colors. Unions between mortals and Immortals are looked down upon in, lest their pure genes be diluted.

Aside from being the only ones who could handle such Monster hunts, it was fitting that Immortals dealt with this problem, as it was "Immortal business." When Immortals died, they became Monsters—terrifying manifestations of the Power they had wielded in life. Their Power in death generally reflected a multiple of what they had in life. They couldn't take it with them, but it could keep going without them.

Without a Mind to command it, an Immortal's Adamant body shed their material form altogether and in death became pure Power. This flame of pure energy was mindless like a beast and gorged itself on any Adamant or sources of power they could get to avoid depletion and a second death. Some developed scales and bones and exoskeletons that could lessen the leaking of their Power and more importantly defend the solid Adamant Core of the beast that had formed from their living form's shattered mind. Their material body became immaterial, and their immaterial mind became material.

Only those with Power could hope to fight these creatures which could range between smaller than a human and the size of an entire city. The Arcosian army who had arranged this hunt were sure to lure in powerful Monsters to guarantee a good fight and plenty of glory for the ambitious youths.

The royal youths gathered on a large meteor, observing the swarm of Monsters coming toward them.

"So Norne von Arcosia, you were impressive at the summit. On top of that, I heard rumors you found yourself quite the monster. Are they true?" Grak asked, approaching Norne.

"Prince Grak of Akkad. It is an honour to be addressed by the next in line to be Lugal of Mesos. As to His Majesty's strength or rather 'monstrous nature,' I cannot say. None of the fights I've seen him in have lasted more than one punch. Seeing him fight these Monsters will probably confirm the rumors for both of us." Norne gave a phony smile.

"I see—" Grak began. Suddenly, Chaos launched up at the upcoming swarm of Monsters. He used the blitz technique to fly so quickly that to most, he appeared to disappear. Only Grak, Norne, and one other could follow his movements and see him reappear right in front of the swarm.

"Impressive." Grak smiled. Chaos was excitedly whooping as he flew towards the Monster swarm only to be eaten by the largest one. Everyone was stunned silent, but Norne just shook her head. The Monster shrieked at them, intimidating everyone.

Shortly after though, it began glowing from within and Chaos ripped his way out! Laughing as he tore the beast to shreds while running up its neck, he charged a punch and with one mighty blow which knocked the Monster's head off.

The beast's head landed in front of the other royals on the meteor who stared at it in amazement before the last of its Power dissipated, leaving nothing but its skull behind. Chaos landed on top of it, smashing it to pieces with a hearty laugh.

"I'm the best!" Chaos flexed. However, instead of praising him, Norne and the others had quickly flown away. Chaos was confused before looking up and seeing all the Monsters surrounding him to fire a massive, combined beam attack. They all focused on their blasts, destroying the entire asteroid. The other nobles had landed on smaller asteroids floating around nearby. When the dust cleared, Chaos didn't have a scratch on him. He just laughed before going on the offensive.

He went through the swarm, ripping the space Monsters apart while the other royals couldn't help but watch in awe.

"Norne…your beast was an incredible find indeed! After this is over you should come with me. I have something you'll probably want in on." Grak landed next to Norne and smiled.

"I'm listening." Norne finally looked up from her book.

"After the battle, come. Everyone else in on it will meet then," Grak said before running ahead to join the fight. Norne rolled her eyes and just sat down, opening her book. Chaos was whooping, jumping around, and smashing the giant beasts with his bare hands.

Crashing next to Norne, he looked at her. "Not gonna join?" he asked while holding a squirming Monster down and wrestling it right next to her.

"No thank you," Norne refused.

She preferred to keep her own Power secret as she was getting a feel for everyone's Power levels. Normally, she would just stay home with Heidi whenever the royal kids went out to fight. As far as everyone was concerned, Norne had failed to inherit her father's Power just as her sister had. Norne was already a national embarrassment to her father in every other way, so joining Heidi in sitting it out never caused much of a stir. This was her first time on the hunt, so surveillance was the name of the game. She took care to know who she could kill in a fight and who to be wary of. So far, she was not impressed.

"Alright. You're missing out." Chaos finally punched out the core of the Monster and it deflated under him. Looking up, Chaos saw a massive Monster swirling above all the others and released a giant smile.

"Got it!" Chaos excitedly shouted before jumping up. To his surprise though, a beautiful green-haired woman in Italic Centurion armor had already killed it in one punch.

"I think I'm in love!" Chaos' eyes widened at the sight as she flew down and burst through another Monster with a single punch, killing it as well. Blitzing around, she shredded dozens of monsters before they even knew they were dead. Chaos was practically drooling at the sight of this powerhouse. While he was distracted though, a massive Monster swooped down, trying to eat him. He managed to react, stand up and forcefully keep its jaw from closing.

"I swear! Why do all these things want a piece of me!" Chaos laughed while forcefully opening the jaw further than it was supposed to open. Suddenly an orange beam of highly focused Power, pierced right through the Monster and it died instantly. Chaos reoriented himself and used Power to fly up and look to see who did that.

Grak waved up at Chaos before going back to fighting multiple Monsters on the ground using his Lugal's sceptre, blasting any Monster in the distance using the gem at the top. He skillfully held off more Monsters than ten other fighters combined. His refined and masterful technique made him stand apart with a mix of both physical and ranged attacks that even surpassed Norne.

Norne took note of their Power. "Grak of Mesos and Aurelia of Italia—two of the strongest fighters in the known Universe. Some say they're already more powerful than most monarchs. What would they want with us?" Norne wondered while continuing to study their fighting. In the end, not a single Monster remained. Like a child, Chaos rolled all the large bones into a pile of potential trophies from his many Monster kills.

"Good job. The Adamant in Monster bones sells for a high price. Guess you do pay for yourself after all." Norne grinned after walking over and hitting one of the high-quality skulls to confirm its value.

"Good haul. You're going to love the team. Norne, I'm sure you recognize most of them," Grak said while approaching with a group of several of the stronger princes and princesses in attendance.

"Like I said. We're listening," Norne replied.

"Alright. Good work everyone," Grak said. "This is Norne and Chaos, the two people who successfully overthrew the former number one Empire in the Universe—Tartarus. If they aren't inspirations, I don't know who is. We have been born in interesting positions. A monarch ascends the throne after their parent falls. In times of war, with the turnover rate high for obvious reasons, we would all have ascended to our rightful stations by now, as many of our parents had.

But now, the Universe has stagnated. Safe, easy wars with the Powerless barbarians of miniscule tribes are all that our nations involve themselves in. No worthy opponent—no risk, no real challenge to their Power. Power and domination are the reason why monarchs are exalted above all others. That was why, but no longer! In this time of stagnation, the monarchs remain on their thrones, complacent and weak. Now our birthright is kept from us. As heirs to vast power and wealth, we are expected to accept it will forever be held out of reach. Our parents are *Immortal*. Their very lives keep what is rightfully ours out of our hands. But no longer." The others in the group cheered him on, moved by his charisma.

"Almost all the preparations are complete so we can *all* get what is rightfully ours," Grak rallied, as they cheered even louder. After his impressive speech, he pulled Norne and Chaos aside along with the green-haired woman from before.

"You've rallied an impressive amount of people to this cause. Everyone here is already in on it?" Norne asked.

"Of course. And this is Aurelia Gaius, my partner in crime for this little mission. You can trust her; she's been with me on this since the beginning and she's the strongest heir among us." Grak grinned while presenting her.

"I'll cut to the chase," Aurelia said directly. "As the one who often ends up as Grak's muscle I suppose we will be working together a lot—so, try not to irritate me," she warned. Chaos suddenly began making strange grunts and primitive primate noises at the sight of her.

"What the Hel? What are you thinking?" Norne raised an eyebrow, communicating mentally. To her dismay though, in his mind, all she could hear from Chaos were the same gorilla grunting and excited noises.

"Oh. That *is* what you're thinking." Norne sighed.

"Grak are these really the aces you promised? A baboon undressing me with his eyes and a munchkin who'd rather read a book than fight?" Aurelia bluntly asked. Norne almost burst a blood vessel at these comments, "Where does she get off with that?! I swear she's just like Heidi!" Norne ground her teeth while thinking about Aurelia's informal and direct speaking.

"Aurelia! Not now. We're talking business," Grak cried.

"Fine." Aurelia crossed her arms and turned away, disinterested. Chaos immediately looked down.

"Back to—business," Grak continued. "So, what'd you think? Pretty interesting proposition? I can tell you are more forward-thinking than most, so surely this aligns with your interests."

"As an affiliate of the Tartarus government, I know civil wars are bad for business. You have solid plans?" Norne coldly responded.

"Plans of attack to eliminate *all* national leaders. Even those whose children didn't sign on will be on the chopping block eventually. You just beat us to the punch with Drakon," Grak explained.

"I see. Well, if you want pointers—it really was a spur of the moment thing," Norne began.

"No. What we talked about there is just for the others. The true purpose is unknown to them, but of much greater concern," Grak interjected.

"Your target is? Requiring all nations together must mean they're a great threat," Norne said skeptically.

"I know it may sound biased, but our ultimate target is my father, Sargon of Akkad. All other battles are just a buildup to that final goal. He is the most ancient being in the known Universe. He claims to be an original Immortal," Grak explained.

Norne's eyes widened but she subdued her amazement with skepticism. "An interesting propaganda technique to be sure." She laughed it off.

"It is true," Grak warned.

"A likely story. My father used to claim to be an original Immortal too, till he gave it up because enough people have records of his father and grandfather to prove otherwise." Norne sighed.

"I don't get it, what's the big deal?" Chaos asked.

"The original Immortals. People had to have come from somewhere. Every religion has their creation myth, but while they diverge in many different ways, a strange commonality revolves around the spontaneous creation of the first beings. Beings without parents or normal births who were created straight by the gods or the Universe or whatever.

The weird thing is there are records all over of people claiming to be that. Saying they were emissaries of the gods made it easy to justify the first planet states. But over time, I thought the consensus was that they all killed each other," Norne explained to Chaos before turning to Grak.

"Some survived. Is it really that unbelievable? Immortals must have come from somewhere," Grak argued.

"Whatever, it's an old tactic for establishing legitimacy. Your father is fueling his old hype. I suggest you not be taken in. Right Chaos?" Norne sighed.

Norne looked over, but Chaos wasn't paying attention.

"Chaos!" Norne shouted.

"What?" Chaos cried out loud as he snapped back to reality.

"Original Immortals—ones without parents. If anyone tries to sucker you in with that baloney, they're lying. It's old fairy tale stuff. Completely unbelievable," Norne told him telepathically so that Grak couldn't hear.

"Why's it so unbelievable? My dad was one," Chaos casually added, mentally communicating with all three.

"WHAT!?" Norne and Grak gasped.

"Yeah. He used to say that's why he was destined to rule, as an 'original person'. It got annoying. That's where I learned about being king and stuff and how it was the best feeling that there is and that only perfect beings like me deserve it." Chaos explained.

"Of course, you're the son of Typhon the Destroyer aren't you." Grak realized.

"Yup. He really was that famous, wasn't he?" Chaos asked.

"Did everybody know about him except me!" Norne huffed.

"My father was the only living leader to meet him, but tales of his might shook all the nations," Grak explained.

"Yeah great, but let's go back—why is your father the end goal? Not to beat around the bush but surely Arcosia is poised to be a more powerful player." Norne stated.

"True. But as you can tell by his absence, my father is set in the old ways. He doesn't follow modern convention. In fact, it was my elder brother Hammurabi who expanded much of our international involvement. Father does things the way kings did in the old times. He prefers the old days. But that means if there is war, he will lead the charge, and in terms of power he is the mightiest king of them all by far," Grak pointed out.

"Maybe, but he was running scared from my old man, and I killed him easily." Chaos laughed.

"True again, but your father was not in his prime when he was exiled. Instead of risking a direct confrontation, the alliance of nations learned of a way to rob him of his Powers instead. The man you met was a shadow of the one everyone else remembered him as. You impressed me today, but you're no Typhon," Grak explained.

"The old man was...stronger than me?" Chaos gasped.

"At his peak, most definitely. From what I've seen today, you are mighty. But you have to remember that we Immortals grow in Power as we age. And though we inherit much of that strength from our parents, their own Power continues to grow independently of ours. That's why we need to work together or else be warned that your nation of Tartarus will not last.

My father has watched the Universe develop and he grows annoyed by its progression. If we don't act quickly, he's going to restart everything again just like the purge of the first generation. He'll take us back to the stone ages. I know you want more, but I really have dangled it in front of you enough for today."

"Forgive me for being doubtful," Norne said to Grak, "but how certain are you of success? Against not just Sargon, but the international community in general."

"We intend to be quiet about this. The deaths will be spaced out and seem unconnected and natural. They can be killed using poison, accidents, sudden Monster attacks, and so on. As long as we control the narrative and not make our involvements known, this should be an easy divide-and-conquer approach. Don't worry, it *is* thought through." Grak confidently grinned.

"I know that rulers aren't exactly known for being the bright-est, but are they really going to stand there as their fellow rulers drop like flies? Wouldn't you fear that they might start conspiring to see your downfall if their heirs begin taking over en mass?" Norne asked.

"We've already planned out the general order of removals, it's just a matter of finalizing them now. However, in general, Sargon is last and all the other leaders that are among the least bright will be saved for later. The most intelligent and dangerous will otherwise be removed before they could make a move against us. Trust me, I have this planned out. Minimal risk for us all and maximum reward." Grak grinned reassuringly.

"And Sargon himself? If he's so powerful, we can trust he is among the least bright?" Norne asked.

"Trust me. He is mighty, but he is also a giant fool. It'd be getting too much into the weeds to explain now, but as Prince of Mesos I handle all the international affairs. Areas under my administration keep his inner areas insulated from what goes on outside. Even beyond his slow wittedness, I will be doing everything I can to ensure news of the outside world never even reaches the isolationist heart of the Empire. He won't even know what we're doing before we're ready to take him out," he assured her.

"We're in," Norne instantly said.

"What!" Grak was surprised at how quickly she responded after exhausting her questions.

"We're in. Sign us up," Norne said before abruptly exiting, calling for Chaos to join her.

"We're in?" Chaos asked, picking up his massive Monster skull as a trophy.

"We'll discuss it tomorrow. For now, based on how he went on, trying to hook us in even if what he said isn't true, we can infer that he needs us more than we need him," Norne explained with an evil grin. The two made their exit, with Norne pulling Chaos by the arm as he craned his neck around to look at Aurelia who already looked back at him with disgust.

The next morning, Heidi confidently strolled through the palace as she hummed to herself with a mischievous grin. Finally arriving at the guest room where Chaos was sleeping, she creaked open the door with a smirk and snuck in.

"Good morning tough guy. I heard the Monster hunting went well last night." She made her way over to the bed. However, when she pulled the sheets off and bent down to kiss him, she was poked in the forehead by something.

"Ow! What the Hel!? I thought you'd be into this kind of—" she began before looking down and instead of Chaos found the massive Monster skull he'd brought back sitting there. The shock made Heidi shriek in horror.

"Norne!" she screamed angrily.

While Heidi cried out, far away Norne and Chaos were trekking through the snowy Arcosian mountains together.

Out in the snowfields, they walked to a nice, deserted spot in an area overlooking the castle. Norne was still in her blue nightgown and Chaos in nothing but his black pants. Shielded by their Power, the snow and ice were nothing to them.

"Why'd we have to go out so early? I wanted to sleep in." Chaos yawned.

"Because we need to talk." Norne answered.

"Oh. About that Grak guy? Can we really trust him?" Chaos asked, mostly just to mimic Norne's incessant skepticism.

"I'm impressed you suspect him so soon, but we can deal with that later." Norne smiled and took out her knife as her Power flared up. Chaos raised an eyebrow, quickly becoming fully alert and looking down at her.

"You wanted a rematch, remember." Norne grinned and tied her hair up in a ponytail. Chaos smiled. In a flash he Powerfully upper-cut Norne so hard that he carried her off the ground with his fist.

"I won't give you the chance to use that Power!" he cackled while putting his full strength into his punch. It seemed that after seeing it just once, he had learned the blitz technique, and his speed was monstrous.

The blow definitely broke a few of her bones, so Norne had put all her own Power into freezing just enough of the attack to not be killed. The slowed, depowered attack had spared her as she pushed herself off Chaos' punch. Using the blitz technique to have a chance of even hitting him now, Norne grabbed his throat with one arm, forcing him to the ground and began freezing his neck.

"That won't be enough to do it!" Norne laughed while wiping blood from her mouth.

The two maniacs were laughing. Norne was freezing Chaos' body again and held her knife ready to finish him off, however Chaos' full Power was too much, and the slow spreading ice quickly began boiling off. Norne gasped in surprise at the sight before Chaos violently grabbed her by the neck and held her up with one arm. She struggled against him, pulling with all her might to get his hand from around her neck, while he bellowed an insane laugh.

"Fine—finish me—" Norne accepted defeat. Chaos however just tossed her up and flopped onto his back playfully so that she landed in the snow next to him again.

"What?" Norne asked.

"You're too much fun, Norne." Chaos laughed.

"You don't say—" Norne raised an eyebrow in confusion.

"There. We're even now. After all, as my equal it only makes sense that we fight again sometime," he explained.

"I see. I didn't put up much of a fight there though." Norne let a genuine smile slip at the compliment.

"Well, I know I'm not that smart…but even at full Power it shouldn't have been so easy to escape your ice. That first punch I landed at full strength must have done a number on you, so it seems that whoever would win between us really just comes down to whoever gets the first hit. If you froze me before I could hit you, I'd be done for and if I hit you before you could freeze me, I'd win.

I mean you're the first person to *ever* survive being hit by me at full strength. I get excited just thinking about it. A friend who is just as strong as me!" Chaos smiled.

Norne, completely red-faced in embarrassment, didn't know how to take all the praise, so just looked the other way to see the castle in the distance.

"You're pretty cool too," she nervously managed to get out.

"Yeah, I am. But wait—didn't you want to talk about Grak?" Chaos asked.

"Right. Grak—let's talk about Grak." Norne calmed herself down while hiding her face from Chaos.

"His deal sounds pretty good honestly. I say we follow along as long as there are things to gain. Regime change is a pain to do by force, but if they will intentionally install monarchs we prefer, it just makes our job easier," Norne explained.

"Awesome! So, what was the sparring for?" Chaos asked.

"Just wanted to define a pecking order. Grak's warning made me want to reaffirm for myself that you were as strong as I counted on. Based on their reaction to your showing yesterday, I think it's safe to conclude that you are stronger than at least the majority of Grak's current allies.

Given your appraisal, I guess we can place me somewhere near that top as well. Basically, we can be sure at least for now that there's no threat of them turning on us just yet. But stay on your guard. Once we outlive our usefulness to him, don't be surprised if he approaches one of us about betraying the other. You're strong and pretty easily manipulated, so if they come to you with anything let me know," Norne warned.

"I'm not easily manipulated," Chaos said in embarrassment.

"Sure." Norne rolled her eyes.

"I'm not!" Chaos whined.

"Listen, even beyond easily outsmarting you, people can use their Power to control your mind. I know this may shock you, but Power has more uses than letting you punch things really hard."

"I know that. I can also use it to run very fast," Chaos retorted, thinking he was clever for pointing out the obvious.

"Very good Chaos. But I mean abilities. I doubt you have the wits for it, but people like me have found that Power lets you reshape reality itself. My Fimbulwinter is an example that you've seen, but I'm sure many people out there have figured out how to mind control. Fighters tend to specialize in one or two key uses—like my knives and freezing. So, you can be sure that if they can manipulate it, they'll be really good at it," Norne cautioned.

"Oh well. I'll just punch them first." Chaos excitedly cracked his knuckles.

"Right…honestly you probably lack the…mental fortitude needed to learn how to plan an ability or learn Runic to program your Power. So sure…for you, just punch the enemy first."

"Alright!" Chaos excitedly punched his fists together which suddenly caused snow to fall on Norne. He childishly pointed and laughed at her, but she blew it all off with a burst of Power around her body and dusted herself off in annoyance.

"Alright, come on, let's get back to the castle. We have business to attend to and I don't want you causing an avalanche," she said before flying toward the castle, Chaos following after her.

When they returned, Chaos snacked on the foreign fruits he had stolen from displays, while Norne cautiously looked around every corner of the stone hallway, which was dimly lit from the dwindling nighttime lamp oil. She could barely see the end of the hall as the blue carpets on the floor seemingly expanded toward nothing.

Heidi could've been down any hall, and the overcast skies ensured no sunlight came in through the tiny windows that dotted the higher ends of the castle walls. Norne refused to let her have Chaos too. It's just like her mother said, 'other women are harlots who are just trying to take away what you have.' Or at least that was what raced through her mind.

"What're you looking for?" Chaos asked.

"Shh!" Norne shushed him.

"But we're talking mentally." Chaos huffed.

"Whatever." Norne rolled her eyes and ignored him, refusing to concede the point. She turned a corner and saw her sister Heidi wandering around looking for Chaos.

"Hey, Chaos? You up?" she asked while looking around with a giant smirk. Norne panicked and rushed Chaos into her open room and closed the door, breathing a sigh of relief. Despite only having her back turned for a second to close the door, she turned around only to see Chaos find her knife collection.

"Ooh. Pointy." Chaos tapped the sharp tips of the assortment of blades. Though many were almost identical prototypes, there were many different shapes and styles attempted—some ceremonial and elaborate while others discrete and better suited for concealment.

"Hey! Don't look at those, they're scrapped prototypes!" Norne panicked in embarrassment.

"Whoa cool! Look, there are big ones and little ones! Even for you, this one is too small." Chaos noticed while comparing two.

"I've been making them since I was a kid. All Nornes make their own sacrificial knives… I was just kinda obsessed with perfecting mine. It's weird, I know," Norne explained before snatching them both away from Chaos.

"Look there's a whole bunch more in here!" Chaos said after opening a secret cupboard where in a stuffed doll (conspicuously with an old portrait of Heidi on the head of it) had dozens of knives sticking in it.

"Hey! Don't look in there!" Norne panicked, closing the cupboard with a bang. Meanwhile, Chaos was already flipping through some old sketchbooks of hers, before tossing them aside and digging through the bin of discarded jewelry.

"Chaos? What are you doing?" Norne asked as she turned around and saw Chaos grin.

"Ta-da! Check this out!" Chaos excitedly showed off a stack of metal rings that successfully fit around his massive forearms.

"Uh—that was supposed to be a corset—" Norne began, both impressed and horrified that it fit around his arm.

"Awesome! Get me another one of these corset thingies!" Chaos excitedly grinned. Norne couldn't help but laugh, confusing Chaos.

After the summit ended, Chaos and Norne returned to the Empire of Tartarus and continued winning over the hearts and minds of their subjects. They were very successful. On one occasion, Chaos used the Adamant bracers on his arm to block a powerful sword slash from a cloaked swordsman who had slaughtered many Tartarian citizens.

The people cheered as their Emperor came to their rescue and in one punch obliterated the enemy warrior and more besides. They brought out offerings to present to the Emperor and his Imperial Knights who they revered as gods. After the celebratory feast was over, Chaos and the soldiers retired to the palace. Chaos entered Norne's room and grinned.

"Alright! Defeating your ice warriors made me even more popular!" Chaos smiled while sitting on Norne's desk until he heard a loud creak and hurriedly stood up instead.

"For the last time, it isn't ice! It's called Vanus, a kind of anti-power. Well, technically Power is Vanus, but you wouldn't get it." Norne shook her head.

"Whatever." Chaos rolled his eyes like he had seen Norne do many times before. Norne continued paperwork. "Either way it's good," she said. "Now that we've run out of genuine Drakon supporters we just need to extend this parading long enough to fully capitalize on the people's hatred for their former king."

"Yeah, but why do we need to work so hard for the peasants? They work for me! Not the other way around," Chaos said.

"Right," Norne agreed. "But it's best they do not know that. They're too small minded to know their place, so they need an incentive to work for you. Besides, groups like Grak tend to take off when a monarch isn't popular, and we don't need that. Don't worry I'll develop more efficient ways to keep them docile later, but for now these spectacles are necessary. The people love you and news spreads fast." Norne signed off on some documents using Chaos' name for him.

"Yeah. Those ice guys you make, and control aren't much of a challenge on their own. But in our next sparring match you can have them backing you up to make it even more fun." Chaos excitedly anticipated their next match.

"I was really hoping my ice puppet ability would be stronger now, to put on more of a show…but at least even though it's incomplete it can still be of use." Norne sighed.

"You just called them ice puppets," Chaos pointed out.

"Whatever." Norne rolled her eyes, before realizing what had just happened. Oh well, monkey see, monkey do. Did she really do that so often?

"They put up more of a fight than those captured Monsters you used before." Chaos laughed.

"Grak said he'd be calling on us soon, so I figured it was too risky to lure Monsters to attack places when you may be indisposed upon their arrival," Norne explained.

The two had been running this scam for a few weeks already to win over territories hesitant to support Chaos, slaughtering the most resistant and earning the trust of those spared.

"I just wish you could come fight with me. That would be fun," Chaos pouted.

"Are you kidding? I have way too much paperwork to get through. But don't worry. Very soon, you'll have someone to hunt Monsters with." Norne grinned.

"Is she hot?" Chaos asked.

CHAPTER 6

Not long after Chaos and Norne's return, Magnus Pompeius Draco, the most powerful man in Tartarus made his dramatic return to the capital of Eizberg. The path to the castle was cleared and everyone stood aside as the procession of knights marched towards the palace. Behind them, the bones of a massive Monster were pulled along by slaves. Following that were large piles of gold, high-quality Adamant and other treasures he had plundered during his latest campaign.

Magnus made his way to the throne room and bowed before the new Imperial throne.

"Welcome back, General Magnus," Norne von Arcosia, his new ruler greeted him. Magnus looked up and found not the giant Jotun he had heard had usurped the crown, but instead a small Arcosian girl sitting on the royal throne.

"I understand this must be difficult for you. A lot has changed since you left for your campaign." Norne smiled.

"So, I have heard," Magnus emotionlessly responded.

He was exactly like Norne had read. Magnus was a nationalist fanatic who lived and died based on his loyalty to the Empire. Yet he was also notoriously stoic and hard to read. If he was on the verge of flying into a rage and hacking her to pieces for revenge, it would be impossible to tell.

Humorously he had just returned from putting down a rebellion attempt against the previous crown only to be greeted by a pair of successful usurpers.

If Magnus was in the capital on the day of the revolt, he would have fought Chaos and Norne to the death in favor of defending the old status quo. But by the time he learned of the overthrow, power safely rested in their hands and so he pledged his loyalty to them. While they were in charge, he would risk life and limb for them, but if he outlived their overthrow, he would serve the next usurper just as loyally.

"Magnus Pompeius Draco, I would once again like to congratulate you on your promotion to High General of the Imperial army. It felt wrong to only christen such an occasion with an impersonal letter." Norne stood up from the throne and began to descend the stairs toward him.

"I was honoured then as I am now," the stoic soldier replied. "I will do my best to bring glory to the Empire."

"Excellent. You'll have to forgive the emperor for not greeting you personally. He is currently indisposed. But please, shed that antiquated armor and don your new commander's set. Once you get changed, you can present yourself to the new emperor." She smiled as an armorer and some slaves entered to assist him.

"As you command." Magnus stood up and followed the armorer to get changed.

"How does the new armour fit, General?" Norne asked as she and Magnus entered the Imperial training grounds.

"It is excellent craftsmanship. Despite the increased defences, it is far more maneuverable than the old armour," he replied as he tested the different points of articulation of the armor and found it surprisingly mobile.

The strength of this new Imperial Knight armor came from its similar design concept to the Italic lorica segmentate. Rather than the old design's large Adamant chunks defending key areas, the armor was made up of many layers of reinforced Adamant pieces that could slide and pass each other in various ways to maximize motion.

"I'm glad you like it. It was the prototype that was intended for the emperor. However, *someone* is obstinate about wearing armour!" Norne said, raising her voice in annoyance at the end.

"Armor is for cowards!" Chaos rolled his eyes.

Magnus looked in shock as Drakon of Chaos, the usurper, stood in the training grounds wearing the royal purple robes of a true king. However, while he had his back turned in order to face them, three Imperial knights leapt forward to attack him. Magnus gasped, preparing to save his new master as he drew his new and improved Imperial knight spear.

"He'll be fine." Norne surprised Magnus by putting her hand out to hold him back. Chaos effortlessly blocked all three attacks at once before roundhouse kicking them all at once. The soldiers in their new armor just barely blocked his attack in time with their spears. Nonetheless, they were still thrown back and fell to the ground—defeated.

"Awesome! You were right Norne, these elite guys are way more fun than those weaklings from before." Chaos marvelled that his opponents' bodies, armor, and weapons were still in one piece after that attack.

"Of course. It'd be a rather large mis-investment if you were still turning them into a red mist while holding back this much. Anyways, peons, get out. There is a top-secret meeting going on," Norne yelled at the three aching knights.

"This girl is overly familiar with the emperor. Is this really the new second in command of the Empire?" Magnus looked skeptically at the small Norne as she chatted casually with Chaos.

"Chaos, this is Magnus. The one I told you about," Norne introduced him.

"It is an honour to meet you in person, Emperor Chaos." Magnus bowed before his ruler.

"Really? You're not mad about me killing your old boss?" Chaos was baffled.

"I am loyal to the crown...and now you are the one who wears it," he declared. Chaos looked at Norne skeptically, but she just shrugged.

"Alright, whatever. You guys do what you're doing." Chaos walked away and sat by the wall, much to Magnus' confusion.

"Magnus, you impressed me by so easily pulling your sword out of all nine layers in your test. I lament a nation wasting talent like yours simply because you lacked the right family connections. You're a cut above the rest of those stuffy bureaucrats who sought this position," Norne explained.

"I am honoured." Magnus saluted.

"But if you're going to work for me, I need to know that I can trust you; and that means we need to understand each other a bit better. Things will work best if I properly understand your capacity and abilities...and if you can glimpse mine," Norne said as she became serious.

Magnus felt an intimidating glare emanating from this tiny Arcosian child but kept his nerve. He figured he already knew her type—spoiled Immortal brats like Drakon II who were born with massive amounts of power but had far too great an estimation of their own abilities. This undue confidence was more irritating than intimidating.

"Let's fight one-on-one. We will test your combat abilities here and now so I can get a precise estimation of what I'll be working with, and you can stop underestimating me as quickly as possible. Seeing is believing after all." Norne grinned. Magnus was shocked.

"She's clearly close to the emperor in some way. I'll have to be careful to not seriously harm her," he thought as Norne began stretching to warm up for the match.

"And Magnus...if you disappoint me, I will kill you." she glared at him and he was once again taken aback.

Norne got serious, powering up to her maximum in front of the head-knight. Her raw power shook the palace as Magnus' cape was blown back. Despite her small stature, Norne had inherited her father Otto's impressive battle Power and even at this young age she could give him a run for his money. The training of the Church had closed the age gap relatively quickly and Magnus stood face to face with a warrior whose raw strength would rank among kings.

However, the knight stood firm, unflinching from the shock-waves and bursts of Power that came off Norne even as she reached her maximum power. With the power that they hoarded for themselves; one noble was strong enough to fight off hundreds of fodder soldiers by themselves. He would not be as easily impressed as a regular plebian.

After the initial shock of how high her Power was for her age, he simply returned to his previous assumption—she was an arrogant kid who inherited all her Power from her parents. Without Otto's years of experience, she was no threat to him. After all, his own battle Power was much higher than hers. He was the spear of the army, the mightiest warrior in Tartarus. While Arcosia's army was mightier knight for knight, even the strongest Holy Moon Knight knew better than going up against Magnus head on. Even Otto would have had second thoughts if he was in this situation. Really, under normal circumstances Magnus would've been head of the army far sooner, but nepotism won the day in meritocracy as it so often did.

Nonetheless, Magnus' talent for analysis and strategy immediately kicked in. Based off the massive amounts of Power Norne released as she rushed to reach maximum Power, the average fighter couldn't gleam much. However, he noticed that she spread her Power around her in a defensive shield to start with rather than focussing it on her fists and legs as melee fighters would. This likely meant she focussed on Type B combat—ranged attacks and blasts.

Next, he surmised that if she was a blast attacker like her father, she could also be an ability user and would use her power to activate bizarre effects and versatile powers. On top of that, she carried no weapon, or at least none that he could see. If she had weapons, she was the kind to conceal them.

All these thoughts raced through Magnus' mind in less than a second as his years of experience had taught him to do. Norne couldn't help but smile at having the Empire's genius tactician actually taking her seriously. And yet, she still felt somewhat disrespected. Magnus was still thinking about how to defeat her in one attack as to not harm the child. His lax posture and failure to match her full Power indicated as much. Just like her father. Her smile faded, and she took a step forward.

Magnus was mid-analysis before his years of experience again kicked into high gear. His warrior's instincts saw him jump high into the air just in time to escape the ice that was spreading all over the ground where he just stood. He surveyed the area, noting that the path of frost extended all the way from Norne to where he had once stood, conducted along the surface.

"That's no normal ice. There is not enough water for that much visible freezing. The air itself must have frozen!" he concluded as he felt something ominously off about the Power he sensed coming from the path, and especially from Norne. The Power she'd withdrawn at the start of the fight had…changed somehow. Converting raw Power into an ability? Magnus immediately noted she was more dangerous than he initially thought. As he descended from his jump, he used his Power of flight to hover above the ground, making Norne smile.

"You were quick to surmise a limit of my ability. As I'm sure you guessed, it's much more difficult to conduct my ice without a solid surface to work with. Much more Power consuming as well. Twenty points for thinking on your feet, or rather off them." Norne grinned.

Magnus grew annoyed that this mere child was appraising him just because of her bizarre Power. Drawing his spear, he prepared to attack as Norne jumped up at him and did the same with her knives.

As soon as they were out, Norne threw her knives only for Magnus to dodge them so quickly that he appeared to vanish. The blitz technique was popularized by Arcosia; however, Tartarus had adapted it as well and Magnus was known as the best user of the high-speed technique in either country.

"You're pretty impressive at using the technique of my people. Not bad for a foreigner—I almost want to give you some points," Norne confidently said as she turned around and deflected an attack from Magnus which was meant to knock her out.

Norne counterattacked with the dodging Magnus now on the backfoot. While she had Powered up, he still hadn't, and so his speed was limited to the restrained Power level he had patronized her with. It was a mistake he severely regretted since this handicap saw him cutting it extremely close with each swing.

With no other choice, Magnus swung his spear and clashed with Norne. The Powerful shockwave sent both flying backwards. As soon as Magnus hit the ground, he immediately Powered up to maximum Power. She was still a kid, but he knew he had to take this fight more seriously. It was just a sparring match, but she seemed like she was out for blood.

"You're finally starting to take this seriously? Good. Then I guess I can too." She smiled.

Magnus thought she must be bluffing. There was no way that she was holding back. That would mean her Power level was even higher than Otto's. Sure enough, Norne did not Power up any further. She was already at her maximum Power.

They clashed many more times in the air with their weapons swinging, dodging, and blocking one another. Neither scored a vital hit on the other but a full Power Magnus now held the advantage... sort of. He knew he was faster than her, but her expert use of the blitz technique almost made her an equal to his incredible speed. He was the master of the blitz, the best in Tartarus. He should've been running circles around her. Was this new armor heavier than he thought?

Magnus grumbled as his many attempts to knock Norne out with a single non-lethal hit kept missing when he could've sworn, they'd have hit. If anything, as things went on, he felt as if he were actually getting slower. The whole time, Norne just had a confident grin on her face as she blocked and dodged these attacks.

Finally, the stalemate broke as Magnus swung his spear and knocked Norne's knife out of her hand.

"It's over," Magnus stoically declared, before swinging his spear to hit Norne with the flat side of his blade. Norne however just smiled.

His spear stopped short of hitting its target. In fact, he stopped altogether as he became frozen solid! Every clash with Norne—every time he remained within that strange Power around her, he'd been losing power, speed, and heat. This was the result; his eyes moved around inside the Magnus shaped ice block, frozen in disbelief.

"Another twenty points for that impressive speed and skill. You're as good with the spear as everyone says. But appears you aren't a very good listener. It was at the start of the fight, but surely you haven't already forgotten—my ability works wonders with solid objects. That includes you." Norne grinned.

"What a dummy!" Chaos laughed at Magnus despite having been caught by the same trick before.

Norne casually walked over to pick up her knife before strolling back to Magnus with a menacing grin. Magnus couldn't move at all. He was defenseless and Powerless even with the armor. Norne grabbed his spear and then effortlessly threw him up into the air.

"Try to free yourself before you fall and shatter," she shouted.

He panicked, forcing out as much Power as he could to try and thaw the ice and mysterious curse Norne had put on him.

Before even beginning to fall back down from his arc, he broke out of the ice in an explosion of Power.

"Wow. For a weakling that's pretty good." Chaos chuckled.

In that ice, he'd lost so much Power that he couldn't even reach his maximum anymore. This permanent reduction also came with the nasty surprise that his recovery was significantly slowed. His analysis of his current situation had immediately become grim. If he was frozen again, he was unlikely to have enough Power left to thaw out.

"This child…is no ordinary fighter." He was filled with dread just looking down at Norne.

"Well, aren't you coming on down for round two, Magnus?" she asked, grinning.

Pushing past his usual limits to save his pride, Magnus could top up at around ninety percent of his original maximum, to survive this encounter, that would have to do. Norne tauntingly motioned for him to come back down, to be up close and personal.

"She's a nightmare up close, but—" Magnus thought as he spun his spear around and began firing spear shaped blasts down at Norne.

Norne grinned and effortlessly began dodging all of the attacks that rained down. She was amused by this shift in tactics. Unaffected by her ice, he definitely held a speed advantage, so attacking from a range was his best chance to hit her. His ranged attack Power was nothing to scoff at, but Norne evaded him just the same.

She knew he must be desperate. If she returned fire, she would destroy him. If he continued to be this disappointing, she figured she'd just shoot him out of the sky and call it a day.

Through the rain of fake spears however, her eyes widened as his actual spear down came. Thrown using his physical strength, rather than his less impressive Type B blast attacks, it presented an actual threat. It was hidden among the swarm, so Norne only noticed it when it was a few feet away from her. With no time to spare, she raised her defenses to block it as the spear made contact with her Power.

If Norne had tried to block it like a regular fighter she surely would've died. And yet, with her Power to remove the Power of others, she had blocked the spear not by pushing against it, but instead slowing it down and freezing it until it had no momentum to block.

Magnus was horrified as Norne held onto his spear, which had been completely frozen solid.

"Nice throw! Twenty more points for sure. If I was a normal fighter, that would've killed me." She smirked before throwing the spear back. Magnus gasped and dodged it, making sure that weird Power of Norne's didn't touch him. When he looked back down to see her however, he found she had flown up and was now inches away from him.

He was dead! All his training had failed him up against the demon in a princess' body.

Norne stopped with her hand only an inch away from his face. It was just a child's hand, yet it was also so much more than that. Hovering around it, like an icy mist, was that otherworldly, unnatural form of Power. As cold as death itself, being this close to the source of the attacks that could freeze him just by being in the general area of it filled him with a primal, inescapable dread. If this girl was in charge, though she was Arcosian, this country had finally deserved the name Tartarus!

Magnus was shocked that that she didn't finish him. It would only take a touch. He was stronger than her by far, but he never had a chance of defeating Norne von Arcosia. He now knew his place in the face of this awful power.

"Another twenty for the dodge. And the final twenty...for knowing to acquiesce to your better. Submitting to the strong is exactly the kind of thing I look for in a number two like you."

She grinned once again and pulled her hand back. Magnus was too stunned to even move. His spear fell back down from her throw, and she caught it for the stunned warrior.

"I believe this is yours. As well as the command of the Imperial Knights. Congratulations Magnus Draco. You've impressed me. Welcome to the inner circle." Magnus took his spear in confusion. She was terrifying. Perhaps just as much as the emperor.

"So, Chaos, any protest about him as our head minion?" Norne asked.

"I guess he's fine. But from the look of it, he isn't that great. If you fought him like you fought me, he'd be dead already." Chaos sighed.

"She was holding back!" Magnus gasped.

"Don't look so glum Magnus. Sure, that was only fifty percent of my true strength, but I'm hardly a conventional opponent. In a normal fight you would've easily won with the skills you showed off. But raw strength isn't everything in a fight." She laughed at his horrified expression.

That insane and completely unfair Power of hers was not to be trifled with. This was the kind of Power that no amount of mere training could prepare you against. He was filled with amazement and loyalty towards his new masters.

"Excellent. Magnus, you can finish up His Majesty's domestic martial duties while he is off handling international affairs." Norne smiled.

"As you command! In justice!" Magnus cried and saluted the two with the new Imperial motto. Now that a champion of the home front was secured, Norne could properly focus on their commitment to Grak's alliance. When the appointed date came, Grak arrived with Aurelia where Norne stood next to Chaos who sat on the throne.

"It's time," Grak announced. "Our first target will be toppling Aurelian the dictator of Italia to install Aurelia," he explained with a strange hesitance in his voice. Aurelia looked at him with a side eye but said nothing.

"Understood. When will this operation take place?" Norne asked.

"Today. We handled all the boring preparations so all that is left is to execute on them," Aurelia explained.

"I see. Well, as pledged, his Imperial Majesty will lend you all his strength," Norne proclaimed.

"Alright!" Chaos cheered as he stood up and dramatically descended the stairs from the throne to the ground.

"For this battle, a brute force approach will be necessary," Grak said. "That's why we've called upon your help. In future it will be hushed up more, but know that today, Aurelia will be taking full credit for what happens. Officially, we will have had nothing to do with this, but it will be a second instance of direct overthrow."

"What happened to being subtle." Norne was annoyed.

"Again, apologies for this, but she is very insistent." Grak laughed.

"I'm not a coward. You can spin excuses for any other battle, but I will proudly own that I won my birthright by my own power," Aurelia declared.

"Anyways, what about you, Princess Norne? Are you going to fight with us?" Grak asked.

"I am not one for combat. I will stay here and maintain the administration. I wish you success in your mission." Norne smiled the phony grin she had mastered.

"I see. No need to worry. We'll have His Majesty back before bedtime." Grak smiled before turning around and exiting with Aurelia and Chaos.

"Chaos—" Norne communicated mentally, "If they do anything suspicious...kill them,". Chaos grinned and nodded silently before following his new "allies."

CHAPTER 7

The Imperial Core of Eurasia was populated by the spinoff nations of the ancient Italic Empire and Mesos Empire. Over a thousand years before this tale, each empire had suffered a tiny little collapse and lost control of their territories. Mesos had handled its collapse far worse and the lost territories in Asia were further flung and had over time lost contact with this little international community's corner of the Universe. Thus, the Imperial Core was mostly comprised of Italia's bastard children.

After the fall, this bastion of civilization played hot potato with whichever dominant power in Eurasia was claiming to be the inheritors of classical society that week. The Arcosians, the Venetians, and other Italic minorities. Even Tartarians at one point or another held it as a sign of their right to rule. Back then, those who had been left behind by the majority who escaped from planet Italia to the planet Ravenna found themselves ruled over by foreign barbarians, and their sacred Reman senate was reduced to a mere city council in the face of foreign despots. They had been colonized by those whom they had once oppressed, while the escapees spent their days bickering over who had the right to reconquer the old capital instead of ever actually doing it.

Yet, one day, the warrior hero Aurelian who wielded the power of the founder returned and recaptured the sacred city for the Italic peoples. And for almost five centuries the new Reme was the Empire of Italia, the one and only successor to the old world.

The old city of Reme was rebuilt as good as new and shone as a beacon on the planet of Italia from which this palingenetic nation was ruled.

Over his long rule, Aurelian had seen to it that that imagined glorious past was brought to life before everyone who had longed for it. The pristine pillared palaces proudly stood as if they were still in the glory days of the old Empire. Their technology was cutting edge by the standards of a space faring medieval society, yet traditional ways of dress, art and even speech were returned in a pseudo-renaissance. Aurelian had made Italia great again! At least that is what his political maneuvering had convinced everyone.

The Dictator put meticulous effort into revitalizing all the classic features that the Remans idolized. That nice coat of paint tickled everyone's nostalgia and kept them blissfully distracted from the fact that the only things that really hadn't changed were the inherent flaws in the empire that had doomed them back then.

In fact, the only thing missing was the actual coat of paint. The only part of the recreation that failed historical accuracy was the marble white everywhere. The paint of the old world had long since faded and the raging war had killed anyone who would be old enough to remember the century's old coloring. In the intervening time, people had grown to appreciate the old uncolored marble and since Aurelian's goal was the return of an imagined past over truth, it was good enough.

In fact, the only change that Aurelian actively reminded his subjects of, was the new religion that Reme was reborn with. During a pivotal battle, Aurelian had a "come to Sol Invictus" moment and he was determined to make sure everyone else did as well. The pagan Olympians were cast out of their own reconstructed temples and the Iconography of the decorated star god was thus everywhere.

In fact, it was from under one of these statues of the sun bird of Sol Invictus (a repurposed Aquilla bird of Jove-Tinia) that Aurelia and the strike team emerged. The secret entrance into the palace that her ancestors had once used to escape the sack of Reme now served as the entry point for those who once again sought to overthrow the Dictator.

"This way." Aurelia led Grak, Chaos, and her elite soldiers into the Italic palace interior.

"I am not going to lie; my father is second in strength only to Sargon. However, he is too crafty and influential to be left around once this starts. So, if either of you want a chance at claiming your thrones, we need him gone. So, this is just as much for all of you as it is for me," Aurelia bluntly briefed them.

Chaos had long since stopped listening and noticed a group of priestesses (the Italic vestal virgins) giggling as they walked to the chamber of the Divine Flame that they attended.

"Word of warning, head-on in a fight, he'd kill half of you. On top of being comparable in strength to me, his unique ability is a pain, so we all need to ambush him at once before he can use it. His Power is great but even he cannot effectively fight multiple opponents at once. Got it?" Aurelia nodded to the assassins. They ran off, but Chaos was preoccupied staring at a group of the beautiful Italic Vestal virgins who walked ahead, carrying urns and artifacts for their rituals.

The assassins expertly moved ahead with purpose; their eyes fixed on the next target while looking out for potential enemies. Meanwhile, Chaos went in the opposite direction, literally chasing skirts. Ironically as he snuck away, he was stealthier than he was for the mission, as he took great care to float low to the ground, for both silence and inconspicuousness.

Those loyal to Aurelia allowed the assassins right into the palace and any others along the route accepted bribes without question. Aurelia's plan was a perfectly executed infiltration and fool proof (though they had underestimated one fool).

"Whoops! Almost forgot why I was here," Chaos said, remembering his purpose. "Gotta go, ladies. But if the princess ever comes by, could you put a good word in for me?" Chaos hastily ran out of the Italic shrine.

Aurelia slipped the palace aristocrats their bribes so that they exited the building with all their guards before the fighting would start. She nodded that they had support for the next little bit.

Chaos wandered around a dark corridor. "How'd I get in here...*feastiary*? Like for a feast! Sweet, it's dinner time!" Chaos stopped next to a sign and ironically misread the word "Bestiary."

He excitedly lifted the door to the cage and walked in.

"What's in here?" Chaos naïvely asked while stumbling into the den of Monsters, unknowingly walking over the bones of those who had foolishly entered previously.

Though Monsters would normally hibernate when not presented with a source of Power to consume, with a Powerhouse like Chaos in the room, they were wide awake.

In the next instant, the massive Monsters caged within, used for public executions, breathed a terrifying beam of energy that melted the very Adamant cage meant to hold them.

Aurelia and the assassins ran ahead, still without tripping any alarms, but as they turned the corner, she motioned for everyone to stop. Past the front guards, the tighter security in the inner palace was a concern.

While looking around the corner at the Italic royal guard in assembly, Aurelia turned to Grak. "The Praetorian guards were too risky to approach with this, because they're too loyal to father. I'll try talking them into it, but if things go south, we have to B-line for my father and take him out before anything happens. Hear that big guy? Stealth is—" Aurelia began before looking and just then realized that Chaos was gone.

"He left us back at the front entrance," an Aurelia camp soldier whispered.

"WHAT!? Why didn't you say anything?" Grak asked angrily while looking around.

"The palace is constantly monitored. He's going to give us away!" Aurelia cried. A loud alarm sounded, and the infiltrators looked around in concern. Just then, Chaos crashed through the door, hanging onto the tail of a massive Monster meant for the Bestiary festival. The panicked and fleeing creature forced the soldiers to dive out of the way, as it demolished everything in its path.

Chaos finally dug his feet into the ground, stopping the beast and began swinging it around before throwing it straight into the air. The beast flew up several stories, collapsing the stairs where soldiers were running down to respond to him.

"That was fun. Ooh! Look, the throne room. That's where the guy is right?" Chaos asked. Aurelia and Grak's jaws almost hit the floor. Casually strolling up to the door, Chaos knocked it over with one hand. Inside, the throne was empty.

"That's weird. It's almost like they knew we were here... how'd they find out?" Chaos puzzled as the entire hallway behind him collapsed from his antics. When Chaos turned around, the Italic royal guards had him surrounded.

"Oh good! You guys are Aurelia's inside people, right?" Chaos asked. Aurelia who was still watching this, despaired. The soldiers all dog piled on Chaos, kicking and hitting him while he was on the ground.

"Hey! Hey! Stop that!" Chaos squirmed under all the warriors' combined attacks.

"Come on...if he's not in there, I know where the bunker is. The oaf will ensure it isn't too heavily guarded." Aurelia sighed and led the group away.

On the first floor, Aurelia led them into a secret room behind the shrine.

"Come on, he's in here." Aurelia nodded and began to open the secret door. Immediately after though, in the middle of the bunker, Chaos fell down from the roof with dozens of chunks from dead soldiers and Monsters.

Chaos fell on his butt in the middle of the room and looked around cluelessly. "Oh hey, a second throne room." He smiled.

"Drakon! You are the one besieging me!" Aurelian demanded.

"Chaos! What're you doing! We were supposed to sneak up on him!" Grak cried and Aurelia ran in after him.

"I see…so you are in on this as well Aurelia?" Aurelian asked. Aurelia didn't respond and simply turned to the royal guards.

"Leave here if you wish to live. If you put your weapons down and join your new Dictator, I will spare you," she confidently ordered them. Several soldiers began whispering amongst themselves, but Aurelian simply began laughing.

"Aurelia… I thought I'd taught you—a dictator does not ask, they command!" Aurelian's eyes suddenly began to glow. Grak and Aurelia knew of this ability and so immediately raised a Power defensive barrier to keep it out. The ability cracked their shields and would have broken in if any average warrior dared try and block it. But prodigious Grak and Aurelia's shields did hold, and they remained unaffected.

"The Power of the Dictator is complete control of those beneath him. Your assassins are now under my complete control! In my foolishness, I taught it to you Aurelia…but it means you should understand your situation," Aurelian monologued. Grak turned around, seeing all the brainwashed soldiers whose shields had failed, staring at him, and preparing to attack.

"We have to deal with them before my father. To break his hold on them we must—" Aurelia began but suddenly all the soldiers exploded in a massive blast. Grak and Aurelia turned around, shocked to see Chaos with his eyes still glowing and surrounded by the residual Power from the beams he had fired.

"What are you doing?! Those were allies!" Aurelia screamed.

"From what I heard; they were dead weight. Let's get this over with." Chaos turned to face Aurelian.

"Oh…it appears I must have somehow missed you. But I like your spirit kid. Tell you what, I'll make you, my herald! From my forefather Aeneas on down, the absolute authority of the Dictator commands you!" Aurelian grinned at his overdramatic theatrics before he again used his mind control ability, this time on Chaos.

Grak quickly brandished his sceptre and created a barrier of Power around both of them to keep the mind control Power out again however, Chaos didn't bother evading Aurelian's beam of influence.

"Now, Drakon of Chaos! Execute the duplicitous Grak and my treacherous daughter Au—" Aurelian began but Chaos suddenly began walking towards him.

"What! Listen here, slave! I ordered you to attack them! I am your Dictator, OBEY MY ORDER!" Aurelian fired the mind control again, but Chaos kept walking.

"I am Drakon of Chaos and I obey no one," Chaos furiously responded before walking right up to the Dictator and towering over him menacingly. Aurelian finally stopped trying to control him and stumbled back in shock.

"Impossible! My power as Dictator is *absolute*! It comes from the gods themselves!" Aurelian panicked.

"Well, my authority as emperor is absolute because I AM A GOD!" Chaos grinned menacingly before his power burst forth in a violent inferno around him. Aurelian froze in fear. His ability required massive focus and Power, leaving him temporarily vulnerable and drained of Power.

"Now obey *my* order. Die." Chaos made a fist. He threw a mighty punch, which Aurelian blocked by putting as much Power as he could into both his arms. The shock to the unprepared dictator shattered both his arms and launched him into the air. Chaos' eyes widened, impressed that someone could even survive one of his attacks head-on.

"Got to get some distance and re-orient!" A panicked Aurelian ignored the pain and focused on Chaos but noticed Aurelia dashing past him. Zooming up at him with a blitz so quick that she seemed to disappear for a second, Aurelia threw a swift punch right for the head kill-shot. The attack was swift, but Aurelian was the one who taught her high speed combat and so dodged nimbly, and her attack only managed to draw blood from his cheek as it grazed him.

The two made eye contact, neither daring to leave themselves open with their ability's long cool down time but nonetheless, the eyes of the dictators glowed not unlike the brandishing of a weapon.

Aurelia's killer intent was palpable—they had to kill Aurelian before he could fully recover from using his Dictator ability. If he did, he could regain control of the fight and counterattack at full strength. A warrior king like him did not survive this long by fluke. He was five-hundred and three years old and had fought more battles than all of them combined, tenfold.

Before Aurelian came to power, an Italia in crisis went through multiple Immortal rulers per century. There were once twenty Dictators who rose and fell in only fifty years. Yet, Aurelian alone ruled for a span nearly ten times that. He had repelled invasions from Tartarus and Arcosia simultaneously in the past and defeated both their kings at once.

This was not an opponent to be taken lightly, even three on one. This fight was to be quick and brutal. Aurelian's anger was clear too, but as he stared at his daughter, despite his best efforts, he faltered. For a second, a great sadness washed over his visage.

There was no time for that though as Grak finally got a hit of his own in, firing a beam from his staff. Sacrificing his leg to block it, Aurelian growled in pain as his shin armor shattered from the explosion. His arms hadn't healed, and he literally had only one leg to stand on while both Aurelia and Chaos came punching towards him. Aurelia threw a punch which he tried to block with what remained of his arms, but they were blown into chunks by the impact.

In that instant though, Aurelian remembered. Many years ago...

"Got you!" a 4-year-old Aurelia yelled, while throwing a powerful right hook, but Aurelian easily dodged her attack in the sparring match and caught her in a bear hug.

"Come on my Tesoro. You always put all your weight behind a right hook. Just because I showed you how to focus your Power for critical strikes doesn't mean you should do it constantly. It's too obvious." He laughed while carrying the little princess over to the table where his queen had brought out some Mensa for them to snack on. It was both of their favorite.

"It's obvious, but it's my strongest move. It makes sense to use it with all I've got!" she bluntly responded. Aurelian had laughed back then, but now in his desperation, it was all he had.

In the present, Aurelia and Chaos were both punching to kill. As expected, Aurelia's punch was a right hook. Viewing the double team attack and gauging the angle and distance of his attackers he powered up to his maximum.

"Vici!" Aurelian cheered, using his remaining leg to try and divert Aurelia's punch to kill Chaos instead. Chaos was shocked and backed off to prepare and redirect his Power to defend himself. Aurelia, however, swung her right arm so swiftly that her father's kick missed. He gasped as Aurelia instead swung her arm to use the momentum to spin her entire body.

With this spin, Aurelia swung her left leg and obliterated her father's! Aurelian gasped as Aurelia spun a second time with that momentum and threw a right punch anyway. This full force hit to Aurelian's head caused a massive leak of his Power reserves which lit the room up in a flash! The attack had such force that even after shattering his defenses it sent him crashing through his throne and the wall, out into the back yard!

All this took place in less than a second.

Aurelia flew out after him to finish the fight. Chaos was eager to follow but Grak stopped him.

"Hey! Why'd you stop me? I thought the mission was to kill him." Chaos angrily pulled his arm back.

"Hold on...you got yours. Everyone gets to kill their own," Grak explained while putting his hand on Chaos' shoulder.

"Really? You didn't hear my speech a while back there?" Chaos raised an eyebrow.

"I thought of this. Norne agreed to this, and I thought you listened to her," Grak pointed out.

"Fine, whatever." Chaos pouted and stepped aside as Aurelia stepped up. He'd had enough fighting for that day.

Outside, Aurelian's body was mangled. He vomited blood but managed to survive. The crippled dictator intentionally rolled down the hill using his half-regenerated arm and leg nubs to try and escape.

Reaching the bottom, he looked up at the sky, breathing heavily. His armor was smashed to pieces and gone forever, but his limbs eventually regrew. They were weak and numb, but he could move now. He forced his barely healed body to stand up on his wobbly new legs. Before he could even get up on his feet fully, Aurelia came crashing down from the sky. Strangely, her confrontation had been delayed slightly. The impact sent her father flying into the Tiber River that ran behind the palace.

"By Sol Invictus! My own daughter! What did I ever do to deserve this?" her father gasped.

"Nothing. You were a good teacher and an even greater father. But, your life robs me of my birthright. You made me grow up in a farcical position, a princess who could never be queen. I refuse to be denied my birthright any longer. I will claim it now," Aurelia said before powerfully knocking his head off. He hadn't even had time to get a last word in.

"Whoa! What a shot." Chaos clapped for Aurelia, after childishly sliding down the hill to witness the fight. A much more considerate Grak went over to console her and ask, "are you alright?"

"Better than fine. Now excuse me... I have to prepare for my coronation." Aurelia walked away without making eye contact.

"Well…thank you for the assistance. Things didn't exactly go as planned but your role in this was important," Grak turned and spoke to Chaos.

"No problem, it was good exercise. I'll head back and tell Norne the good news. See you at the coronation." Chaos waved before flying off.

With Chaos gone, Grak walked over to Aurelia who was leaning against the wall weakly. He watched his friend worriedly and began moving to comfort her, however, she held her hand out to stop him.

"Aurelia… I told you it wasn't worth it. Our situations aren't exactly the—" Grak sighed.

"Stay back, idiot. Something's just in my eyes. It *is* worth it. The Power of a Dictator is worth anything. I've killed before, it's easy. Like breaking toothpicks." Aurelia rubbed her face while refusing to let Grak see her.

"I just—didn't realize that *he* would have—so much blood." Aurelia wavered, even if only for a moment. That soldier's rigor failed to desensitize her when she needed it most, or at least that is what Grak figured.

"Right. Well, if you want to feel even happier, you can come visit Cyrus on Mesos. That always cheers you up. I have a feeling you'll both need it after today." Grak backed off physically but remained supportive.

"I'm FINE. Besides, there's more work to do." Aurelia rubbed her eyes again before standing up and marching off to finish her plan.

Grak watched her silently as she called the troops to the throne room. The remaining commanders and their legions not in the battle had been sent away on a wild goose chase during the assassination and were very perplexed upon their return. At the front of the mass of soldiers, their commanders were assembled and saluted their princess.

"Princess Aurelia—we have returned but something appears to have happened. Where is the good Dictator Aurelian?" the most senior member asked.

"Dictator Aurelian is dead, and I have killed him. As his daughter, I am now claiming my birthright as Dictator of this nation," Aurelia boldly declared. The room fell silent. The shrewd commander looked at Grak who sat and quietly observed.

"Well? Bow before your Dictator. My coronation will be this evening so double time on the preparations," Aurelia coldly ordered.

"You really expect us to take this Power grab lying down! Foolish child!" the dozens of centurions all drew their weapons which displeased Aurelia.

"Puny insects! Acknowledge your Dictator and bow!" Aurelia commanded, her eyes glowing red. Her great Power fell over them and they were cast under her royal spell. Boring into their mind, it stripped them of their agency or will to self govern. Instead, they felt an oppressive drive to submit themselves unto the 'dear leader.'

"Your words are our command! Speak and we will answer, great Dictator!" the centurions fell to their knees in reverence. Aurelia smiled with a euphoric pride overtaking her.

"Excellent. As your Dictator, I speak now. Obey me, for all your lives! Forever my words will be your commands!" she cried, amplifying her Power further to subjugate them.

"Your words are our command, Dictator Aurelia!" they all saluted like mindless drones. Grak closed his eyes and sighed. Aurelia smiled ear to ear, reveling in the moment—it had been worth it.

Back on Tartarus, Norne sat in the guest room that she had converted into her quarters. It was a bare room and even after all this time, most of her things were still packed in the bags and cases she had brought them in. She had buried herself in her work with the desk alone being filled with signs of occupation.

Norne was flipping through reports on government spending while taking notes on reforms. Feeling lonely, she kept looking over her shoulder, waiting for Chaos to walk through the door. She kept doing this, playing a mental game that on the tenth time, he'd be back. She eventually lost count and felt embarrassed as she recognized she rather enjoyed spending time with the oaf.

"What am I worried about—he'll be back soon. Geez, I need to do better in terms of making friends." Norne sighed. Suddenly, Chaos slammed into the newly added glass windows directly in front of her desk and smooshed against it, inches from Norne!

"Coronation party!" Chaos excitedly yelled through the glass which caused Norne to panic and comically fall out of her chair in surprise.

The two made their way to the coronation on slave drawn carriage through the stars. Despite Chaos being able to fly there in barely any time on his own, it was too much of a status symbol to forgo being brought there on the backs of their "lesser". An unnecessary yet popular cruelty.

Inside, Norne was dressed in her very best for her first official appearance as a Tartarian representative. By contrast Chaos was completely shirtless as a reward for winning their last sparring match. Instead, he wore a cape fastened around his waist by his metal belt over his black dyed pants.

"So, you were completely immune to his ability? I'd heard that Dictator Aurelian's power was all but invincible." Norne was amazed as Chaos reported the happenings of the battle to her.

"Yeah, I guess I'm just too cool." Chaos grinned, "Which reminds me, I want a cool ability too like you and the green chick."

"No, you don't. It takes years and years to conceive of, design, and program an ability with Power." Norne cautioned.

"You said that before, but I do tons of stuff with Power already. It can't be that hard." Chaos shrugged.

"Yes, because luckily for you, that comes naturally to people born with Power. Even mortals who get Power later in life can figure it out fairly effortlessly. The stuff I'm talking about is not at all intuitive. You need to manipulate your own power to make it do things beyond what your tiny brain is capable of." Norne sighed.

"Oh." Chaos pouted.

"If you want though, I could make you an Object with an ability. Like my knives, all I have to do is channel Power through them and it carries out the ability I want. I mean, I just gave it my freezing ability again, but I could whip up something different for you." Norne explained.

"Like a mind control ray?" Chaos asked.

"Listen, from what I've heard it would be extremely difficult. I've been working on my Power since I was an infant, and it still has bugs to work out. And yes, that means that as an infant I was smarter than you." Norne glared.

"Hey!" Chaos protested.

"Besides, Aurelia likely has a Meme." Norne sighed.

"...never gonna give you up?" Chaos asked cluelessly.

"What? No, I have no ideas what you're on about now, but a Meme is an ability passed on from person to person and perfected over time." Norne corrected. Chaos looked at her as if she were speaking a different language.

"Listen, it is nearly impossible for a single person to create a power like that, something as complex as controlling a Person's mind. It likely began generations ago and since it is passed from Italic leaders to their firstborn it was improved and modified with use until today. It's passed on by nongenetic memes so if they wanted, they could give it to someone outside the family, but secret powers like that are normally kept close to the chest. Aurelia doesn't seem like the innovative type so hers is probably a one-to-one copy of her father's." Norne explained.

"But how would you change it?" Chaos asked.

"It is all over your head, but just know we have certain ways of visualizing instructions that tell our Power to do certain things. Once you can see it, you can edit it. The new instructions, if they are physically possible are carried out. Like writing instructions and a slave carrying them out." Norne exposited. Chaos looked like he was kind of getting it.

"Over time, clearer and better instructions can be used instead. Imagine that earlier iterations instead of full mind control could only provide suggestions or had tedious preconditions to work. Then after learning the most effective way to do that, the weaknesses were removed and from there it grew in potency." Norne finished her explanation.

"Like a secret recipe!" Chaos' mind immediately went to food.

"Yes, Chaos. Like a secret recipe. They can make copies for apprentices while keeping their own and both keep cooking." Norne sighed.

"Ooooooh. That's pretty clever. So why not just get Aurelia to give me a copy like her dad gave her?" Chaos asked.

"Because Memes are pretty rare. Effective ways of passing them on are secret, even to me." Norne explained, "The Meme of the Arcosian royal family was stolen generations ago by our sister country Prussia so I only know about it from books. Not that my father would've given me one even if he had it."

"...can we steal it too?" Chaos asked.

"NO! When editing a Power's instructions, it can be done in different 'languages. The default around here is Runic. My Fimbulwinter is programmed in my own form of Runic. Other than syntactic changes and Vanus functionality my Runic isn't that different from the modern standard." Norne corrected, "But Memes are often programmed in secret, coded languages that outside people can't even decipher or understand. It'd be useless even if I got my hands on it."

"But I want a Meme! Don't give me up, Norne! My body is ready!!!" Chaos wailed and memed.

"We'll discuss it at a later date. Besides those fiery eyes of yours and this supposed immunity to other Memes might be worth looking into." Norne responded.

"Yay!" Chaos cheered childishly.

"But for now, we're going to a very important event so remember to be on your best behaviour." Norne said worriedly.

Later, at Aurelia's short notice coronation, Norne sat next to Chaos reading her new book entitled, *Aeneas' Odyssey by the poet Virgil Houser*. Norne always was a fan of Italic literature.

Chaos, meanwhile, was busy stuffing his face with the Italic delicacy, Mensa—a strange and unique food of bread topped with cheese, mashed tomato pastes and a variety of meats.

"Norne! This is delicious! Is the creator of this really in that boring book of yours?" Chaos excitedly chowed down.

"Probably not. On top of being boring and predictable, it's historical fiction that seems plagiarized from somewhere else. I'm not reading this for fun, rather to follow up on an irregularity I noticed with Italic records and mythologies. It's just a hunch, but the route of travel doesn't match any actual star maps suggesting that this comes from outside our current known Universe—" Norne began excitedly explaining her analysis and findings.

"Boring! Norne, I thought we agreed, you won't talk nerd stuff with me, if I stop giving you details on all of the action I'm getting," Chaos interrupted her and just then noticed a group of the former vestal virgins waving and giggling.

"Fine! Excuse me for trying to advise you on the best interests of the Empire. Don't know why I missed you anyways." Norne huffed.

Suddenly the army's trumpeter stepped up, playing the signal of the Dictator's arrival.

"Presenting, Her Divine Majesty, Dictator Aurelia!" the announcer proclaimed with his eye perpetually tinted red from Aurelia's spell. Aurelia herself entered, then, wearing a strange half dress and half generalissimo's uniform. Walking to the podium, she cleared her throat and began to speak.

"Brothers and sisters of the Italic states, foreign allies of the nation…it is with great pride and humility that I address you all as Dictator for the first time," she began.

"In the epic confrontation between myself and the former Dictator, I received a divine vision from the old god Maris. I knew him, as you all do, my countrymen as the Fourth of the Pantheon of our forefathers—divine ruler of the harvest and of war. He who led our people out from Ilias, and the hands of the Etruscans grew furious with my predecessors' arrogance and blasphemy. The Etruscan king who enslaved our people was Remus, the man who was Dictator in name only, bore the same title as his middle name. Lazy from the god's welfare he in his degeneracy, erected monuments to a mere star, Sol Invictus, the impostor and usurper of the heavenly realm." she continued.

"I have reclaimed the nation from the false god, Invictis, who will hold power over Italia no longer. Invictus' foolish followers have reaped what they sowed! I have returned us to the ways of the eight who bear witness in the heavens—the gods and goddesses of my ancestors—of *our* ancestors. I have been chosen by them to enact their will on Italia and among all the stars. I have returned Italia to its former glory! Everything within the Empire, nothing outside the Empire and nothing against the Empire!" Aurelia declared in her fiery, emotional, rambling speech. The room erupted into applause and nationalistic cheering.

Norne rolled her eyes. She wrote speeches like this to pander and whip people into a frenzy all the time. After learning how the trick worked, some of the magic of it was lost. After the speech, Norne went off to get a refill of her glass, causing her to not notice Aurelia approaching her from behind.

"Norne von Arcosia," Aurelia said which made Norne jump up in surprise

"We haven't had the chance to talk since the monster hunt, but since I forgot to mention it then, I would just like to say that I find your track record rather impressive. How did you find this coronation event?"

"Dictator Aurelia. Nice speech. Couldn't shake the feeling I'd heard something like it somewhere before though." Norne decided to play coy.

"Cut the pretenses. I haven't been shy about being a fan of your work in Tartarus. Consider us even for your supposedly brand new 'Provinces' and 'Senate' that has everyone so impressed. Personalities aside, I feel we could help each other make our nations as grand as the Italic golden age," Aurelia said much more directly.

"Get Italia's Senate and Provinces up and running again instead of conforming to the lesser systems of our neighbors, and I'd be happy to share credit for being inspired by Italia's past. All human art or achievement comes from cannibalism and theft. I admire everyone thinking I did everything from scratch, but your observation doesn't 'expose me.' I'm happy that another person knows of the ideal past we should seek. As for you—you have to actually live up to the ideals you thunder about before anyone will take you seriously." Norne grinned before walking away with her drink.

"I shall. I am going to return Italia to its former glory so that your foreign forgeries will pale in comparison. To you, I suggest you reign in that perverted oaf if you want to maintain my respect, especially if you want that whole 'god and emperor' are one thing to be believable," Aurelia said.

"Oh yes, that reminds me! Removing the cult of Sol Invictus was an interesting move. I'm sure along with decriminalizing all the persecuted pagans, removing the religion's ban on the government profiting from religion will be a convenient side effect. Not to mention enforcing the idea that the Dictator is chosen by the gods instead of being a servant of the people. Your selfless devotion to the old ways should be applauded." Norne confidently took a drink.

"It should. Why use another priest to head religion? Just like in the old days I restored the Pontifex Maximus position; it just so happens that I feel I am the only one capable of heading the religion from this high office. Every good ruler needs to know who they are devoted to after all. Even the figureheads they prop up." Aurelia grinned before taking her leave to talk with other national leaders. As soon as her back was turned, Norne stared her down with a look of contempt.

"Gods, I hate her," Norne and Aurelia mutually thought to themselves.

"Aww! Isn't that cute, all dressed up like she's actually important?" Heidi walked over and haughtily laughed. Norne spat up her drink in surprise.

"Heidi! Why are you here? It's for rulers and *one* guest," Norne gasped.

"Why do you think dad wouldn't bring me? Aurola and I go way back, so of course I should be here." Heidi confidently got her name wrong.

"Hoping to get a gift despite never knowing her? Unfortunately, Aurelia isn't as stupid as you are," Norne thought to herself, struggling to contain her pure contempt for her sister.

"Additionally, your mother was acting weird about the invitation," Otto walked over with wine and lovingly hugged Heidi with one arm. "Of course, Heidi would be the next logical representative of Arcosia."

Norne raised an eyebrow. "She already recognized the pattern?" she immediately recognized her mother's thinking. "So much so for testing for reactions and hoping no one would notice. The plan isn't to kill anyone here, but it makes sense she'd already start taking precautions."

"Anyway, what are *you* doing here, pipsqueak?" Heidi asked interrupting Norne's train of thought.

"I was directly invited as Super Delegate of the Tartar—" Norne began.

"Aw, you got a pity invitation. That's adorable. Did you have to beg Augustine?" Heidi got the name wrong a second time.

"Aurelia," Norne whispered the correction before opening her book to escape the conversation.

"Either way, why not drink some wine like a grown up if you don't want to embarrass yourself." Heidi poured herself some and waved it in front of Norne to taunt her. Norne's eyebrow twitched in annoyance.

"No, if she gets drunk and makes a fool of herself, it will embarrass Arcosia. Just stay out of trouble," Otto argued.

"Immortals are immune to extreme effects of alcohol either way. Dictator Aurelia is not dropping a fortune on enough Adamant 'sweetener' just to give all her guests a buzz," Norne grumbled under her breath. At that moment though, a small, dark skinned servant girl approached Norne and respectfully bowed.

"Oh good, a waiter!" Heidi said. "Hey, get me some of those weird table shaped bread things the peasants enjoy so much. I want to try some, but the line-up is too long since they mysteriously needed to restock."

"I'm sorry, Princess Heidi, but I am here for Princess Norne. Prince Grak would like to see you," the girl politely explained.

"What?" Heidi looked down at Norne in confusion.

"Guess that's my cue." Norne stood up, overjoyed to get away. The door to a waiting room was opened and Norne entered. It was a dimly lit room with only a lit fireplace to illuminate it. She was surprised to see Chaos waiting inside already, stuffing his face with an entire mini feast.

"Hey Norne!" he waved while stuffing his face.

"Would you go anywhere if they offered food?" Norne sighed and walked over.

"Maybe." Chaos licked his fingers. Chaos finished emptying one of the plates and the small servant girl nervously took it from him.

"Thanks toots." Chaos winked at the servant which made her even more uncomfortable, so she hurried away.

"When is Grak getting here?" Norne asked, but suddenly froze as she caught something in her peripheral vision.

Someone else was in the room, sitting right across from them. Swinging her head to look, Norne saw another young Iryan girl sitting by a chair next to the fireplace.

"Hello," the girl said with a friendly wave and innocent smile. Norne was terrified. Norne didn't know how to react, as she panicked internally. "I didn't even sense her in the room," she gasped.

"Judging by the Mesos styled clothing, she's Iryan… but not as swarthy as the servant. A higher-class noble? If she's nobility, is she an ally of Grak? Then why the deception—making us meet her in such a dark room! If she can hide her Power, does that mean she's here to assassinate us? I couldn't even sense her eyes watching me." Norne continued to panic, immediately projecting scenarios as her mind raced.

"You sound nervous. I'm sorry, I only used my brother's name to ensure you would come here and talk to me. Apologies for the deception," the mystery girl explained.

"Brother's name—so you are a princess of Mesos then? I was under the impression Grak was an only child," Norne cautiously responded while calming down slightly.

"Oh. Can't blame you there. I promise I am Princess Cyrus of Mesos, but we can discuss that later. For now, we need to discuss this…alliance with my brother," the girl continued.

Norne began to sweat nervously. "Sure—" she said before slowly walking over to the empty chair already set up next to Chaos. She carefully watched the girl Cyrus who turned her head as Norne moved. Norne finally sat down, cautiously, and slowly.

"Princess Norne, you really don't need to be concerned. This is a friendly meeting." Cyrus genuinely smiled.

"I can't read this girl," Norne worriedly thought, completely baffled. Cyrus' smile suddenly faded as she had to rub her eyes in pain.

"Oh, excuse me for one second," Cyrus excused herself. "The light is just bothering my eyes a bit, no concern." Norne raised an eyebrow in confusion.

"Milady, if I may, His Majesty isn't here so, feel free to close your eyes," the servant girl lovingly said, while walking over to Cyrus' side.

"I—pardon me Princess Norne. You wouldn't mind, would you?" Cyrus asked hesitantly.

"Not at all," Norne said. "Can I ask why though?"

"Princess Cyrus suffers from blindness. Bright lights can irritate her head," the girl explained while maternally rubbing the princess' forehead after she had closed her eyes.

"Ha! That doesn't make any sense." Chaos ignorantly laughed.

"Thank you Atosa," Cyrus said gratefully. "Apologies again. Many people find it disrespectful, but please know that I mean no dishonor in any way."

"No offense taken," Norne responded.

"She's yielded control of the conversation and taken a role of subservience—what is she playing at?" Norne worried mentally, still skeptically looking at Cyrus.

"You wanted to talk about our alliance with your brother. What exactly were you talking about?" Norne asked out loud.

"I know my brother is planning the assassination of all current rulers. And I know you're in on it," Cyrus said.

Norne and Chaos froze in shock.

"*If* such an agreement existed, could we count you as an insider on it, or as opposition?" Norne felt out for an answer to decide on how to proceed.

"I am completely against it! My brother never tells me anything when it come to this anymore, but he did let slip that he would only progress with the plan if he could recruit the new superstars on the Universal stage. That would be you two. I know Dictator Aurelian's death was not random, nor will it be isolated, so he is clearly starting to test the water in his scheme," Cyrus explained.

Norne and Chaos looked at each other as beads of sweat started to form on their brows.

"So, if you're opposed…what do you want?" Norne asked nervously.

"Please…don't kill my father," Cyrus pleaded which shocked Norne. Chaos and Norne didn't know how to respond.

"If you all dislike the modern rulers so much—and I disagree with many of them too, we should talk things out with them. I know Grak thinks he's doing the right thing, but just using violence and killing them isn't the answer!" Cyrus declared.

"Oh… I can read her now. She's an idiot!" Norne thought while cracking a grin at her response. Chaos began to roar with laughter at the idea.

"Silly girl! That's not how things work in the real world!" Chaos almost fell back in his chair after she spoke.

Cyrus frowned and became discouraged. "Oh, I know it doesn't fully fit with how you do things. But Princess Norne, *please* you have to agree with me. Wouldn't you want this killing stopped before it comes for *your* family too?" Cyrus implored.

Norne paused to think about it. Catching herself starting to daydream ecstatically, Norne quickly snapped out of it and responded.

"I understand your concern. But Princess Cyrus, if you are so concerned, then why not come forward and simply warn all the monarchs who are in peril?" Norne asked.

"Because…if I do, Grak will be killed. Aurelia, the others involved in the conspiracy, and probably even some of the children who aren't involved too. I don't want any of that. I don't want any of them to fight! There has to be another way and I know that you two are the only ones strong enough to get my brother to listen to reason. You're vital to his plan so he *has* to listen to you!" Cyrus begged them, getting on her hands and knees.

"Don't let him kill my dad! Please, I want us all to get along!" she begged. Norne and Chaos looked at her in complete bafflement.

"Thanks for confirming one of my theories, idiot girl. Grak really is right where I want him. She really is more of a liability than Chaos. How to play her for more info?" Norne grinned while thinking to herself.

Suddenly the door burst open and Grak stormed in. Cyrus hastily stood up and inhaled, "Someone's here!" she cried.

"Cyrus! What are you doing here? Father will be furious." Grak quickly took his sister by the arm and pulled her away from

Norne and Chaos. There was a strange silence with Grak holding Cyrus like a parent protecting a child in a crisis. His raised voice may have been confused for anger, but Norne could sense another underlying emotion—fear.

"Grak, you're crushing me! Stop holding me so tight," Cyrus whined, scrambling in discomfort.

"I apologize for my sister. Please ignore anything she has said. The girl is going through a bit of a rebellious phase," Grak said, audible irritation mixed with concern and fear in his voice.

"Atosa, take her back to Mesos. I insist you stop enabling her antics," Grak told the servant girl while handing Cyrus off to her.

"Of course, my prince. Let us go home Princess Cyrus." The servant Atosa took her gently by the arm and led her out.

"Aw… can I at least say hi to Aurelia first?" Cyrus asked.

"Cyrus!" Grak raised his voice as Cyrus sadly left with Atosa, her face downcast.

"What'd she say?" he reluctantly asked.

"Oh! You're not going to believe this—" Chaos began blabbing until Norne interrupted him.

"She was concerned about us being allies, and simply wanted to meet the newest rulers next to Aurelia," Norne lied.

"I see." Grak stared her down, skeptically. Norne stared back, using her phony smile.

"Well then…good night. I will contact you to let you know when the next mission will be. I trust we can count on you when the time comes," Grak said before turning and leaving.

"So…what now?" Chaos asked.

"Now, we wait. We watch and see." Norne grinned while moving a flowerpot to reveal a slip of paper underneath.

"Mee—t m—ee on Mes—ss—os next Wednesday to talk about it further—further—talk about it further—" Chaos struggled to read the paper despite the unbelievably clear and legible handwriting.

"She's pretty crafty and pretty quick with her hands for a blind girl." Norne laughed to herself before folding it and grinning maliciously.

"So, she still wants to meet with us? Why bother, even I know she's a dummy?" Chaos asked.

"That's exactly why we continue. Everyone has a weakness…but we just found a fatal one for the man at the top of the pecking order. Both for our 'friend' Grak and more importantly the mystery man—Sargon. That fool is our key to both of them at once!" Norne sinisterly grinned at Chaos.

"Oh. Oh!" Chaos realized that they just struck gold.

Chaos and Norne looked at each other before both laughing maniacally.

STEP 3

INFILTRATE AND INTIMIDATE

"What is needed is a realization that power without love is reckless and abusive and that love without power is sentimental and anemic. Power at its best is love implementing the demands of justice. Justice at its best is love correcting everything that stands against love."
—Dr. Martin Luther King Jr.

CHAPTER 8

SMASH! A younger, preteen Chaos woke up. Sitting up and looking around he saw the shattered fragments of a boulder that had been broken over his head while he was sleeping. He felt for a bump but of course, there wasn't even a scratch. Even as a child he was practically invincible.

"Damn it! Even Drakon and his men couldn't kill it…now as their final revenge, they've stranded me with it. Why do the Fates conspire against me!" Chaos faintly heard a voice ranting as he rubbed his eyes and yawned.

"Father? You are awake?" Chaos asked and looked toward the cave excitedly.

A shabby and disheveled man sat on the primitive bed fashioned from stone along the wall with his head in his hands.

"You! Of course, I'm awake, you idiot! Why did you follow me again? How do you even keep finding me?" the broken man groaned.

"You called out to me, father. I knew you would never actually leave. That's why you always guide me to you. I didn't want to wake you last night, so I waited here for you to wake up." Chaos grinned at the man.

"Damn it all. It's worthless to me now but this cursed Power keeps drawing this thing to me. This thing that has what should rightfully be *mine*!" the man screamed and smashed the wall of the cave.

Chaos tilted his head in confusion. The man's hand bled from the hit, for he was only a man.

"Are you upset? Are the monsters still coming after you? Don't worry, I will protect you, father!" Chaos excitedly jumped to attention, looking around for monsters.

"They're coming after you jackass. I wouldn't need your 'protection' if you'd just leave me alone. They never targeted me before—you're a literal death magnet. I used to be a god and now, I have a walking, talking reminder of my fall following me everywhere! Words cannot describe how detestable you are. Not that it matters. All this time—this mental link without language barriers means nothing considering how much of an idiot you are. What do you even understand?" Typhon looked out of the shade with hatred at the young Chaos before spitting on his son. Chaos grew silent for a bit.

"It's been years of you following me around! It's more of a torment than this damnable weather. I've wished nothing more than for you to stop. Preferably to die as well. If you're too stupid to understand what I'm saying, you'd think that would give you a hint. Leave! Nobody wants you, you idiot. You were cast out from the palace as soon as you first started infesting this world, and now I am tossing you out again. Leave!" Typhon snapped.

Chaos was silent. He was invulnerable to any physical damage, but he didn't like it when his father yelled at him.

"I don't want to be alone," Chaos whimpered.

"Well, I do. If you can understand, then get lost," Typhon growled.

"But Father... I am strong. Why won't you let me return you to the throne? I can do it if you want. Show me the way and I'll beat them all up for you!" Chaos offered excitedly.

"Save it, you damned brat! A man only deserves to rule if he has made it by his own hands. Others may run his empire—others may destroy his empire, but *he* must build it! Don't insult me. Don't take what little pride I have left!" Typhon screamed, rambling incoherently.

Chaos was silent again. He could tell his father's mind was degrading. Banishment did not agree with him. Typhon would spend every day berating his son and complaining about all he had lost but, to Chaos' confusion he never even considered doing anything about it. His pride was too great for him to admit that his spirit was broken.

"But father...if I help you, that would be nice. And then... after you, maybe I could be king?" Chaos asked.

"Shut up! I'd rather die than owe *anything* to you. You hear me! I'd rather DIE! And you'll never be anything, you—you worthless garbage! You'd take my throne over my dead body!" Typhon shrieked, his voice cracking.

Chaos just sat there.

"Over my dead body!" Typhon screamed again before throwing another rock at his son's head. It broke into pieces without even leaving a scratch. Slowly, Chaos' eyes began to glow red, as he fixed his gaze on his father.

"Okay," he emotionlessly replied.

In the present, Chaos opened his eyes and found that he was buried under a pile of books. Digging himself out, Chaos felt his head in the same spot where his father had tried stoning him.

"What a weird thing to remember. From way back then," Chaos thought.

Standing up, he walked out from under all the books that Norne had piled up and went to sit on the throne in his underwear. Just then, a servant came to attend to him.

"Y'know, now that I think about it, my dad treated me pretty bad," Chaos thought out loud. "Probably should've just killed him sooner."

"Emperor Chaos, your scheduled meeting with Grak is in half an hour." A large soldier approached and bowed.

"Boring. Where's Norne, let her do it." Chaos rolled his eyes.

"My Emperor—as you ordered me to inform you, Dictator Aurelia will be here accompanying him," the soldier nervously continued.

"Alright! Get Norne, we're going hunting and I need a wing woman!" Chaos laughed and excitedly stood up, which frightened all the servants.

"Wait. Where's Norne? Oh right. She said she was visiting the stupid girl," Chaos remembered.

Norne was traveling across the stars on her way to Mesos on her slave-drawn carriage.

"Cyrus of Akkad," Norne reflected to herself, "in all my research I couldn't find anything on her. But then again there isn't much information out there about Mesos in general. The secretive, isolationist people are a mystery to everyone, so her inviting me to the hidden heartland is a golden opportunity." She excitedly grinned at the prospects.

The carriage slowed down as it descended from orbit above the capital city Akkad—a gorgeous oasis in the middle of the desert, the city itself was carved in the landscape between two rivers. At the narrowest point between them, the waters of the Tigris and Euphrates rivers were diverted via a canal. The freshwater streams flowed into a massive fifty-mile-wide square moat. Pumps took the lake water up into the artificial mountain of the city. The rock and dirt foundation of the city were solid chunks taken out of the planet, laid out in a tiered system of square levels.

The base level was the largest with the second lowest being about three-quarters of the size. Each level stacked above grew smaller with a total of six levels in all. The excess perimeter of each level held houses, small farms, and markets. A variety of gridded roads and paths connected areas on each level and the different levels to each other. The bridges to higher levels often had waterways running parallel to them with a bridge on either side. The water would collect in pools at each level for drinking and agricultural uses before flowing down until reaching the water in the moat around the capital below. Great walls surrounded the moat also serving to divide the rich from the poor at every significant point of separation along the tiered levels of the city. At the very top and the center of it all was the royal palace—Norne's destination.

The carriage landed and Norne was let out. As she exited the carriage, she looked up at the massive ancient Mesos palace that stood before her.

The building was unlike any castle she had ever seen. Of course, it was not a castle—it was a ziggurat—or rather a ziggurat-shaped structure, not unlike the city of Akkad itself. The flat-topped pyramid was a 10-storeyed wonder of architecture with tiered floors. To avoid the ziggurat turning into an oven, pane-less windows open to the outside were situated in every room and every hallway. Because of this, even from the outside, Norne could see into the building in places, especially the less important lower floors.

The large bricks on the outside of the building were scalable but Norne could see the massive stairs inside used to traverse the floors through the massive entrance. The recently added doors were open and Norne was confused that the lower levels seemed so open to the public, especially in contrast to the secretive upper levels whose insides were hidden by thick curtains hung in the windows.

Inside the building, on the bottom floor were open hallways, leading to the inside rooms of ascending importance (with the Lugal at the top). The hierarchy of the society was baked into the building itself.

"Alright, can't be too friendly, she knows my reputation and could sniff it out if I'm too phony. Slightly antagonistic works, I guess. Just can't make her mistrust or lose her favorable opinion of me. That way, who knows how much she'll divulge for me." Norne grinned while planning out the persona she would use.

She confidently began her march to the entrance, giving off an imposing and dominant presence. The soldiers by the gate stood up straighter, impressed by the young girl's commanding aura.

They recognized the royal Tartarian carriage and, since Norne was on time for her appointment, prepared to receive her as if she were in fact the queen of Tartarus.

In reality, Norne was in agony under the blistering Mesos star. This was the complete opposite of what she was used to. Immortals were built to survive extreme temperatures, Norne especially with her control of thermal energy could effortlessly have made herself more comfortable. However, it was a well-known rule that no Power was to be used in large cities. Given the destructive capabilities of even weak users, the nations of the Universe generally had a zero-tolerance policy for using Power to do anything within their city limits. Even in foreign countries, it was seen as an act of hostility to disregard this tradition.

Thankfully, Norne finally mustered up the strength to stand up straight and finish walking to the door. Norne entered the Mesos palace, still sweating from the heat. Not wanting to appear rude, she did not ascend the large stairs without invitation and instead walked around them, looking into the connected open rooms as she passed by them. The inside of the palace was far different from the palaces of Italia, Arcosia, or Tartarus.

Bronze was the order of the day, and it was everywhere in the form of iconography on the walls, ceiling, and patterns on the floor along the walls. Vases, plates, and suits of armor decorated the walls with statues and reliefs of former princes—the princes of Mesos who ruled directly under the Lugal. Norne could swear that some looked like Grak.

Clay tablets filled with royal decrees in an older Mesos language that Norne couldn't read were on pedestals beneath each statue and suit of armor. Whoever they were, they are remembered by the people she thought, never having cared much about Mesos or its history.

Norne wasn't that impressed by the foreign art but instead paused when she saw the ornate rugs. She amused herself, remembering that this was where they were from. However, after a short while, she shook her head to focus her attention. She had taken in enough sights for now. She needed to find Cyrus.

"I have to stay on guard. In any political meeting it is important to remain reserved and in control," Norne thought as she looked around for Cyrus.

"She's here Princess Cyrus." Atosa led Cyrus down the stairs and into the room.

"Norne! I'm so glad you made it!" Cyrus ran towards her excitedly after getting down the last step.

In her excitement, Cyrus tripped over a rug and fell to the ground clumsily.

Norne froze, not knowing how to react.

Cyrus began giggling and stood up, dusting herself off. Atosa quickly walked over and took Cyrus' hand to gently lead her the rest of the way.

When they got right up to Norne, Cyrus suddenly gave her a giant hug.

"I'm so glad you could make it! I don't get many visitors, so I was waiting for this anxiously. Or wait, I guess I kept you waiting just now—sorry. I'm just glad you're here," Cyrus said, overjoyed to have Norne over.

"I make it a point of keeping appointments—there's no need to get so excited about my arrival. Please compose yourself!" Norne panicked in the face of this foreign expression of genuine affection.

"Well, we're friends, right? So, it's okay to be so open with each other. No need to be so formal," Cyrus innocently said and finally let go of the hug.

Norne was confused at first until she remembered, in the letter she sent ahead announcing her arrival she generically ended with, "Your Friend and Ally, Norne."

"Could she have really taken it seriously? Maybe whoever read it to her exaggerated? Or was my Mesos wrong? I didn't use a more extreme declaration of friendship than I meant, did I?" Norne's mind raced while Cyrus just felt the soft sleeve on her arm.

"Wow! Your clothes are so silky and soft! I wish I had something that felt this comfortable! I'm so jealous."

"I also…admire your outfit," Norne awkwardly responded, having her thought process interrupted.

"Me? Oh, I'm still in pajamas. I stayed up real late last night reading, so I just got up." Cyrus laughed genuinely.

"I see. Wait—reading?" Norne asked, completely baffled.

"Princess Cyrus…if you're going to admit you aren't ready, let us go and get you prepared," Atosa reminded her.

"Right. Just wait in my room, it's just up ahead when you go up the stairs. I'll be right back," Cyrus excitedly explained before being led away by Atosa.

Norne scaled the stairs, now having her invitation and not wanting to get caught up looking at the exotic decorations of this floor and went right ahead towards the room which Cyrus had indicated.

Norne, left to her own devices awkwardly looked around and slowly made her way to the Princess' room. She had felt Cyrus' directions were lacking, but sure enough, once she was close enough, it was obvious which room belonged to her.

By the stairs was a room that was fully carpeted and filled with furniture covered in pelts or pillows to make it even comfier. Inside, Norne inspected the rather spacious room. No sharp weapons or statues were displayed, like Cyrus, it was very… soft. It was very spacious and filled with copious amounts of stuffed animals such as lions and jackals and leopards. All the ferocious, adorable stuffed animals were lined up in a circle in the middle of which were three other stuffed toys—one of Cyrus herself, one of Atosa, and one of Grak. A happy family.

Norne was disgusted by this collection and reveled in the superiority of her own knife armory instead with a grin. Then she noticed the oddest thing.

Lining the walls, she found nothing but bookshelves with strange and thick tomes in them.

Everything was soft and fluffy but lacked any major decorations. The room was very functional, primed for comfort and access to information. Despite Norne sneakily looking behind every nook and cranny, what she first saw was all there was to see. She did manage to find a drawer of older toys, clay carts and horses, and people tucked away for sentimental value.

On display were more clay sculptures—hideously gross and amateur-looking ones. On the bottoms of them, Norne saw they were engraved with the names Cyrus and Grak in fingermarks too small even for Cyrus now. One fairly decent sculpt seemed to be of a Mesos soldier and had Grak's name on the bottom in a mark definitely made in his youth.

"Well, she *is* blind. No wonder these don't look like anything." Norne mocked the product of what Cyrus had poured her childhood love into making with her brother.

Many servants walking about peered in the door, saw Norne snooping, and just kept moving, amused by her growing frustration at the lack of hidden items. Norne was too focused on exposing the dark side of Cyrus she insisted the girl had to notice them.

Finally, Norne sat down in the surprisingly genuinely comfortable chair out of frustration.

"Clever girl—she must've hidden everything since she knew I was on my way." Norne skeptically continued looking around from her seat.

"We're back! Sorry if you were waiting long." Cyrus excitedly entered, now dressed up in a regal Mesos-style princess dress to match Norne.

"No problem. Now…down to business," Norne began.

"Like the layout of the room?" Cyrus laxly asked as she was led over to sit at her desk by Atosa.

"What?" Norne was confused by the casual tone.

"The room's layout. I change it up every few months for the fun of it. Does this arrangement look nice?" Cyrus asked.

"Sure? Wait, why?" Norne was still thrown for a loop.

"It's the perfect excuse to have my brother hang out with me. Hehe. Even he can't resist a request from his baby sister, so it gets him away from work for a bit." Cyrus did her best mischievous grin, but it still looked innocent.

"I see," Norne said flatly, not seeing anything.

"Great. Well, straight to the point—I stand by everything I said in our last meeting. I really need your help in stopping the fighting," Cyrus stated, sitting down on her bed.

"Right…but as representative of Tartarus, I have to ask—what is in it for us?" Norne asked, snapping back to attention after that casual chat.

"Simple. I will forever be in your debt. Whatever you need I will do for you and your Empire," Cyrus responded without hesitation.

Norne paused, this threw her off even more than the last conversation.

"Your assistance will be worth more than I could ever repay, so I give you my word, my very soul will belong to you," the girl said with one-hundred percent conviction and sincerity.

Norne's brain almost overheated from trying to understand her. She hadn't expected this.

"Uh—hold on! That's a rather hefty promise, are you sure you understand the implications of what you're saying?" Norne asked, completely thrown off by Cyrus' genuine promise.

"I understand because what I'm asking you is equally as serious. You'd be risking a lot to help me so it's only fair I return just as much!" Cyrus did her best attempt at being forceful but could barely raise her voice.

Norne just leaned forward, her normal ability to see through anyone only returned a giant question mark in the face of honesty.

"What is wrong with this girl?" Norne thought in complete bafflement.

"My brother is devoted to his plan…and being crown prince as well as commander of the army, he has the charisma to lead people along with it. Stopping him without conflict will be a Grakean task," Cyrus began.

"Grakean? He is so beloved as to warrant a word on Mesos?" Norne raised an eyebrow.

"Oh, no. His name comes from the Grakean Epic," Cyrus explained. "The oldest surviving literature in the known Universe. It was commissioned by my father as a pseudohistorical account of his life to inspire his followers. It isn't much of a read nowadays though. A lot of it is just a reference to how rich everyone was back then, using taxes of goats to prove it. Still a big thing of cultural pride though." She laughed.

"I see. So, you want to somehow peacefully resolve an internal conflict between a modern hero named after a founding myth of the country, and the first king who wrote that same myth. Did I leave anything out?" Norne asked.

"That the army is already split between crown loyalists loyal to my father and those who prefer my brother. Both are pretty uncompromising in their beliefs," Cyrus added.

"Cool." Norne sighed.

"I know it will be difficult. My brother thinks what he's doing is right. But the old generation won't go quietly. I don't want them to fight. Grak has given up on my attempts to convince him, but I *can* change father. If we talk things out, then everyone can change, and they won't need to fight. I disagree with father a lot and I know he doesn't like me, but I love him," Cyrus told her.

"Oh right. She's an idiot. I really was overthinking this wasn't I?" Norne couldn't help but think after Cyrus' little speech.

"So, tell me…if I'm going to help, I have to ask what it is that your brother wants to do that clashes with the current king so much?" Norne asked, concerning Atosa, by her obvious nosiness.

"The liberation of the poor and oppressed around the Universe. We agree that the best way to make nations better is from the bottom up and that's what he's going to do. The problem is that he forgets that wars, especially civil wars are the worst for the lower classes. If he wasn't so blinded by resentment for father, maybe I could convince him to wait just a bit longer," Cyrus said, feeling sad at the memories.

"Oh, come on, empty promises like that are the thing you use to keep the peasants in line. Everyone uses that fancy talk to drum up their base. I want to know what he's really planning. If you want us to cooperate, then I need the truth," Norne said in complete disbelief.

There was a long and awkward silence. At that moment, neither of the two could comprehend the other.

"Y'know Norne, I get it now. You're super out of touch, aren't you?" Cyrus innocently asked.

"Princess—" Atosa stepped in nervously as Norne almost blew a blood vessel.

"Oh, sorry! I guess I've been talking to Miss Aurelia a lot lately. I appreciate her coming to visit a lot, but she really does love complaining about people in her new government," Cyrus apologized.

"Figures." Norne rolled her eyes and thought internally but never outwardly betrayed her contempt. "I guess it is important though, to be acquainted with future in-laws and all that." Norne shrugged it off out loud.

Atosa gasped while Cyrus tilted her head in confusion.

"In-laws? How?" Cyrus asked.

"What? Grak and Dictator Aurelia are practically inseparable. I'd figured given their age and position, it was only natural they'd be married off to each other," Norne admitted in surprise.

"Ew! No way. Aurelia's like a sister to us, she and Grak are very close, but definitely not like that." Cyrus laughed at the idea.

"I see." Norne rolled her eyes, attributing the answer to Cyrus' naïveté.

"Besides, you're looking at the future queen of Mesos right here!" Cyrus laughed and grabbed Atosa's hand which made her blush in embarrassment.

"The slave?" Norne raised an eyebrow.

"No, the free woman and a good friend of the family." Cyrus smiled up at Atosa.

"No offense, but wouldn't it be wiser for Grak to settle on a...better deal? A former slave turned paid slave isn't much of a candidate for a future queen," Norne pointed out.

"No matter what you or anyone else says, I support my brother marrying for love. We both promised we wouldn't be the same as our parents, so I won't let it happen," Cyrus said.

"Nice sentiment. But in terms of practicality, come on! Marriage is political. You have to ask, 'what is the country gaining from this?'" Norne sighed.

"Hm... Atosa, can I show them?" Cyrus asked.

"Alright. I'll go get them," Atosa said before nervously leaving.

"I'm just saying if she jumps right into her old job after leaving it, isn't she better off serving instead of helping lead a nation? I mean, don't you think she was probably put in that role for a reason?" Norne asked.

"You underestimate people Norne. Get to know them and they can show you wonderful things." Cyrus grinned.

Atosa quickly returned with stacks of drawings and placed them on Cyrus' bed.

"Take a look. Pretty good, aren't they?" Cyrus asked as Norne took a sheet.

On it was a masterfully planned out classical Mesos structure, even more elaborate and incredible than the very palace they were in.

"The building looks incredible...but I didn't see anything like it on Mesos before. Where is it?" Norne asked.

"In Atosa's mind. She designed all of these and many others. You think she's just a servant, but she is a master architect. Is this kind of talent something that should be restricted to the lowest caste? Rob the world of this genius because of an old system? I one hundred percent agree with my brother about changing things, the only place we differ is on the method," Cyrus proudly declared.

"I see where you're going with this and yes, exceptions to every rule exist but to uproot an entire—" Norne began.

"How many other people like Atosa are out there, not living up to their potential because they're oppressed?" Cyrus asked.

Halfway through, Norne had mockingly started mouthing the words and rolling her eyes at the idea.

"You're really running away with this idea, aren't you? I mean, how are *you* even judging how good these plans look?" Norne pointed out.

"The descriptions sound lovely. I can't quite speak for how it would look, but I know they sound like they would be wonderful to live in." Cyrus smiled.

She couldn't see it, but Atosa was turning so beet-red she almost burst with embarrassment and excitement from all the compliments on her magnum opus.

"Thank you, Princess," Atosa covered her face and managed to squeak out.

"So, what do you think now?" Cyrus asked.

"I think our collaboration is going to be…interesting." Norne sighed.

"I know right! Don't you just love a good honest debate between friends? I know I haven't convinced you yet Norne, but just wait, I can prove firsthand to you that my methods work." Cyrus smiled.

Norne, not knowing how to answer, went back to looking at the drawings.

"I'll admit the buildings are good. You should be proud, girl," Norne finally conceded and handed the drawings back to Atosa.

"Atosa! That's another thing. I'll get you to call her by name yet!" Cyrus tittered.

"Fine—Atosa, I was thinking of designing a new capital for Tartarus, something more modern and to my standards. Would you be interested?" Norne asked.

"Sorry, I only do Mesos style. It probably wouldn't fit on Tartarus. Also, I refuse to let my work be constructed by slave labor. No offense," Atosa said with a rare flash of resolve.

"Some taken. It's a big cost sa—oh right," Norne remembered.

"That's the main reason Atosa is staying on as my attendant for now. It pays the bills while she looks for more…ethical construction projects to involve herself with. Who knows, if you want her on board maybe Tartarus could—" Cyrus began.

"No thanks. I have no intention of bankrupting the country." Norne shut her down before she could even finish.

"Aw, shucks." Cyrus childishly pouted.

Norne rolled her eyes.

"Tell you what, why don't you come to town with me! There's no better way to convince you than to show you with your own eyes." Cyrus excitedly suggested.

"Oh no, don't feel forced to go down there on my account." Norne flinched at the idea.

"C'mon Norne, I'm not being forced. I was going to head down there later anyway. It'll be fun and since you're here to gather intel on us it would be useful to you too." Cyrus beamed, which shocked Norne.

"…don't force me there on my account?" Norne didn't know how to respond.

"Oh, c'mon silly." Cyrus motioned for Atosa to fetch the carriage.

"What have I gotten myself into?" Norne sighed as Atosa led her out.

Meanwhile, on a space carriage ride to Mark-Denn, Aurelia and Grak sat in awkward silence. Sitting with them was High General Magnus, the supreme commander of Tartarus' Imperial Knights. He silently sat with an ominous presence that even creeped the driver out.

"So…what's with tall, dark, and creepy?" Aurelia started mental communication with Grak.

"Apparently, Tartarus mandates that the Emperor be always shadowed by one of his guards. Don't worry, he won't be taking any of the credit, he's just here in case Chaos is in danger." Grak sighed.

"What about that?" Aurelia asked while motioning outside the window. Grak looked, and sure enough, Chaos was still flying next to them reclined in a lounging position in the vacuum of space outside.

"'Hey! Bet, I can get there first while asleep! Race ya!'" Aurelia mockingly repeated Chaos' bet before he launched himself and quickly fell asleep.

"He's proven his point. Should someone tell him it's a lot safer in here?" Grak asked while holding in laughter.

"You really want him in here running his mouth? It's better we get some peace and quiet. What's the worst that can happen to him anyways." Aurelia rolled her eyes.

Immediately after, a monster swept in with its mouth open, swallowing the sleeping Emperor whole before flying off with him. There was a long, awkward silence.

"I mean he's proven himself pretty indestructible so far so he's probably fine." Aurelia shrugged. General Magnus sighed before wordlessly standing up.

"I shall return shortly with his Imperial Majesty. No need to wait up," he said stoically before blasting off after Chaos.

"Yay. The strix is gone," Aurelia childishly said out loud as Grak face palmed.

On Mark-Denn, Aurelia and Grak approached the castle. Grak shivered in the cold. "How can anyone live on this ice ball without constantly using Power to warm themselves?" he complained in annoyance.

"You really can't appreciate the suffering I endured while visiting you on Mesos, can you?" Aurelia rolled her eyes at him.

"Pansies! This cold is nothing. Where I grew up this was a warm day," Chaos loudly called out from behind them as he approached.

"Oh god." Aurelia turned around but immediately regretted it and turned around again, covering her eyes.

"What?" Chaos asked while casually strolling up to them, buck naked again.

"Your Majesty—" Magnus reached for something in his sleeves, ran over and got on his knees, presenting a new pair of pants with the corresponding metal belt ring for him.

"Oh sweet! Norne really does think of everything." Chaos smiled, taking the pants and putting them on.

"So, what's the plan?" Chaos asked while walking over wearing his new pants backwards.

"We're here for King Claudius of Mark-Denn. His nephew, the prince has accused him of using witchcraft to ascend the throne. We should beware of a fierce ability," Grak said to Chaos on the way to the Mark-Denn castle.

"Yeah, big deal. You guys just try to get a hit in before I've killed him." Chaos grinned.

"Well…there's no welcome committee, so we can assume the prince's part of the plan has already leaped into action," Grak explained.

Walking through the front door without any opposition, they quickly entered the throne room. Before them, the room was already filled with dead bodies. The Queen, the son of the head advisor, and even the prince himself.

"Well shoot! The job is already done," Chaos said in disappointment.

"We will give him a proper military funeral—he was a good man." Grak remorsefully sighed while kneeling next to his fallen comrade.

"They're already onto us. Look, Adamant poison. Claudius killed the prince before he could kill him," Aurelia said after inspecting the swords from the duel.

The weapon of the dead prince's opponent (whom she recognized as the son of the chief advisor to the king) was poisoned with a potent concoction so strong that it tarnished the Adamant steel of the weapon.

"What in the world could have happened here?" Grak asked while looking around.

"Who cares! What is more important is do you think the whole jig is already up?" Aurelia asked.

"No. Claudius was always paranoid. Given the rumors that he had been trying to do the same thing we are doing, it only makes sense he'd be alerted. He was one of the sharper rulers after all. But with him out of the way, I doubt any others are smart enough to catch on," Grak explained.

Chaos took a closer look at the dead king who began twitching.

"Hey guys—" Chaos began.

Suddenly Claudius opened his eyes, and a powerful burst of energy blew everything away except Chaos who was unphased as the king stood up. Claudius felt all over his body to check he was alive and laughed.

"Aha! That antidote saved me! Foolish nephew. Did he really think the king of assassinations would come in without a backup plan! The little prince-let thought he could kill *me* with my own poison!" Claudius laughed as his sword wound closed.

Suddenly he noticed Chaos standing right next to him.

"Hi." Chaos waved.

"Ah yes…the strong man from Tartarus. I just knew you and the prince were in this together." Claudius scowled while quickly recovering from the failed assassination attempt.

"That's right! The prince-let is dead, so I call dibs!" Chaos flew forward with a punch ready to kill Claudius. However, Claudius smiled and as his eyes glowed white, Chaos was suspended in the air completely unable to move!

"Nice try little King-let. I've heard of your legendary punches that can kill in one blow. However, against me that won't do any good." Claudius grinned while moving his hand to float Chaos higher. Chaos looked around, squirming in the air.

"It's no use! Take this!" Claudius thrust his hand forward and smashed Chaos into the back wall. Chaos shattered the brick and dented the Adamant frame underneath as he groaned in pain. Still, he couldn't move as he felt yanked forward again by the telekinesis.

"This will end it!" Claudius cackled while waving his hands around like a manic conductor, slamming Chaos all over the room using his mind. Chaos was just screaming comically as he pinballed around, destroying most of the castle's inside. Grak and Aurelia skillfully dodged whenever Claudius tried swinging him into them. They looked for an opening, but evading their giant ally turned projectile took precedence over counterattacking.

Finally, Aurelia grew impatient and when Chaos came flying at her, punched him away instead of dodging.

"You can fly, idiot! Take this fight seriously!" Aurelia yelled.

"Oh yeah." Chaos remembered. Without much effort, all Chaos had to do was use his Power to resist the direction Claudius tried pushing him in. Chaos' overwhelming raw Power trumped Claudius' ability by far and the treacherous king could no longer even budge him.

"Ha! Once I figured you out, you're pretty weak, huh?" Chaos immediately boasted, laughing.

He jumped to attack but was surprised when Claudius' used his telekinesis to grant him additional momentum. That extra speed sent him flying up much higher than he intended. Chaos made yet another exit hole in the roof. This time, however, he came smashing back down again where Grak had been mere seconds before.

Grak fired a blast from his staff, but Claudius telekinetically slowed it down enough to dodge it. It was enough time for Aurelia to jump through his defenses and punch a chunk of his side out. Claudius vomited blood but jumped back and put all his Power into a defensive shield that blew Aurelia back.

They were as fierce as the rumors had said and Claudius was no Aurelian—he had to play this safe as he healed. Chaos, however, gave him no time to rest as he jumped at him again.

Getting closer than before, Chaos splatted on a rotating force field that Claudius had raised just in time. Holding on with all limbs, Chaos was spun around Claudius horrifyingly quickly so that Aurelia and Grak couldn't make a clean shot.

"What a fool." Claudius raised a hand to send Chaos flying away.

Suddenly, Chaos head-butted the shield, smashing his head through it so that he was only a few inches from Claudius.

With a grin as he flew around Claudius. "Little weaklings who hide behind shields have no right to brag," Chaos said.

In a flash, Chaos bear-hugged his way through the shield of Power, shattering it like glass. He caught Claudius in the bear-hug and roared with laughter. "So, what now? Speak up quick or I might twitch and crush you to mush!" Chaos noted how little resistance Claudius could put up physically.

Claudius, outraged, focused all his Power into eye beams and shot directly at Chaos' chest. "Hah! That barely even tickled!" Chaos laughed at him—his nigh invulnerability never failed.

Claudius was horrified but out of desperation fired an even bigger blast that extended from the shield that surrounded him. The shield was formed so close to Claudius' body that it was a mere form-fitting cloak thinning out as he projected most of his concentration into killing Chaos with this beam.

The beam hit Chaos' chest, sparking Power in the collision as Chaos laughed maniacally at his invulnerability. He began crushing in on the shield with his brute strength alone, grinding it to a halt and forming cracks.

This time, however, the beam blasted a hole through Chaos' chest, leaving a massive bloody hole right through it. Chaos let go of him and fell to the ground.

"So, it seems you aren't indestructible after all. At a focused enough point even the beast's tough hide can be pierced!" Claudius laughed.

Grak and Aurelia were shocked.

Just then Chaos stood back up and his wound was completely healed.

"WHAT! Even for an immortal—that's impossible! I hit your vital organs!" Claudius said.

"Well, I guess you missed." Chaos tapped his fully regenerated chest.

"All of them!" Claudius panicked. Chaos had destroyed both his arms with a flick as he raised them to block the attack. Up close, with brute strength, there was no competition between them.

Claudius however put all his Power into one final blast to try and finally kill Chaos. This time, instead of blocking it, Chaos grew annoyed and the flames from within his own eyes blazed out to meet Claudius' blast!

"Fool! In terms of long-ranged blast attack, I Claudius reign supreme!" Claudius cackled, believing Chaos' choice of attack had sealed his fate.

However, when the two beams made contact, Chaos' instantly overtook Claudius' and engulfed the usurper in an instant, destroying his entire body! Claudius went out in a pathetic shriek as his entire body was blasted to atoms, leaving nothing but a nuclear shadow of him where he stood.

"Damn shame. The first guy to do any real damage against me other than Norne was that weakling." Chaos sighed as the fires in his eyes subsided.

Grak took note of the 'other than Norne' comment.

"You really are the son of Typhon…no one should have been able to survive that attack you took." Grak nervously laughed.

"What? It almost sounds like you wanted me to die." Chaos cluelessly laughed back.

"Enough about that. What do we do now? Mark-Denn has no royal family, who is going to rule?" Aurelia asked.

"That is where I must step in," Magnus said, finally stepping in.

"What!" Aurelia and Grak had almost forgotten he was here.

"In accordance with the Imperial Territories and Succession Act—any territories encountered by Tartarus without a sitting monarch will automatically be assumed and incorporated as an Imperial territory. Without a monarch, Mark-Denn will be put under the control of a provisional government according to the Senate's appointment and will then be granted junior Province-ship once everything is in writing," Magnus proclaimed.

"You have got to be joking! You are in no position to unilaterally—" Grak began.

"I think you'll find Tartarus is. As a major and *vital* component of your coalition, these are the Emperor's demands, and they are non-negotiable," Magnus coldly responded.

"Norne," Grak cursed under his breath.

"There is no need to worry. The Empire is not in the practice of attacking allies, only territories without leadership and in need of our—protection and guidance. For the sake of peace." Magnus explained despite his statement clashing with the flaming waste they had made of Mark-Denn.

"You have some nerve demanding all this when all you did was stand by the entrance," Aurelia said in disgust.

"I demand nothing. His Majesty scored the killing blow. It is not for me, but like all things it is for him." Magnus bowed to Chaos who giggled like an idiot at the incessant praise.

As they walked away, Aurelia turned to Grak.

"Did…she plan this? Sending him along to make her real goals clear?" Aurelia asked.

"I'll look into it, but if she was going to turn on us, I doubt she'd do it so soon. Norne probably just predicted things would play out this way." Grak sighed.

"Grak, you are the leader of this group. Make sure you don't let them steal that from you. Remember, they work for *us* and not the other way around," Aurelia warned him. As she walked past, Grak looked at Chaos with concern.

CHAPTER 9

Back on Mesos, Norne impatiently tapped her foot on the carriage floor. This was a fancy royal carriage, but instead of being pulled by slaves using Power, it was propelled along by a pair of Caspian horses native to Mesos. Even worse, Atosa, to make the animals move dangled carrots above the creatures so that while they trotted speedily it was nowhere near as fast as they could go by means of a good whipping.

"I could have flown there in an instant. Why do I have to endure this boredom all so this little princess can avoid feeling guilty over something so stupid." Norne stared with contempt at Cyrus who took out a primitive binder filled with some clay tablets to pass the time.

Norne looked with surprise at what she realized were the 'books' Cyrus had brought from her shelf for the ride.

"What is she doing?" she asked in confusion.

Cyrus began tracing the wedges in the clay, row by row from left to right.

"Cuneiform?" Norne asked out loud after noticing the foreign markings.

"Yep. It's a dead language that nobody really reads anymore, but nobles and priests still learn it as a status symbol," Cyrus explained.

"I see. Indents in clay can be felt, unlike ink on paper." Norne quickly understood Cyrus' unique method of reading.

"My brother knew I that got lonely when he was away so when he couldn't be there to read to me, he transcribed stories into cuneiform for me so I could read them myself. He's far too busy now though, so Atosa learned how to do it and now she keeps my library ever-growing," Cyrus explained.

"I see. Let me guess, you are paying her for it on top of attendance work?" Norne sighed.

"Of course! I've heard she has some of the best wedgemanship in the nation. After I buy them though, they can be re-sold to scholars for investment in town. You should be able to see the effects when we get down there." Cyrus smiled.

"If we ever get there. I know this is supposed to show me there are alternatives to slave drawn carriages but come on. Surely you know the distance between planets is too great for a mere beast to carry us, right. It's unnecessary," Norne said.

"Fair point for now. But while you're complaining you could get to our destination faster than the horses, given you are the daughter of the legendary 'Otto King of War.' Surely with your Power you could get to your destination faster than any slave as well." Cyrus grinned.

Norne's eye twitched, unamused by Cyrus' point.

Finally, they arrived at the poor village. Atosa fed the horses the treats she dangled ahead of them and put them into a cool stable. Returning to the carriage she helped Cyrus out before looking back up at Norne who intentionally hid behind the door and looked out skeptically.

"Princess Norne?" Atosa asked.

Norne looked around tentatively.

"Come on Norne, despite what I'm sure you've heard, they don't bite." Cyrus laughed.

"Whatever." Norne sighed and reluctantly stepped out of the carriage. Hopping down, she landed next to the other girls and looked around.

"These are the slums?" Norne asked suspiciously.

"Lower-income res—" Cyrus began.

"Whatever. Where do we have to go?" Norne hand waved and walked over while continuing to look around genuinely uncomfortably.

"I will lead the way." Atosa stepped up but Cyrus put her hand on her shoulder.

"Atosa—don't forget, the royal legion should be back on Mesos today. It would be a good time for family visits don't you think?" Cyrus grinned.

Atosa's eyes lit up and she was almost brought to tears with excitement.

"Thank you, Cyrus!" Atosa lovingly hugged her before rushing away, down the street.

Cyrus waved (though slightly in the wrong direction) as Atosa excitedly ran out of sight.

"Great. Leave me with the blind girl," Norne thought, disgusted.

Suddenly Cyrus held her hand out.

"Come on, now I guess we need each other to find our way around." Cyrus beamed.

Norne was unamused. This was her life now—visiting peasants.

Norne's mother had told her all about peasants. They were lazy, drunken people who were so beset by vices that they would never pull themselves out of their pathetic squalor. And Mesos people were among the worst kind. Not only were they unsightly compared to the pure Arcosian race, but they were among the most pathetic poor. They were secretive and shifty and set in old and outdated pagan ways. Norne shuddered at the thought of seeing even one of them.

The two princesses made their way down the road. Cyrus was cheerfully humming along while Norne nervously hesitated before each step, disgusted by all the filth around her. The slums weren't as dirty as Norne had been led to believe but there were clear signs that they had been at one point. The mud brick houses were crammed with families living under the same roof. The streets weren't paved and the dirt path irritated Norne as she grumbled under her breath, "dirt people," before kicking up some sand.

Worst of all, some poor people would even make eye contact with her so that Norne had to quickly look away and hope another one wasn't around the corner.

While she was preoccupied, Norne didn't notice a group of excited children run over to greet Cyrus. While several went over to hug Cyrus, a little boy with a runny nose, no older than three years old hugged Norne, innocently looking up at her and saying, "*fwend*." She gave a loud shriek of terror which caught the attention of everyone in the area who moved to get a better look, causing her to turn beet-red in embarrassment.

"Come here, Adel. My friend isn't used to meeting normal humans," Cyrus joked while picking up the little boy who laughed.

"I kill city-sized monsters with one hand in my spare time damnit—I have to regain control," Norne thought while she angrily and frantically wiped the snot from her dress with her concealed knife. She only planned to reveal it in the most extreme of situations, and this qualified.

"Princess Cyrus. You're back so soon? You were just here the other day," a man in rags approached.

"Yep. The tablets you ordered are in the carriage," Cyrus announced.

"Alright!" the kids excitedly ran over to the carriage.

"You left it open? What if they steal something?" Norne whispered to Cyrus.

"I brought the things for them though," Cyrus said in confusion at Norne's concern.

"Oh yes, I almost forgot," the man happily handed Cyrus a stack of tablets bound with rope. "The kids were in such a rush that they forgot to present the thank you tablets they wrote for you."

"Wow, I can't wait to read them." Cyrus held them close to her heart which baffled Norne. They had touched poor people!

"The elder is this way. He's at the Eduba right now." The man led the way by holding Cyrus' hand.

"What is happening?" Norne walked up and whispered to her.

"You don't need to whisper," Cyrus told her. "We're just heading to the building I told you about. You're a scholar so you'd be excited to know we're building a school for the children."

"Oh, gods! You're educating them too?" Norne was horrified.

Just then, they arrived at a large, open-aired building that was notably more appealing looking than the surrounding buildings. It was newer with professional uniform bricks not unlike the capital.

"Pretty, right? Atosa said she'd been working on the design since she was a child. I'm so happy that it is finally finished," Cyrus explained while Norne was amazed by the welcome and open-air architecture.

"What did you call this again? A monastery for the poor?" Norne asked.

"The Eduba. I noticed the palace was in need of new scribes and it made sense to recruit more here so my father approved it," Cyrus explained.

"If there's a labor shortage, why not just train a few sla—" Norne began before noticing some disapproving looks.

"For the last five years, Mesos has had a decline in the slave population. There's no need to go back on that after so much progress. I couldn't betray them after all this," Cyrus replied.

"Right." Norne nodded along while counting the number of teachers who stood around looking at her.

"But is it really safe?" Norne reached for her knife, after noticing a large and muscular man by the door.

"Sure. Not to brag but I think they like me." Cyrus grinned.

"True, but you'd be a prime target if they wanted to get at your brother or father. I've played along long enough—this environment is unsafe," Norne said threateningly.

Everyone just laughed which confused her. Finally, the elder sighed.

"Put that weapon away, the children are back." The elder stepped up. Norne put the knife back into hiding as the children excitedly entered with the tablets Cyrus had brought.

Putting them on the teacher's table they excitedly opened them to get a look.

"They love to learn. Turns out all they need is a little help and they can improve themselves." Cyrus turned to Norne who was baffled by the children's excitement over what amounted to nothing more than old, donated books.

"Princess Cyrus! They're all already filled out," one student noticed.

"These ones are all for you to read. After all, I heard you're all good at making your own now so there will be no more templates, just filled tablets for reading. Now that you can understand them, it's time to give you books that can teach you." Cyrus grinned.

"Yeah! Princess Cyrus, we each made the tablets your thank you notes are on. Mines-es is a perfect square," an excited youth pointed out using improper grammar.

"Good job. I can tell you're all going to be great scholars someday." Cyrus held her hand up so they could high-five her.

"Whoa! The Grakean Epic! We get to read that?" a little girl excitedly lifted that tablet from the top and held it out to Cyrus.

"Oh um...well that one might be a bit too mature for you all right now. We'll work our way up to that." Cyrus hastily took the tablet and held it away so that the elder could take it instead.

"I forgot to say, the older students get their pick from the unedited texts. We didn't have time to revise some of the heavier stuff," Cyrus whispered to the elder who nodded.

"Older students? Where are they?" Norne looked around.

"They are...busy right now. They can't attend during the day," Cyrus nervously said, dodging the slavery connection with children in the room. Norne got the point though.

"Princess Cyrus, we wanted to read the Grak story," one child said, huffing loudly.

"What do you say instead we start with, *The Story of the Ten Princes*? It's not in there, but I can tell you if you want." Cyrus grinned.

The children cheered and sat on the mat, waiting for Cyrus to tell them the story.

"So, this is going to be my whole day, isn't it?" Norne sighed.

"To build our great country, Lugal Sargon gave us his ten sons whom each helped develop Mesos. While he was the supreme Lugal, each of them in succession supported him in performing the day-to-day administration of the Empire. Each ruled differently but equally contributed to the great Mesos that we all know and love and are huge inspirations we should follow. His first son, Grak was a great hero who fought off the demons and monsters of the ancient world to make a world where humans could live. His second son, Hammurabi gave us the laws to form the nation and bring the people to work together under the Lugal. He also—" Cyrus began, reciting the mythologized order for rulers whom each contributed to Mesos.

Norne watched from the side as Cyrus moved the children with her dynamic storytelling of the old legend.

"She's something special, isn't she?" the elder walked next to Norne and grinned.

Norne rolled her eyes.

The story had everyone captivated and went on for nearly an hour. Norne yawned.

"And finally, after the ninth prince, Prince Darius Akkad, the tenth prince, Prince Nezzar Akkad reigned the longest of all. He rebuilt the declining Empire and spread Lugal Sargon's influence out to the extent of the old Empire, giving us the star map that we are all familiar with today," Cyrus ended.

The children applauded her.

"And don't forget the eleventh son, Princess! Yeah, our Prince Grak is going to give us freedom!" an excited child raised his hand and cheered.

Cyrus paused for a second. "Yes. I hope so." She nodded with a grin.

"Cavalry is back!" a Mesos soldier shouted, dramatically entering while carrying Atosa on his shoulder. Norne was shocked as everyone got excited as a group of soldiers entered, (less for their sudden appearance but more at how late it had gotten).

The people clapped and cheered for the soldiers' return.

"Back from the war. The return party is over?" Cyrus warmly smiled.

"We head out again after the weekend, so the party is never over," one soldier said while taking time to hug his wife who was a teacher at the Eduba.

"Weekend? Weak-end?" Norne thought to herself in confusion. She had never heard of such a thing. After all, Wednesday was the day of rest in Arcosia—the rest of the time was to be spent toiling away.

Along with the soldiers, many more adults arrived, in a mass meeting in the Eduba. Norne was horribly uncomfortable being surrounded by all the cheer and excitement.

Nervously pushing her way through the crowd, Norne made it to Cyrus and whispered, "what is going on?"

"The debriefing service should have ended at the same time construction hours ended. Now all the kids' families should be here to pick them up to celebrate the troops coming home. It's the first vacation an entire company's gotten all year," Cyrus explained.

Norne was about to add a follow-up but cutting through the crowd suddenly came the soldier who had carried Atosa.

"Oh hey, I knew I heard you here earlier! How's it going mom?" the soldier winked.

"Welcome back Colonel! More exciting war stories to tell?" Cyrus giggled as she gave him a big hug.

"Father! Remember, that is the princess you're speaking to!" Atosa said, embarrassed by the soldier.

"Yeah, but as her current son and future father-in-law it makes sense to be familiar doesn't it?" he said while laughing.

"Dad, you would be Grak's father-in-law, not Cyrus'." Atosa sighed.

As everyone else had a laugh about that, Norne moved closer to Cyrus.

"Mother?" Norne whispered, leaning in.

"Oh yeah. After the nobles tried banning me from using the normal method, I found a legal loophole for freeing slaves. Children of royalty are automatically freed. So, you're looking at the proud mother of four-hundred and fifty-two." Cyrus grinned and everyone laughed.

"Which reminds me. I've finished five more, so welcome to the family everyone." Cyrus handed out five certificates of adoption.

"Whoa! Five at once, you're a god!" a freed soldier cheered.

Others fell to their knees with tears of joy.

"As expected of someone who shares my namesake, you're almost as cool as I am." Atosa's father chuckled.

"I'm sure I'll get there someday, Mr. Kourosh." Cyrus laughed with Atosa's father.

Norne was utterly baffled by what she was seeing.

"Oh yeah, in Mesos, Cyrus is the female name and Kourosh is the male equivalent. Pretty ironic that we're both technically Atosa's parents now, huh?" Cyrus explained to Norne so as to not leave her out.

"Yeah, whatever. Wait—if Atosa is technically your adopted daughter, doesn't that make her engagement with the prince even more of a political nightmare?" Norne asked.

"Don't worry. As soon as they're married, the adoption is nullified, and she keeps her freedom by merit of being married into the royal family," Cyrus explained.

"Great—and wait that engagement is public!" Norne cried.

"Not for anyone outside this room. It *is* a secret. Please don't tell anyone," Cyrus begged nervously, realizing her mistake too late.

"Right," Norne said.

"Speaking of secrets—that reminds me of the time General Grak trusted me with the top-secret mission!" the soldier Kourosh stood up and boldly began recounting.

"Come on dad, if you're going to bluster about fake war stories at least come up with new ones," Atosa was crimson with embarrassment.

"What? Fine how about the time I singlehandedly defeated an army of mercenaries that held the prince captive!" Kourosh grinned which just made her put her head in her hands as everyone else had a hearty laugh.

"Is he *trying* to get killed by his commanding officer?" Norne asked.

"Why? My brother considers himself in his debt. You should've seen him on his knees asking for his blessing to court Atosa." Cyrus giggled.

"Grak the Great did what!" Norne's eyes almost popped out of her head.

"It's late," Kourosh said, "so what can I get for my future princess—oh and current princess, too?" He lovingly swept his daughter up for a piggyback ride then turned to face Cyrus.

"Some patented Darya family bread if you don't mind." Cyrus requested, grinning.

"You're on, Princess." Kourosh picked her up and jovially carried her out too.

They were like one big happy family. It creeped Norne the Hel out, though then again, even she had to admit, a healthy family setting was better than what she grew up with. But she preferred not to think about that.

As the crowd grew, Norne snuck away to the cemetery. The massive graveyard was filled with headstones of various shapes and sizes, all very amateur in style and fabrication, though some stood out as being higher quality and marked by the royal Mesos seal.

Each spot had enough room on either side of them for an average-sized body, so it was clear the deceased were not simply crammed into the ground carelessly. Inscribed on some of the headstones were the names of the deceased, lovingly hand-drawn into clay nameplates in cuneiform for those who knew it. Norne noticed that some were evidently written by children and that the large graveyard looked well attended to and respected in accordance with the extremely religious townspeople's traditions.

"What a waste of space." She scoffed at the sight.

Norne was a proud Immortal. If her lot in life was a mortal body that would grow old and frail, she couldn't stand it. If she were born to die, she felt she would—die. So, she sat alone, apart from them. The moon was high in the sky and she sat alone, reading, *A History of Mesos-Italic Religions.*

"'The dead are nothing but refuse. They are chaff to be cast off and forgotten, not mourned.' Is that what you were thinking?" Cyrus asked.

Norne jumped up in panic and surprise, having been unable to sense Cyrus' approach as usual.

"Thought I was an etemmu?" Cyrus laughed at Norne's uncharacteristic emoting.

"What?" Norne was now surprised and confused.

"Oh right. Ghost is the word in Arcosian, right?" Cyrus asked.

"Ghosts! Please, I don't believe in such nonsense! Superstition is for the poor, not me!" Norne was embarrassed.

"Well, here I am. It was a nightmare to find you here. Y'know, I'm gonna say it, it's really mean for you to wander off and make the blind girl go out looking for you." Cyrus sat down next to her.

"In Arcosia we get antsy about large peasant mobs. No offense." Norne closed her book.

"Fine. Thanks for staying as long as you did. It means a lot. I mean it's still pretty calloused and out of touch. But it's a start." Cyrus grinned.

"None of this helps with what you asked of me." Norne looked up at her.

"It does. You just aren't far enough along yet to see why," Cyrus responded.

"Are we leaving yet?" Norne asked impatiently.

"In a bit. Just let Atosa finish saying her goodbyes." Cyrus assured hers.

"So sentimental. That is why they waste valuable land to cram corpses into the ground." Norne scoffed.

"'The dead are nothing but refuse. They are chaff to be cast off and forgotten, not mourned.'" Cyrus repeated the quote.

"Stop quoting at me, what is that?" Norne asked.

"I thought you'd recognize it. It's a rather famous passage from the Grakean Epic. I was actually explaining to the children the other day how 'refuse' can be used as both a verb and a noun. At this early point in the story, the main character is lacking in maturity and makes bold and arrogant claims he later has to reckon with. Our hero took life for granted until he lost the one that he loved. That tends to set everything in perspective," Cyrus explained.

"How cute. But I'm not a big fan of morality plays." Norne derided.

"You know…they say the story is about my father. That even one as cold and detached as him once loved someone. Is there anyone like that for you?" Cyrus asked to try and keep the conversation going.

"Well, everyone outside my immediate family was purged by my father before I was born. So, I never had to get attached to any relatives. Therefore, I guess not." Norne shrugged.

"It doesn't have to just be relatives. In fact, the cemetery got expanded into its modern form because of Grak. Rather than just some holes dug out back, he wanted to ensure his fallen soldiers received a proper send-off. He speaks at every one of their funerals and makes sure the family never wants for anything. Forging personal connections isn't that hard if you try." Cyrus turned to face Norne.

"Enough trying to beat me over the head with it! I get it. You like the peasants, got it. You and your brother are so intrinsically morally superior to us backward nobles," Norne responded, her voice full of irritation.

"Not intrinsically. We had to learn. In Mesos, the Lugal remains forever detached and distant from his subjects. But the Prince, the one who directly interacts with the people and rules from the ground and not from on high, they almost always go through the metamorphosis you are minimizing there. Grak used to be a lot like you—or at least I've been told he was. Now he more or less aligns with me. You don't have to be weak to have a heart. It may take a while but, appreciating people and appreciating life is a thing anyone can do. That's what I hope to show you. That's how a person as powerful as you can actually do the things a powerless person like me can only dream of." Cyrus grinned.

"Do you always tell people you are trying to manipulate them as you do it?" Norne sighed.

"Well, if I tell you what I'm doing, doesn't it cease being manipulation?" Cyrus innocently asked.

"Are we leaving yet?" Norne complained again.

When the time came, Kourosh and the elder saw them off. Cyrus dropped a bag full of bronze and jewels into the shocked old man's hands.

"Princess…we really cannot receive any further gifts from you. What if His Majesty were to notice?" The elder pleaded.

"Elder… I'm a very clumsy girl so you must forgive me. It seems I misplaced all my jewels and ornaments. Do keep your eyes open for them and make sure they are returned to the proper people for me, would you?" Cyrus said with a big smile.

The tiny girl put all her strength into retrieving a comically oversized jar full of all her royal jewels and handed it to the elder.

"I see. It will be done, Princess." The elder accepted the jar. There was never any use in trying to argue with Cyrus over accepting charity from her. Norne rolled her eyes.

The townsfolk waved goodbye as the horse-drawn carriage chased the carrots back to the capital.

On the ride back, Cyrus turned to Norne. "So Norne, have your heart and mind changed?" she asked.

"You're a strange one, Princess Cyrus." Norne dodged the question.

"I had a feeling you'd react this way. Most nobles have never even seen what their subjects look like. Even my brother used to say that I was weird for enjoying common people's company. But seeing them up close helped change his mind on how the world works—it wasn't common people's company or noble people's company. It was people's company. It'll take a while, but I hope to change your heart as well. Then we can leave those labels behind and just be people. I know that's a long way off still, but for now, I can settle with changing the monarchy we have for the better. I can be content with that change by the end of my lifetime," Cyrus admitted.

"Change to what? You've already tossed the world order on its head." Norne raised an eyebrow.

"I know it probably won't be for a while but—when everyone is at a better place—I hope we can finally end slavery," Cyrus said.

Norne paused. In the next second, she burst out laughing so genuinely and loudly it could be heard outside the carriage. Norne rolled on her seat with her stomach in pain, belly-laughing at the idea harder than she'd ever laughed in her life.

"What! I'm serious," Cyrus stated, embarrassment evident on her face.

"It is the trend of human history that over time there is more freedom for more people! It only makes sense to not fight against that and give people more rights instead of less. That's real freedom—the ability to do whatever they want as long as they aren't hurting anyone else. Don't you agree?" Cyrus elaborated.

Norne's laugh grew even louder until she physically fell over.

"Hey! Stop laughing!" Cyrus, horribly embarrassed, covered her face.

Norne laughed all the way back to the palace. Atosa opened the door to let them out and helped Cyrus descend who was still scarlet faced.

Norne exited the carriage, still laughing hysterically. Suddenly, Grak floated down next to her and crossed his arms.

"What's so funny?" he asked sternly.

"Prince Grak! What a surprise—" Norne panicking, tried to re-orient herself.

"Grak!" Cyrus hugged him excitedly.

"Hey Cyrus. Another message came in from the committee. What do you say you go give it a read?" Grak lovingly hugged her back with one arm before quickly looking back to Norne.

Atosa was moving in to embrace him as well, but after seeing how serious Grak was, she timidly decided not to and grabbed Cyrus by the hand.

"Come on Princess. Let's get you settled in." She hurriedly led the princess away.

As the two entered the palace, Grak and Norne were left alone.

"So…did you get all the info you wanted from her?" Grak angrily asked.

"I don't know what you mean. I was invited here." Norne smiled.

"To sabotage our alliance no doubt. So, what will you do?" Grak asked.

"Don't be ridiculous, your proposition is entirely more beneficial to Tartarus than any agreement with one little girl could ever be. Besides she spent most of the day forcing me to endure the slums below. Other than her proposition nothing was discussed." Norne shrugged.

"Good. Leave her out of this," Grak sternly warned.

"The girl is obviously still a child. I can't fault her for that." Norne pretentiously shook her head.

"She is. A precious, young, and *impressionable* child. Normally I'd tell you to stay the Hel away from my sister, but unfortunately, even before this meeting, she took a liking to you. She sees the best in people and unfortunately can't see you for the awful person you are," Grak angrily said.

Norne paused, looking up at him and making direct eye contact. Rulers often knew each other's dirty secrets, but few ever took issue with them or ever admitted to knowing them in the first place. Cyrus really was his sister.

"Grak I'm hurt; we hardly know each other. But given your past comments—I suppose the Senate and castle staff were in need of a purge for a while now anyway. Leaking is a risky business after all." Norne let her façade slip only for a moment, before quickly returning to it.

"You take yourself so seriously don't you. You think your family issues get you a free pass?" Grak asked.

Norne lost her phony smile.

"Ooh. Magnus used the Sovereign Territories act, didn't he? That's why you're pissy isn't it? Losing control of our little deal Grak?" Norne sadistically grinned.

"What can I say? Keeping on the princely persona gets tiresome when dealing with your kind." Grak glared.

"Fair. I understand, it is nice to share some open contempt with someone once in a while, given our line of work's requirement for personas." Norne laughed.

"Seconded." Grak joined her laughter, then grew serious.

"My sister is still mostly unaware of your true nature, having only your manufactured narratives to go on. Since the cat is out of the bag, it doesn't matter if you keep visiting her, she's scared right now and could use the company. *But,* if you ever harm a hair on her head… Aurelia and the entirety of the alliance, my father—they will be the least of your concerns if I ever find you. Are we clear?" Grak leaned down with palpable bloodlust in his eyes at the mere thought.

"Crystal. Gosh, is that really what I sound like?" Norne asked as Grak calmed back down.

Norne returned to Tartarus leaving Grak breathing easily once again. Setting his royal staff at the altar of the legendary first prince Grak (from whom he had inherited it), he ascended the stairs and approach Cyrus' room.

He found her sitting in bed, cuddling with the stuffed lion, and reading the clay tablets the children had written earlier as Atosa combed her hair.

"Cyrus?" Grak asked after remembering to put on the silver ornaments she got him instead of his usual bronze ones.

"Grak! Perfect timing. I was thinking we need to reorder the room." Cyrus smiled at him.

"I'm not moving all your furniture around again." Grak sat next to Cyrus on the bed and quickly kissed Atosa on the forehead before reclining. Grak was so tall that his feet dangled off, but he ensured there was enough room for the two girls to be comfortable with him there, "I'm here now, though. So, if you want to talk, here I am."

"You've seen through my clever ruse, I see," Cyrus joked.

"At first I was surprised how unlike you it was to take advantage of another person's kindness." Grak laughed at her response.

"Well, what can I say. Writing political speeches does that to a girl." She smirked.

"Oh yes. My thanks again, you did excellent work as always. The crowd loved it. Though I'm sure that is because they couldn't read all the misspellings." Grak grinned.

"Really? So, the rebel faction surrendered with minimal fighting!" Cyrus asked as her face lit up.

"Of course. No show of force was even needed. Once they saw that I'd come personally to hear their troubles and then, heard your words it was in the bag." Grak grinned.

"Alright! I was a bit worried because I realized five minutes too late that I had handed off the rough copy instead of the finished version of the speech," Cyrus admitted.

"I could tell," Grak replied. "But I think I nailed the delivery either way. All they wanted was to be heard so it went over pretty easily." He couldn't help but chuckle. Atosa smiled warmly to see the two together again. Neither Norne nor Chaos would ever have seen Grak this happy.

"All their problems were attended to?" Cyrus asked.

"Most of it could be solved even without throwing money at the problem. As usual, they were last on the list for Monster clearing so it's from that that the other effects sprouted. But then again, being a poverty-stricken area has other problems than merely getting forgotten for Monster protection." Grak got serious.

"But once they're a part of the Uruk autonomous zones, all the benefits that come with that should help alleviate those problems." Cyrus grinned.

"Right. I'll be heading back to get things started, but work has already started on irrigation and housing projects. Plus, the increased tax revenue of the other areas should revitalize their economy in short order. And we can jump straight to silversmithing over there to give them a head start. Turns out the more we do this, the easier it gets," Grak said.

"Told you! Silver is the way of the future. Just you wait, soon this new planet will be outpacing Uruk economically." Cyrus smirked.

"Doubtful." Grak sighed.

"Oh yeah? That's my new mission—make that planet the number one in the Empire!" Cyrus grinned.

"Way to show me up as always," Grak teased. "Also, I took care of the corrupt nobles you noticed. Sure enough, they don't hide things any better than they did under father's administration—if you could call it that," Grak noted.

There was a sudden awkward silence.

"Grak…if you trust me then you'll let go of things like that. Trust me, father will come around once he sees how well we've progressed things," Cyrus promised.

"Cyrus, let's not talk politics now." Grak sighed.

"Why? Politics and Power seem to be all people get killed over these days. Best to know what's going on, to stop that from happening. No one even held a funeral for Uncle Aurelian. He wasn't perfect either, but I think people deserve better than unmarked graves and destroyed legacies, no matter who they are," Cyrus firmly declared.

Grak paused and sighed. "Cyrus—not everyone in this world is like you. I came around but some people are too far gone. Your methods can only work if people want to be good people. And as far as we've gotten, you have to admit that some people don't. There are people who will actively oppose the world you want to create." Grak sat up.

"No one is beyond saving!" Cyrus cried. "And if we play favorites saving some and not others, aren't we the same as them then?"

"Cyrus. You opened my eyes to so much. The world we all wish for *cannot* be stopped because we lie down and let others destroy it," Grak said raising his voice.

"Well, you seem like the one who can't see! I'm not an Immortal like you. I will die someday but I'm patient. By the time I die we probably won't have fixed everyone's problems, but we'll be on the right track. Trust me Grak, there are things I want and believe that are so radical I haven't even told you about them, but the fact is that I'll *never* get to see them happen. It makes no sense for *you* to be the impatient one," Cyrus boldly responded.

"This isn't a matter of patience, Cyrus. You are not an Immortal and if father *kills* you then things go right off the track, don't they? I can't keep leaving home and spend every waking moment dreading that he'll hurt you again!" Grak cried.

"But—" Cyrus began.

"Don't try to stop me, Cyrus. You know I'm right." Grak sighed.

There was a long pause. Atosa had stopped combing and now just looked from sibling to sibling worriedly.

"Yeah. You're probably right." Cyrus gave in, much to Atosa's shock.

"It's surely much faster and certain to succeed doing things the way that you and your friends plan to. But think about this—if I could figure it out after all the lengths you went through to keep me in the dark, how long before dad figures it out?" Cyrus began to tear up.

Grak didn't know how to respond.

"Don't you know that now I can't keep hearing you leave home and spend every waking moment dreading that father sends some people to take you out of the picture? Or worse, does it himself? I remember what happened to mom and I can't lose you too." Cyrus was fully crying now, curling up around her childhood stuffed toy.

"You know that won't happen," Grak said, trying to comfort her.

"Really? I've heard how you talk about him. If you were strong enough to fight father then he'd be in a shallow grave already, wouldn't he!" Cyrus asked.

Grak couldn't respond. He knew she was right.

"I worry about you too. So does Atosa. Don't go running around and get yourself killed while convincing yourself it is for us. Slow and steady wins this race. Do you say I'm smart? Well, I think it's smart to minimize risk and it is safer to keep father and the others with us instead of against us. If you really do trust me then trust my plans!" Cyrus dramatically declared.

"You've gotten too good at giving speeches." Grak sighed, laying back down and grabbing Cyrus to embrace her in his arms.

"Hey!" Cyrus laughed. Grak pulled Atosa in for a group hug.

"I love you two, more than anything under all these stars. I promise, nothing will happen to me, so don't worry," Grak assured them.

"Now, let's get some dinner, we've all had a busy day." Grak grinned and stood up.

"Hey! You're not getting out of resolving this discussion." Cyrus pouted.

"Give it a rest, Princess Cyrus. Remember, he's taking time off to spend with us so we should use it to the fullest." Atosa finally stepped in.

"Alright." Cyrus acquiesced and took Atosa's hand to be led down the stairs.

Meanwhile, in Tartarus, Norne had long since returned and was back to her plotting with Chaos in their very different kind of relationship. That evening, in Norne's still bland room in the Tartarus Palace, Chaos had belly-flopped on her bed (crushing it) and was busy writing on it, while Norne sat on his back, reading as usual.

"Norne! If this is supposed to be *my* signature, why do I have to learn to copy one *you* made," Chaos whined while crumpling up a page of failed Imperial signatures in frustration.

"Because, when I asked you to make one and help with paperwork, *you* spent the time with floosies. It's your own fault, so now you have to imitate the one I made for you. I rather like how it looks, so get it right. Or else we're going back to arithmetic." Norne scolded him without looking up from her book, *Monster Encyclopedia 73rd Edition*.

"Aw! Not that number stuff again! I already know how to count, what more do I need?" Chaos threw a tantrum.

"An Emperor who needs to count on his fingers is a disgrace to the nation! Be glad I hired the greatest educator in the country. You should at least be comparable to a literate child when he's done with you. That will be good enough for now." Norne sighed.

Chaos huffed and crossed his arms. Suddenly, an hourglass ran out.

"Norne, it's time. Can you take the thing out?" Chaos asked.

"Cool. On to the next test." Norne said before taking the needle of a primitive intravenous device out of Chaos' arm.

"Alright—and you are also immune to Mandrakes. Lucky. That one is gaining in popularity among the Senate so I was worried it would be a problem." Norne smirked while checking off a box on a long chart of poisons she tested on Chaos.

"Oh yeah! And my regeneration from critical wounds is just as fast as the others. I was shot through the heart today." Chaos grinned.

"I received the report from Magnus. You're averaging nine times greater Immortality compared to regular Immortals if that makes any sense," Norne explained.

"Then can't we just say I'm unkillable and skip all these trials?" Chaos asked.

"No one is unkillable. Even you need to make sure you avoid critical damage to your head, remember? Besides better safe than sorry, you might still be vulnerable to certain substances, and I'd prefer to not be blindsided," Norne insisted.

"Ugh! Fine, but if we have to do this, I liked it when we tried the poisons in the food better. That way I didn't have to notice it." Chaos rubbed his arm after it had instantly healed.

"Oh, don't be a baby. This is faster and more accurate—well you know what I mean. It's not my fault that so far, you're one-hundred percent immune to any known substance. I know you're strong but what the Hel is your stomach made of?" Norne asked.

"I told you already. My old man tried every poisonous plant, berry, gas, or mystery liquid he could to off me. But none of 'em worked. Even told me so—I'm unkillable." Chaos laughed with a twisted nostalgia.

"He thought that is what got him stripped of his powers and isolated on a barren ice ball with you to begin with. We can never be too careful. Until we find whatever mystery method your mother used to restrain him, we have to always stay alert," Norne reminded him.

"How'd that even happen to begin with?" Chaos asked curiously.

"Dunno. That's a priority thing I need to get to the bottom of—how they did it, and if whoever did it is still at large. Lest it happens to you next. But I'm taking a break from that since, the only books I can find recording Typhon's rule just keep talking about how handsome he was. I don't care how he looked. GIVE ME SOMETHING USEFUL! What a pain." Norne sighed.

With the entire page done, Norne flipped to the next one and put the appropriate poison in the vial to flow directly into Chaos' blood.

"Next up—pure arsenic dissolved in a commonly used castle rat poison."

Norne tried to stick the needle back into Chaos' arm, but it snapped.

"Chaos—" Norne angrily groaned.

"Oh right. My bad," Chaos said before exhaling and lowering his instinctual Power field. Norne finally stuck the replacement needle through his skin—even without Power that was tough.

"There. We'll be done in no time. And once you've cleared all the poisons, you can eat anything you want." Norne sighed.

"Kay." Chaos grinned and went back to practicing his signature.

Norne re-opened her book and sat on Chaos' back while he wrote.

"Grak lets me eat whatever I want," Chaos pouted.

"Oh, for crying out—remember it's only a matter of time before he tries to trick you into something. You must remain vigilant," Norne reminded him.

"Yeah, yeah. I've been keeping an eye open or whatever. The other one is for the hot Italic chick." Chaos grinned.

"Aurelia?" Norne asked.

"Yeah her. Turns out women who can kill just as well as I can are a *huge* turn on." Chaos laughed.

"Oh, gods. We're testing poisons now; don't tell me we need to test for STDs as well." Norne groaned.

"What is STDs?" Chaos cluelessly asked.

"Try not to find out." Norne closed her book.

Chaos crumpled up another page of failed signatures and tossed it away before groaning and giving up. Lying face down on the bed he made more room. Norne decided to lie down on his back and take a nap. Given the size difference between them, she could recline casually. The two rulers had worked hard.

"Oh, and before I forget!" Norne said without opening her eyes. "Before you go out with Grak again, you have to get ready for the winter harvest."

"Norne, I know you don't think I'm that clever but even I know that 'winter harvest' makes no sense." Chaos rolled his eyes.

"You're right. You are an idiot. Winter harvest is when it gets cold enough for the northern ice to move south enough to balance out areas of the molten hemisphere. The temporarily de-lavafied land is safe enough for peasants to venture out into the closer parts of the molten hemisphere and collect the Ambrosia fruit there. It's, one of the most culturally significant things in Tartarus civilization, you know? One of its founding traditions that the ruler always participates in, you know? It is your first year as Emperor, so you have to make a good impression," Norne explained while suddenly sitting up and scribbling down some notes for the event.

"What? Now I have to go fruit picking? I thought that's what the slaves are for?" Chaos whined.

"It is but the peasants don't know that. You just open the event, then you can head home. They harvest the dangerous area for us, feed themselves, and literally make their own bread and circuses so that we can take a break from coddling them while they somehow still give us all the credit for their hard work. It's a pretty sweet deal and we *cannot* afford to screw it up." Norne stared directly at him.

"Fine. I'll save some of the fruits for you. Then we can share that ambrosia stuff from before." Chaos excitedly realized.

"Cool. It's a date—" Norne cut herself off. "I mean it sounds good."

"You seem a bit different after visiting Mesos too," Chaos noted looking up at Norne.

"I have no idea what you're talking about. Just focus on helping Grak with the alliance. We need to make as many allies of his allies as we can." Norne pulled her book over her face.

CHAPTER 10

"True to your reputation, you're quite good at this, Grak." Prince Wilhelm von Prussia smiled at Grak while placing the king's crown on his own head. He looked at the charred remains of the assembled councilmen that Grak had vaporized in their chairs, as well as the shocked Chancellor's head mounted on Magnus' spear.

"Ahem," Chaos coughed loudly, trying to spotlight his successful instant execution of the chancellor's royal guard by smashing his head into the wall.

"And of course, your help as well Emperor Chaos. Your legendary strength was not exaggerated. I'll admit I had my doubts when Grak brought you along in place of the army I requested. But you really were more than enough for dealing with him. Seems the right choice was made." The prince grinned.

Finally, Wilhelm removed his blade from his father's head with a smile and the battle was officially over before it had begun. His father, the King of Prussia had in fact agreed to meet with them over concerns of all the sudden deaths among his ruling peers. However, even the warmongering despot was taken aback by Grak's fierce kill first and ask questions later approach.

"Aurelia was busy, so naturally Chaos was the logical choice," Grak explained.

"Oh yeah! The hot one wasn't here today? Where was she?" Chaos asked.

"The—hot one?" Grak asked.

"Play dumb as much as you want Grak," Wilhelm said laughing. "Everyone knows you don't just keep a catch like that in the 'friend zone.' The sooner you and Aurelia stop denying it, the better."

"Aurelia and I are business partners only. Neither of us is looking to settle down right now," Grak lied unconvincingly (though not about the part they thought).

Wilhelm rolled his eyes.

"Yes! Got this in the bag then." Chaos flexed excitedly with the unappreciated Magnus walking by his side, wiping the blade of his spear clean.

"Onto to business, Prince Wilhelm. Our part of this partnership is done, but are you certain the new administration you have selected is up to the task of replacing this council?" Grak uneasily asked.

"Of course," Wilhelm said reassuringly. "My backers were very excited to take these high positions in exchange for supporting me."

"That does not answer the question though. It would be wise to reconsider just handing out important positions to your friends and supporters." Grak sighed worriedly.

"You said it yourself—your part is done. I'm king now, so I can handle everything. Besides, Norne helped me screen for good people, so it should be fine." Wilhelm smirked.

"I see," Grak noted with a hint of suspicion.

So, this continued for some time, Norne visiting Cyrus and Grak collaborating with Chaos. On Mesos, Cyrus and Norne continued their play dates of sorts.

Grak grew was beginning to get very uneasy about how frequently Norne visited his sister and was curious to see what they did when together. One day, when he had time enough to spare, Grak went to see just that.

To his surprise, he found that on this particular occasion, the girls had gone to see the royal smiths with Norne of all people, leading a class. The experienced bronze workers had all nervously agreed to this and gathered around for the demonstration. After explaining the theory of heat treatment with a rundown of her Kelvin-adjacent temperature system, Norne prepped the metal for use and began crafting.

She showed her Arcosian silver crafting skill to the amazed bronze workers, making herself a new knife in a frighteningly short amount of time. Only a few hours of work before Grak's arrival and a weapon fit to cut Chaos had been minted. The sun was setting by the time it was done and Atosa had fallen asleep, but Cyrus and the smiths were still on the edge of their seats.

Norne proudly waved it around. "Yeah, these instruments will work. I think this may be one of my best yet." She grinned with pride.

"Wow… I come home and find you waving a knife in my sister's face?" Grak asked, surprising everyone present. They turned to see him leaning in the entrance.

"Grak? You're back early." Cyrus grinned.

"Just overseeing some construction and rebuilding in disaster regions, no fighting today." Grak smiled. Noting that Atosa was asleep he gently placed the letters of thanks (on account of her temporary housing designs solving the homelessness crisis that came after a horrible earthquake) from the people on her lap.

"Grak! Grak! You should see Norne's cool new smithing techniques!" Cyrus cheered, still amazed by Norne's expertise. "I could barely understand half of what she was on about, but it sounds amazing! She says she's even one step above the Arcosian priesthood's secret sacred silversmiths."

"Oh really?" Grak was skeptical since he knew how prone Cyrus was to fawn over new things she had just learned about.

"She tells the truth, Prince," the head smith informed him. "I've been in smithing for thirty years and all this 'degrees' talk is practically another language for me. I feel like I'm back in the Eduba, learning all this, but it is quite exhilarating." He chuckled.

"I see. Let me guess, Norne, you are in the mood to sell us some?" Grak sighed. When he looked at Norne however, he was confused to see that she looked confused.

"Is something the matter?" he asked.

"Wait—you actually weren't fighting today?" Norne asked.

"No, unlike you, I have citizens I care about protecting as well. As easy as it is to destroy, a ruler also has to build up their country," Grak scoffed.

"But Chaos went out to meet with Aurelia for a mission today. Grak, if you're here, then where are they?" Norne asked, genuinely surprised.

"What? We just finished in Prussia so we aren't meeting 'til next month." Grak gasped.

The two looked at each other in genuine confusion for a second.

In Italia, a group of rebels loyal to the previous dictator had gathered under Aurelian's flag.

"Hail the dictator! Death to the usurper!" the surprisingly large number chanted.

"Death to the usurper? I am your *dictator*. You drunk peasants. Your revolt over alcohol and taxes are not my concern." Aurelia crossed her arms, standing before the army with one of her own.

"You promised us change. But it's more of the same! Nothing has changed at all!" the rebel leader screamed.

"Sol Invictus tolerated your fool of a father because of his faith, but now you have nothing redeeming you!" a more zealous rebel added. Their previous loyalty to the state would have better been described as tolerance.

"Death to the usurper! By Sol Invictus, the star of righteousness arises with healing in our wings," the army began to chant.

"Wow, I thought the people liked your old man." Chaos walked over while eating a Mensa slice.

"They did. The people that mattered did, anyways. Even *he* had to put down annoying riff-raff whenever they got rowdy," Aurelia said dismissively.

"Ha. You should take tips from Norne. She says her ideas for 'circuses and bread' actually came from Italia, so you really suck at this." Chaos laughed at Aurelia.

"Shut up. Now did you bring what I asked for or not?" Aurelia asked.

"Sure thing." Chaos grinned.

Suddenly a group of Imperial Knights impactfully landed around their Emperor, their blades drawn in his defense.

"We do this in the Emperor's name! He who is mightiest determines what is just! So, we do this in his Majesty's power! We do this In Justice!" Magnus proudly declared the Imperial Knights' motto while raising his blade high in the air.

"In justice!" the other knights repeated, raising their blades as well.

"Just in case any of you felt like running away or siding with the rebels—" Aurelia fiercely addressed her troops who were beginning to lose their nerve, "Chaos so generously brought some babysitters along." At this, the soldiers tightened up and prepared to battle.

"Good. Seems you're good for something after all," Aurelia said before looking over at the Imperial Knights in full armor.

"Knockoffs. But they'll do." She scoffed at their obvious similarities to the ancient Italic warriors, the centurions.

"I don't see why we need 'em. This is only an army of what, a couple of hundred of them?" Chaos casually remarked while doing warm-up stretches.

"Just try not to die." Aurelia sighed.

"I could say the same for you. Now let's—" Chaos set his eyes on a target. In a flash though, Aurelia dashed forward, punching holes through the rebel leaders without warning. At the sight of her strength, Chaos loudly cat-called the dictator. He grinned while watching her powerfully rip through the crowd. He excitedly ran in after her and really, the two armies were only there to prevent anyone from escaping. Not just the army, but after they had been killed, the rebelling towns who supported them were all marked to be destroyed as well.

It was a faux pas to simply destroy planets in their entirety, so their destruction was to be slow and painful instead—systematic personal killings led by the blood-drunk troops of Tartarus and Italia together. In this endeavor, however, Aurelia made sure that Tartarus hung back as cleanup, picking off any stragglers or lucky escapees. This was an exercise to condition her people—Italia led the charge against the civilian targets.

The men and women in armor under Aurelia's command on their own were personally decent people. Few expected that after the battle, they would be winding down by letting the nightmare spill over into the civilian populace. Before today, even the suggestion that they should indulge in such inhumanity, would normally be met by ridicule and rebuke. Many of these soldiers were first-time combatants, drafted by Aurelia's warmongering pushes for conscription and mass enlistments. However, that is not to say they were unwilling to serve. They were young and eager for adventure—they wanted to be heroes.

Armed in the noble steel armaments of their ancestors as the drumming and trumpets of the dictator's proclaimers echoed their beating hearts, something began to stir. As they entered the town along with the literal trumpets, the incessant demagoguery from the Dictator shouting about the glory of their ancestors and how they lived to die continued. Thinking about what they were doing, would be emasculating. As soldiers of the Empire, action for

JAIDEN BAYNES

action's sake was all that mattered, not what they thought was right or wrong—the Dictator commanded it.

To keep their pristine armor clean and safe from the stains of blood, they donned crimson-red cloaks, while casting off their humanity. The noble Italic army ravaged their way through their own territory ensuring that *no one* questioned Aurelia's power. No blood was spared—from house to house, like a force of nature the maddened patriots of Italia did the dark deeds their authoritarian leader commanded of them.

As they butchered all in their path, they didn't bother thinking about the pain they'd wrought. Besides these were the treacherous pig dogs they had been told betrayed the glorious leader. The people of Italia not born on the capital planet of Reme were seen as lesser Italics. They were lesser races compared to the capital bred successors of the founder king Remus. Similar thinking was often echoed in all the other empires (favoring the wealthy residents of the capital compared to the impoverished serfs or plebians of the outer territorial holdings) but ever since Aurelia came to power the sentiments grew much stronger.

In Tartarus they constantly took such actions against any who disgraced Chaos. Here, the Tartarians carried on like business as usual. Should the successors of Aeneas and Remus: Italic peoples, the greatest of all the races (in their own minds), shrink in the face of their peers? If they were doing it too... what was the issue? The justifications could be thought of after.

Walking past the carnage, Aurelia looked with disdain at those who dared to rebel against her and felt no remorse for the slaughter she had wrought. Instead, she felt proud of the strength of her glorious Empire. She was a Dictator worthy of continuing the prelapsarian idealized past of those who had come before her. They were not individual storm troopers in Aurelia's mind, but rather an extension of herself.

Now she had grown up to be as great as the mythologized Aeneas or even her father before he went soft in his old age. She was a hero like the idols of her girlhood dreams—an individual with great power who far surpassed the rest of their contemporaries. Like her troops, despite moments of better character, she reveled in this. Her troops had gone mad with bloodlust and tore apart men, women, and children alike. She had achieved her fascismo.

If a normal person had done a fraction of the atrocities Aurelia and her army committed, they would be branded a murderer and a monster. However, because Aurelia commanded a great force and awesome Power, she was styled Dictator and conqueror.

When the slaughter was over, Aurelia retired to a special red tent marked for her alone as Dictator. What set it apart in designation among the many other identical red tents for her troops was a single, golden symbol of the Italic axe on the entrance to the tent. The golden symbol of Italic power since ancient times—the fasces.

In the tents around her, many soldiers fell to their knees and wept after what they had done. But many more did not. They were not crazier or eviller compared to their compatriots, however. The self-justifications had simply kicked in earlier for them than their traumatized peers. They weren't cruel for killing a child. After all, their fellow countrymen had just slaughtered its parents, so they had put it out of its misery. It being the child. And if it was excusable to kill them—so on and so forth. They weren't at fault, they were just following orders. At least in their minds.

Their hollow consciences cleared; this group felt fit to look down on the shell-shocked, sorrowful soldiers as weak. However, even those who justified it were looked down on by Aurelia's favorites—those who did not bother thinking about justifications at all.

Shortly after entering, Aurelia exited her tent in clean clothes, refreshed. Her pristine white tunic was so stained with the blood of her own subjects in the 'battle' that it had to be discarded. Her blood-soaked garb was burned, and her armor polished back to a shine. When she walked out, she noticed Chaos sitting by the entrance.

"I'm surprised you managed to restrain yourself. Good thing I didn't have to kill you too," Aurelia joked.

"Listen hot stuff, I like you, but you aren't close enough to me to make murder jokes yet. That's only for Norne and Norne alone." Chaos grinned.

"Fine. Remember we are not friends. We are allies. For this mission, I just felt that as a fellow ruler, you were more dependable than any of the 'rulers to be.' You can appreciate…what had to be done in these types of situations," Aurelia said frankly, putting her Dictator's laurel crown back into her hair.

"Ah, I see. You wanted some one-on-one time with me away from your boyfriend." Chaos stood up and walked over, smiling at her.

"The relationship between Grak and I is purely professional and a means to an end. As Dictator, I only continue supporting him because I believe it is in Italia's best interest to have strong allies. Unfortunately, that also includes you." Aurelia pushed him back.

"I think our…partnership could be rather pleasant if you wanted it to be." Chaos got uncomfortably close.

Aurelia pushed him away again in disgust.

"What? You should know a woman who can fight on this level *really* does it for me." Chaos grinned.

"Whatever pig. We're done here so let's get going. And *you* walk ahead. I can tell that your degenerate eyes were looking at me from behind on the way here," Aurelia angrily said.

"Nothing gets past you." Chaos laughed and stood up, walking ahead, chuckling to himself.

Back in Tartarus, he walked into the castle to find that Norne was standing there, giving him a look of death.

"Hi Norne," he nervously said.

He sat on the floor of his room as Norne furiously paced around him.

"Chaos, we do NOT loan our military out for free," she scolded him.

"But you said to stay friends with countries that would be a useful thing to do," Chaos pointed out.

"This is different!" Norne pointed at him.

"You're just mad I did it without your permission. I'm the Emperor, remember that! The laws say that I command the army, so I can do whatever I want!" Chaos childishly yelled.

"For crying out loud! Do you remember *who* wrote those laws? It's just fancy talk to make *you* seem more respectable while I do all the heavy lifting," Norne said.

"That's dumb! I'm the Emperor! That can't be all you're mad about." Chaos crossed his arms.

"And also…you fought with her as a team. I thought that was our thing." Norne blushed, not knowing why she reacted this way around him.

"What? You miss the fighting? Fine, we can go out and butcher some rioters another time," Chaos promised, giving her a thumbs up.

"Okay. Thanks, Chaos." Norne blushed again, content with this brutal offer.

At the same time, Grak was scolding Aurelia, while she in turn ignored him the whole time as she stood posing for her twelfth royal portrait that week. This one saw her in the role of Italic hero and demigod Hercle, triumphantly pointing a club forward while wearing the skin of a lion.

Grak, seeing that she wasn't listening folded his arms and waited. Aurelia side-eyed him as irritation practically emanated from him. The painter, sensing the palpable tension in the air, hastened his finish and quickly rushed out.

"Alright…now what were you whining about?" Aurelia sighed as she removed the ridiculous lion hood and other articles of the outfit that she had appended to her own to emulate the hero. Grak stepped up as she tossed her costume on a table for slaves to clean up.

"That was not the deal! Aurelia, our revolution is to bring about change and not just cause more of the same trouble!" Grak furiously yelled at her.

"Don't confuse your childish ideals with mine. I made my goals clear to you long ago. Don't act surprised." She rolled her eyes.

"Aurelia, you said you could make Italia better. But now you're just acting like—like—" he didn't want to finish the sentence.

"Like what? Like a Dictator? Because I am, Grak. Has it only just now hit you?" She crossed her arms.

"But working with Chaos? I thought you despised him, why work together? Why do things the way he does?" Grak cried, exasperated to see his friend like this.

"I was just making it clear that we used *them* not vice versa. Someone had to step up and make that clear. I used to respect you Grak, but this is why I lost that respect. You've been listening to Cyrus far too much. I remember a great warrior, but she put these childish ideas in your head." She stared daggers at him.

"It's not right. What you're doing isn't right." He couldn't even look her in the eyes.

"I am Dictator. That makes it right. Perhaps you'll finally see it when you are Lugal." She turned to him.

"Aurelia—what happened to you? You sound like Chaos."

"You'll understand when you are Lugal. Power is very enlightening," Aurelia responded.

"Cyrus can never find out." Grak sighed.

"And she never will. Don't worry, I ensured there were no survivors. I've gotten quite good at that. Remember, I am the Dictator," Aurelia calmly said.

"It would crush her. Remember that. She looks up to you," Grak warned.

"Well then…we're both bad role models, aren't we? Plotting patricide and all that." Aurelia scoffed.

"And as you have supported me, I haven't stopped you. She would be disappointed in me too." Grak sighed, finally facing her.

"It doesn't matter. Soon the only one remaining will be Sargon. Then all my goals will be realized," Aurelia said ominously before walking past him.

"So then, was it becoming Dictator that changed you…or were you secretly always like this?" Grak wondered out loud.

CHAPTER 11

In those days, Tartarus was hosting their snow sculpting festival and as a sign of their international collaboration Grak, Aurelia, Atosa, and Cyrus were all invited. The snow sculpting event was crowded with excited families from all over the Empire along with allies of the crown from all over. The day chosen for this distraction was of course a national holiday, formerly in celebration of the pagan god Perun which was then stolen by King Drakon's church to promote him, then stolen once again by Norne to be a celebration for Chaos.

"Welcome, please enjoy the day," Norne said with a fake grin, welcoming the nobility as they entered the palace. She handed passes to the attendees.

"Quite the interesting setup. I always assumed you were allergic to fun." Aurelia entered with Italic Centurions in a slightly warmer set of Dictator clothing.

"Greetings Dictator Aurelia, I hope you enjoy this day. Follow the carpet out to the snowfield or head straight to the banquet hall if you'd prefer." Norne shook her hand with a phony greeter's excitement.

"I see," Aurelia said before walking away.

As soon as she walked past, Norne scowled at her.

"There she is," Grak said suddenly, catching Norne's attention.

"Welcome, Prince Grak—" Norne began.

"Norne!" a muffled voice came out of a giant ball of cloaks, fur coats, and winter blankets with arms and legs. Though buried beneath twenty layers of furs and fabrics, Norne recognized it as Cyrus' voice.

"What in the—Princess Cyrus!" Norne gasped, shocked.

"Yeah. Grak said Tartarus was cold, but I think he went a bit overboard." Cyrus laughed.

"It is very cold, and you *could* get sick from a gust of wind. I'm just making sure you're safe," Grak paternally scolded her.

"I see," Norne said awkwardly.

"Cyrus!" an excited Aurelia called out after hearing she was there. To Norne's surprise, the stone-hearted dictator excitedly ran over and hugged Cyrus out of the ball of coats.

"Aurelia! How have you been?" Cyrus chuckled while Aurelia waved her around.

"Great now that you're here!" Aurelia laughed before engaging in the sisterly ritual of rubbing noses by way of greeting each other.

Even Grak was getting embarrassed at the overly affectionate greeting and whispered to Aurelia, "Just because your men know to look away doesn't mean the other guests do."

"Hmph. I haven't gotten to see my little *Topolina* in so long and I don't care who knows it. You're just jealous." Aurelia childishly smirked at him while continuing her public cuddling with the Iryan princess.

Norne was shocked but just as Grak said, Aurelia's 4 Praetorian guards instinctively knew to all look away, lest they see the dear leader in a state of weakness (which Norne found funny). After all, only a fool would get attached to Cyrus.

Shortly after, the event began. The professional Arcosian ice sculptors created massive, amazing sculptures of Chaos.

Wealthy children and teenagers flooded the field, while their parents watched from comfortable booths guarded by soldiers.

Norne walked around, excited to see the event going well. Many sculptures of animals, people, and buildings were attempted.

When Norne returned, she saw Chaos flexing with the nobles. They were all giving him praise and compliments that kept him going as he showed off the physique that he was so proud of.

"Well, well, well, Chaos, we meet again." Wilhelm smirked as he approached Chaos with a woman on his arm.

After teaming up before, the two royals had become fast """"friends"""" due to their similar interests.

"Whoa! Not bad, Wilhelm." Chaos whistled, inspecting Wilhelm's date like a piece of meat.

"Yeah, I have great taste. A real shame you didn't bring a date though. Even if she would've paled in comparison to the hottest pair of legs in Prussia," Wilhelm boasted.

"Oh yeah? Let me see—" Chaos said before looking into the crowd of gathered Tartarian nobles. After suitably looking them over he smiled.

"There we go," he said pulling a beautiful (married) noble-woman out from the crowd to his side.

"Your majesty—what is the meaning of this!" she asked in a panic, repeatedly looking at him then over her shoulder at her baffled husband.

"What do you think, Wilhelm? I don't do dates. After all, I get so many chicks I could never just pick one to bring around with me. But even this one from last week is at least as hot as yours," he boasted.

The woman put her head in her hands.

"Chaos, my man you're missing all the romance. A real man takes his time with each conquest." Wilhelm pulled his date in uncomfortably close. It took every fiber of the repulsed lady's being to not push him off her.

"I take plenty of time! Plus, it's not like a one-and-done thing—I cycle through. The only reason I didn't bring one with me is that Norne gets all weird about it for some reason." Chaos refused to be one-upped by Wilhelm in this public contest of measurements.

"Prince Wilhelm, I am glad to see you in attendance," Norne, coming over, interrupted them. "Congratulations on the excellent military victory against the rebel forces and uniting your great nation. Truly you are befitting of your title the Supreme War Lord." She smiled.

"Yes...well I suppose I did," Wilhelm replied, standing up straight and regaining his composure.

Compliment a fool and you may make him useful.

Wilhelm then cleared his throat and began to boastfully recount his first successful war as monarch of Prussia. In reality, aid from Tartarus had done most of the work but Wilhelm enjoyed LARPing as a warrior king.

The crowd focussed on his story, giving Norne a chance to talk to Chaos.

"What are you doing?" she asked him. "I thought you were excited to play in the snow too."

"PFFT. Not now. I can't look lame in front of Aurelia," Chaos replied.

"Aurelia!" Norne growled.

"Of course. Plus, I'm sure she saw me with the babe. Now that I've outmanned Wilhelm I'm one step closer to nabbing her. Wilhelm told me that chicks love playboys." Chaos grinned.

"Of course, he did," Norne responded with a deadpan expression on her face.

"Now then, if you'll excuse me," Chaos said before resuming his flexing from before.

Norne was annoyed to see Chaos looking over his shoulder to check out Aurelia's response from her own social group. However, he was disappointed to see Aurelia not even watching his flexing (and Norne was disappointed that he was disappointed). Aurelia intentionally stayed among the generals and academics to avoid Chaos and was quite happy with the success so far.

Norne's mother told her just what to do in this situation...but since Aurelia was too valuable an ally to assassinate, she went with the other thing her mom had always said.

She quickly walked over to Magnus, the life of the party (a silent stone-faced man standing in the corner with a drink and talking to no one).

"Magnus, come with me, I have a proposition," she commanded.

"Marry Dictator Aurelia!" Magnus gasped after hearing Norne's plan in secret.

"Of course. She's been a thorn in…the nation's side diplomatically. Marrying Italia into the fold could be useful," Norne lied.

"My life has been devoted to the army—this old soldier has no romance to speak of," he admitted.

"Magnus, this is an order. She is a distraction for the Emperor that must be removed from the equation. Marrying her off would be the easiest way," Norne insisted.

"But milady, surely his reputation regarding married women also proceeds him," Magnus attempted to explain.

"That can be dealt with! The point is that the Emperor's marriageability will be an important bargaining chip in the future. No offense but while Italia is a useful ally, they aren't worth expending that chip. So, in marrying them into the Empire, you'll have to be good enough," Norne said coldly.

Magnus reluctantly accepted, knowing full well that Norne was making him do it for more selfish reasons.

After her conversation with several generals of other nations regarding the future of armored combat, there was a lull in the conversation as many from the group went to refill their plates. Aurelia who didn't have much of an appetite for anything stayed and watched the ice sculpting while indulging in her wine. Magnus saw his opening and with a not so gentle push from Norne, he was off.

"Nice…ice sculpture, is it not?" He asked, rigidly wandering over. She paused and looked at his awkward approach.

"Sure," she responded, before looking back at it.

"I—you—you drink wine. Do you prefer yours with or without sweetener?" Magnus blurted out things as he saw them.

"With. Since a young age, I've acquired a taste for it," she replied in confusion at his continued conversing.

Another awkward silence filled the air as Aurelia took another sip.

"I read up on your record. You are a master strategist, I felt even I had much to learn from your campaigns on Barr," Magnus said awkwardly, trying again.

"Okay—thank you. Your campaigns have impressed me as well. Beyond single battles or engagements, I can tell that you maneuver your troops as well as the ancient Dictators of Reme. Norne did well in selecting her commander," she answered, her attention now captured by Magnus' out-of-character actions.

"Marry me," Magnus said, cutting straight to the chase causing Aurelia to freeze momentarily and Norne to facepalm.

There was a far worse awkward silence before Aurelia began laughing out loud. Magnus looked at her uneasily—now it was his turn to be confused.

"As dictator of Italia, dozens of people have approached me with offers of marriage. They all boil down to a similar pitch. I know how beautiful I am—I've been told to death. But y'know, at least you have your priorities straight." She laughed at him so hard that she had to wipe a tear from her eye.

"Is that a, yes?" Magnus deadpanned.

"No. Aren't you like sixty?" Aurelia asked.

"Fifty-one. But to Immortals, does it really matter? Age is a number—which—which pales in comparison to my—love for you?" Magnus half asked, bombing his pickup line.

"Most go for complimenting how beautiful my eyes are next. So…interesting subversion," Aurelia teased him, amused by his awkwardness. She could tell something was up.

"What beautiful eyes—" he began before Aurelia held her hand up to stop him.

"Right." He sighed.

"Speaking of eyes. Shot in the dark but…given those purple eyes, you are Italic nobility, right? The patricians are proud of the royal eyes and that shade is definitely identical. Why have I never seen you before?" Aurelia asked.

"My father comes from a part of Tartarus annexed from Italia in the past. Thus, racially I suppose I would have ancestors who once lived in your nation," Magnus explained.

"I see. I was going to joke that you're too tall for an Italic man, but I'll be damned." She smirked.

"All my Italic relatives and acquaintances are of average height. I've never understood the stereotype," Magnus responded matter-of-factly.

"And they say Arcosians have no sense of humor. You're a proud Italic man but it seems you've been around the witch for too long." Aurelia shook her head.

"I find your mutual distaste rather confusing," Magnus admitted. "Any clarification you could offer?"

"Well, I'll clarify that I don't hate you. At least you can be excused for wearing *that* then. You call yourselves knights and wear those silly feathered helmets like Tartarians…but I know a Centurion when I see one. That Norne of yours is a real Italophile, isn't she?" Aurelia noted, pointing at his armor.

"I suppose. But I too love things from Italia. Like you," Magnus bumbled, remembering that he was supposed to be flirting.

"Is that so?" Aurelia burst out laughing, not at all attracted to him, instead, enjoying his amusing failed attempts at romance.

Across the room, Norne grew bored, especially when the cheesy flirting turned into a casual conversation between two people uninterested in romancing each other.

However, at that moment Chaos saw Aurelia laughing with Magnus and could not tell the difference. Storming over, in a jealous fit, he pulled Magnus aside and slammed him against the wall.

"Why are you courting Aurelia! This is revenge for sleeping with your sister, isn't it?" Chaos asked aggressively.

"Of course not, my Empero—wait what?!" Magnus stopped mid-sentence.

"Answer the question!" Chaos yelled at a quivering Magnus. Amused by this turn of events, Aurelia stepped up—she quickly figured out what was going on.

"I'll tell you what boys, as Dictator it won't do for me to be making a decision personally. If you court me, you court the nation of Italia. If you are serious about marrying me, Sir Magnus you must defend my honor on that account," Aurelia said with a mischievous grin.

He began to sweat.

"So then! That's it, we'll fight over her!" Chaos angrily shook his own general.

"But my Emper—" Magnus panicked.

"If you really love me, Magnus, you'd do it. What? Don't tell me it was all an act or something." She grinned.

Magnus panicking, looked to Norne for help. But she was just as stunned as him. She suddenly looked from Magnus to Aurelia who was maliciously grinning back at her.

"Damn her!" Norne cursed under her breath.

"What's wrong Magnus! I'm game, are you?" Chaos stepped up confrontationally before Magnus.

This was the norm among the powerful, whenever conflict arose it was natural to instantly resort to violence. Dueling for honor and killing over petty squabbles… anything became noble when the nobles did it.

"One second! Chaos, calm down." Norne ran over and led a terrified Magnus away.

Once they were out of earshot, Magnus fell to his knees.

"My lady… if I had done something to offend you…all you had to do was alert me and I would have repented without such punishment! I beg you, whatever it is I have learned my lesson!" Magnus was convulsively shaking at the thought of fighting Chaos.

"Calm down, I'm not punishing you! Aurelia is just being petty and turned the plan against us. There's no use pursuing her now but it won't do to disgrace the head of the army in front of everyone gathered here. Even worse we can't make a fool of the *Emperor* with everyone watching." She didn't know what to do.

"Look at her—she thinks she's so pretty and so clever. Making a mockery of me! Just because I'm the younger sister—I mean ruler." Norne furiously bit her lip.

"How can I resolve this fight in a way that works in our favor?" She wondered, getting back on track.

While everyone was whispering about what was happening, Cyrus walked over to Chaos and tugged on his royal robe. "Emperor Chaos," she timidly said.

"What?" the nine-foot behemoth bent down so she could whisper into his ear.

Norne was still stuck on what to do before Chaos began bellowing with laughter.

"Alright! Magnus! Are you ready for our battle!" Chaos laughed.

"Chaos, hold on!" Norne said, panicking.

"Come on! And bring the biggest plates we've got because we're stuffing our faces with the best food we can offer!" Chaos laughed.

"What!" Norne was completely baffled, looking to Cyrus standing next to Chaos, who simply smiled.

That evening, Chaos was still stuffing his face with piles of Mesos dishes. Magnus was slumped over on the table next to him groaning, his stomach stuffed full from all the food he had been forced to eat (after all he was forced to eat, he almost wished he had to fight Chaos instead). Nearby Cyrus sat on a hill, reading a tablet in silence before Norne walked over and sat next to her.

"You saved me back there, why?" Norne asked. "I don't do favors and it doesn't make us even if that's what you're looking for."

"That's not it. Aurelia was being mean," Cyrus replied. "Not to be rude, but His Majesty needs to work on his manners towards the fairer sex. Nonetheless, Aurelia's little retaliation prank would've hurt a lot of people. It was better this way."

"Great. Why did you have so much food on hand anyway?" Norne wanted to know.

"Oh! We had a festival after another one of Grak's victories and with so many chefs together in one place, I commissioned it for today. I was going to distribute it to peasants on their way home from the snow sculpting as an extra day's meals, but I suppose I can do that another time. Besides, you took better care of everyone than I expected today." Cyrus smiled at Norne.

"This was a propaganda tool. The people need to at least think we care." Norne hand waved.

"That works for now. Doing good by accident is still good." Cyrus grinned.

"I still cannot understand you," Norne admitted, laying down in the snow.

"I know. It may take a while, but I can tell that one day when you become the person that I know you can be—you will be able to do more for people than I could ever dream of. All that power has to be good for something other than playing politics. Oh, and I have a better response for why I helped you back there." Cyrus decided to lie down beside her.

"What do you want?" Norne immediately became skeptical.

"I did it because that's what friends are for." Cyrus smiled genuinely.

Norne paused. "I don't understand you," she repeated with a sigh.

"Well, I'm not strong but there is more than one type of Power," Cyrus replied, grinning.

"Obviously. But don't oversell yourself, just because you were useful in this one case. Besides, true Power reigns supreme." Norne shrugged.

"Yeah. Hearing all the stuff that people can do with Power. It sounds pretty cool. It'd be so fun and interesting to use Power don't you think?" Cyrus asked.

Norne paused. She couldn't help but think of Chaos ripping his enemies apart with his bare hands.

"I mean…it really depends on which side of the fight you're on," Norne noted.

"What? Fight? Why would you assume I meant to use Power for fighting? Think of all the heavy things you could help people move. Or all the planets and stars you could go to without needing transport. Remember, there is more than one type of Power and more than one way to use each one of them. Why do you obsess over fighting?" Cyrus asked.

"Because—because. Of course, *you* wouldn't get it." Norne sighed.

Grak watched the girls getting along and smiled a genuine smile.

"So—Grak, old pal." Chaos walked up and put his arm over Grak's shoulder.

"Yes, Emperor Chaos?" Grak asked, worried he'd be in for another Wilhelm-type conversation.

"About the green-haired one…how much does the breast-plate add? I know it's armor, but I got to thinking if it is really thick—what if they aren't as big as—" Chaos motioned to make his point.

"Really? We are not having this conversation," Grak said cutting him off. He guessed correctly.

"Aha! Your sister stopped me from getting her. Now I know why!" Chaos laughed.

"We are *not* courting. For the millionth time! Is it really so hard to believe two people can be perfectly platonic friends? Unlike you, in Aurelia, I see a valued comrade. Unlike whatever you do. Besides, she's never been interested in guys. There are more important things for actual rulers to worry about. We're adults," Grak explained.

"I guess that means you're stupid enough to be trusted at least." Chaos chuckled without any sense of irony.

Grak rolled his eyes.

"But you still know her so…any advice on getting into her toga?" Chaos winked at him which just made Grak despair at the Emperor's incessancy. He didn't hear a word of what Grak had said.

"You two are getting along well," Norne said as she and Cyrus walked over.

"As I see you are as well." Grak smirked.

"Yeah! Look Norne, you're holding hands like a pair of help-less schoolgirls! Leading the blind one around like those dogs they have!" Chaos pointed out, bursting out laughing.

Norne gasped as without realizing that she had kindly helped Cyrus walk over by gently holding her hand to lead her. Panicking at this sign of weakness, Norne dropped the girls' hand and scrambled a few paces away.

Cyrus tittered at Norne's embarrassment while Norne herself gave Chaos the look of death to make him stop laughing at her.

"Thanks, Norne. And by the way, feel free to visit Mesos any time. It'll be lots of fun," Cyrus said.

"Sure," Norne replied before glaring at Chaos to stop him halfway through a laugh.

Watching from nearby, Grak had left the group to finally grab a glass of wine for himself. He'd been drinking buddies with Aurelia since they were old enough to sneak from their parents' stash, but he had stopped the habit for Atosa.

"All's well that ends well." Aurelia walked over with a glass of wine, excited to see him indulging himself.

"No thanks to you." Grak sighed.

"Meh. If all these men are going to be incessantly throwing themselves at me, I say I deserve to have a little fun." She grinned.

"I see. You are pretty scary after all." Grak smirked.

"Well, it's their fault for getting their hopes up. Any idea of a 'perfect bride' is naïve, to begin with." She took another glass of drink.

Suddenly, Grak spotted Atosa walking over to grab Cyrus like a mother picking their child up from the Eduba.

"I'm afraid I'd have to disagree with you there." Grak smiled.

Aurelia was confused before looking to see that Grak was gazing at Atosa.

"Of course… Atosa is just as beautiful as always." Aurelia took another swig and watched her from afar as she always did.

"I know right." Grak laughed in concurrence before pausing.

He slowly turned and looked at Aurelia in confusion at what he'd just heard. She finished downing her glass and pouted.

"Oh. Oh? Oh! Sorry?" Grak said as he just then realized.

"Don't patronize me…*donnaiolo*." Aurelia scoffed.

There was an awkward silence, then the two old friends had a good laugh about it.

The party in all its excesses continued throughout the evening but things died down after the sunset. All over, the city lights came on as the beautiful new Adamant streetlights Norne had built (which secretly doubled as bombs, just in case.)

Norne waved as each slave drawn or in Cyrus' case, Grak drawn carriage flew off into the night sky to return the guests to their home planets.

The snowy field by the castle was silent and Norne finally exhaled, ceasing her phony waving.

"Mother was right: hosting is so exhausting. And expensive." she sighed.

Chaos snickered, sneaking up behind her with a handful of snow. He moved to put it down her back to prank her, but she swiftly moved out of the way and kicked his feet out so that he fell face-first into a snowbank instead.

"I swear you're five years old. Yes...now that they're gone you can play in the snow." Norne sighed and turned to leave.

"But Norne...you've been hanging out with that blind girl all the time. As your Emperor, I command you to stay and hang out with me." Chaos sat up in the snow with a childish grin.

"Pfft. If you read those laws, I wrote for you, you'd know that I made sure you can't actually order me to do anything." She grinned smugly.

"Oh," Chaos said with genuine sadness.

Norne paused for a second at his reaction.

"What? There is someone whom you think of beyond just those meant for fighting or sleeping with?" She laughed at him.

"Hm...that doesn't sound like me. Oh, wait! Are you talking about you?" Chaos pondered.

Suddenly he got a face full of snow.

"You're weird. Why do I always draw the weirdest people?" Norne laughed again as Chaos wiped the snow off himself and picked up a snowball to retaliate.

"Things are going according to plan. I suppose some more relaxation couldn't hurt." Norne dodged before making one of her own, childishly playing with her mass-murderer best friend.

A week later, she went to visit her other, very different pal on Mesos.

It was a nice day on Mesos, the sky was clear, and the cool breeze made the desert heat tolerable for the Arcosian princess.

In the palace's private garden, Cyrus and company relaxed while the castle's inhabitants enjoyed their midday break. Grak had returned from a campaign and so took the time to spend with his family. Relaxing with her fiancé after so long apart Atosa helped Grak build the play-Ziggurat they wanted to put in the village for the children. Kourosh was there too, cheering them on but giving the two lovebirds some space.

Grak was having trouble with assembling the pieces, but Atosa calmly walked him through the whole process in a cute little

JAIDEN BAYNES

scene that while a bit frustrating would be a fond memory for years to come.

"This wouldn't be an issue at all if they just got slaves to do it," Norne thought to herself as she watched on in disgust.

"Norne, you know our opposition to slave labor. We've been over it a million times." Cyrus sighed as if Norne had said it out loud.

"What!" Norne panicked, realizing that Cyrus' proleptic response was to words she was yet to even speak.

Norne hated that feeling, it was just like being with her mother.

"Now let's get back to your cuneiform test. This way we can write letters directly." Cyrus pointed at the tablet she was helping Norne practice with.

"Fine," Norne grumbled.

The last tablet was fairly short and so Norne easily read it. The tale written in cuneiform was the Epic of Sargon of Akkad:

> I am Sargon of Akkad, the true king, and the Lugal. My parents, I knew not, for no father or mother bore me. I arose on the banks of the Euphrates and spent my youth humbly as a gardener of the people of the land. My might was greater than any other and rather than live among them, I was called to live above them. I sat on the throne of that world and ruled its peoples as many other kings did in those days.
>
> A goddess came to me and gave me her love as well as her wisdom. It came to pass that I had an even higher calling. Many ruled a planet, but I would rule them. King of kings and lord of lords—I am King of Akkad, I am

King of Mesos, I am King of the Universe!
Uruk, Sumer, Elam, Marahashi—I conquered
my rivals, and their slaves became mine. In
the young days of the world, I built the first
Empire.

As years went by and most degraded in old
age, all the lands revolted against me, and
they besieged me in Akkad. But I am eternal. I am youthful and strong. I completely
destroyed my enemies and laid low any
usurpers. I had neither rival nor equal.

Nor do I now, I am the greatest of all the
realms, of all the kings, of all the gods. The
one true king who will rule over all! I am
Sargon of Akkad!

"How arrogant can one man be?" Norne scoffed after finishing reading.

"To be fair he didn't write it himself. Big sister Enheduanna
compiled his story in these poems and hymns, so it isn't just father
writing a record bragging about himself. It's father bragging about
himself and then someone else having to write it down," Cyrus
explained.

Norne glared at her and growled in annoyance at the contin-
uation of the girl's perceived psychic antics.

"That time, you did actually say it out loud. I thought you
were talking to me," Cyrus clarified.

"Good. Just know that in Arcosia, mind readers are put to
death for witchcraft." Norne sighed.

"Aw, don't worry. I'm sure I'd be executed for a million other
reasons in Arcosia." Cyrus giggled.

"Probably," Norne admitted.

"Oh! And all of father's children other than Grak and I are dead. I've only read about them in books and stuff. I didn't read your mind again. I just realized my explanation from before was a bit incomplete," Cyrus chimed.

"I don't care." Norne rolled her eyes.

"I didn't need mind-reading to predict you'd say that." Cyrus laughed.

"Well then, I think I've jumped through enough hoops for the day. I'll take my leave." Norne stood up to exit.

"Aw! Already? It's still early," Cyrus pleaded.

"I have way too much work to just sit around like you lot." Norne sighed.

"At least make yourself useful and return those tablets to the royal library where you got them." Grak glared at her when he saw Cyrus frown.

"Fine…whatever." Norne picked up the tablets and went to take them back inside the Ziggurat. However, when she approached the door, someone else blocked the way.

She locked eyes with a tall, musclebound man who was as tall as Chaos with spiky black hair and a full-grown beard. His piercing eyes froze Norne where she stood and for once it wasn't even just prejudices against Mesos people. The towering goliath's glare was fierce beyond anything other than her mother's.

None outside Mesos had seen him for years but seeing his uncanny resemblance to Grak, Norne knew at once.

"Lugal Sargon of Akkad," Norne said in awe at his presence.

"What!" Grak panicked as he saw his father.

"This is *my* palace. Of course, it is I," Sargon bellowed.

Sargon strode out as Norne made way for him. She turned to the others in bafflement and found them all paralyzed in fear. Most pronounced of all, Cyrus was visibly shaking as he entered.

Grak prepared to rush over and get between his father and sister, but Sargon growled angrily.

"Children these days have no respect. Your Lugal is here, and you don't even salute me?" Sargon demanded of the prince.

Grak was incensed at seeing Cyrus in distress but just out of reach. Nonetheless, he complied and clenched his teeth as he saluted his ruler. Kourosh and Atosa bowed immediately.

"Hey, what's wrong?" Norne walked over to Cyrus and asked with a whisper.

Norne put a hand on her shoulder to try and get her to calm down, but Cyrus was silently shaking—her father's mere presence was giving her a panic attack.

"I'm…fine," Cyrus said, lying to Norne for the first time.

"That thing again—you're showing it off to foreigners now too? You want them returning home to mock me? Parading such a failure of a child to make a fool of your Lugal?" Sargon snarled at the sight of his daughter.

Cyrus just wanted to curl up into a ball and die as Grak audibly growled.

"Keeping this contemptible embarrassment hidden away here serves no purpose if you permit such foolishness to happen. But oh well, now that my greatest shame is known there is no helping it. No matter—when the time comes all will be forgotten anyways." Sargon shook his head.

Grak clenched his palms so tightly that they began to bleed. Atosa nervously held his hand to try and calm him down.

"You, thing, just try not to shame your Lugal before I get around to destroying you with all the other worthless insects." Sargon laughed at Cyrus.

"Enough!" Grak screamed.

Sargon looked at Grak with contempt.

"Stupid boy, this is exactly what puts those stupid thoughts in its head. It's nothing but trash. Better off dead. The only reason, it isn't dead is because it's not worth the effort. Any amount of energy expended on killing such a weak thing is too much." Sargon scoffed.

"What!" Grak screamed, as his own Power erupted so violently that the city of Akkad rumbled.

His temper had reached its limit. Sargon gave his son the side-eye as Grak gritted his teeth. He didn't dare move from the spot he stood in but like the flames of Power, his anger refused to subside.

"How insufferably arrogant. Unbelievably disgusting!" Sargon roared.

Grak didn't dare attack Sargon, but this time he wouldn't just roll over either. Sargon was disgusted that Grak dared stand up to him.

"Kneel." Sargon acted first and with the wave of his hand, his own Power extended out.

Norne felt pins and needles in her skin, a primal terror she could barely comprehend! In a flash, she grabbed Cyrus and jumped over a dozen feet away from that man. Grak reacted too and aggressively threw his beloved Atosa into her father to knock them both away. He had shielded her with his Power so she would survive the high speed as she was thrown.

It wasn't a second too soon, as faster than Atosa or her father could even perceive, everything with a twenty-five-foot radius of Sargon of Akkad was pulverized into a crater. The Adamant stone from which the city was built became dust under the weight of his Power and as the massive cloud blasted out in all directions, only the giant hole in the ground remained.

Sargon of course preserved the piece of the ground beneath his feet so that he did not fall, but six feet under, Grak was still being crushed by the incredible weight of Sargon's Power.

Norne and Kourosh each had to protect their powerless civilian with Power lest the sheer energy being released from the distant aftershocks of Sargon would vaporize them. The air around them turned to charged plasma and was blown away like the shockwave of a nuclear explosion. This small, localized supernova of Power came from a single man.

It was all crushing down on the Mesos prince. Grak was slowly sinking ever further as his shield cracked and constantly broke, only keeping him alive as he pushed all his Power out into constantly replenishing it.

"Delinquent brat. Surely you know that it is a crime to use Power within *my* city limits," Sargon growled at Grak.

Grak's wrath only grew more pronounced, and his Power spiked to a level where it almost pushed back against his father's.

Sargon raised an eyebrow and crossed his arms. Instantly, his Power grew even larger and as the area of effect remained the same, the denser crushing force came down on Grak. Grak's shield shattered, and he was crushed within an inch of his life.

The prince screamed in agony as his bones were turned to powder and he started vomiting blood, when Sargon finally stopped. Without throwing a single punch, Sargon had beaten Grak to the brink of death with only the pressure of his Imperial presence.

"Boy, you are lucky that this planet has sentimental value to me—or I would have destroyed it as well as you for such foolishness," Sargon threatened.

Grak couldn't even move to respond, having fallen unconscious as he barely clung to life.

"I thought so." Sargon chuckled at his crippled son's situation.

For a seemingly endless tense ten seconds after, no one dared speak or even move.

"Know your place! All of you insignificant worms! I am the greatest of all the realms, of all the kings, of all the gods. The one true king who will rule over all! I am Sargon of Akkad!" Sargon shouted for all to hear.

The palace remained silent.

"How troublesome. Someone clean this up." He dismissively turned and left.

Just as suddenly as he had arrived, he left and returned to his den at the top of the Ziggurat.

Even once he was gone, Norne didn't even dare move.

"What incredible Power! I have to wonder…is this man even more Powerful than Chaos?" Norne began to sweat nervously.

STEP 4

REMOVE THE COMPETITION

*"Religion is regarded by the common people as true,
by the wise as false, and by the rulers as useful."*
　　　　　　　　　　　　　　　—Lucius Annaeus Seneca

CHAPTER 12

The Kingdom of Strias, one of Arcosia's fellow Arcos worshipping kingdoms had secretly sent word to many other nations. Its King Charles had eagerly summoned in secret the monarchs of the old generation who had not yet been killed by their offspring or increasingly by successful usurpers. The worried king had recently taken notice that over time, over *half* of his old friends had been dethroned and replaced by their children.

Nightmares plagued the King, remembrances of the time of Typhon's ascension in light of Tartarus' recent actions. On one night it returned to him, the message sent out by the new arrival as a mental warning to those who plotted against him in restoring Drakon to the throne. While the nations prepared for war in secret he somehow knew and came to them in dreams, or rather: nightmares and warned any that those who plotted against him would be utterly destroyed. The King would wake up in cold sweats, terrified that Typhon's curse had come to pass through his son!

Now, disturbed by this shocking and totally unforeseeable recent trend, in his infinite royal wisdom he called this meeting. Seated at a roundtable council were many top rulers, assembled with looks of worry and concern on their faces. Fashionably late from a party, Charles was sober enough to disengage party mode for once and attempt to lead this brave resistance.

"Gentlemen… something strange is going on. I believe we may all be in danger." He astutely said before sitting down and looking at the other leaders. He saw one chair for Mesos was left notably empty.

"Unfortunately, as usual Sargon of Akkad isn't here." He sighed.

Leaning back in his chair he turned to address the others.

"Now, I know that many among us came to power by… removing a relative ourselves. Because of this, I know the precedent has been set that we do not bother when the same occurs in other nations nor should we pass judgement unless the new crown opposes our interests. However, too many deaths too quickly make me worry these may not be isolated. This may be some kind of conspiracy. And Wilhelm of Prussia told me that I was being paranoid… but now he is in the ground and his son Wilhelm sits on the throne!" He explained.

The others did not applaud but simply glared at him.

"Seriously! I was worried about Arcosia taking action and trying to reunify Strias and Prussia but now, honestly, I am more worried about Tartarus! It was Drakon's death that started all of this. If this keeps up, we may all be in the ground before long. Hunting trips gone wrong… court assassinations… and even blatant patricide seem to be happening *way* too frequently. Our fellow old generation rulers are dropping like flies. I love the kids and all, but it's a bit worrying, isn't it? At first, I figured it wasn't my problem, but now this is starting to interfere with my finances as I am sure it is with all of yours as well." He explained.

Standing up he looked around at them all and continued his declaration.

"I fear we may be… as the kids say, out of touch. For us few who kept to the well-advised strategy of celibacy… I worry we may be next on the chopping block if something is not done. Like what Strias, Prussia and Arcosia used to do in partitioning. There are enough of these youngsters now that direct military action could overtake us and divide our lands among themselves." He sighed.

Sitting back down, he calmed himself.

"And damn that Otto, he keeps covering for these brats but I'm telling you that woman of his is whispering in his ear again. They're probably in cahoots with them anyhow! That's why Arcosia isn't at this table... I feel that the Imperial Core alliance has been compromised. It now only exists as a liability for us. It restricts our counterattacking those upstart youths and so I say it must go! It may be drastic but in light of their recent actions I feel that Arcosia, Italia and Tartarus must go! We will form our own, better alliance and be rid of those patricidal pests once and for all!" Charles cried. Greedy self interest again found its way to the table of supposedly sensible self preservation.

"But... just because we probably should have seen this coming does not mean we should lose our heads." He began before his own head was blasted off his body and splattered against the wall!

Around him the illusion faded, and all the participants seemingly disappeared. It was all an illusion. No one had ever arrived; his message had been interrupted... by Tartarian spies.

"It was right of me to monitor correspondence between the nations. It would have been very bad for us if the remaining powers had successfully coordinated an alliance against us." Norne grinned.

"Y'know... it's pretty sad that it took them 2 years to even react to us killing them off." Chaos shook the blood off his hand, since he had killed the King himself.

"Oh well. I'm surprised any of them even tried anything. Normally the old farts don't know anything about the outside world if it doesn't affect their bottom line, but then again, I guess he only did because our actions started to. Either way, thank you for the assistance, King Wilhelm." Norne turned to their ally who sat across from the dead king with a smile.

"Of course… that is my power. That's Prussia's power: Utgard Loki the master of illusions. The king's authority is invincible!" Wilhelm confidently put his legs up on the table as the illusion of his Meme fully dispersed. For seem reason he was very happy with himself for showing his secret power off to two foreign leaders.

"Don't forget who got the kill shot though." Chaos said before tipping the chair with the beheaded king over.

"Either way, the thanks for your assistance comes not only from me, but from Tartarus and Arcosia as well." Norne put on her phony diplomatic façade again.

"Hey, what are cousins for? I mean, since Arcosia has no Memes for its royalty at all, I guess I'd better supply for our sister country's rising star." he laughed, despite not even knowing Norne's name before she became a major player through Tartarus. Norne hated him but he was a useful idiot.

"Plus, partitioning up our sister country is a pretty sweet deal too. Tartarus and Prussia will each take halves as an eternal reminder of today. Thanks Chaos old pal, but then what are friends for?" Wilhelm laughed.

"We aren't friends." Chaos flatly responded.

"Sure, thing pal." Wilhelm laughed haughtily.

"You know where the babes are. That is the only reason I have or ever will talk to you." Chaos frankly remarked which surprised Norne who had never seen him like this with anyone else.

"Sure thing. Well, I've gotta go now. As King, I've got a hot date to see who gets to rule Prussia with me as queen. Later." Wilhelm stood up and casually excused himself.

Just as they had done here in Strias before and as they intended to do to Poland after, like minded powers could easily partition the weak between them. Those who were not powerful enough in this new world fell victim to the fate of their previous victims.

"Man, he's annoying. Why do we have to work with him, again? I could've easily brought them down myself." Chaos growled.

"This new generation unfortunately isn't as stupid as the old one. It may work on Wil, but Grak would immediately turn hostile if we set a precedent of unilaterally infiltrating and assassinating other governments. Especially those smart enough to try and replicate our colonial methods. That would be even worse than these idiots allying against us." Norne explained.

"What? You're talking like you do at the meetings again…" Chaos complained about her sophisticated articulation.

"We want to expand in a way that doesn't threaten our allies. Or at least that doesn't draw attention to the threat we may pose. Nobody likes having their government infiltrated and we don't want them suspecting us." Norne sighed.

"Oh. Right. Why are we stalling again?" Chaos asked.

"I'm not explaining it again. When we next meet with the others, make sure to keep your mouth shut and let me handle things." Norne shook her head.

Almost two years had passed since Norne first met Sargon of Akkad. Grak's team met to discuss the next plan of action. By this time, they had all, except him, ascended to their respective thrones and now spent their time collaborating on how best to consolidate their power while waiting for Grak to give the green light to claim his own birthright. A few childless monarchs of the old guard like Charles remained but now they were the minority and no real threat to the emerging titans.

The Imperial Core of Eurasia had sworn pacts of mutual collaboration and nonaggression. In reality, this was just a ploy by the four great powers, Mesos, Italia, Tartarus, and Arcosia to suppress the growth of their neighbors as they rebuilt their strength from the last period of instability. Focussing on the weak barbarian worlds was an excellent distraction to keep other nations from impeding their own recovery while allowing the dominant powers to better control the lesser regimes.

Any nation worth their salt had a functioning intelligence network, but if any was caught spying on one of the big four powers, they would suffer sanctions and international condemnation from all other members of the Imperial Core as per the alliance's rules. As such, the assassinations could go off with minimal interference from the other countries.

Norne ruled Tartarus, Aurelia ruled Italia, Grak handled all foreign policy for Mesos, and curiously, the Church of Arcos had convinced King Otto to stay neutral in this fratricidal fray. Everyone was convinced that they could work the bloodshed to their advantage. It shouldn't surprise anyone that the world order of their parents so perfectly reproduced itself in the next generation. The nature of Empire was a hard one to kick, which greatly pleased the true Imperial Core of this engagement.

The other countries were unable to learn from their own ascension the dangers of their position as stooges for their superiors in the Imperial hierarchy. Nonetheless, everyone trusted Grak and so the meeting was very casual. Although unlike the other parents, more importantly than King Otto of Arcosia, Sargon of Akkad remained.

Chaos and Norne were the last to arrive and take their seats. Aurelia had already started ranting against the alliance.

"This is becoming farcical. We have accomplished *all our goals* except for defeating Sargon of Akkad. Every other leader on the chopping block has fallen, so he should follow! If he is such a threat to us all, we should take him out! The longer we stall, the greater the chance that our foes will recognize what is going on!" Dictator Aurelia protested, standing up.

"You cut your hair? Why! It looked so much hotter before!" Chaos whined upon seeing her.

Aurelia gave him a death glare before looking to Grak for a reason not to. She also had an upgraded set of armor with even more Adamant Power gems embedded in it, but Chaos didn't take notice of that. If he kept pestering her though, he'd see the strength of this state-of-the-art upgrade. Before things got out of hand, Grak spoke up.

 JAIDEN BAYNES

"I've said it enough times—things are not yet in place. To minimize resistance, I am destabilizing Sargon's supporters. Once he's isolated, we can move. Like all of you, I don't want to inherit a broken kingdom," Grak explained.

"You have said it enough times, it's starting to become a *joke*!" Aurelia cried as she slammed her fist on the table in frustration. "Sacrifices have to be made, if someone sides against us, they are removed from the equation. Stop putting this off. *Gah*! This is why I dissolved the Italic Senate!"

"No. If we act carelessly, it will be our undoing. We need to continue to build power to effectively deal with Sargon. Trust me, as long as we continue to lay low, none of the old guards will pay us any mind. Haste and unnecessary aggression are the enemies here," Norne interjected to everyone's surprise.

"WHAT!" Aurelia growled.

"Grak is right. Sargon of Akkad is not to be taken lightly. We must bide our time and build our power. The time isn't now," Norne said calmly.

"What? Did you meet him on one of your playdates with Cyrus and then wet yourself!?" Aurelia glared at her.

Norne and Grak remembered what happened when Sargon appeared on the scene. They hadn't told a soul or even discussed the events of that day with each other.

"This discussion is over. Go home everyone," Grak said, then quickly stood up and left.

Everyone else stood up too and swiftly made their exit, leaving Aurelia to fume alone.

The meetings had been getting more and more brief with time. It was starting to seem that Grak and by extension Aurelia were the only ones taking them seriously.

In the hallway, Aurelia aggressively walked over to Norne who slowed down and turned to face her.

"You really must calm down. You don't dictate to us, unfortunately," Norne said with a smirk.

"I saw him too. Your response isn't unreasonable. Even I used to fear him," Aurelia told her.

"I'm not afraid," Norne deflected. "I would merely like our odds better if we did more to be prepared."

"Sure…but you know Grak says that considering how strong all of us have gotten—if we all fought Sargon, everyone who mattered would make it out alive. HE'S ADMITTED THAT!" Aurelia said.

"He also said he didn't know his father's full power. Any estimations are being made with guesses and incomplete data. I agree with Grak that we need to do more preparation first." She walked away.

"She could at least pretend something wasn't bothering her," Aurelia grumbled before walking away in the opposite direction.

On Mesos, as had been a common occurrence over the past two years, Cyrus, the Princess of Mesos was hanging out with Norne (who was mostly there to spy on her country but also had a soft spot for the naïve girl she befriended) in her palace bedroom.

This time when Norne arrived, however, Cyrus was sitting on her bed with a large box, reading the accompanying message.

"What's this? Business stuff?" Norne asked as she walked into Cyrus' room, unescorted. She had visited so frequently that now she could come and go as she pleased.

"Just the opposite. Our big infrastructure overhaul for a universal postal service was just implemented. I wanted to help with overseeing tests and addressing any other implementation difficulties, but I've been ordered by Grak to take a week off after completing such a massive project," Cyrus pouted.

"A whole week!" Norne being a mutual workaholic despaired with the young princess.

"Yeah, I feel like I could be doing so much more. However, it seems that the committee—my overseas pen-pals, are testing out my postal service idea for me. Wonder what the first package by mail from them will be." Cyrus smiled with anticipation after reading the indented Mesos script on the box with her finger.

"I can at least see this one, can't I? Or is this 'committee' message top secret too?" Norne asked.

She was now beyond spying on another nation and was genuinely curious about what Cyrus had received.

"Don't worry. If it's something cool, I'll probably say it by accident either way. Can you open it?" Cyrus grinned.

"Sure," Norne said as she lifted the box. Unfortunately, she lifted it upside down, and Cyrus heard a strange plop.

"What the Hel!" Norne cried, jumping back.

"What is it?" Cyrus asked, worried by the sounds of the commotion.

"Princess Cyrus, look out! It's headed right for you!" Norne panicked which made Cyrus worry even more.

Suddenly something jumped onto the princess, knocking her down into her cushioned Arcosian pillows.

Before Cyrus knew it, the creature was licking her face and panting excitedly. Norne picked it up and pulled it away. "Are you alright?" she asked.

"What was that? It was so…fluffy," Cyrus said, puzzled.

"You're right. You could make some quality pelts with furs like this." Norne plucked at the fur with a mischievous grin.

It barked nervously after making eye contact with the ice witch.

"No!" Cyrus grabbed the creature from Norne's hands after hearing the plea.

"It's just a puppy." Cyrus cuddled the dog and held it away from Norne.

"I was just joking…mostly," Norne said, taking her husky fur cloak off and tossing it over the chair.

Reaching into the package she read, "Enjoy the…seeing-eye dog? Training instructions enclosed."

"Oh cool! This must be the thing they were telling me about from—another country." Cyrus excitedly held the puppy up above her head which made it bark excitedly.

"Weird. It's so small it doesn't look to be of use." Norne rolled her eyes.

"If it's so small then why did you get so scared over a little puppy?" Cyrus laughed while cuddling the little bundle of fur.

"On Arcosia, we use the Arcosian White Shepherds for hunting. Forgive the association with bloodthirsty hunters. Now that I've gotten a closer look, I don't think I've ever seen a breed like that." Norne noted the matching physique but lack of white fur.

"What color is he?" Cyrus excitedly asked.

"Green," Norne said sarcastically.

"Meanie. What color is he?" Cyrus crossed her arms.

"Like a light brown. What would the Iryan color be—" Norne tried to think of an appropriate translation.

"Don't even bother. The language's color expressions are a disaster, it lacks any real diversity, so Grak says it doesn't accurately describe things of different color. For example, my dress and all my bronze jewelry would both be translated as 'green' in Iryan," Cyrus pointed out. "Such a sadly impoverished vocabulary."

"Well shoot. I was kind of right then when I said green before. He's like a—like a brownish, bronzish color," Norne replied.

"Hm…bronze, the color of Power. I see. Since the dawn of Mesos, dogs have been man's best friend. They represent health, good luck, and other cool stuff. Loyal puppy, I dub thee 'Gula'!" Cyrus dramatically lifted her newly named pet high into the air.

The dog gave an adorable bark of excitement.

"Pfft. The dog doesn't actually love its owner. It'd eat you if the food ever ran out." Norne sighed.

"That was dark. Y'know, we really need to work on getting your sense of humor to be more suitable for all ages." Cyrus smirked.

"Joke? Please, a dog's only use is to hunt animals, then be skinned and fed to the next generation of hunters. The Arcosian phrase 'die like a dog' exists for a reason," Norne stated darkly.

Cyrus paused.

"You're just saying that because you're still mad that your father never got you that dog, aren't you?" Cyrus asked.

"Damn it! I never should've told you that," Norne said, feeling embarrassed.

"Against my better judgment—hold him." Cyrus held the dog out for Norne to grab who in turn, crossed her arms and looked away.

"Come on! You know you want to," Cyrus teased.

Norne quickly took the dog and cuddled it which made it audibly pant excitedly. Cyrus smiled.

"Do you love Gula?" Cyrus asked.

"What is with you today?" Norne asked, annoyed.

"Do you? Do you?" Cyrus asked.

Norne began blushing at the cute animal that literally gave her puppy-dog eyes. Refusing to show any weakness though, she noticed something else had fallen out.

"Hey look at this! One-of-a-kind...photo capture device?" Norne read the label with a shock.

"Oh snap! That one *is* top secret. I was supposed to test it for al-Haytham!" Cyrus panicked.

"How?" Norne asked, looking at the blind princess.

"Well—" Cyrus paused.

"Don't tell me that's what the dog is for." Norne pointed at Cyrus as she saw the princess' look of confusion turn to a mischievous grin.

"I wasn't gonna say that!" Cyrus said, blushing in embarrassment. "You can't prove I was going to say that."

"Of course not." Norne rolled her eyes.

"Anyways, I read his theories and schematics in the past so... maybe I can provide instructions? You'll be my seeing-eye operator, won't you?" Cyrus asked.

"Me? I thought it was top secret." Norne scoffed.

"Well, the cat's out of the bag on that one anyways so, might as well show you too." Cyrus grinned.

"Speaking of dark humor, do you know where that saying comes from?" Norne grinned in response mischievously.

"To operate the device," Cyrus said, intentionally interrupting Norne's train of thought, "point the pinhole at the front and there should be a switch to flip. Point the pinhole at us, flip the switch and come over here. I think that's how he said it worked."

Norne followed her instructions, setting the primitive camera up on a low ottoman footrest before hurrying back over.

"Alright. Now I think we have ten seconds."

"Until what?" Norne asked skeptically.

"Until it copies an image of us onto a page. Like an instant painting," Cyrus explained

"What!" Norne panicked, suddenly becoming embarrassed, worrying how she'd look before the ancient device flashed.

The camera took a picture of the two girls and their new dog.

"How does it look?" Cyrus asked as Norne went to retrieve it.

"Fine?" Norne said, trying not to sound embarrassed at how obviously embarrassed she looked in the photo.

"Let's take another one!" Cyrus excitedly cheered as the dog yipped to match the eagerness.

"Why?" Norne asked nervously.

"So that we can each have one," Cyrus said.

"Why?" Norne asked again.

"Fine, fine. You take it then. If I'm following your implication correctly it would be no use to me anyway." Cyrus shrugged.

"You do know I'll try and reverse engineer the technology as long as I have this, right?" Norne asked.

"Of course. That was going to happen either way after you saw this. But at least this way...you can have a keepsake of us. You're immortal but I won't be around anymore in just a few decades. So, isn't al-Haytham's device wonderful? These pictures capture moments forever. Long after I'm dead, I hope this is something you can remember me by." Cyrus shook her head.

"Fine." Norne rolled her eyes.

"Norne, don't destroy this. Even when you have used it for what you need, please keep it around for my sake. For some kind of proof, I was alive. Some proof that I mattered to you." Cyrus got very serious, much to Norne's surprise.

She didn't know how to respond. Gula just looked from one girl to the other in confusion, not knowing what happened.

"You aren't exactly old and grey yet," Norne noted.

"What can I say, I'm feeling old. I made fun of Grak when he became an adult, so I guess it's only fair. My coming of age ceremony was just the other day and now I'm in the same boat." Cyrus giggled.

"Right. Well, it is on short notice—but—" Norne cleared her throat.

"But?" Cyrus asked, confused.

Norne stood up and politely curtsied before her.

"Princess Cyrus of Mesos, as thanks for repeatedly inviting me to be accommodated in your palace, I would like to extend the warmest welcome to Tartarus. It would be the least I could do to repay your hospitality. To help make your obligated rest an enjoyable one I will do everything in my power to ensure you are hosted at a level of comfort that would be the envy of kings and queens." Norne curtsied.

Cyrus was stunned. Norne awkwardly looked up, nervously anticipating Cyrus' response.

"Yes! Of course, I will come!" Cyrus shrieked, and practically jumped out of bed at the offer, surprising Norne.

Back in Tartarus, Norne was preparing for the first friendly visit of Cyrus on Tartarus. She had figured it was a fun idea at first before her perfectionist tendencies kicked in. Cyrus was coming to visit her, so she was obsessed with making a good impression. The day before, everyone was in a frenzy making everything look as good as possible, even though Cyrus wouldn't be able to see any of it. But Norne was insistent.

Chaos walked in, devouring a massive turkey leg as he walked. "Hey what's happening?" he asked, confused by the preparations. "I don't have another or—party until next week." He'd learned from Norne how to catch himself before he spoke.

"Chaos! There you are. For god's sake, put a shirt on! Cyrus is an…important puppet for my schemes so you cannot ruin this for me. So please, act like an Emperor for ONCE. This is a big step for us diplomatically." Norne speed-walked over to him.

"Democratically, you just want to hang out with your new friend instead of me." Chaos huffed like a child.

"You are a grown man, suck it up," Norne yelled. "Whenever I am free, *you* are always out with some—"

Magnus who had walked over long before awkwardly stood there and watched this bizarre lover's quarrel of sorts. He didn't dare interrupt them directly since he was nearly as scared of Norne as he was of Chaos at this point.

"My Lord and lady…" Magnus nervously fake coughed to try and get their attention. He had walked over long before and had uncomfortably watched the quarrel from the sideline.

"What!" they both yelled at him.

Poor Magnus almost died from terror from incurring their simultaneous glares.

"The…security set up was just approved by Prince Grak… everything has been finalized for the Princess' arrival tonight," he reported, sweating bullets.

"Good. I better finish my room. Get security in on this too. Remind them that like the servants, if they touch anything, they get to be test subjects for my new execution devices," Norne said in a rush.

"It shall be done." Magnus bowed before exiting to inform his units.

"You never clean up when I come here," Chaos pouted.

"You live here," Norne pointed out.

"Oh! Can I sit in on this girl's night?" Chaos asked.

"No. You introduce yourself professionally and then stay a minimum of twenty feet from Cyrus at all times. By the way, if I forgot to mention…if you try *anything* with her, I will castrate you." Norne put on her cutesy smiley face for that chilling threat before walking off.

Chaos was silent. After Norne left the room, he finally asked out loud, "what is 'castrate'?".

That night, Grak, Atosa, and Cyrus arrived.

When Cyrus arrived, she excitedly hugged Norne who came to greet them. As instructed beforehand, all the soldiers averted their eyes (lest they see the Queen of Ice displaying normal human affection). Of course, Norne did not hug her back, but she didn't push her away anymore either.

"Hey, Grak." Chaos walked over with a half-hearted wave.

"It is good to see you again, Emperor Chaos," Grak affirmed with a friendly smile.

"Emperor Chaos, I am honored to have the chance to stay here." Cyrus bowed respectfully. Chaos paused for a second, looking at her in annoyance before putting on a phony grin that Norne had taught him.

"No prob, princess. What do you think? My castle is way cooler than yours—oh right, you couldn't see it anyways." Chaos spitefully smirked.

Grak was furious but Cyrus giggled.

"I suppose you're right. However, I'm sure it is a wonderful castle, your Excellency." Cyrus said, putting on a huge smile.

Chaos, annoyed, prepared another veiled insult (further applications of Norne's teaching in the least important situation).

"Princess, we shall escort you to the guest room," Norne interrupted before he could follow through.

"Of course, Senate Superdelegate." Cyrus bowed.

Norne led Cyrus away and when Chaos turned, Grak walked up and shook his hand.

"We will be leaving now; I leave her in your care. But Chaos—" Grak said pulling him in and whispering aggressively, "Norne has given me every assurance, but to you—I will make this very clear. If you try anything, I *will* castrate you."

Grak let go and walked away.

"Why does everyone keep saying that?" he wondered out loud.

Cyrus unpacked, then Norne led her to her own new, renovated room.

"It took a year to renovate, but I finally got decent quarters outside my office. Cost half a soldier's yearly salary but it was worth it. Now I can do all my work in here." Norne proudly showed off her room.

"Wow—I'm sure it's amazing," Cyrus said politely, nodding.

"Right—anyways, right this way." Norne led Cyrus over to sit on the comfy bed.

Norne's new room was a massive Queen's bedroom with the fanciest accommodations of the era. As she entered, Cyrus then opened one of the bags she had brought along and the noble Gula hopped out and began panting excitedly.

"Why do you keep transporting him in sealed containers?" Norne asked, shocked that he had survived the ordeal.

"It had breathing holes. Besides I had to keep him secret from father or who knows what worse fate would have befallen him," Cyrus pointed out.

"Does Grak know?" Norne asked.

"Of course. How else do you think I smuggled him out when Grak insists on double-checking everything I packed? I swear sometimes my brother can be such a worrywart." Cyrus giggled.

Cyrus got comfortable on the bouncy mattress and Gula got comfortable on her lap while Norne sat on the side chair as this was their usual dynamic in Cyrus' room.

Norne looked up from her book, *The Foreign Algoritmi of Ibn Mūsa*, at Cyrus who was sorting through many delivered messages.

"I thought you said Grak forced you to take time off? I'd criticize bringing homework along, but I'll save the hypocrisy for my political work." Norne said.

"It's not homework if it's fun to get through," Cyrus replied grinning.

"More messages from your friends that I can't read?" Norne asked.

"Nah, the committee doesn't do frequent correspondences. Since the last one was so recent, I doubt I'll hear from them for another few months at the least. For this—I'm assuming these are more proposals." Cyrus sighed while sorting through.

"Proposals?" Norne asked.

"Despite father's best attempts to keep me hidden from the world, it seems somehow rumors got out. Unfortunately, unless Atosa and my brother have been lying to me for years a lot of people would consider me pretty…well, pretty. It's so funny how all of a sudden, the entire Universe seems to care about me, when before I was just Grak's blind sister." Cyrus laughed.

"So, the letters of proposal flood in. Perhaps Lugal Sargon will be pleased," Norne suggested.

"Well, I guess it would be less wasteful than his old plan of just killing me. However, now Grak would probably be upset at the number of his own friends whose names are apparently in here."

"Apparently? You aren't even checking who's writing them?" Norne asked, noticing Cyrus wasn't actually reading any.

"Oh well. I'm not interested in boys anyways. Too much work to do." Cyrus sorted through them more as a formality or consideration of their feelings than anything.

When she picked up a paper letter she shook her head, "the worst is when they send me pictures to try and win me over. After wasting Atosa's time with reading a bunch to me, I've made it a precedent that if they send paper to not even open it." She threw the unopened letter onto a massive pile.

"Of course," Norne said, betraying a bit of annoyance at Cyrus being spoiled for choice, compared to Norne who still seemed to be bound to be an old maid. A strange concern for Norne who noted that it seemed out of character for her other interests. Maybe her mother was right.

Now a fully grown woman, as the rumors had suggested, Princess Cyrus had grown much more beautiful while Norne hadn't grown an inch.

"Norne… I thought you were the one who complained people care too much about appearances. Is that jealousy I just heard?" Cyrus asked.

"You must've imagined it," Norne deflected, covering her face with her book as if that'd do anything.

Suddenly, loud music started blasting from somewhere outside Norne's room.

"What in the Hel!" Norne cried.

The music began blaring even louder as Chaos opened the door. "Sorry Norne, having a super fun party out here without you."

"Damn it, Chaos! Turn the music down. This is not the time," Norne impatiently demanded.

"Sorry Norne, I can't. The Imperial Orchestra insists this is the funnest way to have fun," Chaos lied with a giant grin. Magnus suddenly popped his head in as well and mechanically chimed in, "woot-woot," as he had been ordered to do.

Norne was furious but Cyrus waved.

"No worries. Please, enjoy your party, Emperor." Cyrus smiled.

"Of course, we will. Come on Magnus." Chaos left.

"Woot-woot," Magnus repeated robotically, following him out, also as ordered.

"What a child!" Norne said out loud before remembering Cyrus was there.

"Nah. Atosa made him seem scary, but honestly, I think he seems sweet," Cyrus confided.

"Do not confuse stupidity for innocence," Norne said candidly.

"C'mon, don't say that. You can't forget about his, 'meat grinder abs,' 'boulder-sized muscles,' or 'sculpture esque jawline.' Geez, do you salivate like that whenever you talk to him about me too, or is it only a one-way thing?" Cyrus asked, reminding Norne of her past references to Chaos with a laugh.

"May we never talk of that again either! Not a word to him, got it!" Norne panicked in embarrassment of what she had previously confided in Cyrus.

"Geez, how oblivious can one person be?" Cyrus laughed, finding Norne's response adorable.

"Trust me, you couldn't even imagine. You can't even imagine how annoying it is to have the one you...wish to pursue...be completely oblivious to you!" Norne cried.

"Yeah. It must suck," Cyrus said in response.

"But anyway, I've told you too much. Hurry up and get secrets of your own so that I can leverage them over you," Norne joked.

"Never! I'll take them to my grave!" Cyrus jokingly declared.

The girls spent the night in excellent company, having the time of their lives spending time together.

When Cyrus fell asleep, Norne was sure to pull the thick Mesos blanket over her lest she catch a cold in the Tartarian climate. After doing so, she paused. Quickly she pulled it back off to about as much as it was before.

Then after another moment of hesitation, she pulled it back up to ensure Cyrus remained warm and slept easily.

It was after midnight, but instead of sleeping herself, Norne went to her office to catch up on missed work. She silently walked through the palace halls, passing past the rows and rows of Imperial Knights that stood at attention, defending the high priority guest.

All through the night, they stood on guard, and in the morning when Norne returned to check on Cyrus they were still there.

However, the door to Cyrus' room was wide open and she was nowhere to be found.

"I—what am I even supposed to ask you? Did you think you were posted here to take in the view!" Norne turned to the trembling, unfortunate knight who was stationed right next to the door.

"We beg forgiveness, Lady Norne! We were just following orders!" he squeaked.

"Uh-huh. Where the Hel is Cyrus?" Norne demanded.

"We are not at liberty to say Milady," the knight reported.

"Don't tell me—" Norne looked from him to the others around the room.

Each averted their gaze as soon as her eyes fell on them lest she come over to them next.

"Did I not *specifically* warn you to not let him in there?" Norne growled.

"Milady, he *is* the Emperor," the knight next to her pleaded.

Norne glared at him.

"And! And he insisted he had the purest of intentions when he retrieved her this morning."

"Morning?" Norne was confused.

"Thank you for this invitation, your Majesty. I am honored to eat in the court of the Emperor of Tartarus. You're such a gentleman." Cyrus smiled.

"Of course, it's my house after all. You stuffy types expect this kind of thing, don't you?" Chaos laughed back.

Norne silently watched from around the corner, completely baffled by what she was looking at. Around one of the palace's tables, Chaos and Cyrus sat with a setup as if they were going to eat the world's most overpriced breakfast. Despite the immaculate setup and room preparation, however, Chaos was still shirtless, and Cyrus was still in her pajamas.

Furthermore, Cyrus sat on a mere wooden chair while Chaos had moved his imperial throne from the throne room to the table as if to assert his dominance.

"I'll admit, I'm very excited to try Tartarian cuisine. Norne told me she got the finest chefs in the lands to serve in the castle, so I really do consider it an honor." Cyrus grinned eagerly.

"Yeah, I bet Norne tells you a lot of stuff. But not nearly as much as she tells me. Whatever she tells you, I know a hundred times as much!" Chaos scoffed, hoping to bring out some jealousy.

"Well, that makes sense. National security and all that," Cyrus replied obliviously, much to Chaos' annoyance.

"What in the Universe is happening here! Maybe I should step in—Grak would lose it if he knew they were alone together, but—" Norne began before wondering what they would say about her when she wasn't there.

"Fine. I'll just observe for now. But if that gorilla tries anything on her I will keep my promise." Norne watched intently, holding her knife at the ready.

As breakfast was being prepared, Cyrus showed Chaos that Gula could do tricks.

"Sit, boy." Cyrus pointed Gula did as he was told.

Chaos rolled his eyes, unimpressed.

"How can you even tell the dog is doing the right trick if you can't see anything? Ha!" Chaos thought he was a comedic genius for that one.

"Well, Atosa helped me, so he responds to all commands according to the instructions I received," Cyrus explained.

"Ha! Needing a poor person to help you. So pathetic, right Magnus?" Chaos asked.

"Of course, sir," Magnus called out from out of view.

"Magnus? What is he doing here?" She couldn't see him from her hiding spot.

"Have you ever had any pets, Your Majesty? It's a wonderful experience." Cyrus smiled as Gula ran back to her and hopped into her lap.

"I tried keeping a Monster as a pet once, but it kept trying to eat me, so I just killed it." Chaos shrugged.

"Aw. That's a shame," Cyrus replied.

"Well, I did have other pets, but—I can save that story for once the food arrives." Chaos snickered mischievously.

Norne was becoming concerned.

"Ah yes, it smells great even from here. Even if I didn't know of Norne's staff picks, anyone would excitedly anticipate getting to have breakfast made by the chefs who cook for the Emperor himself!" Cyrus said, hardly containing her excitement.

"Chefs? Oh, you misunderstood." Chaos mischievously grinned.

"The food is ready." Magnus Pompey Draco said dryly as he entered with their meals.

Norne's jaw almost hit the floor. Magnus, the feared supreme commander of the Imperial army came in wearing a comical pink, frilly apron over his armor that read 'please salute the cook' in Tartarian! Before Norne's arrival, Chaos had forced him to wear it and had a huge laugh at his expense (before childishly making fun of Cyrus for being unable to get the visual comedy).

"Oh, commander Magnus? I didn't know you cooked. I'm excited to try it out, thanks for the food." Cyrus smiled as she recognized his voice.

"Good luck," was Magnus' only reply as he gave her a salute and walked away.

"What does...that mean?" Cyrus and Norne both had to wonder.

Chaos was very conspicuously snickering on his throne as he picked up his knife and fork to begin. Cyrus found her cutlery as well and prepared to try what Magnus had prepared.

"It smells delicious, can I ask what breakfast is?" Cyrus asked as she found the food with her utensils.

"My childhood favorite—bear meat!" Chaos cackled.

"Bear meat? For breakfast?" Cyrus was baffled.

"It's an honor if it's from me, right? So, eat up! Back on the planet, I grew up on, I used to hunt and eat bears with my bare hands. I wore bears, I lived with bears, and even had some pet bears to answer your question from earlier." Chaos thunderously laughed.

"Fascinating," Cyrus said, at a loss for what a proper response should be.

"Right before they go to sleep for the winter is the best time to get them. Only pregnant bears hibernated on that planet which is what I called a 'twofer.' Plus, the father bear would often come to defend them, so sometimes I'd actually get three for the price of one. In fact, I think I might've hunted all the bears on the damned planet!" Chaos continued his laughing as he saw Cyrus becoming uncomfortable at his jokes about massacring bear families.

Chaos didn't fully understand court culture or diplomacy, but he did know that people weren't allowed to refuse meals offered by him. He was the Emperor after all, so even though Cyrus would have preferred to abstain, she was going to have to eat the bear meat.

Chaos had been scolded by Norne in the past for insisting on it because when prepared incorrectly, bear meat was known to cause disease (Trichinellosis was its name, but they lacked knowledge of germ theory). However, any skilled Tartarian cook worth their salt could prepare the meat properly.

So naturally, Chaos had Magnus cook the bear meat and present it. Chaos was uncharacteristically firing on all cylinders when it came to avenging a perceived slight.

"Alright, time to step in… I can't have him poisoning our guest." Norne sighed.

"Thank you for the food, High General. I love to try new things, so such an exotic menu is perfect," Cyrus said with a smile.

To everyone else's shock she actually cut a piece and began to eat the bear meat.

Chaos was shocked, Norne was horrified, and Magnus was just glad someone would finally eat something he had made since Norne never ate anything.

Cyrus had heard that bear meat had an extremely gamey taste and was nervous as it entered her mouth.

She ate the meat and was surprised to discover that it had... no real taste at all. It wasn't good or bad it was—completely bland. Chaos and Cyrus ate at the same time and had opposite reactions. Cyrus was relieved and Chaos was annoyed. She ate bite after bite, not wanting to disappoint either the Emperor who hosted her or the chef who'd prepared it. In Chaos' experience, normal people eating improperly prepared bear meat would be gagging and vomiting already.

"What the Hel, man!" Chaos whispered in an annoyed tone.

Magnus nervously backed away. He'd cooked it normally (normal for Magnus anyways) but that somehow managed to be a way that removed its taste while also purging the parasites.

"Thank you so much, you're a wonderful chef, General Magnus." Cyrus was practically beaming as she thanked him.

Magnus paused, at receiving genuine compliments and couldn't help but almost smile back at her, even if for only a second.

"You can't do anything right! Damnit, if we can't poison the kid then at least bring me some more bear meat! You can't cook worth crap, but bear is still bear! Now, I'm actually hungry! Bring me more!" Chaos snarled.

"Of course, sir." The thankless soldier rushed off to fulfill the Emperor's demands.

"I swear—it's so hard to find good help these days," Chaos growled.

"I think he seems nice." Cyrus smiled.

"Nobody asked you. Now eat your non-poisoned food and get out of here," he huffed.

"Sure thing, Your Majesty. Thanks again for treating me to breakfast." Cyrus' unyielding spirit irritated him.

She excused herself from the table and went to get ready for her departure.

"So annoying," Chaos grumbled as Magnus brought his second course of bear meat.

As Chaos reached for it, however, Norne stabbed her knife into it first which made him panic.

"N—Norne! When did you get here!" Chaos was terrified as he made eye contact with her.

"Luck paired with your own incompetence is the only reason this slab of meat isn't you right now. We will have a word about this later," Norne growled.

Chaos looked back at her and seeing how upset she was, simply got upset himself.

"Fine! Whatever." He stood up so aggressively that he knocked his throne over.

Taking the plate with him, he stomped away angrily as he stuffed his face and grumbled to himself.

"Magnus, go make sure he doesn't break anything." Norne sighed.

"Of course, Milady." Magnus saluted and went off once again.

Back in her room, Cyrus was picking out what clothes to change into for her return trip. Each piece of clothing came with a cuneiform tag attached to it so she could identify it. Finding one she liked, she removed the tag and placed it on her bed to change into after her bath.

"I apologize for him. There is no need to play along to the whims of that wild child on my account," Norne said, already in the room.

"It wasn't out of any obligation to you," Cyrus explained. "He seemed really lonely. But I have a sneaking suspicion that it wasn't my company he was looking for."

"Please, he's a big boy. He can entertain himself while I'm busy. We're rulers now." Norne rolled her eyes.

"But weren't you complaining about things not going anywhere with you two? Hanging out some more could really move things along," Cyrus offered.

"This is entirely different." Norne sighed.

"If you say so. Plus… I know it isn't my place, but I've got to say I never would have figured him to be your type." Cyrus admitted.

"Tell me about it! But it's like my mother always says—oh, never mind. I've said too much already!" Norne cut herself off, helplessly embarrassed.

Cyrus couldn't help but laugh.

"Just hurry up and go!" Norne said, covering her blushing face as Cyrus continued laughing.

A little after noon, Cyrus was ready to go back to Mesos, ending the sleepover.

Her return transport was of course ethical—not slave-drawn, but pulled by a professional, paid, and trusted Mesos soldier— Atosa's father, Kourosh. As she was about to enter, Cyrus turned back and waved goodbye, before using her hand to make Gula wave goodbye with his paws. Standing in the door with Magnus next to her, Norne found herself waving back with an unexpected smile on her face. After watching Cyrus leave, Norne returned to her office.

"You enjoyed your visit?" Magnus asked after escorting her in.

"I obtained valuable intel while Princess Cyrus was here. It was strictly business," Norne lied.

"Of course," Magnus replied. He could tell she was full of it but Norne scared him, so he didn't bother arguing.

"In related news," Magnus said instead, "your mother, Queen Beatrix has requested to come and visit. Shall I give her an appointed time?"

"Just do what you always do. Tell her I'm busy. If they show up unannounced, expel them as intruders. I cannot show favorites," Norne ordered coldly.

"And what if they learn of Princess Cyrus' VIP pass that runs contrary to that section?" Magnus asked.

"I don't remember hiring you to do clerical work. Hand this off to a record keeper and do your actual job! I know I'm good at *my* job, but surely there is some threat to national security you could look into." Norne gave him an icy glare that made him shut up.

"Of course, Milady." Magnus nervously bowed before hurrying out.

With the room cleared, Norne opened the letter that Magnus had handed her.

"Hello, my dearest daughter Norne. I hope things have been progressing well. Your father and I are very proud of the work you have done in securing a useful ally for Arcosia. Heidi says hello. Just a tip, when I want to increase productivity, I make sure to remove all unnecessary distractions. Like I used to tell you when you were a little girl, don't play with your food." Norne crumpled the letter up, froze the page in ice, and then shattered it against the wall.

CHAPTER 13

T hat night, while Norne was falling asleep, she suddenly opened her eyes. Strange men in hoods surrounded her bed.

"Alright, this better be good." She muttered as sat up groggily.

"Norne of Arcosia," the hooded man at the foot of her bed said.

"Weird, hooded guy," Norne responded, sleepily rubbing her eye.

"Are you a Contact?" the man in the hood asked.

"What?" Norne asked, clueless.

"God only stayed on Tartarus, in the Palace. Those who had the honor of meeting him in person are Contacts and received divine powers and instruction from him. You are too young to have met him…and yet you have followed his orders to rebuild Tartarus almost to the letter. Are you to be counted among our allies?" they asked.

"God? Oh right, yes. As his right hand, I carry out the Emperor's genius orders as he directs the nation from on high. My loyalties are of course to Tartarus and Drakon of Chaos," Norne recited, remembering the routine.

"I see. You are not a Contact. Drakon of Chaos is not our god," the man said.

"I'm sorry, but in accordance with the Ten Tables, you have just committed blasphemy." Norne stood up and quickly pulled her knife from her pillow.

All the men in hoods were gone except the one at the foot of her bed.

"Damn it—I'm half asleep. But now at least I can focus on one," Norne thought before pointing her knife at him.

"It makes sense. You were not alive at the time of God—the chances were slim to none. We just had to be sure you were not a reincarnation like we suspect of the...other." The man in the hood sighed.

"Can I ask who you are?" Norne asked.

"The Church of the Supreme Being—Typhon. Praise be! Those who truly control Tartarus are tired of you operating without proper oversight," the man explained.

"I see. If you're telling the truth, it makes sense that someone was keeping this patchwork of a country together before I—the Emperor and I came along." Norne smirked.

"The current Emperor is a false god and an affront to the Supreme Being. This shall be your only warning—he will pay for killing our god. He is a marked man so keep your distance and await orders if you want to live."

"Wow. And I thought Tartarian pagans would be my biggest problem. Obviously, you see the absurdity in resenting the son and *heir* to the god you worship. Typhon is the *father* of the Emperor. That is why he is on the throne," Norne explained.

"Drakon of Chaos' crime of killing the Supreme Being over-shadows his divine lineage. So, revenge will be taken," the cloaked man stated.

"Wait, if he's the Supreme Being, how come Chaos killed him so easily?" Norne challenged with a smirk.

"As Princess of Arcosia, you have received your warning. Return home and await further contact if you wish to be part of the New Order," he warned before turning around.

Norne grinned and threw her knife at his back, but the cloak fell down. She gasped and looked around, realizing all the cloaks were empty and laying on the floor.

"They were never even here. But that ability must be local. That means we have a traitor in our midst," Norne thought while inspecting the regular cloaks that had been used by the mystery infiltrator.

The next morning, Magnus stood at attention in Norne's office.

"Magnus, when hiring you, I did a thorough background check. Swear to me that you will answer truthfully—are you a member of the cult of Typhon?" Norne demanded.

"I swear on my life, I am not," Magnus said, bowing.

"But you were approached by them?" Norne asked.

"They approached me in my barracks on an away mission, calling me a 'Contact' and invited me to join. After they learned of my loyalty to the Emperor, they expressed disappointment and left. I came to report these things to you as soon as I could—I suspect you experienced something similar."

"Last night I received a visit from them. It is interesting that they find us both to be interesting," Norne replied.

"We are both high up in the Tartarian government. It would make sense for them to recruit someone of our level if they wished to infiltrate our ranks," Magnus reasoned.

"Well, that's the point, isn't it? Tell me, Magnus Draco, why should I trust you? You are second to only me and Chaos in influence. Not to mention that you were ambitious enough to betray the former monarchy when such an opportunity arose. The meek little soldier Magnus seems to have been very opportunistic. And now you have enough power in the current regime to move around spying and relaying information without being suspicious. Am I wrong?" Norne asked.

"Not at all, Lady Norne. The greatest security liability would always be whoever was in charge of security," Magnus bravely concurred, though internally, his fear of Norne began welling up inside of him.

"I see. You know I designed this army with an extreme hierarchy. The difference in authority between the Head of the Imperial Knights and each mere Century commander is rather vast. The messages you receive on and off the record—with no one overseeing you, who's to say you report all your communiques to me? Who is to say you actually carry out my orders to the letter and not in a way to aid the cult? And so on and so on. So, Magnus, you agree that I must find you highly suspicious." She glared at him.

"Of course." Magnus stood up even straighter, beads of sweat clearly beginning to fall down his face.

"Well then Magnus, how would you convince me that I can trust you?" Norne challenged.

"I suppose…there is no way to absolutely prove my trustworthiness. As you have surmised, I am the greatest threat to the Empire, after all. I could have easily lied about the encounter to deceive you." His voice trembled as he spoke.

"Very good Magnus. Now, this is important and use your brain on this one—what would you do in my situation?" Norne asked.

Magnus bowed before Norne solemnly. He was a brave soldier but his hidden fear of Norne had been growing since he had met her. Now it was boiling over, and he wouldn't dare lie to her at this critical point.

"I would solve the problem by removing the head. If it is for the Empire, into your hands, I surrender myself to your judgment. May my successor serve the Empire better than I ever could have," Magnus declared.

Norne's eyes widened.

"In Justice!" he declared, fearing for the last time. Norne sighed and stood up.

"Stand Magnus. You would be the most suspicious candidate for traitor but…due to past experience it has come to my attention that you are absolutely useless when it comes to acting." She grinned.

"Lady Norne?" Magnus looked up with tears in his eyes from what he thought were his last moments.

"I said stand, you big baby. As I said, I scouted you *very thoroughly* for the position. No red flags in terms of shady contacts and you did side with Drakon I against Typhon in the past, so you have no past loyalties to him. If you were good enough for my standards, then for now...you are fine. Be assured I am reconducting this check even more thoroughly than last time. The head of the Imperial Knights must be above suspicion.

However, so far while you are the greatest liability, it also happens that you are my most trusted and valuable asset in this Empire. And my most trusted ally as well," she said, feeling awkward to be so friendly with anyone other than Chaos or Cyrus. Cyrus' forward friendliness had really weakened her icy exterior.

"I am honored!" Magnus bowed even more deeply before her.

"Hey! I said to stand you, idiot. You're off the chopping block for now because you're useful to me. Now go out and show I wasn't wrong about you." Norne stammered in embarrassment at his response as she sat back down.

"Of course! I shall not fail!" He stood up and saluted her.

"Excellent. But remember, they're high enough in government to track even your movements. If they're not you, they must still have jurisdiction approaching yours," Norne warned.

"Of course. I will personally interview all my troops," Magnus promised. "After that, the files of all centuries in the Imperial Knights will take a day or two to review at most."

"Very good, Magnus. I shall be conducting similar reviews myself once I finish with yours. Oh, and before I forget, as soon as this meeting is over, be sure to lock down all the records. While we look into this, if there are any trespassers kill them on the spot. To cover their tracks, I expect we'll uncover multiple fire hazards or 'accidents' near the library." Norne sighed.

"It shall be done. You believe they are a threat?" Magnus asked.

"Well, they've already declared they want to kill His Majesty, so they will be our top priority for now," Norne explained.

"Threatened His Majesty! Should I increase his security detail?" Magnus asked, shocked.

"No need. If they've infiltrated us already, there's a very short list of people we can trust. It's only you and I at this point. Adding anyone else to the list without caution would just put Chaos in more danger. Oh yeah do that too, make the short list." Norne put her feet up on her desk.

"It shall be done. Only my most loyal men will be allowed near the palace," Magnus began.

"No. No changes to security. That just makes others know something is going on. This may seem strange but, His Majesty can handle himself. The greater threat right now is their influence undermining our own. While they target him, we target them. Playing defensive while flying blind is a waste of time." She stretched casually.

Magnus looked at her, confused by her lax response to this threat to the Empire.

"I'm not taking this too lightly if that's what you're worried about. I knew that as we expanded, we'd have more confrontations with nonstate actors. It just so happens that I worked out contingency plans for government infiltration and this is the perfect testing ground for it. Don't fail me, Magnus." Norne grinned.

"I understand—the Imperial Knights will follow your plan in defense of the nation." Magnus bowed.

"Excellent. No cause to panic, we should have this cleaned up by the end of the month," she declared confidently.

She assertively marched off to alert Chaos of the situation but couldn't find him. Worry began settling in as all his usual spots—

the banquet hall, the training room, and so on—were all missing their usual Imperial resident.

After looking around the entire castle for him, Norne gave in and finally talked to a group of the filthy plebian knights patrolling the halls to see if they knew where he was.

"Where is His Majesty?" Norne asked the group of knights.

"In the royal bedroom. He has ordered that he not be disturbed for the day," a knight reported.

"Oh." Norne sighed.

Shortly after, Norne opened the door to Chaos' royal bedroom.

"Chaos, we have a situation." She entered the room.

When she looked though, she let out an annoyed groan. Reclining on the bed, Chaos was being fed grapes by Leona Vlatka. That woman who had Chaos resting in her lap was a recently widowed Tartarian noblewoman whom Norne was suspicious of. Many had come to try and marry Chaos to rise up the ladder and Norne suspected this Leona was just like the rest. Even worse, the gorgeous noblewoman with Chaos wrapped around her fingers triggered Norne's perpetual hatred of anything that reminded her of her sister. And seeing how intimate she was with Chaos just made it worse.

"Ahem... Lady Vlatka, I need to speak to His Majesty in private if you please," Norne said, making her presence known.

"Of course, Princess Norne." Leona respectfully bowed before making her exit.

"Farewell, Your Majesty." Leona blew a kiss and Chaos waved back with a grin. After she walked out, Norne slammed the door in annoyance.

"Try to have some damn modesty, you half-naked exhibitionist. Some people have no self-respect, I swear," Norne growled and seethed in her usual way (despite the other person in the room being Chaos: a man who never wore a shirt even in public).

"That's why I keep her around." Chaos chuckled.

"Chaos, the only reason Leona isn't dead is because she's rich. She's just an old cougar out to gain influence from being queen." Norne sighed.

"Norne come on. Old? Plus, why would she buy the cow if she's getting the milk for free?" Chaos winked.

"Gross. Anyways, it's not safe, especially now that someone is out to kill you," Norne explained.

"Ooh! If it's fighting time, are we killing Sargon now?" Chaos asked with a notable nonchalance.

"No." Norne cut him off.

"Fine...are they strong?" Chaos asked.

"We don't know. They could be anyone. Right now, I'm not even certain of Magnus, so remember I am the only one you can trust," she warned.

"Fine. While you go looking, I spend my free time however I want. Leona just lost her husband and needs... comforting." Chaos grinned.

"She's using you. Remember what we agreed on. It is an exceedingly important choice when it comes to deciding on who your future wife will be," Norne urged.

"Right. Well, if Aurelia is still playing hard to get, I can settle for now with Leona. You have no idea what it's like with a tall, mature woman who has all the right assets. You're just a kid, maybe you'll get it when you're older." Chaos snickered.

Norne was visibly angered by his comments, though Chaos lacked the self-awareness or intelligence to know why. All he did know was that he was able to get a rise out of her by following the topic of conversation. Finally, he could get even.

"I swear, you really are a damned gorilla." She growled at his blatant lechery.

"Norne, you're older but you're still small. Little ones shouldn't use such fiery words." Chaos teased her, patting her tiny head.

"Damned degenerate." Norne scoffed.

"Norne, do you kiss your mother with that mouth?" Chaos joked.

"I've never kissed my mother," she coldly replied.

"That's a shame, I hear it's all the rage." Chaos smirked while stroking his jaw.

There was a short silence.

Chaos and Norne's eyes met. She gave him a death glare that made him shudder and quickly respond, "I *hear* it's all the rage—I *hear*! I mean she's totally my type—but I'd *never* since she's your mom I swear! Not that she's ugly because boy howdy is she not! You have a very attractive mother—I mean—like if she wasn't your mom, I'd totally—I mean she *is* so I definitely wouldn't—I swear!" Chaos panicked as if his life were flashing before his eyes.

"Just try not to die while I figure this out," Norne growled.

"Oh yeah. What were we talking about before the whole banging your mom thing?" Chaos asked, having completely forgotten about the current threat. Norne just turned around before stomping out and slamming the door behind her.

"Magnus!" Norne shrieked.

"Yes." Magnus surprised her by already standing right by the door, waiting for her.

"Good. Come with me." She led him back to the library.

Magnus had begun to look for records that he thought could be of use but quickly noticed that Norne was instead sitting at a table. Looking around, he saw the room was empty and all the doors had been closed and locked.

"Magnus. Come here." Norne motioned. He nervously approached and as she motioned for him to sit, he quickly complied. He thought she was over her suspicion of him, but perhaps she was upset by something else. Even as allies she was scary to work with.

"So…you're head of Imperial security. Have you anything of use, General?" Norne impatiently tapped her finger on the table.

"Of course. My instincts pointed out our security threat with minimal effort. The former head priest of the Tartarus state religion, Pyotr Simone. He was always a zealot so while retiring at his age may seem normal at a glance, from my knowledge of him it is most unusual. I see him as a prime suspect in this fanatical support for Typhon. However, he retired immediately after Typhon was defeated so our records of him since then are sparse. But that just adds to my cause for suspicion," Magnus reported.

"That was quick. What association led to that conclusion?" Norne raised an eyebrow.

"Nothing. In fact, there is a complete lack of anything incriminating. However, that is the problem. I remember that this individual cooperated with Typhon completely during the occupation, but either I'm imagining things or everyone else seems to have conveniently forgotten that fact. In fact, no one seems to remember those who betrayed Drakon to side with Typhon back then, even people whom I know would have firsthand knowledge like I do. Most convenient. They could be among my men and there'd be no way to tell," Magnus explained.

"Drakon—that idiot should have executed all the traitors back then. Would have saved us this headache now. Get me a list of everyone that you personally remember as being a Typhon sympathizer. Cross-reference that with Pyotr's associates and we should have some prime targets for interrogation," Norne explained.

"Already done. And I tracked down his current residency after leaving his role as head priest." Magnus eagerly presented the two lists with common people encircled.

Norne was impressed, "You took my previous insults, personally, didn't you?" She smirked.

"I am the defender of the Empire. I take my job very seriously." Magnus humbly bowed which made Norne chuckle.

"Well, there, you do great work. You're on the ball today. If you were a dog, I'd scratch your belly. If you were a cat, I'd give you warm milk until you started to purr. But since you're neither of those I'll just say thanks for a job well done." Norne smiled at his desperate need for validation from superiors.

"What?" He was confused.

"Pardon, the Chaos level attempt at humor. I'm very tired. I hadn't slept for days before the cult so rudely interrupted my attempt and I haven't caught a wink since then either." She sighed.

"Milady, I insist you make time soon. Even for Immortals, it is unadvised to stay without sleep for too long," he cautioned.

"I'll keep that in mind. After all, with such a reliable minion, I suppose I can afford to take the night off from time to time." She shrugged.

Magnus stared at her blankly.

"Too much?" she asked awkwardly.

"Only if you deem it so, Lady Norne." Magnus knew his place.

"Alright then, Chief of Security. Follow up on that Pyotr fellow. I will look at these suspicious members on the list which you so expertly compiled."

"Of course, Milady. In Justice." Magnus bowed.

"In Justice." Norne saluted her loyal minion.

The two split up to search for clues, as Norne went to collect suspects and Magnus to pay a visit to Pyotr's residence.

On a remote planet, far from easy observation, Magnus arrived at a remote monastery. The grassy field leading up to the small building was full of playing children, running around. Magnus didn't even respond and simply walked towards the building's entrance.

He knocked on the door. There was a long silence. Slowly a black-haired woman in glasses with soulless eyes opened the door just enough to look out.

"What is the password?" she emotionlessly asked as lifelessly as the alterations to her priestly garb after changing religions.

"I am Magnus Draco, High General of the Imperial Knights. Open the door," He said bluntly.

"Oh. I am sister Sofia. Sorry." She fully opened the door, still showing a bare minimum reaction.

"I've come looking for the priest Pyotr Simone. He is said to be studying theology in private here. I trust it is nothing preaching against His Majesty the Emperor." Magnus looked down on the short priestess.

"Certainly not. As with all members of the clergy, our branch has complied with the change to the state religion." The glasses-wearing priestess reported while adjusting said eyewear.

"Excellent. May I speak with Pyotr himself?" Magnus got straight to the point.

"Right this way." She motioned. Magnus took a step inside, however, she suddenly stopped him.

"Your armor. This monastery is a holy place. Please remove weapons or armor before entering the house of Emperor Chaos," she said mechanically. He looked the priestess over quickly to see if she was complying with this rule.

There were no signs of any weapons, but her bulky dress did make him suspicious.

"I pray you comply. It sets a good example for the children." She robotically motioned at the kids outside.

"Do not forget whom you are talking to, girl. A warrior must always stay at arms," Magnus said, refusing.

"Okay. It doesn't matter. Just procedure anyways." She shrugged with an understated yet resigned sigh.

Shortly thereafter, Magnus descended a long flight of stairs behind the girl. The descent beneath the monastery was dark and silent.

When they finally reached the bottom floor, Magnus looked around.

"Alright where is he?" he asked.

"Short detour. I have to put my glasses away," she said while putting her glasses in an Adamant box.

"Are you saying we have to go all the way back upstairs!" an impatient Magnus asked.

"Commander, you seem very nervous. Are you okay?" Sofia asked and walked over to him. Before he realized what had happened, the priestess hugged him.

"What are you doing?! Get off me!" he growled.

"You seem nervous. As a servant of God, it is only right I comfort you. There, there," she lifelessly said.

Magnus rolled his eyes before suddenly realizing she had hugged him around his arms—an unnatural position. Worse, she had locked her fingers together. Magnus gasped, sensing something was wrong. He moved to shake her off but was surprised that he couldn't break her hold.

Suddenly her grip became even tighter, and Magnus growled in pain as she began crushing him.

"You're a strong one for your size!" he yelled, struggling with all his might to avoid being crushed. As the two struggled, Sofia suddenly began pulsating with a white glow. The room and even the entire planet began shaking. Outside, the children looked at the monastery and were filled with fear.

"What are you doing?" Magnus panicked as he sensed her building up unreal amounts of Power within her own body.

"In the service of God…certain sacrifices must be made," she said before a bubble of power surrounded her head.

Magnus panicking and desperately summoned all of his own Power to desperately escape.

"Praise be to Typhon the Divine. Death to all heathens," she said before her body exploded, and all her stored-up Power burst forth.

The room, the building, the continent, and soon the entire planet was incinerated in a massive explosion that shredded everything down to atoms.

The only thing floating in the space was an Adamant box, caught by the priestess, whose body regenerated from her head.

Opening the box, she retrieved the glasses and put them over her now demonic red eyes.

"Mission accomplished," she said, turning around to see nothing remaining but space dust.

Content with her trap, the priestess flew away.

The news was hushed up of the incident but there was a general sense of dread that fell over the capital. Several days later things had not yet returned to normal and there were whispers among the clergy.

A confident priest sat across from an annoyed Norne in her office over tea.

"Something troubling you, Superdelegate?" he asked, grinning.

"Shut up. You were stupid enough to leave all these damning documents that got yourself caught, so wipe that smug little grin off your face," she growled angrily.

"I see nothing disagreeable with those writings." The priest laughed.

Norne read directly from a secret book of his that had been confiscated. "Brothers and sisters, we have been inactive on this matter for long enough. The blasphemous demagogues on the top have turned a blind eye to the demon who murdered our god—that pretender sitting on the throne that isn't rightfully his. This affront will not be tolerated, for those who neglect their duty as leaders of god's followers, we should remove from them each their dominant hand so that they may be reminded that they are no longer the guiding hand of his will. For the blasphemer who sits on god's throne, the punishment is death. We must rise up and direct the organization's will, no false prophets no false gods! The time to act is now!"

She scoffed. "Now, I'm not one for encouraging blaspheming against the crown, but that last one made me laugh."

The priest remained silent. No visible emotion could be registered as if his mind had just crashed. Norne could tell his mind was racing for excuses or alternate explanations.

Looking up from the page she raised an eyebrow. "Well? Pretty on the nose, isn't it?" She put the book down, growing impatient for his response.

"You caught me. I am an avid writer of fiction in my free time. This is really, rather embarrassing." The priest boisterously chuckled, feigning embarrassment.

"Oh my god, I can't deal with this. Magnus!" Norne groaned at the pathetic response she had waited for. There was a long and awkward silence before the priest began laughing.

"Foolish girl, word has already gotten out! Your little guard dog is space dust now, he isn't coming. That fool *died*!" He cackled.

Suddenly, Magnus sliced the priest's right hand off and snatched it out of the air! The priest screamed, clutching the stump of an arm left in agony.

"I believe that was the punishment you deemed worthy of those who would oppose a god." Magnus rested his spear and crushed the hand while furiously staring at him.

"YOU! You're dead!" the priest shrieked, flabbergasted that he was somehow back.

"According to everyone who'd heard from the cult. I made quite certain no one else even knew Magnus was on a mission to that monastery. And yet, rumors broke out anyways. Someone couldn't keep their mouth shut." Norne grinned.

"What! How?" the priest gasped, recognizing his mistake.

"This armor was made for His Majesty and is beyond anything you traitors could try. Now, Lady Norne's excellent trap for catching fools like you has paid off. The weak link is always liable to expose the weakness in the chain." Magnus pointed his spear at the priest's face, still angry from that near-death experience. The armor had saved his life from the blast, but it still hurt like Hel.

"We've confirmed a few more low-level upstarts who were easy to weed out from our ranks. Fighting over how to deal with us might have just cost you." Norne grinned.

"You—you're trying to use his death to heighten tensions between us radicals and the moderates aren't you!" the priest said, realizing the jig was up.

"Of course. After all, the other new recruits as sloppy as you have only proven the cult organization is well managed enough to ensure idiots don't have much info to share. 'You don't know where the base is,' 'you don't know who the leaders are,' and 'you don't know who is working as a double agent for the Empire.' We've been through that. So instead, you're going to help us find all that out *or* the wife and daughter join the sets of families from those we have dealt with before you," Norne threatened.

The priest began to sweat. As a member of the cloth, his family was supposed to be a secret even to the cult. Norne had been terrifyingly thorough in her search which showed in the confident grin she flashed him.

"If you nutcases really are everywhere, we can work our way through the ranks until we find a…willing volunteer. So please, do consider cooperating with us. And do try to improve your competence at leading a double life." Norne put a bucket of human viscera on the table. These were the remains of the previous conversations like this.

The priest froze in horror.

"I could just report everything to them." He began to sweat profusely.

"Oh, I'm sure they'll trust a radical who defies authority and was suspiciously interrogated and then let go by the enemy. Give it a try—your name, face, and being found out will be made known to them if you do not return in one week with useful data. That is the only way you survive."

The priest held his slowly regenerating hand stub and quivered in fear.

After he accepted the ultimatum presented to him and left to do his new master's bidding, Norne let out a sigh and reclined in her chair.

"Make sure he's never outside one of our people's sights. Again, from the short list exclusively," Norne turned to Magnus.

"It will be done, Lady Norne," Magnus replied, moving to leave through the secret passages Norne had found which allowed him to move through the castle undetected.

As the door silently slid open, Magnus looked back. "That was an excellent performance, but you did seem genuinely upset. Obviously, my 'death' wasn't weighing on you so has something happened?" Magnus asked.

"Of course not. Just with Leona staying here during this palace lockdown, all he ever does is talk about her now. He never talks about me like that." Norne puffed up her cheeks in annoyance.

"Lady Norne, you are an extremely capable leader and servant to His Majesty and the Empire. You are very accomplished for your age and an astoundingly respectable comrade. Perhaps trifling and tying your personal worth to his approval of you is unnecessary." Magnus admitted, remembering Norne was still an unsure youth after all.

"Save it. You're my minion, not my shrink. Now focus and hop to it," Norne commanded, growing indignant.

"Of course." Magnus bowed and closed the secret passage behind him.

After he left, Norne sighed and took out a letter that had been delivered from Cyrus. Despite the lockdown, messages from her had the go-ahead to be brought to Norne. Because of all this cult business, she didn't have any time to visit her on Mesos.

"The kids have been helping train Gula and he can do all the tricks in the instructions now. Can't wait to show you. Hope work is going well. Gula and I miss you," the small message read, obviously in Cyrus' handwriting.

Enclosed was another picture, this time of Gula playing with the village children. Cyrus was in the photo watching and smiling, so it was obvious she didn't take this one either. And since Atosa was at her side as usual it couldn't have been her unless she was fast enough to set it and run over in time. Perhaps Atosa's father,

Kourosh took it when he visited? Why did she remember his name? Norne figured it may be for the best she stayed away from Mesos while figuring out what to do about the cult.

Sighing, she put the letter away. There was no time for that now, there was work to do.

Later, Norne visited Chaos to fill him in.

"Infighting in this new enemy—divide and conquer as they say. Their factionalism will allow us to make them turn on themselves and expose a critical target for us to attack and nip this in the bud," she informed Chaos.

"Cool." Chaos was picking his nose, not paying attention.

"So, as you can see, we should have this handled soon and we can end the lockdown swiftly," Norne explained.

"Can Leona have a room to stay here even after all of this?" Chaos asked.

"What?" Norne asked.

"Leona. It's been a month since no one was in or out of the capital and she's getting a bit cramped in her room. She said if we built her a bigger room then her extended stay could be more comfortable." Chaos grinned.

"She what! You're the damn Emperor and you're letting some hussy string you along and put ideas in your head!" Norne practically blew a blood vessel.

"Hey! She just suggested it and I thought it was a good idea," Chaos retorted growing indignant.

"We both know you're not capable of thinking. If you *must* continue meeting with her, then do what you do best and stare at her chest instead of listening to what she's saying!" Norne growled.

"I can do both!" Chaos yelled back. The two angrily glared at each other.

"Ugh! If you want to act like a wild child, go ahead Chaos." She crossed her arms.

"Child! You're the one who got a new friend and never hangs out with *me* anymore!" Chaos whined, sounding like a child.

"And this is your revenge? You spend all your time with Leona just to try and get back at me? Are you five years old?!" Norne stomped.

"No, it isn't *just* to get back at you!" Chaos walked over and looked down on her aggressively.

"Ugh! You're unbelievable!" Norne stomped again and began pacing.

"No, you're unbelievable!" Chaos screamed, flopping down onto the floor like an angry kid.

"Someone is trying to kill you! And you are acting like a five-year-old!" Norne yelled.

As they were yelling, suddenly a basket flew through the window. Surprised, they wanted over to inspect it. When they opened the basket, two dismembered heads rolled out.

It was the priest she sent to infiltrate and the Imperial Knight who was appointed to tail him.

"Ew! It's on the floor!" Chaos said, unphased by the brutality. but upset by the damaging of his carpet.

Norne crouched down and picked up a note that was soaked in the blood from the heads.

"Infighting?" the note mockingly read.

"So... I thought you said you had this under control," Chaos teased.

"Ooh. Heads in baskets, I gotta try that," Norne said, excitedly and heartlessly poking the heads that had rolled out, ignoring Chaos.

Magnus quickly entered the door with a gasp. "Something broke into the Emperor's room?"

"The idiot got caught. They sent us their feelings on our probing." Norne held the priest's head up.

"That is a direct threat against the Empire Milady. How would you like to respond?" Magnus asked.

"Wait it out. I have things in the works. Besides, what could they do to us?" Norne asked.

CHAPTER 14

T hat night on Mesos, the castle was quiet. With Sargon away for his yearly 'exercise,' Atosa was free to wander the upper-level halls without escort or fear for her life. So, after a romantic starlit dinner, Grak and Atosa went to say good-night to Cyrus, holding hands as they went.

When they arrived though and Grak knocked, the door was already open. Cyrus' window was smashed to pieces and her bed was empty!

"Princess!" Atosa screamed, running in, and frantically look-ing for her. Grak froze in the doorway, unable to believe what he was seeing. Gula the dog scrambled as he had been shoved into a vase in the corner. Hearing people entering he had finally pulled himself free and run over to Grak, before drooping its head and whimpering sadly.

Grak took notice of the creature's expression and in disbelief marched forward to where Atosa was weeping next to the empty, glass-covered bed. Grak put a hand on her shoulder for comfort, doing his best to keep calm. Then he saw that on her bed was a note reading,

"None are beyond the reach of the Church of Typhon. Hail to Tartarus. Praise Be!" The note was written in Tartarian.

Grak immediately lost his cool. He was furious! With rage that shook the castle, he screamed up into the night sky.

That very same night in Mesos, Norne, Aurelia, and Chaos were all called for an urgent meeting.

Grak was sitting on his throne as the head of the group while impatiently tapping his foot.

"Norne, swear to answer with the truth, do you know what this 'Church of Typhon' would want with my sister. This sounds like something *you* got her mixed-up in. May the gods forbid; *you* were the one who sent them," Grak said with a quiet fury.

"I know of them, they're a two-bit cult that's been in our hair lately. They had threatened to take us down, but I had no idea they would involve Princess Cyrus. I thought this was a Tartarus problem." Norne sighed.

"Well, now it's all of our problem. No one is leaving until we have a plan of action," Grak said, his face creased with visible anger.

There was an awkward silence, even Aurelia had never seen him this mad before.

"Boring!" Chaos yawned.

"What!" Grak asked, looking at Chaos as if he was currently in his view less than human.

"C'mon, I thought you were the cool guy, damsels in distress are boring. Call me when you have someone to fight. Leona's back in town so I'm going to be busy for the next little bit." Chaos reclined in his chair with the biggest smirk on his face.

"Aurelia…choose your words carefully before you add anything, I'm not in the mood," Grak said turning to her.

"Calm down, Grak. Cyrus is like a sister to me. You obviously have Italia's support in this." Aurelia sighed.

"And Tartarus' as well," Norne added.

"What!" Chaos whined.

"Cyrus is a friend of Tartarus. It is advantageous to rescue her as well as defeat the cult." Norne sighed.

"Whatever. Just find me someone strong to fight." Chaos said, waving his hand dismissively.

JAIDEN BAYNES

The meeting was adjourned and all three went straight to hunting for the cult.

"This new development complicates things," Magnus said on the flight back to Tartarus.

"When we return, find out if we have any sudden deaths or disappearances in positions of prominence," Norne instructed him. "They've surely recognized their junior members as a threat and will remove them from play one way or another."

"So, what now? We have no clues as to a register of any members of value. Plus, the hiring process of more trustworthy replacements will surely be more difficult than last time." Magnus groaned, just imagining the extensive investigations.

Suddenly, something clicked in Norne's mind. She began laughing.

"Magnus! That's it—the reason we can't find the high-up cult members. What if we killed them already?" Norne said facepalming.

"The previous noblemen!" Magnus cried in realization.

"All that money they were siphoning off, the power they commanded—maybe not all but surely a great number were in the back pockets of the cult who controlled things from behind the scenes." She laughed.

"Of course, when we replaced them, the cult merely ensured the power vacuum was filled by those partial to their cause!" Magnus gasped.

"I can't believe I didn't think of this before but, get me *everyone* in government associated with hiring. Whoever put these traitors in place has a lot of explaining to do." Norne grinned.

"It shall be done! We will destroy them yet!" Magnus stood up excitedly.

"But it's almost a shame about those corrupt nobles. I thought they were scummy opportunists selling out their country for personal profit. Now I find out they were just religious nuts bankrolling their cult. I must admit I'm somewhat disappointed." Norne sighed.

The next day, the third highest-ranking priest of the new Chaos religion, powerful enough to impact administration but low key enough to stay hidden, followed Magnus down the halls. He had a confident gait about him, undaunted by this unusual summoning. He had faith after all.

The man's religious paraphernalia had been only slightly altered from the previous cloaks of Tartarus' old state religion. For it was here, religion of course, where Norne was laziest of all in her makeovers so to speak.

The priest was brought into a blank, empty, white room where Norne sat silently reading, *The Philosophy of the Lesser Religions*, by Priest Pyotr Simone. Seeing that her target was here, she smiled and set her book aside to sit with a professional posture as he sat down across from her. He began to speak but she immediately interrupted him.

"You've many years on you, priest. Do you remember the Arcosia-Tartarus wars?" Norne asked.

"I was but a boy at the time." The priest grinned duplicitously as he settled into his chair.

"Excellent." Norne returned the grin before putting a bloodied metal tray on the table.

"You see, Arcosian inquisitors do more than read scriptures—like you men of the cloak have interesting practices behind closed doors, our specialty was torture." Norne put a rolled-up cloth on the tray before unrolling it to reveal a dozen different terrifying-looking blades.

"I told you I—" he began to lie before looking down and seeing all the weapons. His eyes widened in shock until Norne pulling up her chair caught his attention.

"During the war, inquisitors learned Tartarus had invented many training methods to make people of importance harder to crack. It was a cultural challenge, Arcosia had to innovate the outdated methods of the past. We had to think outside the box for… unorthodox approaches if we wanted to uphold our honor as the greatest torturers in the Universe." Norne explained, putting white gloves on.

"The records of this experimenting fill many interesting volumes. But the last of the half dozen is what interested me most. About halfway through the war, we learned that torture was *extremely* ineffective. Only about a third of your Tartarian brethren would yield reliable information even after the most devious torture Arcosia's best and brightest could think of. Most would either lie to make the pain stop or resign themselves to death. We have a saying in Arcosia, 'there are two kinds of people—those who talk after one nail and those who never talk at all.'" Norne smiled with devious sweetness while touching the knives in front of her.

"I have many knives in my collection. This first one was from when I was still keeping up the illusion it was for animal sacrifices, so I was influenced by butcher knives. Every day...before I was permitted to eat, mother would have me gutting something head to toe. Head to toe—organs, bones, and all—learn how to remove everything with minimal mess and varying degrees of pain. Squirrels, dogs, sheep...people. Cadavers for people of course, but soon enough it was no big deal. I learned to enjoy it and also what types of knives cut best and where. I have many fond memories with these fine instruments." Norne presented a few of her older knives as a feeling of nostalgia began to wash over her.

"This is my newest model," Norne said, placing her favorite blade on the table. "Good for fighting and the dense Adamant slows regeneration to a near halt, making it good for killing Immortals."

"But for our purposes today—*this* one is a bone saw. The Adamant band in the center ensures it will cut Immortals, but the low-quality means regeneration will be very quick. Next is this spike. Adamant tipped to pierce, but again the rest is not, ensuring regeneration. I made it especially for piercing the palms and soles, excellent for fastening a subject in place. And of course, this knife is for scalping. This Adamant will hurt, it will burn and be *very* difficult to heal so selective, nonlethal, functional cuts. Like scalping.

Just as the knights of old would do to the degenerate savages. You are about on their level, so it fits. And… I've been told it hurts like Hel." Norne put those knives on the table as well.

"And? I told you before, I am not with the cult of Typhon," the minister spoke again.

Norne laughed. With the wave of her hand, she directed the music boy to begin playing his instrument.

"In Arcosia, we've known torture is ineffective for over three hundred years. But from every book on the subject that I've read, we all can't resist the excitement of finding out—are you the person who squeals after one nail or none at all? After all, there's another saying in Arcosia, 'there are many ways to skin a cat.' The femur? The groin? Which appendages or facial features? Which organs? What, if *anything* will it finally be that makes you talk?" Norne began to cackle.

The minister was confused before Norne picked up her two opening instruments, the spike and the bone-saw with an innocent grin. His eyes widened—she was serious. He looked down at his arm, noticing she had already stabbed through the palm of his hand with the spike.

He was about to scream, but the sounds of the music boy already drowned him out.

Later, after putting on a fresh change of clothes, Norne exited the torture room and emptied a bag of hair, nails, skin, teeth, fingers, and other excess into the trash.

"Did he yield any valuable intel?" Magnus asked.

"No. It was pretty fun though. Anyways, while I was killing time, did you find what I asked?" Norne asked while cleaning her instruments.

"You were right. Among the financial discrepancies in our hiring process, there was a pattern. It appears running secret groups leaves a rather large paper trail once you know where to look," Magnus reported.

"What've we got?" Norne asked as she walked over.

"Across multiple provinces, trade guilds, and monasteries, resources have been funneled into massive seemingly illogical construction projects out in the frontier that never finish. All transport records go dead in these areas." Magnus pointed to a star map of government buildings that had budgets approved and construction materials allocated and transported but were never built.

"Well, I'll be damned, they're all within spitting distance of this cold spot. Almost a perfect sphere around. Ideal spots to have the materials 'intercepted' once the project was abandoned. It's settled. I thought they'd have multiple bases scattered around, but they were so kind as to put all their eggs in one basket, so to speak." Norne grinned as she drew a circle around a remote asteroid belt out near the edge of the known Universe.

"Wait a minute," Norne paused, remembering something.

A year ago, Norne and Chaos had stood on a remote frozen planet in the middle of nowhere—the dead world of Etna.

"This is the place?" Norne looked around in disappointment at the inhospitable wastes of the sulfur choked hell on which they stood.

The source of the grey skies and the clouds above the clouds was the supermassive volcano of Mount Etna, for which the planet was dismissively named. Nothing else of value had been found there, except the massive rupture in the planet's crust that stood twice as high as Olympus Mons.

To Norne's confusion (and general ignorance of geology) the billowing mountain of fire continued to burn with a fountain of molten rock a thousand feet above its hellish mouth despite the literal, eternal ice age around them. A planet with the makings of a tropical paradise, which was suspended the perfect distance from its star that perhaps, in a different time (many millennia ago) was a beautiful, amazing place. But nothing lasted forever, and with time, Etna was condemned with the rain of enough brimstone and ash to freeze the whole thing into a fate worse than Arcosia's had been. Volcanoes much smaller than this had collapsed entire planets and Empires.

And yet, despite the conditions of this world hosting no human lives, some wild beasts (the most tenacious of them) continued to survive. Creatures clearly fit for warmer climates refused to shamble to a halt, simply because of the march of time and an old volcano. Those who could, made the necessary changes, bulked up, learned to conserve their energy supplies, and went on living.

The ecosystem had collapsed, but the individual plants and animals, they had survived it all, in their own way. It needed them, but despite their loss of luxury, despite what many would think, they could survive without it. They ironically also survived past the self-proclaimed king of that world, Typhon himself. He'd hunt them to eat, but they didn't need him now that he was gone.

"This brings back memories. This is where I grew up. The old man was forced to walk from place to place like a modern peasant, but to me…this planet was one giant exercise area," Chaos fondly remembered, looking up at a mountain he'd blown the top off as a child.

"Out here in the middle of nowhere. There aren't even any settlements out this way," Norne noted.

"There were once. Bunch of weirdos who treated me alright. My old man was furious with all of them though and had me kill them, so I guess the settlement was a failure. That's why it took so long for another ship to arrive so I could use it to fly to the capital," Chaos explained.

"But there's nothing but remote mines for light-years—why skip so much territory and try settling here of all places?" Norne asked while rummaging through the settlement and finding a strange black book, *The Philosophy of the Lesser Religions by Priest Pyotr Simone.*

"Neat." She took it without a second thought, not recognizing the significance at the time.

In the present, Norne realized. Chaos' father had been exiled to the area, and all those old frontier building projects required that someone had already charted this worthless area for some reason. And there it was.

"They were looking for their god, but based on Chaos' descriptions they must not have reacted well to what they found." Norne grinned with understanding.

"What?" Magnus asked in confusion.

"Don't worry. I need to take this and show Chaos. We might be onto something." Norne took the map and quickly left. Excitedly rushing off, she opened the door to Chaos' room with a grin.

"Found them. Just need you to confirm my theory." She entered with a piece of paper.

When she looked up though, Chaos and Leona were in the middle of an uncomfortably long kissing session. Frustrated, and not willing to wait for Chaos to finish, Norne immediately threw a knife in Leona's heart to talk to Chaos.

"What the Hel!" Chaos panicked as her lifeless body fell off him.

"Focus! I think I found the cult!" Norne pointed at the map.

"You just killed my go-to—" Chaos began, enraged.

"Shut up! Remember that time—" Norne started.

"Where am I gonna get a new squeeze at this time of year!" Chaos demanded, crossing his arms.

"Are we really doing this now? *Again!*" Norne growled.

Suddenly there was a loud thud! Chaos and Norne turned their heads to see Leona put her hand on the dresser to shakily pull herself to her feet. A normal Immortal would have died but Leona's regeneration kept her going. Spitting out some blood, she wiped her mouth as a black mist hung around her knife wound. Tearing the blade out, she threw it to the floor and clutched the opening with a groan.

"Damned brat…that hurt." She gritted her teeth, furiously.

"Oh. What are the odds." Norne noted the coincidence.

Norne watched in amazement as, inside the wound, her vital organs reconstructed and then the bone and skin around it! Regenerating as quickly as Chaos, Leona's eyes began to glow red as the strange black and white energy around her wound glowed brightly before vanishing as the regeneration finished.

"So… Chaos, unless you've been flirting with your sister, I think we've just found a cultist." Norne picked up the bloody knife with a grin.

"Damn you all—those radicals might have been onto something when it came to removing you both!" Leona's eyes glowed a brighter red as she furiously glared at Norne and Chaos.

"Today keeps getting better and better. Go get her Chaos," Norne motioned.

"What! Why?" Chaos was confused.

"Weren't you listening!? Because she's part of the cult that is trying to *kill you*!" Norne yelled.

"A cult that what!" Chaos gasped.

"Have you not been paying attention?!" Norne shrieked.

While they were distracted, Leona jumped for the window as Norne threw a knife after her. Chaos however caught it and scolded Norne.

"Hey! You killed my eye candy once, that's enough!" Chaos threw the knife down.

Norne was forced to watch as a cackling Leona jumped out of the window and flew away at top speed.

"You *idiot*! She must have been a high-ranking enemy and you let her escape!" she shrieked at him and angrily shoved him into his bed, destroying it.

"Ow," Chaos groaned as the frost on his chest from where Norne had pushed him melted.

"Shut up! You're obviously useless unless we're killing something, so come on. We're playing the last lead we've got and you're going to make up for making this headache." Norne growled.

"I have desired this throne since I knew what it was! If anyone thinks they can take it from me, they have another thing coming! Don't say I'm doing nothing!" Chaos yelled.

"You are doing nothing! Are women all you think about now? You used to salivate over being the 'big man' and now some crazy cultists are after your head and you're *here*! Lounging around!" Norne shrieked.

"I'm Emperor," Chaos whined angrily.

"Oh yeah? But are you the man that I—that I—decided to support?" Norne stopped short.

"Let's find out. Y'know what Norne, I need to punch something. What do you say we have a rematch right about now?" Chaos punched his fists together, unable to refute her insult.

There was a tense silence and the air seemed to crack with tension as the two stared each other down. The imminent danger was palpable before the two suddenly noticed Magnus had rushed over and was standing in the doorway.

"Is this a bad time?" Magnus asked awkwardly.

"No. Perfect timing. Save that fight in you, for now, Chaos. We're taking the fight to them." Norne calmed herself down.

"We are?" Chaos asked.

Norne confirmed her theory with Chaos—the planet he had grown up on was visited by people who seemed to have been connected to the cult. For some unknown reason, Typhon had ordered Chaos to kill them, so technically they had never found their savior despite knowing the general area of where he was. It stood to reason that they would put their base somewhere in that general area and the spot on the map Norne had found matched up perfectly. This was their best lead.

Within an hour, the three left the palace to confront the cult, and shortly after, Grak and Aurelia joined them. United, they went to the area that Norne had identified.

"Well then, great job. They're on any one of these million asteroids," Aurelia quipped as they floated on one of the billions of space rocks in that remote area.

"There are millions of millions of millions of asteroids in the Universe. Lady Norne's efforts exponentially narrowed down the scope of our search to this one area," Magnus corrected stoically.

"Whatever. Even at our speeds, it would take forever to check each one. Assuming your hunch is even reliable." Aurelia crossed her arms in annoyance.

"My 'hunch' is the best lead we have. Either this asteroid field or we search everywhere in the Universe for Cyrus." Norne grumbled at Aurelia's sass.

"It doesn't matter! If Cyrus is here, we're going to find her," Grak fumed.

His mental state was deteriorating the longer Cyrus was missing.

Norne and Aurelia both looked at the prince's twitching eyes worriedly. Chaos, however, groaned.

"This will take forever. Here, let's just smoke them out this way!" Chaos opened his mouth and with a mighty yell, fired a massive beam that shredded the field, destroying all the celestial objects.

"No!" Grak snapped and attacked Chaos, but Magnus intercepted, deflecting Grak's staff thrust with his spear.

"You just killed her, you idiot!" Grak thundered.

"Oh. Oops." Chaos realized and stopped firing the beam from his mouth.

Grak was furious but Magnus held his spear at the ready.

"Hey Magnus, for your own good, I'd suggest not standing in Grak's way when he's angry. It never ends well." Aurelia stood back and her confidence wavered slightly as she began sweating.

Grak's eyes were bloodshot, and he was ready to lash out at anything. Things were tense but suddenly Norne noticed something.

"Wait—look there!" She pointed.

Everyone looked in surprise.

"That asteroid there was in the line of fire—it should have been reduced to dust but it's still in one piece. That could only be possible with an insanely powerful shield. Chaos, I think you might have accidentally found what we're looking for." Norne was shocked.

"Hehe. All according to plan," Chaos proudly lied.

In the next instant, Grak flew off to the meteor and instantly shattered the barrier that appeared around the asteroid.

"Y'know, I really thought it'd be harder to find them," Norne remarked as everyone flew off one by one.

Magnus picked her up to carry her there.

Flying around at high speed, Grak looked restlessly before stopping when he found a giant metal vault door on the ground. The others quickly joined him.

"So...asteroids don't have vaults, do they?" Chaos asked.

"Of course, not. With all those building materials they took, I expected some kind of compound. I guess it's an underground fortress of some kind. Be wary, they have two decades' worth of construction equipment so it's probably a labyrinth down there," Norne warned.

Magnus bent down and tried pulling the door open.

"It opens from inside. This base could sustain His Majesty's attack so breaking this down is no small feat." He gritted his teeth and struggled to open it.

"Move." Grak pointed his staff which began to glow.

Everyone cleared the way as Grak fired a massive beam that melted the door. As air from inside began rushing out, suddenly a second door began closing from within to seal it off. Aurelia was swift enough to catch the doors and hold them open.

"In! In!" she cried. Everyone jumped down into the 'aster-oid.' Inside, everyone was falling down a tube, until however, the gravity suddenly changed, and they slammed into the wall which quickly became the floor.

They all sat up as Adamant cylinders lit up releasing energy which illuminated the room.

CHAPTER 15

"We're in. And from here on in, I'm sure we can expect resistance," Aurelia noted while everyone looked around.

Before them, was a massive white gate with a symbol of a shadow man holding his arms out. The entire secret lair was colored in only black and white.

Chaos, Norne, Aurelia, Grak, and Magnus stood by the entrance of the enemy base.

"Aurelia is right. The cultists likely won't be very welcoming. If we have turncoats from the Tartarian troops and priesthood, the average strength level we're up against is of no concern for you all. Just like slaughtering the average army of mortals. We can split up and look for Cyrus. That means minimizing damage to the structure itself—Chaos. However, save for the head cultists, there is no need to spare the others." Norne laid out the plan of attack.

Grak normally would have raised an issue, but he was so filled with rage at the kidnapping of Cyrus that he merely Powered up to attack.

"Mark my words cultists, you will regret incurring the wrath of—" Grak began his monologue.

"Bored now, going ahead," Chaos said before instantly smashing through the giant metal doors.

The cultists inside that were waiting to attack couldn't even swing their Adamant blades before Chaos tore through their liquefied bodies like a whirlwind.

Laughing insanely, he looked down a hallway of other terrified cultists and charged headfirst into them, killing them with the ease of a wild animal wreaking havoc.

"Well, I suppose we should go after him. Can't let Chaos have all the fun," Norne said.

Magnus lifted her up and flew in along with Aurelia and Grak to lay siege.

Chaos was far ahead cackling like a mad man while painting the building with blood and viscera. After reaching the end of the hall, he entered a grand atrium.

This room was empty, but Chaos cautiously stopped and looked at the massive opening up ahead.

"So...there is someone here worth fighting after all." Chaos grinned, sensing a massive amount of Power up ahead.

Then, four shadows flew out and attacked at once making Chaos frown slightly in disappointment. Chaos simply puffed out his chest and weathered the combined attacks of all four with a grin, two blasting him, one slashing across his chest, and the last kicking his stomach.

He grinned and looking around, saw that one of his swift attackers was indeed Leona. She smirked back at him but, in a flash, Chaos went from nonverbal flirting to fighting. With dizzying speed, the Tartarian Emperor threw a swift punch at Leona's head. She panicked and jumped back.

The four landed together by the entrance they'd emerged from. Chaos finally got a better look at them, seeing Leona, a scarred Tartarian soldier, Sofia the girl in glasses who attacked Magnus, and an old man wearing the cult's matching black and white robes—Pyotr.

All four of them had the eyes—Typhon's eyes, just like Chaos had. The glowing red glares between the two sides were almost like each staring into a mirror.

"Man, two for four. That's uh—half and a half! You guys have some hotter members out back I can take instead?" Chaos smirked while pointing at the two men mockingly.

"The son of our god is formidable as expected—we might have to fight him seriously after all," Pyotr the old man said cackling, noting that their opening attacks hadn't even scratched Chaos.

"Pfft, what's wrong Leona? I thought taking a hit was all you were good for?" the soldier scoffed.

"If you want to test surviving one of his punches head-on, be my guest Mikhail," she chastised.

"Fear not. I will create an opening." Sofia stepped up.

Chaos chuckled while charging at them at full speed. Powering up to her full-strength Sofia put her hands out and clashed with Chaos, both pushing each other with incredible strength.

"Y'know, it's common courtesy not to hit people with glasses. But then again, they also say not to hit women so who cares! Don't expect me to be a gentle little lady!" Chaos grinned as his eyes glowed an evil blood red.

"Worry about yourself," she said emotionlessly before Powering up and tightening her grip to squeeze the skin between Chaos' fingers!

Her own eyes glowed in the same way as her Power began to build.

"Hey!" Chaos groaned. Before he knew it, a massive slash to his back knocked him to his knees.

"Double hey," he groaned before looking back angrily at the soldier.

With his eyes off his opponent, Chaos was taken by surprise when Sofia swung him into the air by holding his hands. Once Chaos' feet were off the ground and she held him up above her head, she slammed him down into the ground.

"Oof!" Chaos sank into the floor as the girl jumped back.

As soon as Chaos peeled his face off the ground, Leona and old man Pyotr dive-bombed massive blasts at him that shook the entire building upon exploding.

The four cultists stood around the dust cloud of the explosion, looking in at Chaos.

"Did we get him?" the soldier asked.

"Shut up Mick! We can still sense his energy!" Leona groaned.

Sure enough, as soon as she said it, Chaos' demonic, glowing red eyes could be seen through the dust.

"My turn," Chaos growled as his Power burst forth and blew the dust and debris away. The four cultists struggled to remain standing as the force began blowing them away.

"He's strong, but stay in formation, even he cannot take us all," the soldier said, smirking.

"Should I sacrifice myself to create an opening? My Testament of Sacrifice should be able to disable him without further issue," Sofia asked without hesitation.

"Not with us down here too, idiot! You'd take us all out with him!" Leona scoffed.

As they stood in a stalemate with Chaos, Pyotr, the most experienced one sensed something coming.

Suddenly, Aurelia flew in and within seconds threw a punch right at Sofia's head. Her last thought was, "oh god," before her head was blasted clean off her shoulders and smashed to paste.

The other three jumped back, shocked at the sudden arrival of this other opponent but more annoyed than grieved for their fallen comrade. Pyotr stared at the mangled corpse of his subordinate and descendant but didn't even shed a tear. She'd died for the cause like a good member of the flock.

"Apologies. I saw an opening and I took it." Aurelia rotated her wrist to shake the blood and viscera off her fist. The three remaining cultists focussed their gaze on her.

"No! You killed one of the hot ones!" Chaos cried.

"Shut up! And don't run ahead you idiot." Aurelia swung her arm to get the blood off before heartlessly axe kicking the headless girl's body to destroy the rest of it. "You got me?" she asked looking up at him with an icy cold death glare.

The rest of the raiding party arrived right after, entering the open area where the battle had begun.

"What are you standing around for! Where is Cyrus?" Grak impatiently demanded.

"Ah...the little prince has come looking for his sister. To think a mere outsider would force his way into the house of our god. She shall be punished on your behalf." The old man grinned.

Without hesitation, Grak fired a blast at him, that the other two cultists blocked while he just laughed.

"So, we found our head honcho," Aurelia remarked, cracking her knuckles angrily.

"I believe that is our man—Pyotr Simone," Magnus reported to Norne.

"I see. So, he leads not just from the shadows, but from the front lines as well. I can respect that." Norne grinned.

"Whatever! Dibs on the hot one!" Chaos quickly said, eyeing Leona.

"Hey! Don't we still have a score to settle?" the soldier with the face scar asked grinning while motioning at Chaos and Norne. The two looked at each other in confusion.

"You know this guy?" Chaos asked in a comically loud whisper.

"Do you know how many useless, faceless peons I have to deal with every day? Why would I remember this one?" Norne asked, sighing.

After hearing that the soldier was furious which made Chaos and Norne even more confused. Norne and Chaos didn't even recognize the former soldier.

"Magnus, who is this pissant?" she asked.

"Mikhail of Tartarus. Half-Brother to Drakon of Tartarus and longest-serving general of the army before my appointment. My former commander," Magnus explained while saluting.

"Ooh!" Norne said. "What, were you mad about me firing you, or were you always into death cults?" she asked with a smirk.

"Lemme guess, you're pissed that I offed the old king? Tell ya what, that's a pretty cool looking scar you've got though, so kill the old bag and swear your loyalty to me and you get to live," Chaos offered, grinning confidently.

"The only one who is fit to rule Tartarus is the man who gave me this scar. You are no true king, *usurper!*'" Mikhail pointed to his rare feature: a scar on the body of an Immortal.

"Everyone shut up! Where is Cyrus!" Grak screamed impatiently as his Power flared up.

The two sides prepared to battle.

"He is right, the time for talking is over. However, given Sofia's carelessness, the numbers seem a bit skewed for this battle, so if you don't mind—" The crafty old man grinned.

With the snap of his fingers, suddenly the roof opened up. Everyone looked up as a massive dragon dove towards them, shrieking with a force that shook the entire asteroid.

The dragon landed in a crash as the five invaders jumped back. The dragon shrieked again. It's awesome Power made Aurelia and Grak, experienced monster hunters feel like they had pins and needles in their skin just being near it.

Aurelia gasped. "What is that!" she asked.

"When Drakon I made his cowardly escape, one of his generals sacrificed his life to keep our god busy. Admiring this soldier's virtue, our god gave him a second chance at life as a servant of his will. Behold the results. Praise be!" Pyotr cackled while motioning towards the terrifying beast.

"Impossible. It takes decades, if not centuries for monsters to be born even from the strongest Immortals. Everyone knows that.

If you're going to lie, try using a more believable story." Norne smirked.

"Hm…the ways of our god are beyond your measly understanding. Some of the secrets he revealed unto me serve as a pathway to many abilities you would consider to be—unnatural. Through Faith, anything becomes possible, little girl." Pyotr grinned as his eyes glowed an ominous red.

In response, the dragon shrieked again, stomping toward them.

"Dibs on the big lizard!" Chaos excitedly ran towards the giant Monster and jumped up to kick it in the face. As he did though, the dragon opened its mouth to eat him. Chaos grinned, going for his usual strategy of dealing with Monsters.

However, the dragon's powerful jaws shut while he was still halfway in. Its teeth were each as large as Chaos was tall and so he was fully caught between them in his awkward kicking position.

"Oops," Chaos said, stuck in between its teeth, with his head sticking out but his body unable to move. He squirmed but found he couldn't get anywhere.

"Those teeth are tipped with Adamant which was among the sacred Adamant that god granted us. Praise be! Even you cannot break it fool. His entire skeleton is indestructible!" Pyotr laughed.

The dragon stood up as Pyotr raised his hand.

"He's fallen for our trap. Well done beast. Take him to the alter. We can now begin…the ritual." Pyotr made eye contact with the Dragon. In acknowledgment, it jumped up and flew away through the ceiling which closed behind it.

"Now then…with him out of the equation, what will you do now? Accept your deaths peacefully or continue to resist god's will?" Pyotr asked.

"Norne? You like nagging us with orders. Any input?" Aurelia asked while casually stretching.

"It would be nice to take them alive, please. As a non-combatant, I am of no help to you all here so please at least leave me a sample to observe that strange regeneration Leona displayed earlier. That's all. Don't go easy on my account." She shrugged.

"Alright." Aurelia punched her fists together with a grin. Grak furiously Powered up and stepped forward as Leona and Pyotr stepped up with their own Power flaring up. They had been holding back to test Chaos, but now both sides knew they had to get serious.

"Magnus, find Chaos," Norne ordered while the others prepared to battle.

"It will be done." Magnus bowed. As he flew down the hall after the dragon, the other general stood in his way.

"Where do you think you're go—hey!" the general said as Magnus flipped over him and continued flying off while he was mid-sentence. Mikhail swung his massive sword but missed even slicing Magnus' cape as he flew away.

"Get back here!" he yelled before flying after Magnus to chase him down.

"Prince Grak—what say you we let the girls have some privacy?" Pyotr asked seriously.

"Fine." Grak stomped forward to face the old man.

"You seem rather upset, is it about the little girl we took earlier? Apologies, that action was meant to get at Norne for her meddling. Any distress you received was merely a side effect, my young prince," Pyotr admitted.

Grak, furious, fired a blast that engulfed Pyotr and sent him flying across half the base, leaving a path of destruction behind him. He angrily Powered up again and flew after the old man to further communicate his rage to the old priest.

Meanwhile, Magnus, went along with his eyes trained upwards as he sensed the Dragon flying nearby.

"The walls here are incredibly thick, but with a beast that powerful, following its trail should be easy!" Magnus thought while eagerly flying along the path he sensed.

As he flew though, he suddenly sensed something coming from behind and jumped out of the way as the general's sword flew past him, embedding itself in a wall. He looked back angrily.

"There! Got your attention! Isn't it rather cowardly for the Emperor's right-hand man to do nothing but run away? Fight me like a man, Magnus!" the general taunted, pointing at him.

Magnus furrowed his brow but ultimately, turned around and without a word flew away again to continue chasing after Chaos.

"Damnit!" Mikhail growled before flying to retrieve his thrown sword from the wall to chase Magnus down.

Meanwhile, Norne and Aurelia faced down Leona. Aurelia confidently approached Leona, her confident gate showing that she had no fear.

"So arrogant, human. I'll kill you in five seconds," Leona boasted while immediately powering up to her max Power.

"Fine...from my guess, I'll kill you in three," Aurelia said coldly.

Leona was charging an ability of some kind but to her horror, before her own speed would even allow her to comprehend, Aurelia had closed the distance between them.

Reflexively, Leona channeled all her Power into defense and just in time. Immediately Aurelia went for an uppercut to the jaw, dazing her opponent. While she was stunned, Aurelia went for a mighty kick to the side of Leena's head which lifted her off her feet.

Aurelia scoffed in disappointment that it wasn't even enough to break her neck but quickly continued the onslaught. Punches to all four limbs broke them easily preventing a counterattack, then Aurelia wound back and viciously punched a hole right through Leona's stomach.

Leona was set flying and splatted against the wall with everything but her head being mangled. Powering down, time could resume as normal, and the rubble fell around from the vicious attack.

"Well then…that wasn't even one second, was it?" Aurelia confidently grinned while standing inches away from her as she stuck to the wall and blood flowed down into a pool below.

At the location of Grak's battle with Pyotr Grak arrived where the enemy landed. There, Pyotr's body was a mangled mess after Grak's devastating attack. Grak was hyperventilating but slowly calmed down.

"What? You think it's over?" Pyotr's voice asked. Grak gasped and when he looked again, a regenerating Pyotr stood up and dusted himself off. Even his clothing hemmed and stitched itself back together out of whatever odd, otherworldly material it was.

Grak was horrified, watching the old bones, and rotting flesh reassemble themselves, reanimating the priest as if nothing had happened.

"You look surprised. Our god gave me this immaculate, Immortal body you see. It far surpasses the mundane regeneration of you mere humans. The title of Immortals you lot wear is an insult compared to the divine! Praise be to Typhon who keeps and sustains this old sinner! Praise be!" The old man regenerated from the obliterated body.

As the priest regenerated, Leona similarly healed from the onslaught.

"That's the regeneration you were referring to?" Aurelia asked as she watched in disgust.

"It's even more potent than the example I observed," Norne noted.

Leona's skin-tight outfit similarly regrew to ensure she remained clothed and (at least in the cult's mind) fashionable. Norne took notice of the strange Adamant—the almost organic substance that they wore. Leona casually stretched as if she were warming up for a jog while confidently smirking.

"Sorry, but I'm much harder to put down," she said after fully healing.

"Yes, but I noticed significantly more defense around your head. Perhaps you aren't so unkillable after all." Aurelia pointed at her.

Leona Powered up again, just like at the start of the fight for some high-cost ability, however, Aurelia didn't give her any time, another punch for the jaw sent her flying across the room but didn't kill her.

"Need to get some distance, she's too dangerous close range." Leona coughed up blood as Aurelia flew after her for a follow-up. Leona extended her hand to fire some of her Power as a beam, however, Aurelia quickly grabbed her hand and crushed her wrist. Leona growled as Aurelia made a fist.

"I know that a 'delicate flower' like you isn't a brawler like I am. Do you think I'd ever give you some distance to snipe at me?" Aurelia Powered up her fist to attack. Leona panicked and began charging up the same ability, but once again was forced to convert it to defensive Power as Aurelia held onto her wrist with one hand and began pounding her with a barrage of punches using her other hand.

Leona was being pummeled. She took damage even faster than she could regenerate.

"The Dictator's ferocity—Aurelia's power in one-on-one combat has not been exaggerated," Norne noted, observing the one-sided battle.

Seeing she was dying faster than she was healing, Leona panicked. Her Power barriers would shatter with every punch—she was not suited to a fair, close-quarters fight.

"I need some distance. She won't even give me a chance to attack!" she desperately thought as the Dictator was thoroughly thrashing her. Suddenly, she got an idea and grinned. She intentionally stopped using Power to protect the area around the arm Aurelia held.

Aurelia noticed too late and gasped as she punched Leona. Since the arm was unprotected flesh and bone now, the force of the attack tore it apart. Leona's arm was taken off, but she flew away with her arm left behind in Aurelia's grasp. She had her distance now.

"Damn it!" Aurelia threw the arm away and jumped after her.

"Now!" Leona Powered up for her long-awaited move. Aurelia yelled and created a blast in her hand.

"You think you can beat me with beams?" Leona cackled while firing a beam to keep Aurelia away. Aurelia however fired her blast up to propel her downwards. Once she hit the ground, Leona gasped as Aurelia kicked off the ground with such force that the Adamant fortress shook, and she caught up to Leona in a flash.

Appearing behind her, Aurelia smashed Leona in the back with enough force to stop her punch-induced escape.

Leona's spine snapped. Aurelia grinned.

"Die!" she yelled while repeatedly punching and kicking Leona without restraint. The solid wall of attacks shredded Leona's body to the point where her tight outfit was all that kept her in one piece.

Aurelia gasped. This was far less resistance than before. Leona's torso turned around—she had forgone defense to charge her long-awaited ultimate move once again.

"Fool! My win!" Leona screamed as she fired a massive heart-shaped blast at Aurelia.

Aurelia flew back, glowing white but as the light faded, she was surprised to find she was unharmed. "That...didn't do any damage?" Aurelia was confused.

"And like that... I've won this fight." The fully regenerated Leona confidently grinned while dusting herself off.

"What did you do!" Aurelia flew at Leona and grabbed her by the throat to extract an explanation.

As she held her up though, Aurelia gasped, it was as though *she* was the one being strangled. Leona grinned.

"There we go." She raised her hand but knowing she couldn't harm Aurelia's hand grabbing her, she smashed her own corresponding arm.

Aurelia screamed in agony, being forced to drop Leona as something broke *her* arm! Clutching it in pain, Aurelia clenched her teeth. "What the Hel!?" she yelled.

"You dismissed my regenerative abilities earlier but with my toolset, they came in handy." Leona showed off her fully healed arm.

Aurelia furiously kicked Leona in the stomach and sent her flying, but she too was sent flying back as if someone kicked her in the stomach with equal force.

"There's no way! An ability like that shouldn't be possible," Norne gasped. Aurelia vomited up blood, but Leona just flipped her hair back.

"I'll admit, you made it a real pain to activate my ability. But none have ever bested god's Testament of Love—Leona," the fully regenerated Leona said, smiling.

Aurelia felt her armor, noticing there wasn't a dent or scratch on it, the damage went straight to her body.

"Armor will avail you nothing. Anything my body experiences will be shared with yours. No way around it!" Leona laughed.

Then for good measure, Leona kicked Aurelia down and began kicking the wounded warrior while she was down. Norne just stood there and watched.

Meanwhile, elsewhere in the fortress the old man Pyotr and the vengeful prince Grak flew around, firing blasts at each other. With a maniacal cackle, Pyotr fired blasts in every direction within the confined space of the base, but Grak still skillfully dodged each.

Once up close he didn't bother dodging and slapped one away with his staff before firing a rapid-fire volley of blasts from his hand. Pyotr raised a shield to block it as the explosions sent him flying back.

"Where is she!" Grak screamed as he fired hundreds of Power projectiles which pushed the old man back while cracking and damaging his desperate barrier.

As the blasts stopped and the force stopped pushing him away, the old man was surprised to see Grak, without hesitation, jump through the flash of an explosion and catch Pyotr by surprise with the swing of his staff. Shattering Pyotr's already weakened barrier with the swing, Grak aimed for the head, but Pyotr just barely dodged the attack by leaning back.

He put his hands together and fired a focussed beam of Power that Grak easily avoided by dashing to the side. His eyes barely followed him, but he instinctively jumped back to get some distance as he sensed Grak's inevitable counterattack.

Grak kept up the pressure and thrust his free hand forward in preparation to keep the heat on with another attack. Pyotr raised an energy barrier that tanked one of Grak's blasts before Pyotr himself raised both hands and summoned massive orbs of Power above them. Cackling insanely, he threw them one after the other.

Grak jumped over both attacks and thrust his staff forward, firing a focused beam that punched a hole through Pyotr and roasted the nearby flesh around the wound. Pyotr felt the missing cavity in his body with surprise as Grak rushed him and kicked the old man to the ground. As he coughed up blood and several teeth, he tried to get back up only for Grak to place his foot at his throat. The furious prince stomped the old man onto the ground furiously.

"Where. Is. Cyrus." he repeatedly stomped on the old man's head. Pyotr raised an energy shield and began firing dozens of smaller blasts straight up at Grak who was forced to flip away for safety.

Pyotr stood up, coughing up blood but still had an evil grin on his face. As he began to regenerate though, Grak thrust his staff forward again.

"No! Divine Authority of the Lugal—Marduk! Seal your power!" Grak yelled.

The seal, similar to the Power Leona used on Aurelia, was placed over Pyotr similarly to the power Leona used on Aurelia. However, Pyotr was only amused.

"Foolish man... my Power comes not from strength but from faith. This is god's power you are fighting against. With it, I can do all things! Pyotr Simone: Testament of Faith! Praise be!!!" he cackled as his body fully regenerated not by his own Power.

Instead of stopping him, Grak simply fired another massive beam that obliterated Pyotr's midsection and sent his remaining upper body into the air. Grak was notably furious and crueler than normal since they had kidnapped Cyrus.

As the old man's upper body pathetically fell to the ground, oozing blood, and viscera, Grak walked to him and looked down.

"Give it up old man. I'll just keep killing you until you stay down," Grak coldly said.

"Prince Grak of Akkad—the ultimate mage in terms of attack and defense. Your reputation has brought me shame in this battle. This body is not a suitable temple for the lord's power," Pyotr said, coughing blood. Grak glared at him, still waiting for an answer about Cyrus, however as the shrewd old man was floating in the air, he suddenly grinned.

"Let's fix that," he said as his legs reattached to his regenerated midsection.

Suddenly the priest's Power burst forth. His body grew into an absurdly huge, musclebound form that towered above Grak and would even stand taller than Chaos. Even Grak was impressed.

Suddenly the buff cackled insanely and charged at Grak frighteningly quickly. Grak jumped back and raised an energy shield, but Pyotr shattered it with a single punch and closed the distance, getting in position to kill Grak with his next punch.

As he smiled, preparing to kill Grak with a physical attack, Grak remembered something.

When he was much younger, about fifteen, in the Mesos palace garden that sat atop the roof of the ziggurat, he had been sparring with Aurelia.

As he hit the ground, a five-year-old Cyrus who sat on Atosa's lap, kicking her feet excitedly tallied off, "Aurelia, fifty-one—Grak, zero." She giggled while marking another tic on her clay tablet.

She smiled and held her hand up for a high five which Aurelia obliged by high-fiving her before going to grab her flask of water.

"Hey, why'd you automatically assume I lost?" Grak sat up while clutching his stomach.

"Ahem… Aurelia, fifty-one—Grak, zero," Cyrus cheekily repeated with a cocky smirk.

He stood up embarrassed as Cyrus laughed at him.

"I must get stronger," he resolved, angrily making a fist as his thoughts immediately turned to protecting that innocent smile from the wrath of Sargon.

"Don't be sad Grak. It happens like this every year." Cyrus patted him on the head after she had Atosa lead her over to him.

Grak looked up at her as she excitedly presented a graph she had compiled.

"Based on your win to loss ratios against Aurelia for the past three years and given the rough averaged estimates of your con-flicting accounts of the third year it seems like every few months or so, one of you reaches a plateau and will consistently lose before a dramatic breakthrough. Your rivalry is based on constantly need-ing to improve to surpass the other." The very articulate young girl presented her observations.

"I see," the very impressed prince replied.

"At a distance, you're unstoppable. But up close you're a pansy. I've spent all my training to ensure you never get enough distance to even *blink* before I take you out. Thanks for making me invincible," Aurelia said, walking over with a confident grin.

"Hm. When next we meet, I will be—" Grak began.

"No—if you fight a physical attacker half as strong as me, you slip up once and you die. C'mon, no more bandage fixes." She motioned for him to stand up and come back to the tile makeshift arena.

"We're going to fight again. This time, no blasts," Aurelia explained which made Grak gasp. In an instant, her fist was inches from his face.

Back in the present, Grak grabbed the cult leader's wrist before the punch could land.

"Oh please... I was put through Hel for just this situation." Grak grinned. His opponent's eyes widened in shock that the mage was strong enough to counter him.

"Aurelia's punches are a lot faster. Try again," Grak said before swinging his staff at Pyotr's hand and completely obliterating it on contact. Pyotr stumbled back, looking in disbelief as Grak threw away what was left of the pulp that had once connected been to his arm.

Grak powered up, converting the Power into mass, so that his staff became like a club. Swinging repeatedly, he blasted off one of Pyotr's legs and then his other arm. Pyotr hopped on one leg, unable to balance and so Grak finished him off by thrusting his staff into the leader's stomach with enough force to send him flying. Grak fired dozens of beams which all converged on and blew up their target.

Pyotr regenerated and coughed up blood, hacking and gagging on his knees from the devastating attack.

Grak stood over him. "What's the matter? Find some dropped donation money on the ground down there? You wanted to do this up close and personal so come! Bring it on!" he said to the furious Pyotr while assuming a martial arts stance with his staff as a melee weapon.

By contrast, things were not going as well for Aurelia. While she was on the floor, Leona finally stopped stomping on her and turned to Norne.

"Little girl. Are you a Contact?" Leona asked.

"Why do you keep asking that?" Norne demanded in frustration.

"Nothing…just looking for reasons to spare you if you're no threat. Your mother is an idol of mine after all." Leona shrugged.

"I'll keep that in mind," Norne said as she looked at Aurelia groaning in agony while trying to stand.

"My Power is basically invincible, but the one thing that kind of sucks is that the nature of it tends to make battles drag on." Leona sighed, looking down at the gagging Aurelia.

"I can see that." Norne did her best to hide a smile as her lips began curling up into a grin.

Seeing Aurelia getting up, Leona brutally stabbed her hand through her own stomach which while not harming her, instead made Aurelia vomit up blood.

"Damned Immortals. Their inferior regeneration just drags out the inevitable. My Power makes me invincible so just hurry up and die already." Leona sighed as her gaping stomach wound healed while Aurelia still flailed in unbelievable agony.

"I am going to pay this back to you a hundred-fold! I'll kill—I'll kill you a hundred times!" Aurelia shrieked, convulsing on the ground, her agony only matched by her unyielding rage.

"Please, this is far from the worst thing I've put into my body to get ahead in life. Surely you can handle it, *Dictator Aurelia*," Leona mocked, as she shook the blood off her hand.

"Your Power…can't be that invincible." Norne smiled suddenly.

"What was that?" Leona turned.

"If it was…you would've just crushed your head to end this at the start. A sure-fire way to kill a regular Immortal." Norne grinned.

Aurelia's eyes widened at the realization. Leona froze before laughing.

"Please. With a face as gorgeous as mine who would even think of such a thing. I *am unkillable*, I just chose not to." Leona laughed.

"Do it then," Norne said coldly. "Tell you what, you can place your Power on me to try it."

"Please, I know you just want to give her an opening to kill me before I could blink," Leona said, groaning.

"So, you concede that under normal circumstances Aurelia would make short work of you. Then there is no helping it." Norne smiled.

"What!" Leona gasped.

Norne walked over to Aurelia and bent down.

"What are you doing!" Leona yelled.

Suddenly Norne froze Aurelia solid and stood back up.

"That Power!" Leona began to sweat in terror.

"I don't usually let anyone see it but given our matchup of abilities I wasn't certain it would lead to victory. This was the only way." Norne sighed.

"Ah…coming to the winning side?" Leona asked arrogantly.

"You could say that. Kill her." Norne grinned.

Suddenly, Aurelia broke out of the ice and dashed at Leona, still covered in wounds.

"Fool! Don't you remember where this goes?" Leona intentionally put her own right hand out to be destroyed by Aurelia's right hook.

Aurelia's amazing strength obliterated Leona's arm but this time, no harm was reflected to her. Leona froze in horror as Aurelia smiled.

Without needing to hold back anymore, Aurelia went ahead with a barrage of punches and kicks which pummeled Leona. Within seconds her body was smashed to pieces with an especial focus on her head.

"What is happening?" Leona thought.

Leona had murdered the previous Testament of Love in the Typhon cult to secure her position. She was tired of being victimized, of being the subject of others' whims. Instead, she would now pursue her desires. She would never be acted upon again. Not without extracting what she wanted from the exchange anyways.

When she first met with the other Testaments, things were tense.

"Don't think we haven't figured out why you're here girly," Mikhail threateningly whispered to her after the meeting ended.

Leona scowled at him as he left.

"Don't mind him. He's just insecure that he'll be next." Pyotr grinned.

"So, it's an open secret then?" Leona laughed.

"This isn't a regular noble alliance where nobody notices." Pyotr chuckled.

"But you're not upset at all? I figured you liked the last girl," Leona remarked with surprise.

"She was fine. But I admire you. You saw an opportunity and took it. Our god would be happy with you. After all, given your role, love is not merely of people. The love of Power is the root of many good things. Praise be." Pyotr smiled at her before walking away.

"I suppose it is. Whatever I want." Leona's eyes glowed an ominous red.

In the present, Leona died brutally with her prideful grin tenderized into a paste by the full force of Aurelia's strength before she even knew she was dead.

As the mangled, once beautiful corpse fell to the ground, Aurelia looked at Norne.

"You enjoyed watching me suffer when you could have dispelled her curse at any moment?" she asked.

"No. It is a matter of national security that I can even fight. Just be glad I intervened at all. Even Chaos doesn't know of my ability to neutralize any ability by freezing it. With my Powers now known, I've put myself in significant danger going forward." Norne said, not looking.

After a few seconds, Aurelia sighed.

"My ability is based on this Centurion armor," she began, surprising Norne.

Showing off the gems embedded in the metal, she continued. "When I get serious, I shift the burden of bracing the recoil of my punches onto the armor so I can convert all my Power into attacking. As I'm sure you've already guessed, destroying these Adamant gems Grak made for me would disrupt my Power," Aurelia explained.

"I see. Then based on my comments, you became aware of my weakness in longer-range combat?" Norne asked since she was apparently in a sharing mood.

"Based on you needing to touch me for your freezing to work and your partiality to throwing knives I figured as much." Aurelia shrugged.

"I see," Norne awkwardly responded to this exchange of secrets.

"There. Now we're even. So, let's meet up with Grak. He's going to get an earful for forcing me to deal with such a bad matchup." Aurelia cracked her knuckles.

As they said that, Grak savagely beat down Pyotr in a close-quarters fight, using Aurelia's techniques. Pyotr's punches were hefty, but Grak could dodge and counter with a fierce attack of his own.

But every time Pyotr would regenerate almost instantly. Grak didn't mind, as an outlet for his anger was welcomed and he consistently held the upper hand in this long slugfest.

After a solid punch that made Pyotr hobble back, Grak fired another blast from his staff that sent his opponent flying.

Pyotr stood up but stubbornly flew right back into the fray, fully regenerated, to continue fighting. Grak, getting annoyed at his persistence, powered up.

"Divine Right of Enki," Grak said as his Power burst forth.

Pyotr charged straight ahead and threw a left hook. Grak prepared to match with a right hook, however, to Pyotr's shock he felt something else hit him first. From Grak's Power, a section moved and directly struck him. Grak punched with pure Power instead of enhancing his fist.

"I can handle myself physically but there are other ways to deal with close-quarter fights." Grak snapped his fingers, and his Power took another shape, extending out in the form of blades that diced up Pyotr's body.

The chunks fell to the ground and Grak kicked the pile so that pieces of the buff old man were sprayed everywhere.

"You are hard to kill...but I know you feel pain. Give up now and you can have this go over more easily," Grak warned as his Power returned to the usual shape of amorphous flames around him.

"Boy, for my master, no pain is too much. *You* are the one who should be begging me. Praise be!!!" Pyotr reformed and cackled before running at Grak, pieces of him still flying over and reattaching.

"He isn't even bothering to defend himself when I attack now," Grak noticed.

So, the clashes continued. Pyotr was stronger and faster, but Grak's superior skill was more than enough to make up for the difference. However, as time dragged on, Pyotr's punches began hitting closer to their target and Grak's retaliations staggered his opponent for less time.

Finally, in one exchange, Grak noted that he was moving slower than before and had to jump back as a blow almost hit him directly in the face. Retracting his Power back to conserve it, he saw Pyotr's smug face and became suspicious.

"Getting tired?" Pyotr smugly grinned.

"This is your genius strategy? Just keep fighting until I tire out?" Grak asked angrily.

"My line of work does not expect much mental acumen. It just works." Pyotr chuckled.

"Uh-huh." Grak crossed his arms.

"Come on Prince—your punches are damaging, but how many more can you throw before your evasion can no longer safely escape my fists." Pyotr grinned while making two fists.

"Hah. You're not the only one with a secondary source of Power." Grak held his staff up which glowed with intense light. Pyotr rushed at him, throwing a punch at his head, however, Grak flew up at an angle at max speed. Missing the punch, Pyotr looked up as he flew away.

Grak thrust his staff out which obliterated the part of the wall he had flown through. Not stopping, Grak continued flying away until he was no longer even visible.

"Hahaha! He ran away! The Power of god prevails again!" Pyotr cackled. "A wise decision. Now to deal with the other heretics." He Powered up to go attack Norne and Aurelia.

Suddenly, he sensed something, and just as he turned around, a bolt of lightning came down and blasted him. His body melted and mangled, Pyotr crumbled to his knees (literally) and growled like a wounded animal.

By focusing his power, he regenerated and quickly stood up. As another bolt came down, he jumped back just in time.

"Playing the range game? Fine. Can you snipe me from there before I catch up and kill you!" Pyotr screamed insanely before blasting himself off into the air after Grak.

Bolts of lightning came down and Pyotr just barely dodged each one, continuing his pursuit. One he couldn't dodge came right for his face and so Pyotr raised his arms to block. They were charred and fused together in a molten flesh glob, but Pyotr persisted.

Flying away at high speeds, he was shocked to find Grak just floating there, pointing his staff. Pyotr slowed down in surprise. "Done running?" he asked as his arms healed from a recent blast.

"Of course. I just needed to put some distance between us and Cyrus. Unlike Chaos, I have the sense to do that at least. Look around, this is the place where you will die," Grak said coldly.

"Those bolts of lightning are fierce…but they will not keep me from crushing your head and killing you instantly. All I need to do is hit you once to win. And the more you tire, the easier it will be." Pyotr grinned.

"Same for me. You just got acquainted with the secondary use of secret ability—Divine Authority of Enki. Lightning is the fury of the clouds of water in the sky. In Mesos, the three realms are guarded by the deities Enki, Marduk, and Anlil Utu.

Enki's waters below represent death; the earth and sky of Anlil Utu represent justice and life and the stars represent omnipotence. That is the affair of Marduk. You observed a part of the ability inspired by him in my attempt to seal your Power before. But now you will taste the true Power of Marduk's authority when combined with Utu's Powers of the sun."

"I have no interest in your false gods, boy. What was the point of all that? This is a fight, not a friendly chat," Pyotr spat angrily.

"Well, my ability is great…but it has a rather large charging time. Thank you for patiently waiting until it was ready." Grak motioned to the gem on his staff which began glowing, having fully charged.

Pyotr was shocked. He'd just fallen victim to one of the classic blunders. He braced himself for the attack in a panic. However, instead of a large attack being emitted, a small spark floated out from the staff.

"When Aurelia and I were younger, we once entered a remote star to understand these objects that were often the subject of worship. Inside was pure, compacted heat. Churning and compressing with nightmarish Power," Grak explained as the spark flickered on its path toward Pyotr.

"Stars are not Adamant. They are regular matter and yet, very potent. Observe a star made with pure Power! Divine Authority of the Stars—Marduk-Utu!" Grak announced.

In a flash, the small spark expanded out into a massive ball of pure Power. Pyotr began shrieking. Instantly, the force of the power, acting like intense heat seared his flesh! Before the attack had even reached full size, he was melted down to mere muscles. Melting both inside and out, the old man couldn't even regenerate quickly enough to keep his body from crumbling.

"I don't know how hot the natural Universe can get, but I assume that what you're experiencing is around that." Grak folded his arms and watched Pyotr dying right in front of him.

The pressure crushing down from the attack made it so that Pyotr couldn't even move. And so, he simply vibrated in place, experiencing untold agony.

"I—I—" he said in a futile struggle to save himself.

"You're weak." Typhon told him many years ago.

Back in those days, Pyotr was a sickly mortal man, coughing violently as his worried granddaughter, Sofia helped him stand before Typhon.

Korova was asleep on the royal bed as Typhon stood by the window looking up at the moon.

"I beg your pardon?" Pyotr asked after he finally stopped coughing.

"You want to do so much, but never can ever get around to doing it yourself can you? Typical for anyone who worships anything that isn't me." Typhon scoffed.

"I may be a weak old man... but I have faith that-" Pyotr began.

"But that's just it!" Typhon was instantly inches away, staring him in the face.

Pyotr almost had a heart attack right there and fell back!

"You have faith! Oh! You chase whoever has the most power and devote yourself to them wholeheartedly! Drakon's father died but you supported him! You devoted yourself to Drakon because he was mighty! And might makes right, you have faith that might makes right! Because might can make your 'magic wishes' come true." Typhon paced back over to the window.

"You want the moon so to speak." Typhon put his finger against the glass, looking up at the celestial body.

"You want the moon but you're just a weak little man. Being old isn't the half of it, you have no Power. I can't even imagine. But I've heard it before. It is nourishing to my very soul when people like you put that faith in me. It's a feeling that surpasses even the carnal. I crave it and old fools like you are the best at giving it." Typhon turned around and paced back over to Pyotr.

"What do you want from me!" Pyotr cried.

"I want you to serve me. Your power will be my power. Your goals, mine. I will grant your wishes and you will grant me endless faith and reliance. I want you to worship me. Kiss my feet." Typhon smirked.

"You cannot be serious…" Pyotr defiantly stood up using his cane.

"Drop the cane! And kiss my feet." Typhon declared, spreading his arms out triumphantly as he was silhouetted by the moonlight.

Pyotr was hesitant, "That will give me what I desire?" he asked.

"Have faith old man." Typhon smirked.

Pyotr finally acquiesced and bent down to kiss Typhon's feet.

"Now stand up." Typhon smiled.

Suddenly Pyotr felt a surge of energy! At the microscopic level, his body was rejuvenated and changed! Pyotr stood up, his eyes blood red as Typhon looked at him.

"All that you have is mine. And in exchange, you are afforded some of me." Typhon laughed, crossing his arms.

"From now on. Ask anything of me and it will be yours. Your faith is payment enough you old fool!" Typhon cackled.

In the present, Pyotr was being vaporized.

"Lord Typhon! Save me!" were his last thoughts before every atom in his body was blasted apart at a subatomic level.

The star collapsed in on itself into a massive super explosion that destroyed every trace of Pyotr. Even Grak could not appreciate how completely his opponent had been destroyed—down to the atoms themselves.

For almost a minute on end, Grak floated nearby to make certain that the deed was truly done. Even Pyotr could not regenerate from that.

"Good." He turned around satisfied, as he flew away, content with his victory.

CHAPTER 16

As the fights settled down, Chaos was brought to a large ritual cultist room by the dragon.

He struggled uncomfortably in the beast's mouth. The constant biting pressure kept him unable to move, but he could feel the dragon's readiness and willingness to splatter him if he made any sudden moves. He regretted so casually going in for the attack. Now he was left with only the Power he had used in the attack, which was barely enough to prevent being crushed by the maw he faced.

The troublesome stalemate that Chaos found himself in was that if he moved to Power himself up, the beast would instantly splatter him. If only he had attacked more seriously in the first place, he may have had enough defense to get serious. But his head was exposed so he was left alone with his thoughts, hard-pressed for how to use them.

However, Chaos wasn't very good at planning and so, just got bored. The Dragon continued walking and finally entered a prepared den where it lay. Like a creepy dollhouse. From this high vantage point, Chaos spied several cultists already in the room, preparing things. On top of that, there he also spied Cyrus who was all tied up.

"Oh! The little girl that Norne is friends with." Chaos tried to wave but only his head stuck out of the dragon's mouth.

"Mr. Chaos! Is that you?" the tied-up Cyrus gasped after hearing his voice.

Chaos didn't respond, because he was still mad at her for being friends with Norne.

"Don't worry Emperor Chaos! I'm sure Grak and Aurelia are on their way to save us any moment! I promise!" Cyrus cried to reassure him. He was furious. She had the nerve to try and reassure him and make sure he was fine, while she was pathetically shaking in terror. She who was so weak dared to imply that he, Chaos, was a weakling in need of *comfort* or *consoling*!

"When I break out of here, I might *accidentally* teach her a lesson when I rip through the others!" Chaos growled out of earshot.

"I promise, we're going to be just fine—" Cyrus continued, frustrating a cultist.

"Shut up girl. Now, answer the question. What color hair did this friend of yours have?" the frustrated interrogator asked.

"For the last time—I don't know! I'm blind!" Cyrus yelled back at her captors for the dozenth time.

"If you don't plan on cooperating—" the leading cultist snarled, taking a knife out.

"Hey! I know you, don't I?" Chaos asked when he saw the cultist.

"Indeed, my prodigal nephew. I am Steir von Ard of Arcosia. A former minister of Tartarus and current messenger of our god, the Supreme being Typhon. I'll have you know that infiltrating your new government was a tedious endeavor. Your maneuvers nearly tore our web of communications to shreds. I hope you're happy about all the extra work you caused me," The white-haired man growled as he dramatically took off his cultist hood.

"Yeah, neat. But hold on…nephew? That means you'd have to be my mother's brother, right? Wait—so now you pray to the dude who used to bone your sister? What a loser." Chaos scoffed at him.

"Lord Typhon honored me by choosing Korova as his primary source of pleasure. Do not diminish the honor that our family was granted. The honor that produced you. The honor which you shall be repaying now," Steir said before snapping his fingers.

"Get things ready for the ritual. There isn't a moment to lose," he told an underling.

"Hey! What do you say you let me out of this giant lizard so we can throw down old man? You're a pretty big guy so it might take more effort to kill you than it did mother, dearest." Chaos grinned menacingly.

Steir was as tall as Chaos and angrily turned to face him at that insult against Korova.

"I'm not a barbarian like you, fighting is not for a nobleman. My service to god is in my intellect and organization skills. I will be focusing on that for his return. However, I will still get to kill you. You took everyone I loved from me, so just know nephew, that I will enjoy it." He grinned at Chaos.

"Oh yeah! Just wait till I get out of here!" Chaos growled.

"You can't get out yourself and no one is coming to rescue you. Now sit still and die like a good sacrifice." The man put his cult hood back on and left to prepare for the ritual.

"Sacrifice? What could you possibly get that was cooler than *me*?" Chaos chuckled.

"Why…your father of course." Chaos' uncle laughed back, presenting a disgusting mass of brain tissue that sat on a pristine pillow. The growing mass of bulbous pulp had tendrils and mold-like appendages that expanded from the brain to the pillow, onto the alter itself.

"No way! I killed him, even his brain should be dust, there was no body!" Chaos screamed in panic, instinctively recognizing the remains of Typhon.

"Well, it seems you missed a spot. And with ten years, he has had plenty of time to recover from dust to this. But to speed things up, *your* body will do just fine!" the cultist cackled as Chaos snarled with rage.

"Damn you, old man. Even when you're dead, you're nothing but a pain. This time, I'll make sure there isn't even dust left." Chaos growled as his eyes glowed the demonic red, he had inherited from the target of his rage.

Opening his mouth, Chaos began gathering Power to fire a blast and destroy everything. Steir panicked, but all the cultist knights drew their swords, ready to slice off Chaos' neck! The dragon bit harder and Chaos felt pain, diverting his beam's Power to defend himself from being crushed.

"Remember, Chaos. A fighter is most vulnerable right after they have attacked. Be careful to never leave yourself open," Norne had cautioned him during a sparring match. Now Chaos sat both surrounded by and literally inside hostile forces.

Furious at being deprived of a chance to act, Chaos seethed where he lay.

"Not even dust," he snarled.

At that same time, Magnus was navigating the labyrinth of an underground fortress, following the trail of Power left behind by the dragon. Sharply turning and dashing around, he made it to the lowest levels while looking around for Chaos.

Suddenly he slid to a halt. The trail had reached a dead end.

"Curses…does this mean it slowed down and landed somewhere nearby or was this all a ruse to lead me away?" Magnus thought furiously.

As he stood there wondering though, the general Mikhail quickly caught up and swung his sword down which Magnus dodged by stepping forward to open one of the doors in the hall. "Emperor Chaos? Are you in here?" Magnus shouted into the room.

"Ha! Drop the bravado Magnus. I've got you trapped in this dead-end—there's no more running away. This is the end of the road, Magnus!" Mikhail pulled his sword from the massive crater in the ground and grinned at him.

Magnus ignored him and checked the next door while Mikhail laughed, watching him.

"My regeneration from Lord Typhon makes me unkillable. No matter how you attack me, you'll never win! Now fight me!" the general Mikhail finished monologuing.

When he had finished his monologue though, he saw that Magnus had just walked away and was calling out for Chaos.

"Emperor Chaos! Where are you?" Magnus asked, uninterested in fighting.

When his back was turned, the general jumped forth and swung.

"Ready to die?" he laughed while swinging with full force. The blade came down at Magnus' neck, but his sword snapped on his armor. Magnus didn't even budge from the attack.

The whole time the general kept attacking Magnus who used his incredible speed to search room by room for Chaos.

"No! He's making a fool out of me!" Mikhail screamed in humiliation.

Reflecting back on the past, he remembered that not even Lord Typhon had respected him or thought highly of him. He then remembered a few years ago, right after Chaos and Norne had killed the old nobility!

"Those brats have ruined everything! They've set out plans back a decade!!!" Leona cursed.

"Calm down Leona. They've actually made our job much easier. Drakon of Chaos' body contains everything we need right now as a matter of fact. The only matter is making preparation to seize him and extract what we need." Pyotr calmed her.

"Pfft. Alright, I'll head out and bring the brat here myself. Then we can finally fulfill our goal." Mikhail confidently stood up.

Suddenly Leona and Pyotr began roaring with laughter.

"What the Hel!? Did I say something funny?" Mikhail furiously clutched his sword.

"Sorry Mik… but there's a reason you've been benched for so long. The only purpose for even keeping you on is that god took pity on you in giving you the Perseverance Factor." Leona shrugged.

"How dare you! I'll have you know I was the first to be called by god! Do not disrespect me!" Mikhail yelled.

"'In use to the lord, the first and last may be used up as one and the same'. Besides, these two have made an alliance with Grak of Mesos and his group. We're still not in a position to act recklessly regarding what such a coalition of nations could mean for our plans." Pyotr quoted to correct him.

Mikhail growled but noticed the Sofia sitting silently in the corner, staring at him. "And, what do you have to say for yourself?" Mikhail furiously asked.

"Really… we're all just waiting for you to die so your power can be passed on to someone more useful, like what happened with Leona. You're very easily controlled so you're not a threat but even I, a mere sacrifice has proven to be of greater use to god than you have." Sofia coldly responded.

Mikhail stumbled, shocked by everyone's lack of faith in him. He couldn't help but remember back to his youth.

"Brother… with father's death, I'm sure you know that things will surely get complicated within the family." A 42-year-old Drakon I told Mikhail.

"Of course, brother! Our eldest brother will try to claim the throne, but everyone knows You are the only one who deserves to be king. Whatever you ask of me, I'll help you get it!" An excited 30-year-old Mikhail cheered. He still had that boyhood admiration for his brother.

"Good boy Mik… I knew I could count on you. Just renounce your claim to the throne forever and we only have the others to deal with." Drakon shrewdly grinned.

"Right! After all, us two brothers are all we need right!" Mikhail grinned.

"Whoa! Whoa! Not just us brothers… Dracona and the girls get to stay. But I mean in terms of brothers yes. We're the only Brothers needed in this family. Brothers forever!" He nodded.

Then on the day when Typhon came, Drakon panicked and tried to flee with his friends.

"Go get him Mik!" he called out while running out of the castle, leaving his wife and brother behind!

"But brother!" Mikhail chased after him and put his hand on Drakon's shoulder.

"Get off me! You stubborn idiot, you promised to be of use to me, now do it! Fight for your king! Go!" he kicked him off and flew away.

Mikhail looked up at his brother in shock.

Then he looked back in as the ominous presence of Typhon approached him.

"How pathetic." Typhon exited the palace with his arms covered in the blood of the last few knights who tried stopping him. Mikhail let out a mighty yell and jumped forward swinging his sword with all his might.

Typhon, with the flick of a wrist, shattered it to pieces. Mikhail threw the sword aside and threw a punch at Typhon's face, but the atoms in his arm simply unraveled into a swirling mist before he could even touch Typhon!

"Oh god!" Mikhail screamed at the top of his lungs, falling to his knees and clutching the stub.

"Yes?" Typhon answered with a chuckle.

Mikhail was furious and jumped up to attack, but Typhon simply sighed and without moving a finger cancelled Mikhail's momentum, freezing him in place. There was no getting away, so Mikhail resolved to face him head on and jumped forward to attack!

Typhon was amused and effortlessly swatted Mikhail away with his bare hand. This made contact with the knight and split his face open with a massive gaping wound! Mikhail screamed in agony while he clutched his face. His hand had regrown so he could feel this wound, yet no matter what his face would not regenerate!

"Such fire you fight with. The others were cowards when they died but you are damned determined to get yourself killed aren't you?" Typhon asked.

"I am determined!" Mikhail screamed while holding this unhealable wound.

"You're stubborn. And you really can't think for yourself. Your brother abandons you to die and you follow his orders anyway, just because you are devoted to him. I like that. You can't select a task for yourself, but when given one you stubbornly follow it to the end. You'd be useful, now rise. Come and serve me." Typhon condescendingly smirked at him with his eyes glowing red.

In the present, Mikhail looked at his shattered sword.

"Even he didn't respect me... then, what has my perseverance been for?" Mikhail realized after some self-reflection.

Dropping his weapon, the stubborn man finally gave in.

"Magnus—I—" he let go of his pride and began to concede.

The instant he did this, however, Magnus swiftly decapitated him, leaving his head floating there, wide-eyed and horrified Mikhail thought, "This is what my perseverance gets?".

Those were his last thoughts.

Magnus without mercy, thrust his spear through the general's jaw and up into his brain which killed him instantly. The general fell over, dead.

"Perfect timing," Magnus said before looking into the next room. He had found Chaos at last! Inside, the cult had him and Cyrus in an elaborate ceremonial ritual room. In the back, the dragon has its mouth open enough for Chaos' head to stick out.

"Hey, Magnus!" Chaos called.

"My Emperor!" Magnus cried.

"Ah good. You're just in time." Steir grinned and motioned at a minion.

Magnus gasped when he looked up and saw a massive guillotine blade set up right above where Chaos' head was sticking out of the dragon. Before Magnus could warn him, suddenly the giant guillotine blade came down and broke on his neck. The blade shattered into pieces on contact and Chaos just scoffed at them.

The dragon's teeth were the main threat, and even while pushing back against the crushing, he had enough energy to spare for this.

As men in cloaks raised it back up, a series of others worked away, slashing, and blasting the back of Chaos' neck as he just giggled, claiming that it tickled. Chaos' neck was red and inflamed but they hadn't even broken the flesh yet.

Magnus moved to help, but Steir walked over, holding Cyrus, tied up with a knife to her throat.

"One move and the girl dies," he warned.

Before he had even finished though, Magnus had made a B-line for Chaos with his spear ready.

In a flash, a rather large and muscular man in a cloak intercepted Magnus, pausing with an intimidating presence. Floating there, the two swiftly exchanged blows. Magnus skillfully maneuvered with his spear and the cloaked figure threw swift punches and kicks to counter, evenly matched.

In a stalemate, the two jumped back to reassess the situation.

"This is our masterwork. A contact whom we have made to replace this fool as the son of our god. He is superior to Immortals, does not tire or grow weary, is immune to pain and any poison, and has the Power to kill with one punch!" Steir laughed.

"Not impressed! I could do that too!" Chaos yelled. However, the next blade which came down finally broke the skin on his neck. Blood began flowing from his head.

"What the? Magnus, did they break something?" Chaos squirmed around, futilely trying to see the back of his own neck as it bled.

"I have to hurry. Do not fear my Emperor! I will be there soon!" Magnus said before unleashing his full Power and flying over again. He repeatedly clashed with the cloaked figure. With each swift exchange, Magnus failed to deliver a killing blow but always sliced away some of the cloak.

Finally, as the two dashed past each other, Magnus landed as the cloak was torn to shreds. He confidently turned around—having swung for the hood he was confident in another swift decapitation.

To his shock and horror though, beneath the cloak stood a muscular man without a scratch on him—and no head to begin with.

His eyes widened in shock before barely blocking a punch from this attacker using his spear. He was sent flying and crashed into the wall, rolling out of the way as the headless man charged through the wall to try and crush him.

"You utter fool! This warrior was given to us by the lord god himself! Directed by my fine abilities, he is as dangerous as a Testament. Even our strongest members couldn't hope to defeat him. Praise be!" Steir declared with tears coming to his eyes as he praised Typhon.

Magnus gritted his teeth, narrowly dodging and parrying the headless attacker's swift punches. He figured it was just his luck, getting the easiest enemy and now facing the strongest.

As he dodged, however, he did notice a faint link of Power connecting this body to the alter that a dismembered brain sat on. Somehow the cult was channeling Power from the brain to this defender.

As such, trusting his dodging abilities, Magnus threw his spear right at the brain only for a force shield to deflect his attack.

"Oh, come on!" Chaos groaned.

Dodging a few punches from his attacker, Magnus dove to retrieve his spear only for the headless man to grab his leg.

"Uh oh." Magnus knew what came next. He was smashed all around the room as the blade came down on Chaos' neck again, cutting down to the bone.

"Yeowch! Did something bite me?" Chaos asked as Magnus began to panic. However, the headless attacker grabbed Magnus by the head and smashed him through the Adamant wall.

"Again!" the cultists yelled as the guillotine was lifted back up. Screaming with all his strength, Magnus kicked his attacker off and attacked the energy barrier again to no avail.

The headless warrior grabbed his cape and flung Magnus into the ceiling.

"Magnus, you wuss! Tag me in, I bet I could take him," Chaos barked thanklessly.

"I think you should worry more about your own situation." Steir walked over and used his finger to dip into the open wound at the back of Chaos' neck.

"Oh yeah." Chaos finally realized how much danger he was in, just in time for the blade to come down and slice his head clean off!

"Emperor!" Magnus screamed in horror.

Norne, Grak, and Aurelia raced towards the high concentration of energy where Magnus was.

"Cyrus!" Grak zoomed ahead.

As soon as he entered the den, a bloodied Magnus was flung back, sliding to a halt using his spear before impaling the enemy with his spear and sending him crashing into the barrier.

"We're here, what happened?" Grak asked in complete bafflement.

"Oh look. Stone face made it first." Aurelia pointed out.

"Magnus!" Norne yelled.

Noticing Norne and disengaging from battle, Magnus flipped back and landed next to her, covered in blood.

"Milady—the Emperor—I—" a shaken Magnus began reporting.

"Your beloved Emperor is dead!" the cultists laughed.

"What! How—what did you do to him?" Norne asked in a panic.

"Cut off his damnable head! Look for yourself!" Steir pointed at Chaos' head which rolled past the bottom of the stairs (and notably rolled through the energy barrier).

Norne bent down and picked it up.

"You fiends!" Magnus screamed.

"Now then, begin connecting our god to this Mongrel's body so that he may be reborn!" Steir cackled.

Cyrus was unconscious and thrown to the floor. Grak immediately saw her and couldn't be bothered by the decapitation before him at all.

"Cyrus!" he yelled and charged a blast so powerful it cracked the barrier.

Steir scoffed at his failure before lifting up the brain on a pillow and walking over to Chaos' body. Aurelia dashed forward and began punching the barrier as Magnus did the same with full Power spear strikes. However, all of them were too exhausted and damaged to do much of anything.

"You'll pay for what you did!" Magnus screamed.

Things were tense as the ceremony continued before suddenly Norne began cackling insanely. Everyone stopped what they were doing and turned to see the insane girl laugh with the decapitated head in her arms.

"You cut off his head. You cut off his head! Is that it?!" She shrieked in a louder laugh. Everyone was disturbed and confused as her unhinged insanity showed itself.

"Wake up you moron. You've slept long enough." Norne threw Chaos' head to the ground. Suddenly the eyes began moving and the head began glowing.

"In the early days, I was afraid of letting him out to play without supervision. But his Immortality is in a league of its own," Norne explained as atom by atom, Chaos generated a new skeleton that grew from the stump of a spine connected to his head.

"Poisons failed, so I went to stopping his heart directly. Even with Adamant to keep it stopped, he went the whole day without even discomfort! Taking his head off was equally ineffective. He must be sluggish today because his best regen time is 5.4 seconds," she explained.

Chaos generated muscles and tendons, quickly getting to his feet as inch by inch, new skin began to grow.

"If it *were* possible, I'd say you were still two or three steps away from actually killing him. The word Immortal has been a gross overestimation—until now. He is unkillable." Norne grinned.

Chaos finished his regeneration—good as new. Back to prime form, Chaos roared like a beast, so loudly that the building shook. The cultists were frozen in fear.

"Here," Norne said before taking her cape off and tossing it to him like old times.

Chaos fastened it around his waist and began walking forward.

"End this. No more holding back. End this!" she commanded.

"Right." Chaos began to grin as he hastened his walk into a brisk pace as Power burst forth from his body in a blinding inferno of Power that glowed around him.

"Not so fast, dear nephew." Steir smirked, powering up to use his remote manipulation ability. The headless warrior that had caused Magnus so much of a problem leaped into action. The shadowy figure charged him, smashing his fist into Chaos' face!

Everyone was shocked, however, Chaos stood strong and barely even stumbled back after that direct hit. He recognized this body as a perfect copy of Typhon's own; (plus a severe workout and glow up from the condition Chaos had seen it in).

"Father...it seems that scraggly old living corpse of yours finally got back into shape. But as always, your attacks are nothing! I am not a child. I am a god now! And you are nothing—you're like the buzzing of flies to me!" Chaos chuckled an evil monologue as he stood up straight, pushing back the shadowy fighter's fist with his face.

Steir panicked, ordering the headless warrior to retreat. However, as the beast was still going into effect, Chaos grinned and punched it into chunks in the blink of an eye. Chaos began laughing as everyone, except Norne, was shocked at his power.

"It's fine—the barrier—" Steir began before Chaos with the casual swing of his hand shattered it like glass. Walking through, unopposed, his laugh grew louder.

"Kill him!" Steir ordered from the safety of the back of the den. All the cultists began firing blasts at once, but Chaos walked forward, unphased by everything. Walking through the dust cloud, Chaos confronted a senior Arcosian knight wearing cult colors. Confronting him head-on, the knight broke his sword over Chaos' head.

"Nice. Now, my turn!" Chaos responded before putting a hole through his midsection with such force that he burst into a mist.

Walking up to where he was decapitated, he yanked his prior, decapitated body out of the dragon's mouth and held it up to inspect. Steir dove out of the way, cowering in the corner as the nephew he had threatened now stood within spitting distance from him.

"I am one handsome devil. Waste of a good body, but oh well, guess I just need to break the new one in," Chaos said before violently slamming it down the dragon's throat! The Monster flinched, trying to get away before Chaos held onto the edge of the hole he made in its teeth before punching it with enough force to blast everything off except the bare Adamant skeleton which he had been unable to break out of before.

"Just like I thought. How ridiculous, a beast that's tougher on the inside than on the outside. Only dad could think of something like that. Speaking of which—" Chaos mused.

When he turned around, the cult was terrified. He looked down and saw the dismembered brain that was to be connected to his body, fallen to the ground from its pristine royal pillow in all the ruckus.

"And of course, father, this all comes back to you," he said as he loomed over the brain.

"Don't do it!" Steir shrieked, leaving his cowering corner to finally step up. All the cultists rushed at Chaos in a desperate bid to save their supreme being.

Before any of them could close the distance though, Chaos grinned with demonic red eyes.

"There can only be one, father!" Chaos screamed as he focused enormous amounts of Power into his fist before squashing the brain under it. The shockwave of the devastating attack blew everybody back.

He slowly stood up and as the dust cleared, the cultists looked for Typhon. All they found was a crater in the solid Adamant floor, melted and flowing down as a ready-made tomb for the pulverized grey matter that lay crushed in it.

"No!" the cultists screamed.

"*That* was your god. How pathetic. He was a puny man. He was a fool! If you want a real god—I'm right here!" Chaos pointed to himself aggressively with his brain-covered hand.

Laughing like a roaring beast, his Power vaporized the brain chunks off his hand and whatever was left staining the floor bubbled and boiled in his mere presence.

At once, many stabbed themselves with poison daggers at the sight. Many more fell to their knees and declared, "all hail Chaos! Our one true Master!"

"The—supreme being—" Steir who had met Typhon was horrified, looking at his melting brain.

He remembered in the past before Chaos had been born. In those days when he served in the Tartarian palace, he saw Typhon in all his glory in the throne room of Tartarus with the Queen on his arm and the first fruits of Tartarus' harvest as his feast of offering.

"Serve me and you will become as god," Typhon enticed the Tartarian nobles. Before their eyes, he performed many works. He turned dust to silver and gold, granted the most loyal invincible Powers on a whim, and slew anything he desired just by thinking it.

Now, he was a brain, fizzing into nothingness. As Steir watched the pathetic display he held out hope. As he was holding out hope the bubbling mass then burst apart into debris so small it couldn't be seen, tissues shredded to atoms and atoms shredded to quarks in a rapid deterioration of existence. At this point, the microscopic particles couldn't even be recognized as part of Typhon anymore.

In his arrogance, his god complex had convinced him that he was the Adam Kadmon; the divine man who transcended the world's crude matter. But in truth, like everyone else, he was a man who came from the dust, and to dust he returned. Even Typhon couldn't regenerate from that.

Steir drew his own knife to join many of the followers who fell on their swords. But he hesitated. He couldn't do it. Despite this, as he held his knife out but didn't move, Norne quickly snatched the weapon out of his hand, freezing his entire body except his head.

"Sorry, however, you are going to be very useful to your new gods. After you've outlived that usefulness, then I will give you permission to die." Norne smiled cruelly at the destroyed man.

Magnus, Aurelia, and Grak were shocked.

"You seriously couldn't have gotten out and saved us the time?" Norne asked Chaos, while casually walking over to untie Cyrus.

"Pfft. If they weren't here, I could've handled this myself." Chaos rolled his eyes which caught Grak's attention.

"Nonetheless, even *you* couldn't get out of the dragon. You ended up being useless for this entire mission. Be more careful from now on. I ended up having to expose my Powers as well." Norne sighed as she helped Cyrus stand up who was still too shell-shocked to speak.

Grak, who was so hell-bent on rescuing his sister before, couldn't even move from where he stood after what he saw.

"Truly! I serve the one true king!" Magnus ecstatically joined the born-again cultists in bowing to the Emperor of Tartarus.

Grak and Aurelia looked at each other in confusion. Things were so bizarre that no one even noticed Sargon of Akkad enter the room and stand right behind them.

By the time they did, there was no greater shock that they could undergo so they only slowly turned around to face him. Aurelia and Grak were intimidated but Norne didn't even flinch.

"I'm impressed...you handled things already. I doubt this was the kind of contact they had in mind," Sargon declared, betraying a bit of annoyance that everyone was so dazzled already that his presence did not fill them with awe.

"Welcome, Emperor Sargon. I hope you didn't have business with anyone here." Norne grinned as Cyrus alone desperately clung to her friend in fear at his intimidating presence. Another Saklas.

"I see. You took care of things for me. Good job, brats." He looked at what was left of the smashed brain and saw that his work was already done for him. Without even saying a word, he simply turned and left.

"Well...that was random." Chaos chuckled.

The Imperial Knights were called in to secure the fort, arrest cultists, and attend to any injuries. More importantly, they immediately began ransacking the place and securing everything the cult had in marked boxes as evidence. Piled in all the rooms, the multi-day job would take all the evidence needed to fully understand the cult.

Doing a small part to help, Norne and Chaos sat down casually. Chaos helped by watching them clean up, and pretending to supervise. At the same time, Norne tried collecting chunks of the bodies from the cult's strongest members after the Imperial Knights brought all the corpses to her. Chaos watched like a child in a science classroom as Norne cut to pieces and packaged the corpses for future study.

Aurelia was out of her armor after receiving medical treatment and sat down to rest. Grak walked over, having taken far less damage than she had.

"Should we just let them take everything?" Grak asked.

"Who cares. What would either of us do with this?" Aurelia said while holding her forehead.

"Your fight was that bad?" Grak asked, surprised that a warrior as mighty as her had had such trouble.

"Shut up. Don't talk to me 'til this damn migraine is under control," she growled still clutching her head as she angrily felt the aftereffects of fighting Leona.

Just then, Norne finished up her dismembering.

"Magnus, take these back to my lab. Ensure they all make it and none of the samples are damaged," she demanded.

"It will be done." Magnus bowed before taking them and running off to do as commanded.

Watching them from afar, Grak had a paternal smile as Cyrus slept peacefully in his lap, recovering from the trauma.

"Grak…listen up. It's obvious Norne was hiding her strength. But solo she still wouldn't stand a chance against either of us, let alone Sargon," Aurelia said.

"She will still be a useful ally in the fight against him." Grak stroked Cyrus' hair lovingly.

"But that's not the point. I always thought she was afraid of Sargon but…she has one-hundred percent faith in her pet monster. After seeing him in action today, I hate to say it, but he may be damn near invincible. She knew…and she knew how strong he was," Aurelia noted.

"Chaos is even more powerful than I anticipated. That's true. I'd probably have to use *it* to contend with what we saw today." Grak became uneasy.

"Right. But then for fighting Sargon, I don't care how scared you are of him, all of us together would have it in the bag," Aurelia whispered.

Grak rolled his eyes.

"I'm serious. We're ready. Given what I saw today, we've *been* ready for a long time." Aurelia said.

"So?" Grak asked.

"So! So, what is she waiting for? Soon enough, she wouldn't even need our help to face the likes of Sargon," Aurelia asked, skeptically looking at Norne.

Grak's eyes widened as something horrifying suddenly occurred to him.

"Aurelia, you're right. Now I have to wonder…is this man even more powerful than Sargon of Akkad!" Grak began to sweat nervously.

Outside, Chaos and Norne watched the Imperial Knights packing up all their plunder to take back to the capital. These spoils of war outclassed any mere hoard of silver and gold.

"Oops…do you think I showed them too much of my full Power back there?" Chaos asked.

"There's no helping it. We had to make sure Typhon wasn't revived. You're sure he's actually dead this time, right?" Norne asked.

"Of course! There's no way he'll be coming back from that." Chaos flexed.

"Good. Then with that crisis averted, I suppose it was worth it." Norne shrugged.

"Sargon wasn't even here for that part, so he should still be in the dark. That's all that matters right?" Chaos asked.

"Hopefully," Norne said cautiously.

She stood up as the plundering was completed.

"But it doesn't matter. No matter what comes our way, we can handle it. In the pursuit of Power, *nothing* can get in our way!" she declared.

"That's the spirit! First Sargon, then the Universe, right?" Chaos stood up with her excitedly.

"Of course. This *is* me that we're talking about." Norne grinned.

STEP 5

OUT WITH THE OLD, IN WITH THE NEW

"They plunder, they slaughter, and they steal:
this they falsely name Empire, and where they
make a wasteland, they call it peace."

—*Calgacus*

CHAPTER 17

When Grak was ten years old, he returned from military service to see the birth of his sister Cyrus. Sargon wasn't there. In truth, his mother was only there because she literally had to be. Neither parent cared about either of their children. In their absence, Grak decided that he had to take on that role for his sister.

She was seen as broken or worthless but having served in the armed forces from the age of five, Grak had learned to respect and care for his many wounded and disabled comrades. Paradoxically it was his time spent killing the enemies of his father from such a young age that taught him to care about people beyond what either of his detached parents could have taught him.

Grak loved people, which was a curse for anyone in his position. He did not want the same to befall his sister, but when she asked him to take her to see the people, he obliged. When they were caught the first time, it did not end well. Sargon of Akkad took the authoritarian style of parenting very literally.

The planet-shattering punch smashed the young Grak so violently that he was flung back and smashed through a boulder before rolling to a stop. He vomited up blood and struggled to get to his knees. He hit the ground as thunder blared above and lightning crackled through the air. Rain was rare at this time of year on Mesos. Shortly before, Cyrus had thanked 'Mr. rain' for waiting until they came home. But now, Grak was soaked, bleeding, and barely conscious outside the palace gates. He could hardly stay awake but just as loud as the thunder, Sargon of Akkad's voice blared out.

"Taking this *thing* out of *my* palace against my orders! Have the youth of today really lost even the most basic of obedience?" Sargon growled.

Grak continued vomiting profusely. He felt as if his insides were barely in one piece after sustaining his father's punch. But far more important to him than this, as he raised his head to look up with all his might was Cyrus.

When they were walking back from their little trip, Sargon fired a blast to destroy them which Grak just barely blocked. The shockwave was enough to leave a several-foot-wide crater. By now storm water had all but filled it as it continued to pour. Ignoring this, Grak needed to be sure—he had to be certain that Cyrus had survived the attack.

Sure enough, exactly then, a lightning strike illuminated the area and Grak could see Cyrus lying on the ground a few feet from the crater.

"What were you doing out there, you impertinent brat? Showing off my shame to everyone?!" Sargon demanded as he stomped over to Grak.

Grak used all his might to look up. Sargon helped him up by grabbing his throat and lifting the boy up as he choked and gagged for dear life.

"What in *my* name were you thinking of, boy?" Sargon demanded as he shook Grak.

Grak could not respond because he was still choking. His father growled angrily and hurled him across the area into the brick gates of the palace. He was thrown so hard by Sargon that he sank into the brick and was embedded into the gate by the force.

Sargon snatched the boy out of the wall and held him up again as he continued.

"Well! Why would you disobey me?" Sargon repeated. He had never overtly forbidden taking Cyrus outside; however, he had instructed Grak to never do anything that dishonored him, and apparently, this counted. Either way, Sargon expected an answer.

Grak, however, as soon as his head stopped spinning, turned his head to see Cyrus and make sure she was still okay.

"Listen to me when I do you the courtesy of speaking to you!" Sargon yelled.

Grak looked back but didn't dare make eye contact. A furious Sargon turned around to see what he was looking at before. Sure enough, the little helpless Cyrus was coughing in pain as she struggled to stand.

"Of course," Sargon said in a growl.

He dropped Grak to the floor and stomped over to her. Grak hit the floor, coughing now that he was able to breathe again. Just then he heard Cyrus scream. The ringing in his ears and the spinning of his head ceased at once as he sat straight up to see what happened.

Sargon of Akkad held Cyrus up by the scruff of her shirt, not even wanting to touch her directly.

"You disgust me," Sargon told his daughter bluntly as she cried out in fear. "Silence!" he ordered and she stopped crying at once, for fear of her life.

Sargon calmly exhaled now that the noise had stopped.

"Tell me, boy...why shouldn't I kill her right now?" He turned around and glared at Grak.

Grak was stunned silent.

"I thought so. Honestly, there never has been any good reason. It just seemed like this thing wasn't even worth the trouble to kill. But if she is distracting my servant from his duties—one must spoil the rod to spare the child." Sargon released his Power as he held Cyrus.

"Father!" Grak pleaded.

Sargon reared back for a punch even harder than the one he had hit Grak with as his Power burst forth. Grak, sensing this, jumped forward right at Sargon.

Sargon slapped Grak to the ground, obliterating that section of the road. Whatever Sargon didn't break with his previous attack was broken now.

"Boy! Tell me you didn't just try to attack me!" Sargon furiously yelled at Grak as Cyrus quivered in horror.

"Of—course not—great Lugal," Grak managed to get out through clenched teeth.

"Good," Sargon said, scoffing.

Then he reared back again, this time to finish things! Grak didn't have the Power to do anything. He was too weak to save her and so…he bowed down and prostrated himself before the Lugal to beg.

"Father! I beg you! Spare her!" he cried.

Sargon paused.

"*Please!*" Grak screamed again, groveling as if to a deity.

"Children these days have no respect," Sargon growled. He reluctantly released the girl by heartlessly tossing her to the ground. The tiny Cyrus was in agony after dropping face-first to the ground from several feet up. However, she didn't dare cry.

"Damned kids. Look at what they make me do." Sargon scoffed as he stomped away.

Grak crawled over to check on Cyrus. Now that Sargon was out of earshot, she could cry. Grak with the last of his strength, cradled her in his arms as he did his best not to cry himself.

"Is it true that he hit Cyrus again?" a young Aurelia demanded a few days after.

"Yeah," Grak was pained to say. His physical injuries all healed thanks to his Immortality, but the emotional scars remained.

"I'll kill him!" Aurelia furiously made a fist.

"Aurelia! Not so loud! He might hear you," Grak said in a panic.

"Not now—but Grak, we are young. If we train hard enough, before we reach our primes, we can surpass our parents. Think about it. Then he won't be able to hurt Cyrus ever again!" Aurelia cried.

Grak looked away.

"Be a man, Grak. God." Aurelia scoffed.

"I already…thought about that. In my darkest moments, I remember how she looked, barely alive. And I want to kill him. Thoughts of it even invade my dreams, where I imagine wielding my Power to make him suffer. Asleep or awake, I want to tear him limb from limb and make him feel how powerless she felt—I want it more than anything in the world," he confessed.

Even Aurelia was surprised by the visceral hatred that came over him.

"But—she wouldn't want that. I'd be no better than he was." Grak sighed.

"Please, she couldn't hurt a fly. You need to take action for her. Listen, when I am strong enough, I'm going for the throne. I want to be Dictator. Help me with that and I promise Cyrus will be safe from Sargon. I don't have your patience, so my father gets the chopping block first. But when you need me, just say the word. When it's time, Sargon dies," Aurelia swore.

In the present Grak awoke from his dream, remembering what brought him to this point. All those thoughts had been racing through his mind lately. As he sat up at his desk, he noticed that Cyrus and Atosa had come and lovingly placed a blanket on him so that he wouldn't be cold. He looked at them with a genuine smile, those memories aligning with the peaceful sight he saw.

"It is time," Grak said.

It was time.

"Happy Holy Day!" Cyrus cheered in a complete change of locale the next day. She was handing out Koloocheh biscuits to guests as they entered the festival area reserved around the palace. The biscuits were not native to Mesos but from the Prince

Cyrus civilization which had ironically grown from Mesos in the past. Nonetheless, it was a favorite of the Iryan people and Cyrus had brought a comically gigantic cauldron of the ingredients as an event attraction that could simultaneously feed the masses.

Outside the Mesos ziggurat palace, a massive crowd had gathered to celebrate the holy day.

"Happy Holy Day." Cyrus grinned and handed a set of the biscuits to a happy family.

"Happy Holy Day?" Norne asked, with audible disgust in her voice. To make up for the lack of visits during the cultist incident, Norne had been visiting even more frequently than normal. Now, she stood right next to Cyrus as she manned the entrance and handed the snacks to each person as they registered and entered. Norne inspected the biscuits as if they were some strange foreign specimens. She didn't eat, so she just looked at the treat Cyrus had given her in utter bafflement.

"This was once celebrated as father's birthday," Cyrus began.

"Doesn't he claim to have no parents?" Norne asked.

"Hence that aspect's falling out of favor. Now, it's more a fun excuse to get together and get a day off work." Cyrus grinned.

"Why would you encourage your subjects to be *less* useful?" Norne asked in bafflement. "Only the nobility should afford to take time off for observing religious festivals. This, on top of your 'week endings,' is going to crash the Mesos economy. Lazy people are useless."

"Nah. That isn't even remotely the point, but I think if you were willing to try it out, you'd find happy people are productive people." Cyrus smiled while handing out more Koloocheh.

"Whatever." Norne rolled her eyes as she did nothing but scoff at the festival attendees for not doing anything. Even Gula the dog was doing more to help than she was, by virtue of adorably sitting on the table and thus enticing children to bring their families to go in.

After the crowd had been let in with their complimentary baked goods, Cyrus and Norne entered as well. Atosa led Cyrus by the hand through the mass of people with friendly hellos and casual conversation. Norne, however, was doing her best to avoid touching any peasant filth as she followed behind them.

It was a joyous occasion. The festival itself was fairly non-specific, instead offering a collection of ways that Mesos planets and cultures observed the Holy Week at the end of the Mesos year. As Norne and Cyrus sat on a couch brought from inside the palace to watch the children play with Gula, Norne finally spoke up.

"Cyrus, I figured you were too smart for religion," she said frankly.

"What?" Cyrus asked, confused.

"Nothing. It's just an unspoken truth that royals lead religions, and the peasantry follows it. The supposed god of Mesos is your father. Doesn't that take the magic out of it for you?" Norne asked.

"Um—I—wait a minute. I know this is a personal topic, so my lips are sealed. You guess what I think, Atheist Andy," Cyrus suggested with a grin.

"Guess? Well, I figured like any good statesman, that you see any religious festivals' utility in controlling these sheep. You mentioned the supposed economic utility of rest, so perhaps this is a test of that concept. Let me guess. Even the slaves get the day off?" Norne asked.

"I'd be letting my namesake down if they didn't. Sets a great precedent that laws can conditionally help slaves for any future schemes of mine. So, you're getting some points."

"And the Mesos religion in an earlier form did promote the freeing of the enslaved," Norne pondered.

"Correct again! So, your conclusion is?" Cyrus asked.

"I don't know! All I can tell right now is that you aren't an Arcos worshipper." Norne sighed in frustration.

"And how do you know that?" Cyrus asked.

"Well, I did thrash the moon worshippers pretty hard in conversations with you. I doubt a zealot would take that sitting down." Norne rolled her eyes.

"And? That's what you believe." Cyrus grinned.

"But the followers of Arcos—" Norne began.

"That's what they believe," Cyrus responded.

"Now you're being difficult on purpose, I give up." Norne scoffed.

"I don't know why it matters so much to you. We believe different things and we're friends. My brother and I disagree all the time. If I was an Arcos worshipper, I'd welcome the critiques and all problems you had. As far as I'm concerned, ideas are only made stronger when challenged. When debated in a dialectic, I can learn more about the things other people believe, the things I believe, and hopefully the truth somewhere in between. Introspection is good for the soul and that's why your critique is invaluable to me!" Cyrus passionately declared.

"Definitely not an Arcos worshipper. Their tiny brains would have overheated by now," Norne joked, missing Cyrus' point entirely.

"Then are you an Arcos worshipper? Because by your logic there, you've still failed to apply my method. That'd mean you're as dogmatic in your thinking as any Norne of Arcos. Is your way of thinking *your* religion?" Cyrus rebuked.

"Whatever." Norne scoffed.

"Not *whatever*. You just did it again—refusing to question your beliefs, the thing you make fun of Arcos worshippers for. You don't get along for some reason, but you and Aurelia really are a lot alike. Remember you still haven't answered my question. Why do Empires need more?" Cyrus pointed out.

"You know that isn't what I meant. It isn't a binary. Your way of thinking is foolishness as well. It just requires far more brainpower than the sheep I mentioned could muster. Now quit it, you're not a philosopher. Is this how you spend your festivals?" Norne asked, growing irritated.

"Yeah, you're right. I've just been reading too much of—one of the committee member's things again." Cyrus giggled.

"Now what else is there to do here?" Norne demanded, her mood spoiled by the threat of introspection.

"The kids are putting on a play about Grak, the potters are demoing how to make pottery and tableware last longer, the royal gardeners are giving out seeds and lessons on how to grow your own food, and ..." Cyrus began, listing off the events she had helped to plan.

"No, something that isn't boring." Norne sighed.

"C'mon Norne, get excited! It's a festival, anything can happen!" Cyrus cheered.

Just then, the doors to the palace slammed open. Sargon of Akkad exited the building and the entire festival fell silent.

"Why are these ants festering outside my house. The noise is infuriating. Explain yourselves," he demanded. No one dared speak to him, but his demand was clear. There was no pleasing him.

"Worthless worms—contemptible aliens are all I see. Back in the good old days, there wasn't an unfamiliar face on Mesos whom I didn't know belonged to me. But now they've bred like rabbits. When I return things to the way they should be, this is the first thing I shall rectify." He growled as he looked over the group of his own citizens.

"Hello, father." Cyrus approached the towering Emperor with a smile. Sargon glared at her as if she were something undesirable, he had picked off his shoe.

Cyrus approached with a loving smile, though, Norne saw that she was shaking in his presence. She loved everyone and she loved her father the same, but even that was not enough to mask the justifiable fear she held.

"If he kills her, Grak will go ballistic again, won't he? Well, can't piss him off," Norne thought to herself.

"That foreigner is back here." Sargon scoffed as he took notice of Norne.

"I am honored to make your acquaintance Emperor Sargon." Norne curtsied.

"What a pathetic sight, you are truly a contemptable creature. Those who praise me must do it sincerely. And they should be honored too. This generation has no manners, not like it used to be." Sargon complained about Norne's impeccable acting.

"I apologize that my introduction was not to your satisfaction." Norne bowed more deeply and suppressed her seething anger.

Sargon glared at her. Without another word he simply turned to Cyrus.

"Clean this degenerate filth up. The noise disrupts my slumber. I will not have my palace grounds disgraced, girl, do you understand?" Sargon ordered.

"But your majesty, you approved this event yourself. Would it not be a violation of your word to renege on the promise to hold it?" Cyrus asked.

Everyone in attendance felt their hair stand on end. Cyrus had just talked back to the Lugal.

"Is she trying to get herself killed!" Norne panicked internally.

"Did you accuse me of foolishness or deceitfulness? Which imperfection have you levied against your Lugal, insolent brat?" Sargon made a fist.

"Neither one, father." Cyrus innocently smiled up at him.

"Good. I cannot stand your whining whenever you make me strike you." He snarled as the crowd became even more on edge.

"Of course not. As you said yourself father, no one can *make* the great Sargon of Akkad do anything." She grinned sweetly.

Sargon paused. He was unamused by her statement but lacked the desire to even bother responding.

"Enough. Now pack it up!" Sargon authoritatively demanded.

"Of course," Cyrus replied.

Sargon turned and stomped off. No one could even breathe until he had returned to his lair and the doors had slammed shut behind him.

After he had left, life returned to the crowd who swiftly left the fairgrounds. As they had heard, the people fled in a silent panic, being sure to speed walk out but do it in a way that did not make noise.

"What a commanding presence," Norne remarked, impressed.

"Well, that's why he's the Lugal I guess." Cyrus shrugged, trying to mask her sweaty, hyperventilating terror with a smirk.

"You were the one giving him lip, so don't even complain about the terror." Norne rolled her eyes.

"Yeah. I promised Grak I wouldn't talk back to him. But father needs to see that talking is a two-person affair. If people are too scared to speak up, he'll continue to live in his own world. You can't make connections—you can't grow close to anyone if you choose to deny the existence of everyone but yourself. If people are too scared to talk to him when he's grumpy, then he'll forever be alone," Cyrus explained.

"You sound even more arrogant than he does—a child telling their parents what to do." Norne sighed.

"Well, father's going to be around a whole lot longer than I am. I'd like to think maybe he can work on being more of a people person before I kick the bucket." She grinned.

Made even more uncomfortable by Cyrus' response, Norne changed the subject.

"What does he even do up there all day?" Norne wondered.

"Sleep? Be fanned and fed? Dunno." Cyrus shrugged, not knowing.

"Typical." Norne immediately thought of Chaos the monarch lounging around and taking the credit as she and all his ministers did all the work.

"But Norne, before everyone leaves, can you help me with something?" Cyrus asked.

As the crowd shuffled their way out, as their downtrodden faces looked down, Norne lifted Cyrus and flew above the masses with her.

"Don't leave everyone, the festival continues! We're just relocating! Follow us to the after-festival!" Cyrus shouted loud enough for everyone to hear. The people all regained their smiles as Norne flew to where Cyrus instructed for the day of fun to continue.

"This is not how I intended to spend my day," Norne grumbled.

Cyrus had a giant smile on her face though, and Norne looked at her. "I could drop her—and she would die. Why does she trust me so much?" she wondered, almost becoming upset that she couldn't understand.

"Norne…sorry from before, I wasn't trying to be confrontational," Cyrus said as they flew.

"Good. You are terrible at being imposing." Norne scoffed.

"Wow, thanks. But scaring you wouldn't help my plan. If my words are to have any meaning, I must always stay genuine," Cyrus explained.

"It's hilarious that you think that," Norne scoffed, "but when dealing with the likes of Sargon, intimidation is the only language worth speaking."

"Nah. I've gotten pretty far without any of that. Y'know back in the day, my father would try to kill me just for leaving the house. Back then if I talked back like I did today, I'd be a goner. But after a few years of wearing him down, I can go anywhere on Mesos, and I'm even allowed to go off-world if I get his permission first. Just plain old talking is a lot more powerful than you'd think sometimes." Cyrus smiled.

"Years of work, for that pittance of progress?" Norne ridiculed.

"For people like me, this is the best we can do. You have many accomplishments you're proud of and this is one of mine. Though I'm sure it all comes down to craving some sense of con-

trol—my comfort and achieved safety are worth being proud of."
Cyrus reflected.

"And that's why you've deluded yourself into going against
Grak's plan to quite literally save you?" Norne asked.

"Yep. One day with enough time... I know I can change
father. Don't get me wrong, it's unlikely he'll be up for counseling
or whatever. After all this, I doubt I'd ever want to see him again.
But at the same time, I don't want anything bad to happen to him.
Grak does but—I don't believe in revenge as a form of justice,"
Cyrus explained.

"I see. So, with Sargon you are engaging in a similar failed
project as you think you are with me. Is that where your confidence
came from when you were grilling me before? Is my presence that
unintimidating compared to Sargon's?" Norne scoffed.

"Oh definitely." Cyrus giggled.

"I could drop you; you know." Norne grumbled from 100 feet
above the ground.

"I know. Anyways, before I wasn't trying to 'grill' you. All
that conversation was for... was getting you to think about things.
I don't have all the answers, I can't tell you the conclusion. I'm not
as smart as you. I just hope that... I can get you to think. That can
be how I'm of use to you." Cyrus professed.

"Okay? Get me to think?" Norne was confused given her
determination for something she was certain she was already
doing. Was her message for someone else? Norne had thought, and
she thought she was right.

"Why?" Norne asked in bad faith, smirking at her. Cyrus
paused for a moment and Norne smiled a smug grin. However,
shortly after Cyrus responded.

"Because maybe you can learn more about yourself and the
world. Isn't that wonderful? All by yourself you can make yourself
more able to help yourself and others. There are applications that
can only be achieved by thinking because thinking is the combination of both knowledge and wisdom. The use of wisdom to apply

what you know to questions. And when I'm dead maybe what I've thought of can be useful to them and so on and so on. This way, my thoughts aren't just my thoughts, but they can inspire, challenge or even improve the thoughts of others. That way the whole of humanity can grow from single thoughts by single individuals. Just conversing with people about what you've thought about can change lives and help people understand each other better." Cyrus grinned.

"Was that a scripted answer? Were you just dying to get that one out there?" Norne asked.

"Nope. Thought of that just now. See, even thinking about thinking is useful." Cyrus smiled at Norne.

Norne didn't reply, focussing on flying as they neared their destination.

"Hey, Norne…why are you all so obsessed with gaining Power?" Cyrus asked.

"What?" Norne asked.

"Have you thought about that?" Cyrus asked.

"What?" Norne asked again.

"Have you ever thought about why people seem so obsessed with gaining more and more Power?" Cyrus eagerly awaited an answer.

Norne felt her mind go into autopilot, her mother's instruction had conditioned her for this.

"It is the nature of human beings to seek Power. It is the way of the world for people to claw their way up in the hopes of surmounting the natural order of things," Norne said automatically.

"No good! It has to be in your own words too. No fancy rhetoric just what *you* can think of. If you try to make it snappy then all I'd have to do is, ask *why* again and again," Cyrus interrupted.

"What? It is the way of the world to separate the wheat from the chaff! And it is degeneracy to be among the chaff! Why ask such an obvious question?" Norne complained.

"Well, it isn't obvious to me. Why does being 'natural' justify it by itself? I could argue that death is natural, so is that good? But fine, if it is so natural what would happen if there was a world where humans didn't have Power?" Cyrus asked.

"There isn't! Stop using made-up examples! Hypothetical scenarios are a waste of time. We live in the real world, and *this* is the way things are!" Norne replied defensively. The whole time she had been scrambling to think of a better, more substantive answer and became upset when she couldn't deliver one.

Norne grew upset. In that moment she considered using her power to drop Cyrus right there. Since she had no answer, Cyrus spoke up.

"Is it because Power is the ability to *do*? To enact one's will and be secure from others enacting their own will on you? Is it that drive for security and desire rather than any intrinsic value in power itself?" Cyrus asked.

"Maybe?" Norne responded.

"So, it stems from weakness? You do count fear as a weakness, right? So, Power stems from weakness. It is weakness and subservience to fear and to 'the way of the world,' whatever that is?" Cyrus asked.

"What? No! Power is the absence of weakness!" Norne cried.

"Then you should—" Cyrus began.

"Let me guess, you just want to argue that knowledge is superior to Power. Yes, you're so great and superior for picking the better thing." Norne rolled her eyes and interrupted.

"It isn't a competition. In fact, Grak would say that knowledge *is* power. He would give the answer I provided you. Because he's thought about what he wants and why. You're smarter than the two of us put together, Norne. I honestly expected a better showing than that just now. If it's so important to you, then a better response should be easy. So, I think it's just a matter of taking a moment to stop and think about why." Cyrus grinned.

Norne glared at her.

"That's my challenge to you. Prove you're more powerful than me in terms of knowledge by answering any question. Just by taking a nice stop to think about why. Why anything, really." Cyrus explained.

Norne dropped her.

But they had arrived at the beach and Cyrus fell comfortably into a chair that was set up there.

"Just think about it, Norne," Cyrus said, smiling genuinely.

"Just think about it, Norne," Norne mockingly repeated.

"I know it seems silly, but I think there are two ways to change people's minds. You can put a sword through it, *or* you can put a new idea in it. So yes, do think about it Norne," Cyrus declared.

At the end of the day, Norne returned to Tartarus where work quickly distracted her from slipping any further into introspection.

Back on Mesos, Cyrus flopped down on her bed, completely exhausted. In her room, Grak and Atosa wrote down ideas and lists of people to invite to the upcoming wedding.

"You're the one who was so excited to help with wedding planning, so what's up?" Grak asked.

"Holy Day stuff was a lot more work than I expected." Cyrus pulled in her rabbit plushie to snuggle with.

"It seemed to be a big success, so I should've expected you to work yourself to the bone as usual," Grak replied.

"That's great, it was all worth it then," Cyrus said, then smiled.

"Of course, it was a success. Everyone loved it, so get some rest for now. You can lend us your skills later." Atosa giggled.

"No way! Now I'm pumped! What have we got to do?" Cyrus sat up, still holding the toy close to her chest.

"Listen to Atosa, you've done far too much today already. We'll pick things up tomorrow." Grak told her.

"Ah, I see, Cyrus said. "Fine, if you didn't want the blind girl ruining your plans you could just say," she joked. In response, however, there was an awkward silence.

"What?" Grak asked, taken aback.

Cyrus' facial expression changed as she remembered she wasn't talking with Norne.

"Cyrus! Don't talk about yourself like that," an exasperated Atosa quickly responded.

"Sorry—Norne normally goes for that kind of joke." Cyrus frowned.

"I see," Grak said, making a mental note of that as he and Atosa exchanged concerned glances.

After saying goodnight, the two left Cyrus' room with concern.

"Norne is a bad influence on her," Grak immediately said.

"I can't disagree...but Cyrus is an adult now, remember. She picks her own friends Grak," Atosa reminded him.

"Right, it's just—I don't know. She's had to put up with so much of that. I never expected to hear it coming from her now." Grak sighed.

"I know what you mean. That plus, ever since you told me the truth about Norne, I've never seen their friendly chats the same. I'm just glad that *thing's* dark sense of humor is all that rubbed off on Cyrus." Atosa worried, feeling sick to her stomach just mentioning Norne.

Grak saw the visible concern on her face and took her hand.

"Atosa, don't worry. It'll be taken care of. I promise," he reassured her. He took Atosa into his arms and hugged her to help ease her nerves.

With the preparations finalized, the call was put out. The wedding was to be held on Uruk and all the members of Grak's alliance were invited.

It was time.

CHAPTER 18

The day before Grak's wedding, most rulers were making final preparations. For their part Chaos and Norne flew side by side through the starry heavens of Tartarus. It was considered beneath a ruler to fly to their destination themselves, but the two had a schedule to keep and they were each many times faster than any slave drawn carriage.

Chaos was giddy to have Norne for the entire day. Norne, ever mindful of utility had scheduled their day to take care of everything that the army didn't have the resources to do. They had already laid waste to the last known outpost of Typhon cultists, slain all the vengeful rebel armies of the newly incorporated territories and now they flew towards their final task.

Chaos for his part was casually chatting Norne's ear off about all his many exploits out in the field while she was "wasting time with Cyrus".

"And I'm being serious. All the other rulers are doing it. Wilhelm says to go all in now and you will make a hundred times what you ingested!" Chaos mispronounced, "You're always talking about how to make money, we should do the tulip mania thing with him."

"Don't put a single coin into that scam. Wilhelm is just trying to sucker you in because the only way anyone makes money is if someone is left holding the bag." Norne sighed.

"What!? You don't know it's a scam. He just said not to question where the money comes from. It's not fishy at all. People are making money so it must be legit." Chaos cried.

"It's a scam." Norne insisted.

"How could you know that?" Chaos huffed.

"I know it's a scam because I'm the one who started it." Norne revealed.

"Oh." Chaos pouted in disappointment.

"Empires are expensive to run and foreign investors can help ease that. By request or swindle, that foreign cash will keep flowing no matter what." Norne grinned.

Perfectly on time the two arrived at their destination, dramatically landing in the middle of a field.

"We're here. Look alive the target should be nearby." Norne said while immediately looking around.

"This is an enemy so strong that you needed *me* to handle it? This has got to be good." Chaos grinned.

"Precisely… and an excellent warmup for Sargon of Akkad." Norne shot Chaos a serious glance.

"Right, right. Now where is this guy?" Chaos asked as he punched his fists together.

A fog descended on the dark field. Chaos and Norne turned in unison as they sensed a large Power approaching. The clopping of hooves echoed through the fog and jingling of chainmail ominously heralded its arrival.

A horseman clad in ancient pre-Tartarian armor glared down at the two with his spear drawn. The armor was damaged, and war torn but jagged Adamant crystals protruded out and filled in the damaged sections. Though no man wore these armaments: it was a flaming mass of Power kept under control by a molten Adamant shell. It had the shape of a human being, but it was truly a Monster.

"So, thou hast returned Sosruquo! Our rematch is upon us, this meager fog will not aid you! There shall be no quarter this time." a voice blared from the Monster's helmet, "I am Totrash: I am your doom!"". The Monster released waves of Power that carried this signal since no voice actually came from its corpse.

"Who? I've never met this guy before and that's not my name." Chaos turned to Norne in confusion.

"I don't know. Magnus said he recognized it from some obscure mythology thing. I don't care. If it isn't Italic myth, it's basically dead to me." Norne shrugged.

"Ha! For once something even you don't know." Chaos laughed.

"Right, but the point is: there is your opponent. This Monster killed 5 Imperial knights by itself. Only one escaped to report its existence to us. Any who approach it are attacked and killed so you are responsible for ridding this planet of it." Norne briefed Chaos.

"Monster? But he's so puny." Chaos was shocked by what he saw.

"Size isn't everything." Norne began.

Chaos snickered like a child.

"The point is, despite his size he is stronger than most monsters we've encountered. He'll be the perfect test to see if you're ready for Sargon." Norne finished with audible irritation.

The Monster that called itself Totrash rode a horse with its jaws torn out by the reigns and slowly clopped its way closer to Chaos and Norne. Though Norne took a closer look and quickly determined that the supposed "horse" was in fact just a construct of the Monster. It was rare, though not unheard of, for great warriors to reanimate as Monsters within the armor they had worn into battle during their lives.

Littered around the area were the remains of dozens of fallen foes. He had slain them before and when they resurrected as Monsters he slew them once again for good measure. If they died so easily, they weren't the one he was waiting for.

"So, thou hast returned Sosruquo! Our rematch is upon us, this meager fog will not aid you! There shall be no quarter this time. I am Totrash: I am your doom!"". The ghostly rider repeated robotically as its horse came to a stop and pointed his spear at Chaos.

"Lookit Norne, if you're right that means we found the first Monster ever that can talk!" Chaos excitedly pointed.

"Don't be ridiculous. The Monster has no actual intelligence. It is likely just endlessly recreating the last few moments of its life. That little soliloquy is exactly the spiel our scout heard before it attacked him." Norne explained.

"Ooh. Neat." Chaos grinned.

Before Chaos could turn back around to respond though, Totrash rode forward and skewered him through the stomach! Lifting Chaos off his feet, Totrash hoisted him into the air as he continued riding ahead with his horse. Then the Monstrous rider thrust his spear up into the air to launch Chaos off it. And in short order as the Emperor of Tartarus fell, Totrash removed his head!

Chaos' headless body fell to the ground as his head rolled away. But Norne just sighed impatiently. She knew how this song and dance went.

As Totrash rode his horse back to where he began and reset to how he was when Chaos and Norne arrived, Chaos' eyes already glowed the bright red of Typhon. Springing fully formed from Chaos' neck stump, a new body stood up and casually stretched.

"Damn... for as much as you like running your mouth, you think you'd give some warning before attacking!" Chaos smirked.

"Or perhaps, you can remember to actually stay on guard for once." Norne shook her head.

Walking over to his decapitated body, Chaos nonchalantly undressed the headless corpse and began to put his clothes back onto his new body.

Norne worried that he'd be attacked again, however Totrash did not react and merely began reciting another monologue.

"I am victorious! As expected, the greatest warrior is none other than I! All of Caucasia fears my might and skill, woe to any challengers." The corpse of Totrash recited the victory speech he had prepared all those ages ago when he still lived.

It appeared that this odd quirk of pausing for long monologues was older than Norne thought.

This was to be expected though, after all the survivor that reported was only able to escape because the Monster paused to give that exact same gloat upon killing his compatriots.

In this peculiar halftime of Totrash hyping himself up and Chaos getting dressed for round two, Norne just had to watch in disbelief… followed by tense anticipation. Norne didn't even bother looking away anymore, even after all this time circumstances seemed to conspire to keep Chaos the flasher that she met him as. Plus, she wasn't complaining.

"So, thou hast returned Sosruquo! Our rematch is upon us, this meager fog will not aid you! There shall be no quarter this time. I am Totrash: I am your doom!".

"And I'm the one who's going *to trash* you!!!" Chaos posed dramatically with his best "witty" retort.

Totrash swung his spear, but Chaos blocked it with his arm this time.

"No, you don't!" Chaos grinned before throwing a swift punch to counterattack.

Totrash leaned his head out of the way to dodge before pivoting so that his horse smashed into Chaos and made him stumble back. Totrash repeatedly swung his spear as Chaos skillfully dodged. To get some distance, he jumped back several times until he was more than 20 feet away.

Chaos fired two fiery beams from his eyes and quickly melted his opponent's head! Content in his attack, he put his hands on his hips and declared a premature victory with a haughty laugh.

"Be careful you idiot! He's a Monster, not a person! Destroying the head won't do anything, you need to hit the Core!" Norne screamed.

Chaos saw the reason for her urgency as while he was distracted, Totrash had begun charging at him with his spear pointed. Chaos caught the spear this time, but the force still saw him being pushed back as the horse charged at full speed.

"Nice try, but I'm not getting dressed again, again!" Chaos growled while pushing back.

Digging his heels in, Chaos stopped Totrash in his tracks and with his amazing strength even began pushing the horse back. However, Totrash's head reformed, just as it had after death.

"Nice try Sosruquo, but that won't work this time!" the Monster let out a ghastly roar as his starry eyes glowed as brightly as Chaos'.

"That's a new line." Norne noted that wasn't in the report.

The Monster's body began glowing as the flames of its Power spilled out from within the armor. This was its full Power and final form. Efficiency be damned, Totrash was pushing out all the Power it could to win! His lingering will was enraged and Hel bent at not dying again.

Totrash pulled Chaos in by yanking his spear back. As Chaos staggered forward, the Monster grabbed him by the face and rode away, slamming his head into the ground as he went! For miles and miles, he dragged Chaos along the ground, face first in the dirt!

Chaos growled angrily before tearing Totrash's arm off and leaping up at the Monster. Totrash thrust his spear at Chaos' face, but the Emperor smirked and swiftly dashed to the side at his real target. In a flash, Chaos killed Totrash's horse with a mighty punch that blasted its head off!

"Ha! Like they say: if you want to kill a general, use some force!" Chaos misquoted the adage confidently.

However, since it was just another part of the Monster and not a real equestrian companion, the headless "horse" stood up on its hind legs and began repeatedly punching Chaos in the face with its hooves.

After taking enough of a beating, Chaos grabbed both hooves to stop the attack. The horse just jumped up and double kicked him in the stomach which sent him flying. Chaos clutched his stomach in pain and angrily glared at his enemy with red eyes.

"My mistake was only melting the head... I'll make sure there's nothing left!" Chaos yelled.

Totrash rode forward with his spear pointed at Chaos again as he built power for his final attack. A flash of his flaming eyes scorched the landscape! The armor of Totrash's last victims vaporized. Totrash began to vaporize and come apart as well, but nonetheless remained determined and uncompromising in his charge towards the enemy.

Chaos saw that his foe was still in one piece and so turned up the heat quite literally as he flashed a bit more of his seemingly endless Power. Totrash began to expire at a faster rate but nonetheless continued his charge.

At the moment of truth, Chaos dodged the spear thrust and leapt forth to punch through his enemy!

"Piglet." Totrash heard the voice of his previous killer.

That and that: that was that. The Core of Totrash was blasted out of his undead body and fell to the ground. Chaos tore his fist out of the Monster's body as he finally wasted away and scattered into atomic dust and pure Power.

Norne bent down and picked up the cracked Adamant Core of the Monster.

"Victory!!!" Chaos threw his hands into the air excitedly.

"Complete failure!" Norne yelled at him.

"But why?" Chaos asked.

As they arrived on Uruk for the wedding Chaos was still pouting as Norne lectured him about it.

Uruk was the planet Grak was granted regency over as a reward for his service to Sargon. It was as beautiful as the capital, perhaps even more so. Many almost considered it a second capital especially due to its religious significance in connection to the first prince Grak.

It was the seat of power in the unofficial region of Lower Mesos which Grak governed. The regions that Sargon ruled were unofficially referred to as Upper Mesos and were the heartland of Mesos that survived the last collapse of the Empire. By contrast Lower Mesos was the collection of worlds that Grak had reconquered in the name of the stay-at-home Lugal. The two regions were almost equal in size now and with a wealthier capital of Uruk, many felt that Lower Mesos should have been on top instead.

However, detractors despised Lower Mesos' so-called backward views, such as outlawing slavery within all areas under Grak's administration.

As Chaos and Norne approached the front door, an announcer formally declared their arrival to the others.

"Norne!' Cyrus, who was walking nearby with Grak called out and waved.

"Princess Cyrus, Prince Grak. Congratulations on the upcoming wedding, your highness," Norne said respectfully.

"Thank you for attending, Princess Norne and Emperor Chaos," Grak replied.

"We arrived early it seems. What are we to do?" Norne inquired.

"Go and get ready. The wedding is tomorrow. Tonight, we celebrate! Chaos, you're coming with the boys and me for a bachelor night," Grak announced.

"Hel yeah!" Chaos shouted, in excitement.

"And Lady Norne, Princess Cyrus has invited you to join her at Lady Atosa's bachelorette party.

"Bachelorette party?" Norne, the anti-socialite groaned.

That evening, Norne found herself in the royal dressing room as Queen Atosa was being put into her elaborate wedding wear. They were already calling her Queen on Uruk.

"Great—girl talk all night. The kind of mindless dribble talking about *boys* or *fashion* or whatever that Heidi indulges in. Kill me now," Norne silently seethed while looking around the room.

Surprisingly, the only women even in attendance were Norne, Cyrus, Aurelia, and Atosa herself. The women brought as dates by the other guests weren't really her friends, so instead of leaving them at the bachelorette party, the royals had them left in their quarters like objects not in use. Truth be told, Atosa was not even friends with all of those in attendance at her party.

Grak had recently helped her get closer to Aurelia after their relationship became more public. But that wasn't much of a conversation starter, especially considering Norne's obvious dislike of Aurelia, Aurelia's dislike of Norne, and her usual conversations with Cyrus being of no interest to either of them. Atosa was stuck knowing each of them well enough individually but at an impasse concerning group activities.

Norne was bored to death, the only one there she even cared about was Cyrus. It was horribly awkward. A professional hairdresser, Aisha Bechdel was performing the several hour-long hair preps for Atosa's wedding attire.

"Such an overly elaborate wedding preparation. She just got up and is going to be preparing from now until she goes to say her vows," Norne thought as she vindictively stared at her as if on instinct hating the beautifying process reminiscent of Heidi's daily routine.

Aurelia had an equal lack of interest and instead spent her time petting Cyrus' hair like her star pet kitten. Atosa felt really awkward, getting dressed up with people she only tangentially knew silently surrounding her. None of the girls really got along with anyone other than Cyrus.

The bachelorette party was a long awkward silence until Cyrus suddenly smiled.

"So, Princess Atosa. Now we can be real sisters. As the shame of the family, I never got to do much but what's the first thing you're going to do with your newfound power?" she excitedly asked to strike up a conversation. This caught Norne and Aurelia's attention as well.

"Oh. Well within my authority of course—I want to help everyone from the back on Mesos and around the whole kingdom too! With the new authority I get, maybe I can make the difference I have always dreamed of. Having come from nothing, I can sympathize with them and maybe be the difference I was always looking for!" Atosa declared triumphantly.

Norne and Aurelia both rolled their eyes, their interest was betrayed.

"Aurelia, I can't see, but I can almost feel you rolling your eyes." Cyrus giggled.

"Oh no! It's not mocking. I just would do something different," Aurelia said quickly, not wanting to upset her.

"Well, what did you do with your new power Aurelia? Any tips for Atosa?" Cyrus asked.

"The first order of business is always securing the nation," Aurelia offered. "The extent of that national territory is connected to the security of the nation. Fringe tribes of the un-loyal must be—assimilated. Furthermore, the consolidation of power over territories requires the—replacement of any administrators who are not loyal to you. To ensure the nation can run smoothly, your own safety is priority. National security is your own security. Your enemies, the state's," she thundered, going into her rallying cry speech mode.

Cyrus clapped excitedly.

"Wow! You're even better than before. Are you sure I can't come to your next rally! You're so cool when you get all passionate like that." Cyrus beamed.

"Afraid not, *Topolina*. At such serious events, some topics come up that are—too mature for you." She went back to petting Cyrus like a child.

"Aw. Don't forget, I'm a grown-up now." Cyrus pouted like a child at the patronizing response.

"Too mature?" Norne scoffed at Aurelia's wording.

Aurelia was irritated but suddenly gave a mischievous grin.

"What about you, Norne? Any advice for our soon-to-be royal?" Aurelia asked.

"Basically, the same as you said. But I'm not afraid to be blunt. To secure your administration, execute any opposition. The entirety of the previous administration is a good place to start. Whoever might have it out for you or is holding loyalties that compromise your dominance of the government. Honestly, you can never be overly cautious. Some admittedly reckless executions on my part ended up saving Cyrus' life just the other day with that whole cult situation." She shrugged.

"How many people had to die?" Cyrus asked worriedly.

Norne only burst out laughing. The bone-chilling cackle made the hairdresser stop her work as her own hairs stood up on end. Not a single soul remained alive in the Cult of Typhon.

"Don't worry about it. But in Atosa's case, I'd suggest focusing on the old nobility-obsessed puritans in positions of power who would have it out for you as a principle. In a situation like that, it's them or you," Norne casually advised while looking at her nails.

Aurelia pulled Cyrus closer to her, or rather, further away from Norne.

"What? At least I'm being honest with her. She's right, there's no use treating her like a child here to melt our hearts." Norne laughed.

There was an awkward silence. Norne grinned, eager to take revenge for how she had been increasingly on the losing end of any discussion or debate with Cyrus. Finally, she had asserted dominance again and could feel at peace that she was better than the Princess of Mesos.

"Wow Norne, you're really intent on making it as hard as possible to bring out the good in you. Oh well, when it comes to melting your heart, I guess I'll just need to burn as hot as the sun to melt the ice, so to speak." Cyrus grinned optimistically.

Norne gasped. She was almost disturbed that Cyrus was still unphased.

"Don't worry girls, as weird as it may sound, flaws and all, you're the best friends I could've asked for. I'm working with what I have so no need to pretend for me." Cyrus smiled.

Now both Aurelia and Norne felt a strange sense of unease from her unrelenting positivity. They stayed and chatted, but the two were forevermore on guard around the innocent, idealistic princess.

Since Grak was busy entertaining guests and Atosa had to be up all night for the rest of the wedding prep, Aurelia took Cyrus to bed in her new room in Grak's palace.

Helping the Mesos princess into bed, Aurelia lovingly pulled the blanket up to tuck her in. Cyrus was taller than Aurelia, but that childhood protectiveness was still there.

"Good night, *Topolina*. I'll wake you up to get ready for the wedding tomorrow." Aurelia grinned.

"Fine, but I don't need to be tucked in, geez." Cyrus yawned.

Aurelia smiled. All she could remember was a 6-year-old Cyrus protesting much the same at one of their childhood sleepovers.

"You are an adult, but you will always be my baby sister, Cyrus. Blood-related or otherwise," she declared.

Cyrus paused for a second.

"Aurelia…you're a wonderful person to those you love. You mean a lot to Grak and I too. You're always so kind and devoted and I've always looked up to that—" Cyrus began.

Aurelia was beaming as she couldn't help but smile.

"But—" Cyrus continued, "I wish everyone else could see how loving you can be. Aurelia, why can't you show them? Why isn't the Aurelia I know, the one that everyone else talks about?

Why is my sister known to others as *The Dictator*?" Cyrus held back tears.

"Cyrus," Aurelia said, beginning to panic.

"Norne is right. You have to stop babying me! I know what life has been like in Italia under this new regime." Her voice trembled.

"What I do, I do for the good of my Empire. Trust me…it is the burden of ruling. It's just the way things are, I'm afraid." Aurelia used her patronizing 'big sister' voice.

"Grak and I don't always see eye-to-eye on how he does things…but none of his men are driven mad by the voices of the women and children they'd been ordered to massacre." Cyrus wasn't having it.

After a few seconds of silence, Aurelia sighed.

"I stand by my answer. I would never lie to you," Aurelia reassured her.

"Lying by exclusion is still lying," Cyrus commented.

"Well… I'll be more upfront from now on. You may not like it, but everything Norne said back there was true. That is just a part of running an Empire," Aurelia responded coldly.

"Would you still be so okay if it was me they killed? Many other people had sisters they cared about, blood-related or other-wise. Other people live and love just like we do. They also tend to have empathy." Cyrus tensed up.

"Don't even say that as a joke! I will always protect you—that I swear! If they aren't strong enough to even protect what they care about, then perhaps they didn't deserve to have it at all. Love is a luxury for those who can protect what they care for." Aurelia stood up and walked to the door.

Cyrus paused.

"What happened to you? When we were kids, I know you saw things the way I do. If you don't lie, then remember you used to agree with me back then! You and Grak both were the only ones who listened to me. Why did you go back on everything we agreed on?" Cyrus cried.

"Because I grew up." Aurelia hissed through gritted teeth.

"But—" Cyrus began.

"Good night, Cyrus. See you at the wedding tomorrow," Aurelia said quickly before exiting.

She loved Cyrus but hated how a person so weak could be so confrontational when she wanted. She didn't have Power backing her up, instead she had the ironclad belief that she was addressing someone who was wrong. Against anyone who talked with their fists, she was the most dangerous type of person.

Cyrus sat up and wiped her eyes. After letting out a sigh, through force of will, she got her smile back.

"She's gone now. If you insist on tucking me in too, now is the time." Cyrus smirked.

Norne was silently sitting in the window as the cool night air flowed into the room.

"Given how you were abducted from just such a window in the past, you'd think Grak would have gotten better security," Norne remarked, scoffing.

"There you are. You're so quiet I almost didn't hear you." Cyrus turned her head to face Norne.

"Like Hel I was going to let her get the last word in," Norne retorted, still sitting in the window.

"Yeah, but now I can't help but imagine you jumping around doing acrobatics outside to get in here just to one-up Aurelia." Cyrus giggled.

"Whatever. You really laid into her there," Norne said, immediately changing the subject.

"She can be just like Grak sometimes. But it's more troublesome here. I guess she found my way of thinking didn't line up with claiming the power she wanted." Cyrus sighed.

"Well, I guess she's smarter than I thought." Norne laughed as she jumped down from the window and sat on Cyrus' night table next to her bed.

"Figures you'd say that. Heck, you're worse than either of them in that regard." Cyrus laughed.

"Why thank you," Norne smirked.

"Ruling that way, you all do some pretty messed up stuff. And then you laugh with family and friends without a care in the world. How do you do it—why do you do it?" Cyrus asked.

"It's only messed up for people with weak stomachs." Norne shrugged.

Cyrus paused.

"Hey Norne…all nations have problems with pirates, right?" Cyrus asked.

"Oh! Don't get me started! The manpower I have to expend guarding ports and securing—UGH! You lose more money to those cretons than any of the worst of Drakon's stooges."

"The enemy of humanity. That's what people call them," Cyrus responded.

"Yeah, and what of it? As long as there is distance between destinations, there is room to have resources stolen. What? Are you going to try and sell me on how pirates deserve respect now?" Norne rolled her eyes.

"Nope. I don't like pirates at all. No one likes a bully. That's why the general public doesn't like them," Cyrus began.

"Well, that, and the anti-pirate messaging every government is sure to push. Their reputation as the enemy of humanity is the successful outcome," Norne agreed.

"Nations can't agree on anything but are all united in hating pirates. It's a bit impressive. But you may be overestimating the success and even necessity of your propaganda campaign," Cyrus pointed out. "In the far reaches of any Empire, you're liable to find some undefended civilian areas being dominated by these gangs. Anyone whose had a run-in with them will be sure to end up hating pirates all on their own. And not for the economic reasons that rulers do."

"And… I assume you're going somewhere with this." Norne raised an eyebrow.

"Well, Empires often employ pirates and other nonstate powers to do their bidding. You can call them privateers or nonstate actors or whatever you want but using pirates like that is an age-old tactic to strike at enemies and keep from blame. So, in reality, Empires have nothing wrong with pirates as long as they plunder the 'right people.' Put yourself in the shoes of the regular Tartarian. We know why *you* hate pirates but why do they?" Cyrus asked.

"I don't know what peasants think about. I can't imagine their pea brains have anything of value to offer though." Norne shrugged.

"Well people talk about them as being thugs, thieves, and murderers. When they don't destroy and plunder ships that don't fly their flag, they pillage towns and enslave their enemies, they take all resources of value from people and use them for their own purposes in ways that only ever negatively affect people who have the misfortune of not being affiliated with them. 'Pirate nations' are nothing but colonies of open season targets for those villains," Cyrus said angrily.

"Pirate nation. That's oxymoronic. What arrogance, thuggish pirates thinking they can rule over nations. No wonder everyone hates them, you're right." Norne chuckled.

"I never said *everyone* hates them. I've also talked with people…who like pirates. They say they preferred their tyranny to the tyranny of the Mesos government. I had to reassure them that things would be different, but honestly, I had a tough time finding ways in which my father's Empire was any different from the rule of pirates. So, help me out Norne—in what way are Emperors different than Pirates?" Cyrus asked.

"What a stupid question. Pirates are criminals. Everything an Empire does is legal." Norne dismissed the question.

"Everything a pirate does is legal according to their laws. Pirates have constitutions and they enforce them as strictly as any state. So, what's the difference between a pirate and an Emperor?" Cyrus asked again.

"I already answered your question." Norne sighed.

"Well put a different way, why is a pirate a criminal for crossing the stars in a ship and using Power to terrorize people? Meanwhile, you command a great fleet of ships that do the same thing. A pirate plunders ports and ships, but Empires plunder the whole Universe. When you get down to it, it's just a matter of scale," Cyrus explained.

"Are you calling me a pirate?" Norne raised an eyebrow.

"Nope. It's a matter of scale—you're an Empress," Cyrus responded.

"Exactly. We invade areas within our jurisdiction. If it isn't within our own borders, it is in areas agreed to with the international community." Norne shrugged.

"Pirates only attack within their 'territory.' They have systems of marking out turf with other factions," Cyrus pointed out.

"But that's different," Norne quickly said.

"Why?" Cyrus asked.

"Because." Norne responded.

"Why is it different just because of the number of ships you use, or how strong the commander is, or how good your PR spin is?" Cyrus persisted.

"Because!" Norne cried.

"Because what?" Cyrus asked.

"Because they're different. This is insanity. By far your stupidest idea yet." Norne crossed her arms.

"I thought you were here to one-up Aurelia. At least she had a response to my questions. Insults aren't points," Cyrus insisted.

"Whatever. It's late, and I won't have you blaming me for being tired tomorrow. So go to sleep." Norne sighed.

"Wow, nice exit strategy. Just be sure to ask the next pirate you catch what the difference between you is." Cyrus giggled.

 JAIDEN BAYNES

"Good night." Norne groaned before jumping out the window. Another loss—or rather a lack of victory to compound Norne's growing frustration.

Cyrus waved at her, but as she lay back down, she was troubled. She had no Power. All she could do was try to win people over with words. Despite how confidently she consulted with Norne, Grak was right, the former was much easier. However, Cyrus was hopeful and so she dreamed of a future world. Norne and Aurelia didn't need to agree with her, even Grak didn't fully. Cyrus just hoped that they would stop being *pirates writ large*. So, Cyrus and the girls slept peacefully meanwhile on the male side of things, everyone but Chaos had hangovers all around.

The next morning, the boys were guzzling jugs of water. The Adamant in the wine ensured a mighty hangover. Grak spent the entire morning, walking around in bafflement as everyone would snicker at him. In exchange for little to no hangover, by a twist of fate he alone had forgotten everything from last night.

"Grak, I had you all wrong. You're the man." Chaos gave him an emphatic thumbs-up as he walked past the busy body with more food he had recently raided from the kitchen. Like all poisons alcohol had no effect on him, so Chaos was as high energy as everywhere.

"Thanks?" Grak responded but was even more confused.

However, that was the least of his worries. He had the list from Atosa's father of *everything* he'd been recording about his daughter's ideal marriage since she was a child and he'd only filled in two thirds of the requirements with limited time left.

In truth, as an adult Atosa would have never demanded so much, but Grak was insistent on going above and beyond to make it was a day she'd never forget. Final preparations were underway and Grak was scrambling to ensure that everything was perfect for Atosa's dream wedding.

Grak was so frazzled looking down at the list that he didn't even notice the door opening. It nearly hit him in the face. Coming through it was Kourosh, his soon to be father-in-law. He stood up straight, saluting his inferior officer.

"The preparations for the wedding are on schedule sir! All the valuable intel you provided me has been implemented to ensure this is a day Atosa will never forget!" Grak reported.

"Right?" Kourosh didn't quite know how to respond.

"Well…to be honest there are a few more things to prepare for but I assure you everything will be in place by the time you walk her down the aisle!" Grak promised.

"Good…work? I brought the bread for the meal if that helps." Kourosh for all his usual bluster felt odd with Grak actually grovelling at his feet.

"Of course! I'll have it set up for the wedding feast." Grak took the bagged, freshly baked loaves from his hands.

"I'm glad you're getting so into things, but you shouldn't worry about 'perfection.'" Kourosh offered. "I know my daughter, and Atosa truly loves you. She'd be just as happy getting married out on the streets or in a stable or not at all—just as long as she could be with you." He couldn't help but smile.

"I am honored that you think so." Grak smiled back genuinely.

"Not just think so, I know so. But, instead of all that… shouldn't we be worried about what comes after?" Kourosh asked, becoming more serious.

"All the preparations have been made. For you and your daughter. Enjoy the day. Leave the messiness to me," Grak responded.

"But Prince, I have fought by your side from the start! It would be an honour to help put the right man on the throne of Mesos!" Kourosh saluted his prince.

"I understand, but instead I have to insist that you have an even more important duty. When I go to do what must be done—I can only do that if I know Cyrus and Atosa are safe. I leave their safety to you since you are the only one I can trust with such an important job, father." Grak placed his hand on Kourosh's shoulder seriously.

"I understand." Kourosh nodded. "Give 'em hell, Your Majesty."

"Of course. I will make a world where Atosa can be happy, I swear on my life," Grak proclaimed.

In the royal bedroom, the hours-long wedding prep was nearly complete. Atosa stood uncomfortably holding a pose that allowed the attendants to fasten all the bells and whistles and priceless jewelry that her royal wedding dress was outfitted with. Sleeping nearby, Cyrus was already in her fancy, wedding day attire. She was sure to be up early enough to keep Atosa company, but her overzealousness left her too tired to stay awake for the whole outfitting.

Atosa let her rest though, smiling at the sleeping princess curled up on the couch with her pet dog. As Atosa lovingly looked down on the girl she had basically raised, the door opened, and her own father entered.

"Wow, you look even more amazing than usual," Kourosh complimented, walking over.

"I hope so…all this time would hopefully be worth it then." Atosa grinned.

"Well, the future queen of Mesos needs to make a good first impression, right?" Kourosh smirked.

"I suppose," Atosa said, at first excitedly but then her countenance fell.

"I'm so happy you're here today. And… Cyrus was excited to have her father here today as well. She still has no idea," Atosa said sadly.

Kourosh sighed. "I'm sure she's still holding out hope. But that's why we're here to protect her from a beast like him." He looked down at the dreaming princess.

There was no need to be subtle around the crew working on Atosa. They knew what was coming and they anticipated it.

Everyone was waiting for Grak to kill Sargon, everyone was hoping for it. All except Cyrus.

"But hey, you and Grak were more like parents to her than he ever was. Just make sure this union of families can heal whatever sadness she may feel because of...what needs to be done," Kourosh said.

Kourosh stood next to Atosa and saw why she had been positioned here to wait out the dressing. Centre stage on the balcony view they faced houses that were being built for the poor according to Atosa's designs and Grak's policy. Mesos' choice of ruler was obvious and what came today was just a formality. Kourosh, like many of the people supported everything taking place wholeheartedly.

As if on cue, he arrived. Sargon of Akkad entered the Uruk palace with everyone's eyes on him. The palace fell silent as everyone watched him walk over to Grak.

"Hello, father." Grak saluted him.

"I'm here as requested so can we get this over with. I'm not made of spare time you know." Sargon scoffed.

"Of course. Take your seat in the temple and the ceremony will begin soon." Grak bowed.

Sargon walked over to take his seat but as he passed Chaos, he stopped. Standing directly across from Chaos, the two locked eyes, being about the same height.

"What? Like what you see, old man?" Chaos chuckled.

"Chaos!" Grak panicked.

"Insolent child. I can tell from those eyes alone—you are Typhon's son. How annoying," Sargon said, coldly assessing Chaos.

"Pfft. How'd such a crusty old fart end up having such a hot daughter?" Chaos sighed.

"Chaos!" Norne impatiently looked back at him.

"Huh?" Chaos was confused.

"My warning from back when she visited us still stands." She stared daggers directly into his eyes.

"What? That 'catracing'? What was that even about?" Chaos asked into Norne's cold, dead, and borderline murderous eyes.

Shortly after, Chaos and Norne entered the wedding hall with Chaos looking like a terrified puppy.

"What happened to the big guy?" Aurelia asked and noticed Chaos' expression.

"Don't mind him. Larger words just tend to hurt his brain a little." Norne innocently laughed.

"Well, hopefully, that means he'll behave himself for once. You're just in time, Atosa is coming down now," Aurelia explained.

They looked and coming down the stairs, being led by her father who was in full military garb came Atosa. She descended the stairs in a beautiful Mesos dress fit for a queen. Regal music played as she reached the bottom of the stairs and was handed from her father to Prince Grak so the two could head to the alter.

Chaos immediately snapped out of his trance of terror and began drooling over her. Norne growled angrily.

Atosa's father handed his daughter off as Cyrus handed her older brother to meet her. The two lovers exchanged vows and after the rites and rituals, embraced before a cheering crowd.

Chaos whooped along with everyone else's genuine congratulations. Norne simply grumbled to herself and looked around. To her surprise, Sargon of Akkad was also not entertained by this development. While Norne was looking at him though, Sargon looked back at her. Panicking, she tried to look like she was clapping and cheering for the happy couple, worrying Sargon would keep looking at her.

The wedding feast came shortly after. Things moved very quickly. Around the room were stands set up with fancy assortments of delicacies from around the Universe for all the guests to enjoy. All guests in attendance sat at satellite tables but surprisingly, Norne had a seat right next to Cyrus, who was sitting directly beside Grak.

The whole time, Norne could feel the eyes of the guests on her and felt horribly uncomfortable.

"What were they thinking?" she thought to herself as she began sweating.

To get away, she did the unthinkable and asked, "does anyone need any drinks or something?"

Everyone froze in surprise.

"Wh—what! Is there something on my face?" Norne asked, worried by their reaction.

"Are you drunk already Norne? Or sick or something? You never ask other people for stuff." Chaos put his hand on her forehead to check.

"Forget it then. I was trying to be a good guest. I'll be back." Norne slapped his hand away and got up to go get food.

Standing by a food stand so that a plant hide her from view, Norne took out a book she had concealed earlier, *Who were the Star People,* with a mischievous grin.

"These stupid celebrations are going to go on forever, but at least I can have some fun," she thought to herself.

"A glorified potluck filled with the stench of peasants—only the boy would think of that," a deep voice groaned behind her. Norne panicked and slowly turned around, only to see Sargon.

"Lugal Sargon of Akkad—I didn't see you there." Norne nervously laughed.

"Of course, just as they intended, I'm sure. My son invites me to his wedding and gives me a side table while you get to sit with him." Sargon looked down at her.

"We can exchange seats if you'd like," Norne suggested.

"No. I'm just here to eat and depart. Assuming the food isn't poisoned." He glared at Norne.

"What!" Norne began to sweat.

"Well, the attempt on my life—when will it be?" Sargon asked.

Norne froze, she wasn't expecting direct confrontation.

"First Emperor, whatever do you mean by that? We're all just here to have a good time." Norne slyly grinned since the time to strike was not yet here.

"This always happens. The boy gets too greedy for his station. Be it from infantile altruism, envy of my Power, or whatever, it always happens around the peak of their careers. I've been killing rebel sons all my life, and I think I've gotten quite good at it," Sargon explained.

"Very impressive," Norne said. "You know, it's lonely at the top. That's why it is best to work together. We could be great allies." She smiled.

"I am not a fool, despite what my son would believe. Insolent child, I conquered this Universe countless times before, I don't need you, to do it again. Come back when you are more interesting as a challenge to pass my boredom," Sargon said.

"Conquered the whole Universe? Surely even if you can be believed, you know that we aren't cavemen anymore." Norne smirked.

"True…but none of you were worth the waiting for re-conquering my Empire. Every time it grows, I let it collapse, see which new enemies can emerge in time, but Typhon—he told me of lands beyond Eurasia and my daughter in her foolish transmissions confirmed them. When I next begin the destruction of the Universe, I intend to go to Typhon's kingdom and test if they are of the same stock as their ruler." Sargon grinned.

"You're an interesting man, First Emperor. I anticipate setting up a playdate for you and my Emperor Chaos. I think you two will find each other's company enjoyable." She grinned.

"We will see. He shall be my warmup for my conquest." Sargon dismissed Norne.

Norne left, panicking. Should she tell Grak that the jig was up? Or should she jump ship and try to ally with Sargon. Her mind was racing but something else, even more, pressing caught her attention.

When Norne returned from talking to Sargon, she saw Chaos hitting on Cyrus who giggled at his weirdness. Norne was furious and began stamping over there.

"Now listen, I don't normally go for egg-head types, but between you, the bride, and the Italic chick there's too much babe energy for me to not try something. I know you can't see but trust me I'm quite the looker." Chaos winked at her.

Cyrus did her best not to but ultimately burst out laughing at the comment. Used to either the indignation of Aurelia or the fawning compliance of his usual mistresses, Chaos didn't ever expect this response and was totally confused.

"Are you mocking me? I'll have you know I've gotten *way hotter* girls than you, so I'm doing *you* a favor." Chaos said defensively.

"Apologies Your Majesty, I meant no disrespect, it's just that you and Norne really do make an unusual duo is all." Cyrus smiled while wiping away tears from her intense laughter.

"Oh. Well, whatever, they're out of food so wanna get out of this place and—" Chaos began but Cyrus interrupted.

"Sorry, Emperor Chaos but I can't do that. 'Sisters before misters.' It wouldn't be very supportive if I stole her man away from her." She smiled innocently.

"Stole her man? Who are you talking about?" Chaos asked in dense confusion.

"Snip, snip," Norne menacingly whispered while standing right behind Chaos and doing a scissors motion with her fingers.

She was right behind him, and he didn't know how much of that she had heard.

"Norne! Didn't see you there!" Chaos physically jumped in terror after seeing her furious expression and remembering her threats.

"Oh look, something over there!" Chaos panicked and ran away.

Norne let out a sigh of relief.

"So, you've met father?" Cyrus asked.

"Yes. Are you the one who told him?" Norne got to the point.

"Of course not. I want everyone to live, not to save him by ensuring my brother's death. Which reminds me—it's been years Norne and, you haven't even been trying to stop Grak have you?" Cyrus asked.

"Why would I? We are killing Sargon. Deal with it." Norne growled.

"I figured as much. Thanks for trying at least." Cyrus held back tears.

"No! I was never trying *anything*. I tricked you. I've been manipulating you this whole time!" Norne began losing her patience.

"I know. But you were a good friend." Cyrus smiled.

"Friends! I was using you! Your childish games of trying to control me backfired! You don't have *any* power over me!" Norne shouted, surprising Cyrus.

"Oh. That's what it is. You're right I don't. Only you can decide to do the right thing." Cyrus replied.

Norne stormed off. As Norne left, Cyrus broke down into tears.

The party wound down as everyone, but Grak and the other royals remained with Atosa and Cyrus.

Slowly the regular guests left as the evening went on. Sargon was escorted out by his guards and looked back skeptically as only Grak, and his inner circle remained.

"Ladies and gentlemen, thank you for assembling today. To new beginnings!" Grak raised a glass to a double meaning.

"To new beginnings!" everyone toasted back.

There was much eating and merriment to be had, but when it reached midnight, Grak turned to Atosa.

"My Queen, please take Cyrus to her bed, she needs her rest." Grak kissed her hand romantically.

"Of course." Atosa nodded and went over to Cyrus.

"It's time for bed princess." Atosa smiled and took Cyrus' hand.

Atosa left with Cyrus as Kourosh received the pair and escorted them out.

"Ladies and gentlemen, it is time. Tonight, Sargon of Akkad dies." Grak declared, suddenly becoming deadly serious.

Everyone else followed suit, with a palpable tension filling the room.

"His ship should be returning to Mesos now. But he's deep in my territory. I know his route and we will intercept him. Sargon is mighty but he cannot fight us all. Chaos and Norne—you lead the charge as a diversion and the rest of us ambush him in a pincer attack. With our strength combined, he will fall before he even gets a chance to fight back!" Grak dramatically rallied them.

Everyone cheered.

"Wait—we lead the charge? I wasn't informed of this," Norne noted.

"Your pet monster has proven himself more durable than any of us. He's a safe bet to take Sargon's opening attack, allowing us to ambush him once he's off-balance. It's that simple," Aurelia explained.

"I see." Norne skeptically agreed.

"Now! Let us go and seize what is ours!" Grak declared.

The others cheered but Chaos annoyed that Grak was the clear leader and people weren't fawning over him decided to make a scene.

"Alright! Let's mosey!" Chaos tried to be as impressive in his declaration, but only managed to kill the mood.

"Did—did I do well?" Chaos asked Norne, noticing his propensity for dramatic speeches was severely lacking, especially next to the charismatic Grak. "Norne?" Chaos asked after Norne abstained from commenting.

"I don't know you." Norne hid her face in embarrassment, while all eyes were now on them.

Nonetheless, the time had come. The nobles embarked to carry out the plan and finish ushering in the new generation of great powers.

They had gone, but as Kourosh led Atosa and Cyrus to the dining room to distract them with some fun, Cyrus paused.

"Who's there?" she asked and turned around.

"A friend—with a message. Princess Cyrus, there's something you'd probably want to know," a mysterious voice responded as they approached the naïve princess.

CHAPTER 19

After the wedding, Sargon sat on his flagship to fly back to Upper Mesos. This wasn't a mere slave-drawn carriage, it was a bronze age warship. Instead of being pulled by slaves, it operated on devices called slave-generators—chambers that directed the Power of dozens of enslaved people into propulsive forces out the back of the ship, pushing it forward.

Just as always, Sargon lived off the power of others while giving nothing back in return. He just sat on his throne within the ship, thinking back to the good old days.

He remembered his past with the one who invented such a horrible system for him. But why was he thinking about her at a time like this? Sargon opened his eyes from his dream to look out the ship's front window. A smearing wall of blue light from the rapidly approaching stars was all he could see with his eyes.

Even with the combined strength of all these slaves his warship was moving at a snail's pace for the Lugal. With his own Power, he would've been home already.

But that was beneath an Emperor. Kings could walk just fine but carrying chairs such as palanquins, sedan chairs, and litter were a common invention of countless human cultures.

Sargon sat there, bored as he always was, looking ahead into the vastness of the territory he controlled when he suddenly noticed something.

It was moving far too fast, so the ship wasn't approaching it—it was flying at the ship. Sargon used his Power to get a better look and found Drakon of Chaos flying at him.

In the next moment, Chaos collided with the ship head-on and destroyed it. All Sargon's servants got caught up in the middle of this conflict and died instantly: they were scattered into atomic dust.

Sargon had blocked Chaos' attack when the giant came smashing through the front of his ship to punch him. Now the Lugal found himself standing in a crater in the middle of a deserted planet, surrounded by dozens of usurpers.

"I see—so the straightforward approach then." Sargon floated out of the crater and stared Grak down.

"It only makes sense when dealing with one as simple as you." Grak scoffed.

"Fine. Come to your slaughter! I'll kill all my enemies just as I did so long ago!" Sargon screamed as his Power burst forth. The many royals were shocked to find that Grak did not at all exaggerate his father's strength.

"Even if we all attacked him at once, a great many of us would die. I think it's only just now setting in for them." Norne smirked as she stayed calm.

"Well, that is why we brought him," Grak said as he sensed Chaos' Power approaching.

Chaos crashed down right in front of Sargon of Akkad. He stood up before the Lugal with a confident grin, unphased by his Power.

"Hey, there big guy. Time to die." Chaos stood up face to face with Sargon.

"So, the frontal decoy. Let me guess, my treacherous son and his allies will move to kill me the second I drop my guard to focus on you." Sargon looked around in annoyance.

However, when Sargon looked back at Chaos, he was surprised to see that instead of sneak attacking, Chaos had placed his open palm facing down at the top of his head before extending his arm out to measure the top of Sargon's head. At a time like this, during the epic final battle, Chaos was more concerned with who was taller. Words failed Sargon as Chaos compared and like a first grader was ecstatic to find that he was indeed one inch taller than Sargon of Akkad.

"Ha! How do you like that shorty! You like to talk, but small fries don't scare me!" Chaos chuckled and pointed at Sargon with an unbelievably childish expression.

"I am going to enjoy killing you." Sargon was incensed at Chaos' constant antics and made a fist.

"No, you." Chaos grinned as he Powered up to match Sargon.

This was the amazing level of strength he had displayed during the cult incident. Their clashing Power rocked the planet like forces of nature. The inhospitable world seemed like a paradise before these two monsters faced each other. As planned, Sargon was isolated on this remote rock without help or cover and there were no civilians to worry about. Norne figured this was in the bag. So did Grak.

In the next instant, Chaos smashed Sargon in the face with his full strength. The epic, planet-shattering punch made Sargon stumble back, but not fall. Norne was amazed when Sargon just laughed and in return, smashed Chaos in the face at full strength.

Chaos stumbled back and fell to his knees.

"Good. He knows his place." Sargon grinned, looking down on Chaos.

Chaos, however, began laughing insanely.

"Finally, an enemy worthy of my strength!" Chaos roared with joy, as he had fallen to his knees in excitement rather than fear.

Sargon gasped when in a flash, Chaos pounced at him, throwing a flurry of punches so fast they couldn't be seen by anyone else! Sargon Powered up, throwing his own punches to match. The epic clashes of might rocked the world they stood on and reverberated through the rippling muscles of both combatants.

The other usurpers took to the skies watching from a safe distance of several miles as the raw energy being thrown around made it too dangerous to even approach.

The explosive collision blew the observers back. Chaos and Sargon slid away from each other, both evenly matched. Both grinning. Chaos energetically charged headfirst at Sargon and threw a mighty right hook that made Sargon slide back. Sargon clutched his chest in pain. Chaos ran towards him again for another punch, but Sargon caught this one with his left hand. Throwing a swift punch with his right hand, Sargon cut Chaos' face as he barely dodged the attack.

"First blood!" Sargon laughed.

In response, Chaos smiled and opened wide to chomp on Sargon's left forearm. He bit through the bronze gauntlet protecting him, shattering it into pieces with his beast-like jaw strength. Sargon gasped as Chaos ferally sank his teeth into the king's arm.

Sargon snarled like a beast in his own right and kicked Chaos in the face to send him flying away. Still, Chaos took a chunk out of Sargon's arm with his fangs and spat it out, laughing like a wild man.

"Second blood," Chaos quipped as Sargon's rage built.

The two ran at each other before clashing once again. The calamities in human form shredded the surface of their planet-wide arena.

"It seems that sending Chaos in first was the right idea," Norne noted, watching the awesome display below.

"It does. The two of them are on a completely different level. Either one of them could probably conquer the whole Universe with that kind of Power." Grak looked at them both with disgust.

Norne was confused by his tone but nervously laughed.

"Of course, that's why it's a good thing he's on our side." Norne laughed.

"On your side," Aurelia cut her off.

Norne paused, seeing the fear on the others' faces.

"What are you talking about? We're all allies, there's no need to—" Norne began.

"We're allies to defeat Sargon. As soon as that uniting fact is gone, we'd be left with someone just as dangerous still roaming free." Grak stared Norne down.

"I don't think I like the implication of that. Come on, he's worn Sargon down enough, let's go help Chaos get the finishing blow!" Norne cried.

"Why? The two are both existential threats to our Power. It's best to just let them take each other out." Aurelia watched as Chaos and Sargon simultaneously punched each other in the face.

Norne was horrified to see everyone looking down at Chaos as being no different from Sargon.

"He is the spawn of Typhon—his mere existence upsets the balance of power!" one of the others cried.

"Once he kills Sargon, what's to say we aren't next?" his own 'friend' Wilhelm joined in.

The others agreed.

Norne gritted her teeth and slowly began building her own Power.

"I wouldn't if I were you." Grak menacingly looked down at her.

Norne stopped as she found herself surrounded, with Chaos indisposed.

"Cyrus likes you, so I'm giving you a choice. Leave that monster down there and we will let you live. You can continue to rule Tartarus, you can incorporate it into Arcosia, or you can find a new puppet. We don't care what you do, but Drakon of Chaos must die," Grak told Norne plainly.

"Damn you Grak! You turned them all against him!" Norne cried.

"Norne, decide. Are you with us or the beast? Are you in or are you out?" Grak yelled.

Norne shook in a silent rage.

"Chaos! They're backstabbing—" Norne began to mentally scream so Chaos could hear.

However, the second she turned to communicate, Grak pointed his scepter at her and fired a full Power blast! Norne was blasted out of the sky as Chaos looked up in horror.

"Never take your eyes off your opponent!" Sargon threw a punch, but Chaos dodged it by jumping up to go catch Norne.

Norne was barely holding onto consciousness as she fell into Chaos' arms.

"Norne! Norne! Are you alright?" Chaos panicked as he saw her injured state.

While Chaos fussed over his only true friend, however, Sargon rushed him and punched them both into the ground.

Chaos smashed into the ground and dropped Norne as he vomited up blood from the direct hit.

"Norne," Chaos groaned as he saw her lying on the ground, covered in blood.

Up above, Grak and the others all flew away at top speed. Sargon saw their retreat and began laughing.

"Well, well, well, isn't this interesting. The boy is a lot craftier than I thought. All the threats to his plans are now conveniently together and at each other's necks." Sargon roared with laughter.

Norne struggled to her feet as rage built inside of her. This mistake was uncharacteristic, even for her. But all these years she had made the mistake of gradually starting to trust Grak and his cohorts. However, she agreed with Sargon—this was a setup.

"He dared to deceive me?!" Norne was furious. It made sense, Grak feared both Sargon and Chaos so having them kill each other would be best for him. After all, humans were self-interested creatures.

Sargon of Akkad loomed over the injured Norne with an evil grin as she looked up at him with rage burning in her eyes.

"Sargon of Akkad! How about a truce like I offered you earlier? Let us go and teach that ingrate a lesson," she fumed.

"A truce? No. You two dared to attack the First Emperor. Your deaths shall be my warmup for killing Grak." Sargon cracked his knuckles.

"Damnit. Grak knew there'd be no talking him down once we engaged! I can't believe I fell for this! How could I have been so distracted that I didn't realize—" Norne began before suddenly getting a flash of Cyrus' smile.

Norne growled like a wild animal as her Power burst forth to its maximum.

"That puny amount of Power is supposed to scare me? No wonder you were so desperate for my aid. But unlike you pissants, I don't need help." Sargon made a fist.

"Be careful who you talk to, you old bastard!" Chaos threw a punch that sent Sargon flying away at ludicrous speeds.

"Don't worry Norne… I didn't intend on just backing down either. This Sargon guy looks like too much fun!" Chaos smiled at her while doing stretches.

Sargon regained control and landed on the ground only a few feet away despite Chaos' punch. Having finished stretching, Chaos began to casually stroll toward his opponent.

"You dare to approach the Immaculate Sargon of Akkad!" the ruler asked.

"Well, I can't exactly punch you from over here, can I?" Chaos grinned.

"Is it bravery or stupidity with you youngsters? I really can't tell. Back in my day, brats had respect for their elders. Now they openly defy me and wish to do battle? This Universe was in more dire need of resetting than I feared." Sargon chuckled and shook his head, monologuing as Chaos approached him.

"Whatever. Norne, now that the others are gone, I can go all out, right?" Chaos asked.

"What!" Sargon was baffled.

"Let him have it! Give him everything you've got so we can go kill those traitors!" Norne screamed.

Chaos smiled.

Without a moment of hesitation, he began screaming at the top of his lungs as he forced all his Power out at once. It was like exercising an atrophied muscle. He'd never had a fight where he had to go all out in his entire life. Except of course against his partner in crime, Norne.

Sargon was taken aback, being pushed away just by the Power coming off Chaos! He growled, he too was holding back to reserve strength, but now it seemed more prudent to give it his all and end this quickly.

He released his maximum Power as well, but it was like a candle in the wind next to the amazing energy being put out by Chaos.

Sargon of Akkad was in disbelief. Chaos was even stronger than him.

Chaos yelled at the top of his lungs and punched Sargon in the face at full strength, breaking his nose and knocking him to the ground!

Sargon pulled himself up and wiped the blood away, but Chaos slammed his fist into Sargon's jaw. A left hook, then a right, and an uppercut to keep him dazed. Sargon tried and failed to counterattack with punches of his own, but Chaos simply continued wailing on him.

A punch directly to the stomach had Sargon vomit up blood and fly away into a raised area of the celestial body, obliterating it from his sheer momentum. Sargon was embedded into the rock, coughing violently. When he looked up, Chaos had already flown over and condescendingly grinned at him.

"Grak hyped you up a lot, but I can tell you haven't had a good fight in years. Out of shape old-timer?" Chaos grinned.

Sargon moved to attack, but Chaos simply kicked him in the chest which sent him flying into the planet's moon, destroying it. Within moments, Sargon furiously flew back to counterattack, but Chaos easily blocked him.

"I never get to go all out on most jobs…but fighting Norne keeps me more than in shape. She doesn't have your brute strength, but it still requires me to give my all and grow even more powerful! Unlike you, I'm not a poser." Chaos grinned.

"In my day, I slaughtered entire armies! No one *could* challenge me!" Sargon screamed.

The two exchanged vicious punches to vital areas all over the body. No fancy techniques, abilities, or strategies—the two berserkers simply went all out in a head-on fistfight.

"A Power, rivaling *mine*!" Sargon couldn't help but think excitedly.

Sargon and Chaos were both floored at finally being able to go all out.

However, after one of the many times their fists clashed, Sargon got a strange feeling.

"Amazing! I have always wanted to be evenly matched—I—I *wanted* my Power challenged." He began to waver, realizing perhaps the 'pursuit' of a rival was a front for perpetually picking on those beneath him.

With pain in his fists, for the first time in years, Sargon quickly felt fear. He had felt this fear only once before.

Twenty years ago, Sargon had entered the Tartarian palace, looking around in the throne room. It was empty, at least in terms of people. Otherwise, stacks of books piled up several feet high all over the room.

"Down the hall," a mysterious voice told Sargon.

When Sargon looked around, however, he felt an odd sensation as the world around him seemed to be distorted.

"You're taking too long." The mysterious voice sighed.

Sargon gasped, as he found himself right in front of the door to the royal library, several halls and floors away from where he started. The doors opened themselves from the inside to the darkened and messy room.

An ever-confident Sargon entered the room and looked around but still saw no one.

"Books—scrolls bound with a spine for ease of use. Such a wonderful invention. Rolling up the longer scrolls without crumpling was always a huge pain. But I'm sure you remember that," a shadowed man said while walking towards a bookshelf with a large space chartbook open.

"Who are you?" Sargon asked in annoyance.

"You are Sargon of Akkad. It is nice to meet a fellow first-generation," the man concealed by shadow greeted him. Instead of turning, he began casually walking up the bookshelf walls with the book open.

"So, the rumors are true, Drakon abdicated?" Sargon asked while looking at the sideways man.

"Yes. Don't worry, your main competition is no longer in the picture for your—reconquests," the man said patronizingly.

Sargon was confused, watching the man bend down and place the book back on the top shelf before walking back down and emerging from shadows in the nude while reaching for another shelf.

"Really?" Sargon asked.

"Oh, that's right... I forgot I had guests." The man grinned before gaining black pants as if out of nowhere. He immediately pulled another book from the shelf and cracked it open to read.

"Again, I ask who you are. Or does it even matter?" Sargon asked.

"Typhon. The *true* First Emperor. My territories lay beyond here in Helle but that will mean little to you. Though in all this time, they are probably unrecognizable," the man introduced himself before closing this new book and pulling down another.

"The *true* First Emperor? How arrogant. You seem to know a lot about me. Did those books of yours tell you that? Because I assure you, the youngsters' records are full of gaps." Sargon walked forward.

"Not the books, no. You think about yourself a lot. And if you want to compare Empire sizes, wait until my...vacation is over." Typhon closed this book and was onto the next.

"Humph. Truly you are an arrogant man." Sargon scoffed indignantly.

"Of course, I am arrogant. Unlike you, I am not a mere 'man.' I am something *much* more." Typhon approached, unnerving Sargon somewhat.

He walked right past him to get a book, but in the next instant was putting that away while pulling another out, on the other side of the room. Sargon grew tired of what he perceived as some kind of optical illusion and began to focus on the lax Typhon, with killer intent.

Typhon didn't care and did not even bother to look at his aggressor.

"Drakon or anyone else doesn't matter. Tartarus has become arrogant and will be destroyed," Sargon warned.

"Go ahead. I'm not very fond of it myself—when I begin to reassert myself on this Universe, it will wither away like everything else." Typhon sighed.

In the middle of their tense conversation, the two were interrupted when Queen Korova of Tartarus rushed in excitedly.

"Typhon! Me and the girls found a great hill for sliding. Come out honey, it's great!" she cheerily ran over and gave Typhon a big kiss while he sorted through some books.

"The girls and I," Typhon groaned.

"What?" Korova cluelessly asked.

"The correct sentence was—*the girls and I*. You are the native Tartarian speaker here, remember," Typhon corrected her condescendingly.

"I'm Arcosian, remember silly." Korova giggled.

"That does not negate the point. You are lucky your appearance has you among the chosen. Anyways, read the room. I was in the middle of something." He sighed again.

Korova tilted her head in innocent confusion.

"Ahem," Sargon loudly cleared his throat.

Finally, Korova noticed Sargon and panicked.

"Do not fear him my dear—I will not permit him to lay his hands on any of my possessions. That includes both you and this castle," Typhon casually remarked. Korova clutched him closely, hiding behind him.

"Really? Your husband was ousted only a few weeks ago and you've already fallen in line with the usurper?" Sargon laughed.

Korova prepared to bite back, but Typhon interrupted, not letting her speak, "She knew her place. This Universe is mine and those who recognize that should be praised not admonished." Typhon patronizingly patted Korova on the head.

Sargon rolled his eyes.

"Now if you don't mind, be gone, Sargon. This one's antics are high maintenance, so I have other things to do. And it turns out that you aren't worth my time after all," Typhon said before literally sweeping Korova off her feet.

"Yay! Sledding!" Korova childishly cheered.

Without any hint of fear, he carried the giggling Queen past the other Emperor.

Sargon, feeling an assault on his pride, moved to attack Typhon raising a fist to strike him. Typhon smiled and moved his hand, making Sargon hesitate. Even for an instant, Sargon could feel Typhon's Power flare-up.

Sargon was paralyzed. In that instant, he sensed a Power that eclipsed his own by orders of magnitude. That ominous feeling kept him in his place as Typhon smirked.

"For you my dear," Typhon suddenly said, presenting a ring to Korova.

The bronze and jeweled ring suddenly changed into pure black, solid obsidian (in a feat of alchemic chemistry the bronze age people couldn't properly appreciate)! Only then did Sargon recognize that one of his rings, one of them exactly like it, was gone! Looking in shock, he saw Typhon dangling the stolen jewelry in the air before seemingly, affectionately putting the solid black ring on Korova's finger.

"Oh Typhon, you're spoiling me!" Korova blushed as she received the ring.

Typhon walked to the door and without looking back, taunted, "you know the way out, Sargon. You were much less interesting than I had hoped but I shall choose to spare you. From your thoughts you aren't worth fighting personally, but when I return my loyal subordinates deserve a gift. Try not to die before I can offer you as a warmup." Typhon sighed.

The two locked eyes and Sargon stared into the piercing, demonic gaze of the Destroyer. Without even needing to move, Typhon forced Sargon to back off nervously as he just laughed. Sargon was furious but wouldn't dare move until Typhon left. He had felt true fear and back in the present, this eerie similarity haunted him.

"I outlived Typhon—he died, and I was left, the strongest! I don't want a rival! Bring back the peons I can easily crush!" Sargon began to unravel as his fists were slowing down.

In a flash, Chaos landed another hit on Sargon's face. It cracked and shattered with blood spurting everywhere. Then another punch and another and another left Sargon dazed and disoriented. Sargon could feel his consciousness fade with each successive smash to his face.

"I'm—going to die," Sargon thought in desperation. When push came to shove, the great Emperor was not as great as he believed.

"Pathetic." Sargon recalled another voice saying. This time it was a woman's voice; it was his goddess' voice. It was what she said before she abandoned her disappointment of a partner: Sargon of Akkad.

No! He wasn't dying! He couldn't! His pride wouldn't let him. He'd show them, he'd show them both!

Chaos' vicious assault was still smashing the old Lugal to a pulp, yet Sargon caught Chaos' next punch, surprising him.

"*I* am the First Emperor. *I* am the Lugal!" Sargon screamed as he Powered up past his limits.

Chaos was blown back and when he opened his eyes, was shocked to find Sargon of Akkad grown to the size of a giant. The 500-foot-tall man laughed maniacally. This was the invincible ability his goddess had given him—the Lugal.

"I am Sargon of Akkad ruler of the Universe!" the Lugal screamed so loudly the planet shook.

Chaos excitedly hopped up and down while shadow boxing, ready to fight the giant.

"Mind if I tag in? This hardly seems like just a fistfight anymore," Norne said as she stepped up, now fully healed.

"Yeah! Just like old times, we'll take him out together!" Chaos excitedly grinned.

The two both released their full Power and took battle stances to face Sargon.

Sargon tried to stomp on them, but they dodged in opposite directions. Punching with both fists, Sargon growled as he once again missed both.

Chaos and Norne flew around Sargon's giant body, attacking in sync. They covered for each other, attacked in unison, and perfectly complimented the other's movements.

Sargon saw Chaos and Norne's teamwork and was incensed. They fought just like he had back in the good old days. To conquer all those people in the first place, it didn't hurt to have a friend.

While the giant Sargon tried in vain to hit either with his massive body, Norne smashed into the back of his leg, tripping him up. As Sargon lay flat on his back, Chaos dove from orbit and shattered his giant body. All that was a mere projection using Power.

The real Sargon was inside, now being tackled by Chaos. Sargon desperately kicked Chaos off and stood up, ready to fight mono-e-mono again. Chaos laughed and attacked with a simultaneous right and left hook.

Chaos, however, smashed both arms with his own swinging out. Sargon leaped back in fear, his broken arms flailing in the wind as he flew back.

"I—have to get out of here!" Sargon panicked and looked up before jumping to try and fly away.

While flying away, Sargon noticed Norne trying a sneak attack and blocked with his knee just in time.

"You insolent fly! How dare you!" Sargon screamed while moving to head-butt her while his arms healed.

Norne just grinned and in a flash, Chaos appeared, slamming his fist into Sargon's head which knocked his teeth out. Sargon was sent crashing back down from Chaos' punch and violently vomited blood.

"What the Hel! He isn't that fast—why couldn't I react in time?!" Sargon screamed.

Just then, Norne threw her knife into his back and channeled her Power through it. Sargon stood up, but by the time he was on his feet, Chaos was standing next to him and viciously buried his fist in his face again.

Norne was using her ice powers to freeze the Lugal, giving Chaos an opening to attack. Their teamwork was perfect. Sargon couldn't comprehend this and stumbled backward as Norne jumped behind him, grabbing her knife which was still embedded in his back.

His eyes widened. Again, Chaos smashed his face in with Norne holding the knife in his back, stabbing it deeper and stopping him from flying away again.

"Mercy! I beg you—stop!" Sargon pathetically wept.

"Now Norne, hold him nice and still." Chaos insanely grinned while making a fist.

"Sure thing!" Norne cackled.

"I relent! I'll do whatever you want! Please!!! Let us work together to punish my treacherous son! We can work together," Sargon groveled.

"Too late!" Chaos repeatedly screamed while punching Sargon's head over and over. Norne braced him so he couldn't fly away, and Chaos cut loose without restraint, blow after blow. The brutal rush pulverized him, and down to his brain, nothing was left.

Norne removed her knife and dropped the corpse.

"Even a 'first generation' Immortal can't recover from that." Norne used her cape to clean off the blood.

"Meh. I probably could." Chaos looked at the bloody pulp of a body that lay at his feet.

"So then—what do you say we pay a visit to the son next," Norne said.

CHAPTER 20

Norne and Chaos arrived on a frozen mountaintop where an abandoned castle fortress stood. This was the rendezvous point agreed upon after the mission. It was right next to where the final battle with Sargon had been, so it was convenient. As such, Chaos and Norne stayed there to rest.

"So... I assume Grak will come to ambush us here while we're recovering from fighting Sargon. We're deep in his territory, so trying to escape or call for help would be useless. We have to make our last stand here once our strength returns," Norne explained.

"So Grak betrayed us... I can kill him too, right?" Chaos asked.

"This whole stupid alliance business has outlived its usefulness. Let's just do what we should've done from the start. If they combined feared a battle with Sargon, let's just kill them all and go from there." A thoroughly fed-up Norne sat down on a couch in the foyer.

"Can't we keep Aurelia though? She's *really* hot," Chaos whined.

"Betrayal must not be countenanced!" Norne turned and screamed at him, her anger at a breaking point. Chaos froze, surprised at how badly she was taking this.

"Alright. I'm gonna explore the castle. Call me when the fighting starts," Chaos said before strolling off. Left alone, Norne took her knife out and began cleaning it for the fight.

"If they aren't here yet, they likely underestimated us—but still they may be spending this time to collect armies to make this even more of a pain," Norne thought.

"Norne?" a voice innocently asked. Norne jumped and saw Cyrus standing next to her.

"Cyrus!" Norne shrieked, forgetting that without any Power, Cyrus couldn't be detected like others.

"I learned that this was your main base for secret meetups. After all the info I gathered—you're going to kill father now, so I have to make my last plea!" Cyrus cried.

Norne wiped what was left of Sargon's blood off her knife awkwardly.

"How'd you even get here?" Norne asked.

"Some guards told me you'd be here, so I rushed over as quickly as I could," Cyrus explained.

"Some...guards?" Norne asked, confused. How would they know?

"Norne, please. If our friendship means anything stop the killing, *please!*" Cyrus clasped Norne's hands, in tears.

Norne paused.

"You don't have any power over me. You're just a distraction." She looked away.

"Norne, please!" Cyrus began crying all over her.

"I must take her back to Mesos before this gets messy. It would break her—well Sargon's death would already. I know! Grak and Sargon killed each other, that's how to get out of this. I can salvage it—things can get back to—" Norne thought before stopping.

Her mind ceased all processes and entered a state of complete confusion.

"Why do I care?" she asked before slowly looking at Cyrus with soulless eyes.

"Why am I jumping through hoops for this girl? Why do I care what she thinks about me? About what makes her happy or sad or what would make her hate me? She has *no* power over me. She's a distraction. She's useless." Norne's eyes began to twitch in a deranged way.

"Distractions like 'friends' are of no use. A ruler's greatest threat is a distraction—a needless obstacle with power over them. When I want to increase productivity, I make sure to remove all unnecessary distractions. Kill the girl." These words raced through her head, but they weren't hers.

"You, selfish girl, you're nothing but a distraction. You're useless," Norne said coldly.

"I know. I'm sorry, this was selfish. But it is in line with everything else I try to do. I know you can be a great person—I'm excited by the potential! I believe in you Norne. That's why I like you." She smiled at her.

The radiance from Cyrus' innocent smile paralyzed Norne. Her fist trembled in a confused fury.

When Norne was a child, she could smile like that. In the Arcosian palace's winter garden, the young princess was simply beaming as she watched an innocent bunny rabbit hopping by. The tiny creature was amazing to Norne, as, despite its tiny size, it hopped around free, without a care in the world. At that moment, it was the most precious thing in the world to her.

Arcosians had learned rabbits were lacking in nutritional value as the dreaded 'rabbit poisoning' fate was well known for those who ate them expecting the benefits of normal carnivorous appetites. On top of that, there were so many of them that their pelts weren't even a valuable sell. This made it common knowledge that they weren't worth hunting in Arcosian society, so people just let them be. They weren't strong enough to be any meaningful threat and the propagation of rabbit-kind meant only further weaklings of no concern even if there were as many of them as were stars in the sky. What dangerous ideas could come from a rabbit anyways?

There was no reason to kill a harmless bunny rabbit.

However as little Norne watched the creature with admiration and adoration, a figure loomed behind her. Taking one look at the scene before her and surmising what had transpired, that woman spoke up.

"Norne, my little snowflake…it's almost New Year. What type of sacrifice does Arcos like to go with his burnt offerings during New Year again?" she asked.

"Rabbit?" The infant princess of Arcosia helplessly looked up with worry.

"Very good. Now, go catch that creature and bring it to the temple. I want you to practice your sacrifice preparation for the big day. Then you can be just like me." The woman bent down and patted Norne's head.

"Of course, mother." The little princess knew to do as she had been programmed.

Taking out the knife she had hidden at all times, Norne, without hesitation lunged forward and killed the helpless creature. She had been trained to strike quickly like a Church Inquisitor and she ended its life before it even knew what was happening. The deed was done.

"Very good, Norne." The woman smiled. Norne wanted to cry.

There was no reason to kill a harmless bunny rabbit.

The winds howled outside Sargon's Mountain fortress. Later in the day, Grak arrived with a confident grin. Though a smile was not all he brought—the other rulers and matching armies had been assembled for this meeting, just as Norne had predicted.

The doors violently burst open as an army moved to cover them. It was with a specific intention that they had chosen this place to meet up. Either way, things had gone, and the final enemy awaited inside.

Grak approached, looking inside. "So…which of the two survived?" Grak wondered as he stepped into the entrance.

"Grak. So, you came after all. And all of you who have
betrayed me as well, welcome," Chaos greeted calmly as he stood
atop the stairs with a glass of wine and his crown on his head, tilted.
He was doing his best impression of the self-righteous monologuing egotists among them as a joke, but in truth, he was extremely
intimidating.

Unphased by his appearance, Grak stepped up.

"Your regeneration really is a cut above the rest. But I doubt
your stamina is doing so well after fighting Sargon of Akkad,"
Grak boldly declared.

Suddenly they heard someone writing in pen and saw Norne
furiously writing on official papers.

"Oh, don't mind me. Your little trap left me behind on some
paperwork. I'm just working on national budgets and resource
management. And in my spare time writing a new play on, 'Grak
the treacherous.' I'm sure the kids will love to hear about it," Norne
casually said as she continued writing on the floor next to the stairs.

"Norne! Not going to lie, but I doubted you would walk away
from the encounter," Grak admitted, keeping up the casual façade
that all pretentious royals expected.

"Obviously. But I think you'll find we handled ourselves
much better than you anticipated. After all, *we* have been waiting
for you." She smiled before getting up and walking over to Chaos'
side.

"I'm disappointed. We all ran home to grab some troops,
while you two didn't bring any of your armies. You came alone,
even after knowing that this was coming? Norne, I thought you
were some sort of genius." Grak laughed, coming further into the
castle.

"Yes. I am. Smart enough to see why you selected this attack
date to be during the busiest time of year for our troops. Though

I'll admit I was uncharacteristically slow to note that little scheme of yours." She shrugged.

"I categorized you two as a threat to match Sargon of Akkad… if not surpass him. I'm sure you can acknowledge this as fair play, rather than foul play." Grak took a step closer, confidently.

"I suppose," Norne smiled. "After all, there is another reason that I didn't even bother trying to recall some troops. Just think how impressive it will be when, with only the aid of his most trusted advisor, Chaos slew not only the original Great Conqueror but also all his enemies in a single night."

"Why throw away your life so recklessly? You're brilliant, you'd do just fine without Chaos! What in the world could compel you to answer to a bumbling idiot in the face of your own brilliance? Cyrus likes you, accept my offer and be spared! What would make Chaos worth opposing us?" Grak cried, growing frustrated by her sustained confidence.

"Simple. I love him. And our chances of coming out on top are pretty good too." Norne smiled again.

"Wait, what—" Chaos asked.

"You're insane. Kill them! We have the advantage!" Grak yelled as everyone charged. Through the entrance, they sought to flank Chaos and Norne from both sides of the stairs.

Norne and Chaos stood back-to-back, Powering up and preparing to fight.

"Alright Norne, *this* is what I'm talking about!" Chaos laughed.

"I swear, you can be such a headache. Just try to survive this. I'll take the hundred on the left, you take the hundred on the right." Norne sighed.

"Just watch! I'll take one-hundred and one!" Chaos laughed.

The army charged but Norne suddenly remembered something and reached for an object in her cape.

Grak slowed his advance, cautiously observing Norne as she grinned.

"Before I forget, weirdly, I'm glad you betrayed us. Now I don't have to feel bad about doing this," Norne said before tossing a basket down the stairs. Dropping and rolling down the stairs, it hit the ground and opened with the severed and frozen head of Cyrus rolling out of it. The hacked-off corpse piece continued the roll and landed at Grak's feet at the bottom of the stairs.

The army all halted to look in horror at the sight of the girl's dismembered head. Aurelia froze and her eyes widened as much as Grak's.

"No…it's a trick! I told her to wait back on Uruk with Atosa," Grak said in a panic.

"But I told her to come to her best friend for help if she was ever in trouble." Norne grinned, taking complete credit for this.

"I'll kill you! Why would you kill her?!" Grak roared.

"Because… I wanted to make it extremely clear what happens if you cross us. Now die." Norne grinned.

In a flash, Chaos flew forward and sent Grak flying with a planet-shattering punch that obliterated the entire front of the castle that many had flooded into. The shockwave splattered the first five rows of soldiers who had followed Grak in. The army froze, shocked by his horrific speed. Unfortunately, the most skilled troops had been in the front. Aurelia didn't flinch from surprise or the shockwave after, instead, she stood unphased as blood covered her left side.

"Why are you so surprised? You think we *hadn't* been training this whole time?" Chaos smirked confidently banging his chest.

"Also, it might've helped that from the start. I instructed Chaos to *never* use more than half of his Power in front of you." Norne smiled, hopping down from where the stairs used to be.

Chaos grinned before, with a mighty roar he drew out his true Power, shaking the entire army.

Some more soldiers were vaporized just by being too close to his massive Power. Even Norne had to float far away with a shield up to protect herself from the horrifying amount of Power that Chaos put out at full strength. The sheer Power vaporized what was left of Cyrus' head.

Many in the allied force froze in terror, but it was at that last sight that Aurelia gritted her teeth in fury.

Despite Chaos' big show, Aurelia screeched like a wild animal before pouncing at him and tackling him through the castle.

Smashing through the other side, she slammed him down by his throat and painfully pinched it with her iron grip.

"Damn you!" she screamed and began slamming Chaos around headfirst with all her might. To end her wrath, she punched him in the face across the field.

"You never disappoint," Chaos said, sitting up and wiping blood from his mouth.

"I'll kill you!" Aurelia pictured Cyrus' severed head and stared with a furious look of death at Chaos.

"Hey—y'know it was—" Chaos began to correct her assumption after realizing the cause of her fury, only for Aurelia to fly over and punch him away at an insane speed.

All the green Power gems on her armor glowed, enhancing her strength as she flew after Chaos to tear him limb from limb. Jumping up, she grabbed him and slammed him to the ground, flying across the planet in a rage, dragging him through the ground, face first.

Even Norne couldn't help but think, "better him than me," after seeing that.

"Grak is down, but all that's left is Norne—we can handle this," Wilhelm thought with a malicious grin.

Norne smiled back, taking out her knife. Her bloodlust was palpable as her Power burst forth with a chilling air that terrified everyone.

Then one of Grak's few remaining soldiers noticed that Norne stood beneath him in a posture of having already swung her knife. Then his midsection opened, and he died. Everyone else turned to see Norne's new location and was disoriented by her lightning-fast speed.

Wilhelm, among others, however, also took note of the frost that was appearing on their bodies and brushed it off. Another attacker moved to slice Norne, but she cackled while dodging past him and carving him up with her blades.

In response to that, a dozen warriors from different kingdoms and armies all united in their simultaneous attack. They surrounded Norne so that they could attack from all sides, but she just smiled.

"Get back! If she touches you, you're dead!" Wilhelm cried out. But he noticed that even in moving his hand forward to warn them, he felt slower than usual.

Norne touched the ground and as soon as they were close enough, she froze the ground and them all with it.

Norne smiled, but quickly shifted her eyes to look behind her. Wilhelm had seized the opportunity and as everyone knew a warrior was most vulnerable right after an attack. Wilhelm had his sword pointing directly at the back of Norne's head, but he didn't dare make contact until his planned killing moment.

"I never took Aurelia for a blabbermouth, but I suppose it only makes sense." Norne grinned.

"Don't move. In your attack, you left yourself wide open! There's nowhere to run!" Wilhelm Powered up. Though of course, like an idiot, he wasted time talking rather than just killing her when he thought he had the chance.

Without a word, Norne created five copies of herself made of her anti-Power, Vanus. They all jumped up and killed Wilhelm's guards before knocking him to the ground and pummeling him into a bloody pulp in a united curb-stomping.

Norne casually stood up, looking down at him with a sadistic grin. Then she raised her gaze to everyone else who had assembled to kill her and Chaos. They all nervously backed away, but Norne's smile only grew.

Meanwhile, Chaos flew through mountain after mountain before finally his momentum slowed down enough and he fell out the other side, rolling to a halt in an empty field.

Getting to his feet, he wiped his nose and mouth. Looking at it he saw blood drying on his hand.

"Wow…she's pissed." Chaos laughed to himself before looking up. Aurelia was flying at him, screaming furiously. Chaos widened his stance and summoned all his Power to clash with her.

Aurelia swung her arm to break Chaos' neck, however, he raised his own arm and blocked it. The force from the attack was incredible and as Chaos' arm shook in the struggle, he noticed his own Adamant bracelet beginning to crack.

Disengaging from that, he tried to pivot around her and strike with chops from both directions. However, a furious Aurelia caught both his arms. Recognizing he'd been overzealous in putting energy into offense in his hands, she tore both his arms off to capitalize on his vulnerable defense.

Chaos groaned before Aurelia began slamming him in the face with his own arms, wearing them down to the bone as she smashed his head over and over. It would almost be funny—a man being beaten to death with his own arms if it weren't so horrifically violent. When the arms disintegrated and left Chaos stumbling back in a daze, she threw his arm bracers at his face one after the other.

Chaos was bloodied, but his amazing regeneration granted him two new arms in no time at all, which he skillfully put through his bracers as they were suspended in the air from recoiling off his face.

However, despite his arms being re-armed, Chaos stepped up for a full Power headbutt. Aurelia reeled back from having her face smashed, but her feet never left the ground. Still standing, just as quickly, Aurelia retaliated with a brutal headbutt of her own that knocked Chaos onto his back.

The normal restraints a fighter had were gone, she was using one-hundred and ten percent of her mind, body, and soul to kill Chaos.

"Incredible—I'm using my full strength and yet you still aren't dying. A real challenge!" Chaos laughed, excited by the struggle.

Aurelia wouldn't even humor him with words and flew forward with a punch to destroy his head. Chaos blocked the punch before throwing one of his own. The two fought in an all-out brawling match, slugfest with their strongest punches and kicks being pitted against each other.

The two warriors skillfully attacked, blocked, and dodged with insane precision and speed. With each clash though, Aurelia's armor cracked and fell apart, but any damage Chaos sustained quickly repaired itself.

As Chaos smile widened though, Aurelia scored a punch to his face that broke his nose. Then she grabbed him by the hair and threw him into the planet's star. She snarled at him before stopping. She was foaming at the mouth like a beast—the picture of anger that she always pretended to be as Dictator. The idea of rage was always more attractive, more ideal when it was an act to inspire the masses. Now her war-frenzy made her look just as mad as any of them.

Aurelia looked at her hands which had started to bleed but looked back at Chaos with rage. Her overwhelming Power—her righteous anger was unlike anything she'd ever felt before. This was not the meaningless yelling she'd work herself into with fascist speeches griping about nothing from her privileged palace. For the first time in her life, Aurelia actually had something to be truly angry about.

As blood came from her furiously closed hands—her own fingers digging into her flesh, she longed for the days of being the angry Dictator who would yell about imagined plots and the amorphous enemies that needed to be destroyed. Now before her stood an enemy worthy of that hate and it felt awful. In truth, Chaos wasn't the one to kill Cyrus, so her anger was somewhat misplaced. However, given the genuine suffering she felt and had convinced herself to project onto Chaos, at least she got to feel how those duped by her rhetoric did. It felt awful. If she couldn't smash his face in, she'd break down and cry.

But she didn't have time. Chaos returned from his brief sun-bath completely unphased. Unlike kicking down on the weak, this real enemy was much harder to kill.

"I'm almost disappointed. I go full Power for the first time and you're showing me up. You must be pissed." He grinned as he casually walked forward.

When he was within range Aurelia remembered Cyrus' innocent smile and punched through his abdomen with viscera and blood spewing everywhere. However, as she yanked her arm out, she was in pain.

Chaos fell to his knees and vomited up blood but quickly stood back up, fully healed. Unlike kicking down on the weak, this real enemy was impossible to kill.

While Aurelia flinched in pain from her own punch, Chaos reached forward for her face. She couldn't afford that, she was fighting for her life, so she dodged quickly enough that only her laurel crown was crushed, and her beautiful green hair rendered a mess.

Her gems let her hit like a truck without fearing recoil but as much damage as Chaos was soaking up, one good hit would be the death of her. Chaos smirked and crushed the crown with one hand. This was the problem with Aurelia hyping herself up by beating up on her own citizens or native populations without proper weapons. This time, she'd bitten off more than she could chew. Fascists tend to overestimate themselves.

Chaos came back from whatever she had thrown at him. Aurelia focussed her strength and Powered up to a level she'd never reached before in her life. If she was going to win, she'd have to go for the head. Chaos lumbered towards her again, cackling at the upcoming challenge.

Aurelia directed all her Power to her right fist—her signature opener. Chaos grinned and did the same before throwing a punch of his own. The two met with a clash that shook the planet. Aurelia's full strength however was enough to shatter Chaos' arm as she punched through him and delivered a devastating right hook to his jaw.

The concussed Emperor was dazed, and so Aurelia screamed at the top of her lungs, forcing her Power to unreached heights that began wrecking her own body. Her Power gems began glowing so brightly she couldn't even be seen—they began cracking from the strain.

Then she put all her strength into a machinegun volley of punches and kicks directly at Chaos' head. After the first dozen, she saw that his neck was broken—but after what she'd seen him survive, she knew it wasn't enough.

The punches and kicks didn't let up until Aurelia saw that she had punched a chunk of Chaos' head clean off—there was a piece of exposed skull on the gory, visceral lump of head Chaos had. There was her winning chance. She screamed, putting all her strength into a punch directly into the left side of Chaos' head.

With this she had intended to completely destroy his brain and put an end to him, the same way Typhon had been disposed of. The explosion was a detonation so great that the whole continent cracked and was blasted flat.

As the dust settled, Aurelia panted in exhaustion and Chaos fell to his knees, blood pouring out of every hole in his head both natural and Aurelia made. Aurelia panted and almost fell to her knees as well before noticing something. Her hand was broken from the impact, but it still rested on a hard surface.

To her horror, when she looked, she realized that she had failed to penetrate his skull. As his face reformed, he coughed up blood but began laughing. Aurelia stepped back in dismay as Chaos stood up to tower over her. He'd lost more blood than his total body mass, but he kept coming back.

JAIDEN BAYNES

"Strong hit…but not strong enough." Chaos tapped his skull, showing he was just fine.

Aurelia gasped and Chaos began to approach again.

"His brain! If I can't smash my way in—" Aurelia growled before focussing her Power. Even now she wouldn't give in. Her fists were bloody and taking longer than she wanted to regenerate.

Aurelia threw a swift punch at his head again, but he ducked under it and Powerfully threw an upper-cut into her in the stomach which cracked her breastplate and made her central Power gem flicker.

She kicked him in the face, but the force spun him around, so he grabbed her arm with the remaining gauntlet and putting all his strength in it, shattered it. Blood gushed out from where Chaos was crushing her arm.

Aurelia furiously kicked him in the jaw before axe-kicking the top of his head, repeating these up and down kicks to his head repeatedly. He finally caught her foot, panting as he looked up with an almost toothless and bloody smile.

He began insanely cackling as from the root to the crown, even his adult teeth began to grow back in. Aurelia was horrified. She kicked him in the face with her free leg, but it was too late, he crushed her boot with one of her remaining Power gems.

In a panic, she swung with a kick at his face, but he dodged past it.

Swiftly maneuvering behind her he grinned while pinning the warrior in a chokehold.

"Incredible! Earlier, I clashed with Sargon, and yet you are still the greatest opponent I've fought in my life! Aurelia Gaius! You were a woman worth having! And tell you what, give up now and you get to survive this," he menacingly whispered in her ear.

Her eyes widened in shock, and she stammered not knowing what to do. She hated him! She loved Cyrus. But she loved herself more.

Meanwhile, Norne was cutting and shattering her way through what was left of her former allies and their armies. The only one to have clashed with her and survive was Wilhelm. Lying in the snow with his back propped against fallen debris from the castle, Wilhelm held his bleeding side. The clone-induced pummeling had really done a number on him, and that severe wound was the last major one to go away, forestalled by his attackers' freezing property. As his breathing stabilized, even as the cries of his comrades ran out, he took the time to hold out his prized Prussian saber and look at it.

The proud sword of his nation was broken in half and frozen at the tip of where the break was. Prussia's symbol of masculinity and strength did not compare to Norne's knife when it came down to it. It killed natives without armor just fine, but in a real fight, it had failed. Wilhelm considered himself to be a real man, but in truth, he was just lucky he had never fought Chaos. After one good hit from Norne, he could barely stay awake, let alone fight.

Another set of death throes shook him awake again. The Prussian Empire was often called, 'not a nation with an army, but an army with a nation.' War and fighting were the beginning and end of a proud Prussian man's life—the only way to be a real man. Wilhelm himself had espoused many great speeches about fighting for your Empire and being a hero. People were born to be heroes, like his many elite soldiers who had given their lives to fight Norne off and even give him the time to consider any of this.

So, Wilhelm, as his wound finally regenerated, stood up and bravely ran away.

"Damn it Grak! You said this would be easy!" The bravely bold Wilhelm fled.

At that same moment though, Norne sliced open the neck of the last Prussian troop and sighed in disappointment. The Prussians, though it varied from soldier to soldier, lived up to their reputation in part. They believed they were supermen, so they charged in with more conviction than even mightier warriors and were slaughtered for it.

"What a waste of good soldiers. If only they weren't taken in by the lies of a fool like Wilhelm. Speaking of which—" Norne lamented as she was surrounded by hundreds of bodies before turning around and seeing her unfinished business.

Prince Wilhelm had given up and run away, but Norne quickly flew over and slashed at his neck. The coward already had his blade raised to defend himself. Norne was impressed as she landed, having failed to kill him.

"How irritating." She sighed.

Wilhelm was shaking, but with this sign of luck perhaps good fortune smiled upon him. He raised his blade to try and attack Norne as a diversion to escape again, however, half of his half blade fell off from a clean cut.

He froze up as he realized Norne had cut through his sword itself and sure enough, right where she had been aiming to slice, a massive cut in his neck opened. He vomited up blood, desperately covering the wound with both hands.

"You should count yourself lucky. My swing was meant to remove your head." Norne pointed her knife menacingly.

"This girl isn't human!" Wilhelm was horrified as he saw Norne approach.

She confidently strode forward to finish him off, seeing that he was sufficiently broken in both body and spirit. However, he steeled himself.

"Stay back! I am the King of Prussia!" He Powered up to his maximum. All his Power burst forth, blowing Norne's cape in the wind but doing little else. Norne was unimpressed.

However, after a flash of light, Norne instead saw a towering giant where Wilhelm had been. The mighty creature looked down on her and gave a frightening scream. This was Utgard-Loki! Norne was again unphased by this, however.

"You know, Wilhelm, perhaps you would have done better if I didn't already know your ability." She shook her head in disappointment.

In the next instant, she dashed through the illusion and pounced on the fleeing Wilhelm. She grabbed him by the back of the neck, and he froze in his tracks, terrified.

"H—hey! Norne, wait up! We're cool, right? The best of pals, I mean we're practically bosom buddies—" Wilhelm stammered.

"To be fair, I hated you before we even allied for Grak's little rag-tag group. You are incredibly stupid," Norne said plainly.

"Wait! Hold on, you needed us to kill Sargon! You were terrified of him like the rest of us!" Wilhelm pleaded.

"Yeah, then I went home and checked his Power against Chaos'. You forget I have a certified monster under my command, even I forget the depths of his Power from time to time. Chaos probably could've killed him without me. Gods, you really are stupid, do you not know what acting is?" She grinned as her hand became cold.

"No, please! I don't want to die!" he pleaded, before being frozen solid into a block of ice. Norne shattered him with a smile and turned around seeing the corpses littering the planet around the wreckage of the castle.

"Just wait right here, I'll be wanting to take a look at that Utgard-Loki Power you stole from us, later," Norne said before placing his head, the only unshattered part of his body, on a rock for later testing. Right now, she had other people to kill.

All the while, Grak was still reeling from the first attack that had caught him off guard. Fading in and out of consciousness, he dreamed of a peaceful life with Atosa; raising his kids with the woman of his dreams in a paradise of the Universe after his plans. Then of course the kids would wait excitedly for their aunt, Cyrus. Even concussed, Grak snapped awake as the dream fell apart. The last thing he saw while under was Cyrus' severed head.

Grak was awake and his body was fully regenerated. He didn't know how long he had been out and so he quickly sat up to get his bearings. He dug out of the debris and struggled to his feet in horror at what he saw. All around, he was the only one left alive.

"Grak...you started all this. Feeling any regrets, Mister Lugal?" Norne asked as she approached him. He swung around to face her after hearing her voice.

"Do not mock me! I am Lugal!" Grak said in a very Sargon way.

"Oh yeah? Bring it on then, big man!" Norne laughed in his face.

"With pleasure!" He Powered up to the maximum. Norne darted towards him, reaching to freeze him before he could do anything. Grak, however, released a burst of energy from himself that blew her back. She flew away but stabbed her knife into the ground to slow down.

"Divine Right of the Lugal—Marduk!" He pointed at Norne to seal her Power.

Norne kept running, however, completely unaffected.

"She's immune to my seals!" Grak gasped before dodging past a knife strike and swinging his staff which sent Norne flying.

Norne landed, then fired several blasts.

"Divine Right of the Lugal—Utu!" Grak pointed his staff and fired a focused beam of stellar Power that split and shredded through Norne's blasts. Norne flipped over the attack and threw her knife.

"Divine Right of Lugal—Enki!" Grak said, as his Power became an amorphous, almost liquid field around him and caught the blade before it could hit him.

Norne however grinned.

Suddenly her knife began freezing his very Power! He jumped back, retracting everything he could to save it. However, much was lost as Norne froze it and he could not retrieve what was already frozen. She grabbed her knife from the ice and began spinning around.

"I spent years researching you, Grak! Stories of your 'miraculous power' may help rally your troops but they also give a strategist every weakness you have!" Norne laughed.

She clashed with his staff. He was much stronger, but with her swift attack, he struggled to push her back as her blade was inches from his neck.

"I have eyes everywhere." She threw his own words from long ago back at him.

"I'm going to kill you. Smite!" Grak yelled as a beam of Power came down.

It struck the frozen Power Norne's knife was in. He gasped but looked down at Norne's smug grin.

"I know all your abilities. It's useless—useless! *Useless!* Give up and die now!" Norne's madness burst forth as a frosty mist began condensing around the point where the knife and staff made contact.

She innocently grinned to mock him as her ice began freezing his staff. Even before going for him, the ice froze over the Adamant gem at the top of the staff. It cracked and shattered, losing Grak his access to his divine right abilities stored there.

Before it could reach him though, Grak furiously Powered up which sent Norne flying back again.

When she looked up, Norne was shocked to find Grak floating inside a massive replica of his body made of pure Power.

"Behold! You did well to counter my normal move set, but *this* is a combination of my other techniques. None but Aurelia have seen it and lived, so I doubt you could prepare. This is the Power I had developed to slay Sargon," Grak explained.

It looked familiar.

"Alright then." Norne launched herself at the giant and took a swing at it with her knife. The knife was deflected off the surface and there was no sign of freezing.

"Impossible! There's no way his Power is higher than Chaos' so how did he resist me!" Norne gasped in surprise at her attack's lack of effect.

Grak grinned and moved, punching the air so that his giant moved to punch Norne. She flipped over it but intentionally landed on the giant's forearm, pressing both her hands on the surface to freeze it. Then she suddenly realized. "Ah...that's how you're doing it. Utu's power of compacted Power." She grinned.

Her focusing on that, though, made her fail to notice a second massive punch, which sent her flying and crashing into the ground. Her eyes widened as the foot came down on her.

Grak moved and began stepping on the ground where Norne lay.

"Die!" he yelled repeatedly, stomping.

After a while, he finally stopped and looked down.

"Victory—of course, the gods would shine on me to be the one true Lugal of the Universe. Now to kill Chaos and be done with this," Grak said.

When the dust cleared though, Grak was shocked to find nothing but a puddle of water from where he had attacked Norne.

"What! She escaped!" he cried.

"No...you killed her," a voice snickered.

Grak looked around in confusion, only to see Norne walk over and bend down to pick up her knife which was floating in the puddle.

"How! I just stomped you to death!" Grak screamed.

"Me? Don't be ridiculous. Though I must congratulate you on defeating your opponent, a lifeless double doesn't count for much." She grinned while holding her hand over the puddle and freezing the water to create a copy of her head, even taking on her skin color, eye color, and everything.

Norne released her ability and the ice melted back into water. She stood up and wiped the water off her knife.

"That's impossible—I was just fighting you!" Grak still refused to believe.

"You were fighting the double I left to clean things up here. While you were taking a dirt nap, a bunch of your soldiers tried to make a break for it, so I left to make sure that didn't happen. *Now* you can say you're the last one standing against me in this battle." Norne confidently grinned while swinging her knife around.

Grak fired a beam from the giant's hand that created a massive explosion. Norne, however, landed on a chunk of rubble nearby with a smile.

"Or perhaps I should say that in a language you'd understand—*let's get down to business*," she said in that pretentious ancient cuneiform she had learned from Cyrus.

Grak remembered the innocent and trusting way Cyrus would talk to Norne and in turn talk to him about her. All that was betrayed by the smug monster grinning at him from down there. Grak furiously tried to stomp Norne again, but she jumped out of the way.

"It's curious but fighting my double which really should have made things easier for you, just sealed your fate!" Norne laughed, flying up directly at Grak in the chest of the giant.

Grak swung so that Norne had to redirect, land, and then fly up again.

"Because it was made of my Power, I learned exactly how your ability works!" Norne warned as she reached right outside Grak and slashed, again not even scratching his ability.

Norne landed. "Convection—you cycle your energy out from you then bring it back to be reignited, keeping the surface at perpetually maximum output. Anything I do to the surface; one second won't matter because new Power will take its place and the old will have my effects reversed. Like a star, am I right?" Norne had studied astronomy as well.

Grak was furious that she saw through his Power so quickly. It was as if she'd seen it before.

"Don't worry. I am more Powerful than the double you fought before but apparently not enough to break through that convection barrier you have up." Norne laughed.

"Die!" Grak yelled and punched down. Norne jumped past it, flying straight at Grak again to attack him.

"But that just means all your Power is maintaining your giant! Through the surface, you have no protection at all!" Norne screamed excitedly, knowing that through one breach she could end him.

Grak panicked, taking a step back out of fear. Even worse, a massive burst of Power was flying right toward him. Both Grak and Norne turned to face the massive source of Power approaching them.

"No! Aurelia!" Grak gasped.

"It's about time." Norne grinned.

Zooming over at horrifying speed, a Power approached that was even greater than Grak's ultimate form.

"Grak! You were holding out on us?" Chaos yelled as he flew past Norne and punched a hole through his giant body in one shot.

There was a massive gaping hole where Grak was in the center of the giant's chest.

"I did it!" Chaos laughed.

"No...look again." Norne pointed as Grak had dodged it by moving around to the arm of the giant. Suddenly the giant became opaque so they could no longer see inside.

"He only pretended to be stuck in the center to make our pattern of attack predictable. In truth, he can likely move around anywhere within there almost instantly!" Norne explained, so Chaos could follow.

Grak's giant built back up its Power as the hole in the chest sealed up.

"Yeah but—I'm sure making it opaque is eating into your Power reserves," Norne pointed out, smirking at Grak's general direction.

"Shut up!" Grak yelled and stamped down on Norne. In the nick of time though, Chaos flew down and blasted through the foot of the giant to land in front of Norne and stop the stamp with one hand.

Grak was horrified by Chaos' herculean strength.

"Tell me Grak…you thought through how to counter my ability rather well. I'm impressed. But how do you deal with Chaos? Surely you didn't think just brute force could defeat the Strongest Man in the Universe!" Norne dramatically pointed as Chaos grinned and pushed the giant's leg so hard that it stumbled back.

While his guard was down, Chaos launched himself towards the chest of the giant again.

"You idiot! I already told you I'm not there!" Grak yelled.

Chaos Powerfully punched through and yelled, "fine! I'll just check everywhere!" He laughed and dove down again. Grak slapped him over the horizon, but in half, that time Chaos was back and barreling towards him at full Power.

Chaos blasted through the shoulder, then knee, hand, head, groin and stomach, thigh and foot, finger, and all over the giant. He moved so quickly that even as the Lugal regenerated, multiple holes were still open at once.

Chaos swung his arm through the giant's neck and landed. He sniffed blood and looked at his hand seeing that he managed to tear off Grak's left hand.

"Hahaha! I'm getting closer." Chaos tossed the hand away.

He flew back up, punching holes all over the Lugal again, looking for Grak.

"If I were fighting you, I'd feel around the giant. Its convection comes from you at the core so the level of energy now that you're not in the center would give away your general location. The opposite would work for finding a weak point that I'd finally be able to break through and kill you. That would work. But this works too." Norne grinned.

Finally, on his eight-thousand five-hundred and twenty-first fly through, Chaos grabbed Grak by the neck and ripped him out of the giant Lugal. All this occurred in less than one second.

"Y'know Grak, the funny thing is that this 'ultimate Power' of yours is the same party trick your old man tried before I killed him. And he was *much* better at it." Chaos grinned.

Grak gasped in shock. It seemed in the end, a Lugal was still a Lugal.

"Impossible." Grak cursed his luck as the only one left.

"In his last moments, Sargon groveled like a weakling. Will you be doing the same now?" Norne asked.

"No." Grak grimaced.

Norne's haughtiness suddenly turned to fear. Grak's eyes had a renewed will—a drive and determination that long faded from Sargon's or even Cyrus' in their last moments.

"Everyone else in this battle is already dead. This cursed planet will be all our tombs! Fighting and killing each other for power? Cyrus! Perhaps you were on to something!" Grak cried as he began to glow.

Norne stepped back in shock.

"If there is a Hel, I'll see you two there." He pointed at Chaos and Norne.

Norne stepped back as she sensed the massive amount of Power he was building up. All that he had welling up inside of him. His Lugal form was incredibly Powerful, now Norne was dreading how much force he could output if he released it all at once. Not just one summoning either but all the Power he'd accumulated for years to use it and all his other Powers. *This* was everything Grak had.

One did not need the Testament of Sacrifice to self-destruct. Typhon's blessing was more efficient to be sure, but it was like intentionally overheating an appliance. In this case, the explosion was all-natural. It was rare and seen as unsportsmanlike but still, a possibility Norne recognized. And a possibility that now filled her with fear.

And so Grak with a great yell released all his stored Power in a blast that destroyed the planet, the star system, and beyond in an awesome, awful explosion. The blast was so great that all around the nearby nations, Power users couldn't help but turn and look in the direction of the cataclysmic glow.

As the light faded, Grak floated in the vacuum of space, not a single atom survived around him. That was the absurdity of Power. Now he had only enough left for his fading Mind to feel his body slowly freezing in the vacuum without a shield protecting it.

He felt he was now fading away, ready to pass on as from his legs up his body began shutting down. His Mind, unfortunately, retained his speed and so this one second before death stretched on. He had time to have a good think about everything. Cyrus would be ashamed but at least he got to avenge her. He slowly closed his eyes and prepared for the end.

"Hey, let go of me! You're embarrassing!" Norne cried.

Grak's eyes widened. Before him, Chaos held Norne tightly and shielded her from the explosion by facing her away and getting between her and Grak. Taking it point-blank for Norne, his back burnt down to the muscle and bone as a result of the blast. Even after all that, Chaos survived. Sometimes it seemed easier to imagine destroying the Universe rather than ever destroying Chaos.

"Well *sorry* for saving your life. That really hurt," Chaos pouted after Norne pushed him off.

Grak was horrified. Even in the moment before his death, he couldn't be rid of them.

"Well…that was a bit concerning. But as I was saying Grak, are you going to beg now." Norne sneered at him and got up in his face. He was too weak to even move as Norne mocked him.

He just wanted to die in peace as his heart stopped beating.

"Well?" Norne smirked.

"Forgive me Cyrus, Atosa—everyone. I was right, Norne, you found yourself quite the monster." Grak resigned himself. He wouldn't give her the satisfaction. Her face contorted.

"I'd joke that you'd see her soon, but the afterlife doesn't exist. Goodbye." Norne dismissively beheaded him with her knife.

He wasn't even allowed to die in peace.

At the end of the day, the people of Mesos had gathered outside Grak's palace to await his return. As the people nervously awaited the result, Atosa tensely looked up towards the stars with her hands clasped in anticipation. While they were waiting, Koroush emerged from the palace and made his way through the crowd to Atosa.

"I can't find her anywhere," Koroush updated her.

"Where could Cyrus have gone?" Atosa turned around, now even more worried.

As soon as she turned around though, a bright light descended from space and dramatically crash-landed in front of everyone. The dust dramatically blew into the crowd, blinding them. However, when the smoke cleared, the people saw that it was Chaos and Norne. The crowd silenced themselves before they could cheer. What could this mean?

With a smug grin, Chaos confidently strode towards the palace as if the crowd wasn't even there.

"What's going on? Where's Grak?" Atosa asked in confusion.

Koroush however, froze in terror as he knew what was happening. The crowd parted so that Chaos and Norne could pass. They began to ascend the stairs before Atosa yelled after them.

"What happened! Where is everyone?" Atosa surprised everyone by confidently demanding.

The two paused their climb up the stairs and turned around to face the assembled crowd.

"Sargon of Akkad is dead!" Norne triumphantly declared.

The people let out an uproarious cheer! They laughed and cried tears of joy, many falling to their knees in awe and excitement.

Chaos snickered at them before turning to continue climbing the stairs. Norne, however, smiled. Seeing all this joy in one place, she just couldn't help herself—she couldn't let their happiness ruin hers.

"And Grak of Akkad is also dead," Norne declared with a vile, sinister grin as she haughtily looked down on them all.

"What!" Chaos panicked as he looked at her. That wasn't in the plan.

The crowd was silenced by her words. The people looked up in disbelief. Norne's smile only grew as she saw the despair wash over them.

"And… Cyrus of Akkad is also dead." Norne could barely contain her sadistic elation, as her face visibly contorted to show a fraction of the evil in her heart on her face.

"Cyrus of Akkad is dead!" Norne repeated, shouting even louder than her proclamation of Sargon.

Atosa froze, she couldn't believe what she was hearing.

"Cyrus of Akkad is dead!" Norne screamed again, laughing insanely. She laughed so hard she cried. Tears flowed down her face as she turned and walked past Chaos to ascend the castle while continuing her maniacal laugh.

Atosa was so shocked she couldn't speak. Koroush held her in his arms as the two cried and wept with the others. As she looked back up the stairs, she saw Chaos smiling down at her. Winking at the distraught widow, Chaos turned around and followed Norne up the stairs.

The people of Mesos stood at the foot of Grak's palace, distraught as on cue the Imperial Knights Chaos and Norne had ordered arrived and occupied the city. It was all over for them.

The Imperial banner was hung from every roof as they moved in without resistance. Magnus had been very busy while Chaos and Norne fought Sargon himself. The Old Capital had been seized before they even arrived and the entire nation of Mesos had fallen to a full-scale, surprise attack.

Inside the palace, Chaos obliterated Grak's throne with the swipe of his hand and sat on the bronze foundation as a low seat. Norne casually lounged by his side on the ground, drying her tears from her laughing fit.

"We've done it, Norne! We won! What do we do now?" he asked as he looked down at Norne.

"Oh, Chaos…there's still much to do. We've only just begun. So now—now we gain further Power, we plot further, and we finish what we started! We conquer this whole damned Universe!" she declared dramatically.

STEP 6

TIE UP LOOSE ENDS

*"This elder of the church said: we know that when
you die, you will be reunited with your whole family.
And I said: what happens if you're good?"*

—Stephen Fry

CHAPTER 21

"Happy birthday Norne!" Norne's mother clapped excitedly for her daughter's birthday.

Her sister and father were far less enthused, being there only because Beatrix had forced them. The little princess Norne was overjoyed nonetheless. It was the first time ever her own family had held such a celebration for her. Norne was turning eight years old, and this was the happiest, most meaningful day of her little life.

Kinderfesten parties were common in Arcosian culture as extravagant ways to celebrate the birthdays of noble youths. Then she saw it, her very own slice of the festive layer cake she'd always dreamed of having.

"Come on, Norne, your birthday cake, enjoy." Norne's mother smiled and handed her the plate. Norne could hardly contain herself at the sight.

"Thank you so much!" Norne cheered. After saying a quick prayer as was customary, she prepared to dig in.

Norne took a bite with a huge grin, almost tearing up at this moment. However, as she did, she looked around. She noticed her father audibly sigh and her sister cover her mouth to keep her giggling quiet.

Then it happened, Norne felt spiking pain and nausea. She fell to the ground in agony, vomiting, convulsing, and crying from whatever she had just eaten. It was poisoned.

The vomiting came up bloody and her head was splitting. It was the most painful experience of her life. When she looked up, her father just shook his head in disappointment as her sister almost fell over from laughing so hard.

Norne could do nothing but cry more audibly. Were they finally trying to kill her? That was a possibility she had to honestly entertain.

As she lay there sobbing in agony, Norne's mother walked over to her and looked down at her daughter like she was something she picked up off her shoe.

"Stop that noise at once. Five—" Norne's mother angrily began.

Norne immediately knew to be silent.

"Don't worry…you'll live. But don't walk away from this without learning a lesson, child. Do you think all that survival training before was for you to just go and eat the first thing you were offered? Just because it was handed to you with a smile doesn't mean it couldn't be poisoned. Always remain vigilant." Beatrix sent a shiver down Norne's spine.

"Well, that was thoroughly disappointing. Let's get out of here." Norne's father stood up and left, ashamed of how pathetic she was.

Norne's sister followed him, looking back and giggling as she went.

So, she was only left with her mother who looked down at her.

"Mama," Norne cried and tried to reach out for her mother. Her hand fell limply to the ground.

"I expect more from you. Do better." Norne's mother turned and left as well.

So Norne was left there, convulsing and crying as the other three left her. The poison she'd ingested was the stuff of nightmares, reserved for torturing the church's most hated enemies. It was a poison reserved for the enemies of god. And Norne's suffering did not end that night until the star had risen the next day. At least when the star had in the parts of the planet been spared from the moon's eternal shadow.

From that day on, Norne ate neither food nor drink, except for wine. At first, she figured she could eat food that she prepared herself. But the moment she raised a fork to her mouth she would suffer severe panic attacks and nightmares for days afterward. Eating at all was out of the question.

Yet, wine was made for general consumption—she could pour it herself. If it was served to her, she would still refuse but under the right circumstances, she could stomach it. There was some vague, religious justification she found in the Arcosian holy text to exempt herself as a Norne. Nobody read the damned book anyway so who could challenge her assertion.

Norne was an Immortal, so she needed no sustenance at all. Quite literally, Power alone could sustain her. But ever since a very different party, wine had a special sentimental value to her. It was the first drink they shared after all. And her mother always said—never mind.

After the final battle, Norne managed the immense administration required for absorbing all the recently ruler-less nations into Tartarus while Chaos got to put down any rebellion, they dare to wage in resistance. Almost overnight, Tartarus was five times its previous size.

Everything was going to plan—even better than planned.

Intent on keeping the ball rolling, Norne invited Chaos to return to Arcosia with her now that they were both on top of the Universe.

As Chaos and Norne arrived on the planet, they were greeted by a massive crowd applauding and cheering them.

Norne returned to Arcosia for the first time, and everyone loved her now. She didn't care and immediately called up a servant, asking him, "have the preparations been made?" she asked.

"Of course. Right this way my lady." The servants led her away.

The next day, all the surviving Eurasian monarchs attended Norne's massive birthday party. Chaos was annoyed when he arrived but couldn't see Norne. For the whole day, she was away but everyone suspiciously kept telling him how amazing Norne was and how much they wish they could marry a woman like Norne. Chaos being an idiot, missed the point.

The entire thing was a giant celebration of how wonderful Norne was including a cringey, if Norne were my Queen, speech that each attending ruler had to cite (except her father, of course). They all waxed poetics about her being invaluable to the nation and all the features she had that made her indispensable as a royal advisor and wife. Chaos still didn't get it.

At the height of the party, Norne made her dramatic entrance. She dazzled everyone in her over the top dress. The flowing, Arcosian blue fabric was a match for the extravagant attire of her mother and sister and equally bejeweled with sapphire blue stones, silver ornaments and highlights. Everyone clapped as the bejeweled princess descended the stairs. Heidi was overcome with jealousy as everyone finally paid attention to Norne.

King Otto loved being able to show off his successful daughter to the other rulers. However, mixed in with jokes of how stupid Chaos was, Otto continued to miss obvious hits at his impending death.

Everyone except him was a governor...of the Tartarian Empire. Otto was the only one of the old generations left.

Everyone in Arcosia got the memo, they cozied up to their new Emperor, Chaos, paid the king less mind in order to better serve Chaos and even openly asked about their positions after the upcoming 'change in management.' It seemed to just be generally understood by everyone but the poor fool Otto himself (and his daughter Heidi with whom he shared the one brain cell between them) that it was only a matter of time before Chaos took over.

However, the doomed idiot king didn't matter, this was Norne's night, and she made sure everyone knew it. Wearing dazzling gems from the latest expeditions and only the finest silk and silver, Norne made an important point on how much she achieved in such little time. By no means did she possess the societally conventional beauty of her mother and sister but if outfits could kill, even Chaos would be fearful.

When things died down, Chaos was sitting alone stuffing his face with food as usual. Norne sat next to him on the couch and slide over till their thighs were touching.

"Norne?" Chaos turned.

Norne however was so overwhelmed from simply touching his thigh that she panicked and immediately walked away, stumbling in the high heels.

"What was that all about?" Chaos was confused.

A beet-red Norne sat in dismay in a corner as Magnus tried to cheer her up.

"Fear not, Lady Norne! You will be victorious—I just know it!" Magnus claimed.

"Damn it all—I had everything planned out in my head, but I just can't stick the landing! Everything is in place so why can't I do it!" Norne agonized over her own awkwardness.

She looked around the corner at Chaos who was sloppily eating food and went even more crimson, blushing from embarrassment while watching the target of her affection. Seeing this was going nowhere. Magnus loudly cleared his throat before offering a suggestion.

"Lady Norne, would you like me to go over with you this time?" he asked nervously.

"What?" Norne glared at him.

Magnus immediately regretted his patronizing request. He closed his eyes and braced for the worst, however, to his surprise Norne became more embarrassed and in a half-whisper uttered, "yes please."

Magnus breathed a sigh of relief. He was growing tired of this teeny-bop romance nonsense, but she was his boss. Magnus, now the royal wingman, had to keep her on the rails and led her over to Chaos again.

"Hey, there you guys were. What's happening?" Chaos asked while still chewing.

"Princess Norne has something to ask you," Magnus immediately said.

Norne began nervously shaking and looking around awkwardly.

"What is it Norne?" Chaos asked in dense confusion.

Norne began stammering uncontrollably. Magnus sighed and refusing to let this drag on any longer, reached into his pocket and flat out handed Chaos an engagement ring.

"A gift from the lady." Magnus bowed and Norne covered her face as it went red as a tomato.

Everyone's eyes were on the Tartarian trio now.

Slowly she lowered her hands from her eyes to see Chaos' reaction, but he just laughed. "Hey Norne! Check this out! It has jewels and crap all over it! How much do you think we could get for this bad boy?" he obliviously asked which made the entire room facepalm at his obliviousness.

Norne was utterly embarrassed and stormed off.

"Lady Norne!" Magnus ran after her.

People fled the drink table as Norne went there to seethe.

"He is a mighty foe, Milady. Perhaps it is best to retreat for now and—" Magnus began. Before he finished his sentence though, Norne slammed a goblet on the table and began immediately pouring out bottles of wine into it.

"Magnus where is the Adamant sweetener?" she asked.

"It's this grey powder in the center of the table. But—" Magnus panicked at the sight of how much alcohol she was guzzling down.

"Shaddap! I did this once before and besides—I'm the future Queen of the Universe!" she drunkenly threw the goblet at him.

She then turned and set her sights on Chaos. Stomping over she grabbed him by the arm.

"You! My room, *now!*" she aggressively yelled. Everyone was shocked and Heidi was angrily jealous as she watched Chaos stand up and be led out by Norne.

As she dragged him to her room he asked, "what? Are you sleepy or something?" still not fully understanding.

Smash cut to the next morning. Norne woke up in her bed but looking up she noticed the ceiling was significantly further away then she remembered. Sitting up and looking around she noticed that sure enough, the bed was broken.

"No way…did it happen?" Norne blushed excitedly.

She looked around but found she was alone. Norne awkwardly exited her room, looking around for Chaos. It didn't take long, she found him stuffing his face at the breakfast table with Heidi sitting next to him.

She wouldn't let her sister get to her this time especially since—well she had to confirm it first. She was too drunk to remember what had happened last night. In Arcosian machismo, that kind of thing was seen as perfectly acceptable.

"Hello Norne." Heidi grinned before Norne could say anything.

"Hello Heidi. What are you doing here?" Norne demanded.

"To save you some time—you tried seducing Chaos last night but were so smashed you couldn't even make it down the hall before face planting. When you passed out at the party last night, Chaos was such a dear and brought you back to your room to sleep. You didn't get any, sorry. But hey, I went to check in on things and well one thing led to another and—oh wait, we didn't wake you did we sister?" Heidi mockingly asked.

Norne's eyes widened as she realized what was going on.

"Happy belated birthday sis. Don't worry, the majority of it took place outside your room. Didn't want to destroy any other furniture." Heidi slyly smiled.

Norne was fuming. She hated being home.

Chaos finished downing the whole plate and laughed excitedly.

"Wow, you really worked up an appetite, didn't you?" Heidi laughed.

"You know it! It's like after a big fight!" Chaos laughed.

"Glad to hear it. I'll make sure to have your favorite dish ready for next time." Heidi pushed her luck.

Norne sat in disbelief.

Sure enough, a few months later in the Arcosian palace the clergy successfully delivered Heidi's child. Norne saw the unnaturally large creature open its eyes—sure enough, those were the dreaded red eyes of Typhon.

"Congratulations, Your Majesty. Your firstborn and heir," the clergyman proclaimed after the successful operation. The notably large baby was lovingly handed to Heidi.

"Yeah, right. 'Firstborn.'" Chaos snickered under his breath.

"I'll name him… Drakon II." Heidi looked up at Chaos.

"Didn't I kill him?" Chaos asked.

"Right. Drakon Junior. Yes, that's what peasants do as their equivalent right? Drakon Junior of Tartarus." Heidi smiled.

"Meh, whatever you say, lady. But now that's over, we can start again, right?" Chaos immediately asked. Heidi giggled. "Of course. But first, here." She lovingly handed the baby to Chaos who quite frankly didn't know what to do with it and just nervously tossed it to Norne.

Norne caught it like a log and didn't even look at this monument to her failure. Her mother would be so disappointed.

"Congratulations Norne…you're an aunt." Heidi grinned at her spitefully.

Norne's face didn't even register emotion. She had mentally checked out long ago.

Ever since that night, Chaos and Heidi began their degenerate cavorting more publicly. How long had it been going on behind

Norne's back? She had been so absorbed in ruling the Empire that she had missed that vile woman ensnaring her Chaos. Norne felt ashamed and humiliated and angry.

Chaos never looked at her like that. She felt so ugly. And Norne's mother had always said that ugly girls—well, never mind. At least Chaos' interest in Heidi had seemed to wane after they had learned of the pregnancy ironically enough. However, for all Norne knew that just meant he'd found a new squeeze somewhere else, and it wasn't Norne. It was never Norne. But Norne's mother also had taught her solutions to this issue.

CHAPTER 22

The next morning, Chaos put his shoes on by the front door with a slave-drawn carriage waiting. He was off to massacre some Grak loyalists who were trying to ally with a bordering nation to prevent further expansion.

"May the gods of fortune smile upon you in war. Make our son proud." Heidi waved while holding the baby Drakon Junior.

"Come back any time m'boy. It's good to finally have a son in the family!" Otto excitedly patted him on the back. Otto fussed over his technical son-in-law as if they were long-time acquaintances. Chaos was annoyed by his doting and looked to Norne for what to do.

Norne sat on the steps reading her book, *Treatises on Colonization: The Tartarian Man Who Went Up the Hill and Came Down with All the Strawberries by Scallion Gerald*. She didn't even bother saying anything, the two just shared a knowing look and nod. They knew what was up.

"Uh-huh. Bye." Chaos couldn't wait to get out of there and flew away.

After they watched Chaos go, Otto excitedly walked over to Norne.

"My big-shot princess Norne, back with us at last. It'll be just like the old days. It's so good to have you back here." Otto excitedly grinned with that 'new grandpa' joy still overwhelming him.

"Right," Norne emotionlessly responded.

Then, the three women all went away, wordlessly leaving him.

At dinner, Otto was confused by the women remaining quiet. Heidi was taking care of Drakon Jr. while Beatrix removed her priceless ornamentations which she wore more frequently than usual for Chaos. After all, it was only Otto. He felt awkward, repeatedly trying to start up a conversation but the responses they'd give were brief and impersonal.

Norne stayed a while but since she did not eat, eventually stood up saying, "excuse me. I have work to attend." She bowed before leaving.

"Excuse me, father but this little one seems to be getting hungry as well. I must take my leave." Heidi lifted the baby and left.

"Dear, I have some priestess duties to attend to. Don't wait up." Beatrix smiled before leaving as well.

The women all left Otto for different reasons to do their own thing. Even he began to notice something was off and became worried.

Either way, Norne had returned to her room and was at her desk, reading. There were piles of reports on the Empire's findings in the unearthing of ancient hoards. Norne was coordinating the searches for these hoards in all the Empire's new territory ever since the number of provinces more than doubled.

Before the invention of banking, wealthy figures of the past would store their wealth in massive hoards—caves and craters or other concealed cavities with money and artifacts. Great kings and warriors hid their plunder in these hoards until such a time as they needed to be spent for the lavish expenditures of such icons. Treasure hunting was a common result of many of these caches entering myth and folk tales but ever since banking made them obsolete, they passed from popular discussion.

Norne however, as a lover of the classics, saw all this untapped wealth as a huge potential payday to aid the Empire in finishing the absorption of all that new territory. Through part grave robbing, part archeology, Tartarus had extracted billions of silvers in wealth from the sites they had uncovered.

But all of that was small potatoes compared to their main goal—Andvari's hoard.

Andvari's hoard was said to be equal parts massive and cursed. Any who found the hoard were blessed with a mountain's worth of gold but at the cost of a horrific spell cast on it by its original owner. To Norne, however, superstition was for fools and money was real, so the true purpose of all these expeditions was to find that specific hoard. Tartarus dug around suspected spots to try and find it, while digs elsewhere were used to determine the best practice for not damaging artifacts and maximizing cost efficiency. The nobility was way into this resurgence in 'archeology.' Their private enterprises had decentralized the effort and generated massive wealth for the provinces on their own dime instead of Norne's, so she was in favor of this emerging private sector.

The Empire offered cash prizes for hauls of a significant enough size. But there were already issues of Provinces keeping some of the finds for themselves and taking the prize anyways. It was so annoying—the massive influx of money and power was making Norne's new aristocracy act almost exactly like the old one. In her mind, corruption was fine but only if she intended for it.

Either way, Andvari's hoard was within sight, Norne could feel it. The slaves were now digging in shifts, for twenty-four hours of searching the most likely planets. The Provincial leaders were filing constant updates and managing the day-to-day. And Norne— well, she re-read the *Nibelungenlied* as the origin of the myth to see if there were any clues she might have missed the first seven times she had read through it.

The infamous treasure was originally thought to be a myth, but Norne had found a concerning number of myths to at least in some part, be based on reality (especially after raiding the graves and holy sites of Italia). Plus, if it was real, the Empire would finally have enough money to…have more money.

Norne finished the story once again. It was a lot of hard work. Setting it aside on her desk, she stood up to stretch.

At night, she was sneaking through the halls to the royal library again.

"Norne!" Otto said excitedly, making her jump in shock.

"Hello, father," she responded with the most fake enthusiasm she could muster.

Norne knew that Otto was trying to spend time with her now that she was powerful and useful to him.

"Norne, come with me! I have something exciting to show you." He grinned.

He led her to a wall and pulled the hidden lever to open a secret door.

"Oh. I always wondered what he hid in this secret room," Norne thought to herself, having easily uncovered this as a child.

"Behold…our family's history of sorts." Otto presented a room of old books and paintings and other assorted ancient items such as chests and jewels.

Norne opened a book with a strange *T* on the front and observed the ancient scripts.

"Ancient Arcosian…before the great migration?" Norne wondered aloud.

"That's right. Chronicling the Arcosian people's journey from the land of the ice and snow." Otto recounted their people's legendary immigration.

"And our new home was *very* different." Norne sarcastically sighed before closing the book.

"Well, that's the funny thing! Despite what the legends say, known only to the royals is a secret I pass on to you! This planet we call Arcosia is actually a different world than the one our ancestors started on. All that hogwash about 'bringing home with us' was just to impress the mortal peasants. The old planet was smashed to space dust at some point in the attempt to move it." Otto laughed without considering what that would mean for Arcos' moon.

"Obviously…that's why I said, 'new home.'" Norne raised an eyebrow at his expectation that people had actually bought that one.

"Oh…right. You and your mother are into this bookworm stuff, so I guess it'd make sense that you knew." He was disappointed that she wasn't blown away.

"No, that's just common sense. Even the secret library surely has nothing on these texts. What other topics are in here?" Norne asked.

"Huh? I dunno. I never learned how to read the ancient script, everything I know is word of mouth from my father. Seemed boring, I was out fighting instead." Otto shrugged.

"Of course," Norne groaned, setting the book down.

"You want to read this?" Otto asked.

"Knowing of Arcosia's past could be useful. Would the clergy know about any of this?" she asked.

"Oh, no. The ancients worshipped a different set of gods called the Ass-ear or something. When Arcosia converted to the one true god, my father killed the heretics off. The only ones who knew any of this was the royal family," Otto explained with a chuckle.

"Lovely." Norne tried to hide her growing frustration. Looking up at the old runic painting of a one-eyed man in a cloak wielding a mighty spear with a strange, winged helmet to match the ravens on his shoulders, she raised an eyebrow. Sure enough, he had white hair to match the Arcosian royalty, a curious coincidence to Norne. Though in truth, his hair was simply old and grey (which had ironically been seen as a lesser form racial purity for lacking the pure white beauty standard which he supposedly inspired).

"I know at least that is Wodan or something. Their head god. And Hel—the underworld of modern beliefs gets its name from one of the Ass-ears as well, I believe. They were of the Jarls as you and me, and they followed that eyepatch fellow as their king. How ridiculous. To think they believed a 'mere man' created everything and was meant to rule over them." Otto scoffed.

"Yes, as opposed to praying to a space rock," Norne thought but didn't say, as she rolled her eyes.

"Anyways, wish I knew more, but consider this an early birthday present. You love this bookworm stuff, right? So, enjoy." Otto grinned.

Norne looked at the painting again, the ancient runic script was indecipherable to her but thankfully beneath the bottom inscription she noted an old Arcosia title which she could read as a form of the modern runes. It read, *'King Odin-Grimnir the All-Father of the Aesir.'* If that latter title was accurate, it would be extremely useful in translating the above language. Though Norne was skeptical if it could be trusted given that it was recent enough that she could understand it, but it matched decently well with what her father had said. The mysterious ancient runes, the archaic old runes, and the modern language of Arcosian that came from it, these were all part of the secret Norne could uncover.

Otto got excited as Norne smirked while noting the codes but suddenly she turned around.

"Right... I'll begin deciphering. I'll be going then." She took an armful of books and left. Otto, expecting a more robust response frowned.

The next day, he tried and failed to get the attention of his wife or daughter similarly. Since the day before, Heidi had been much more skillful in evading him, and Otto was starting to get the strange feeling that they were ignoring him.

He hung his head, walking back to his throne room, dejected before Heidi ran over.

"Dad! The girls and I had a party planned but Norne is squatting in the dining room!" Heidi complained. She may have grown but she still knew how to get him to do things.

Otto became excited to be needed and followed Heidi to the dining hall. When they opened the door, they saw Norne and her guest. Otto gasped as he recognized the man as Georgiy Aleksandrov Yesfir Kovaleva, the greatest assassin in the Universe. But to most, he went by his infamous pseudonym, Mr. Vickers.

"What is he doing here!" Otto panicked, as his mind began racing. He hadn't used his services in years. Was this payback time? Coming after Otto's golden goose just as he could smell the freedom of being in the black?

Norne tied a napkin around her neck and put her hands on the table.

"As you observe, the salad, fish, then dinner fork are to your left with the corresponding knives on the right. The smallest points are quite useless as weapons, so you need not fear them as attacks. That said each of them is next to useless as you can observe. It is a true faux pas to create cutlery out of Adamant since they can easily kill a target while their guard is down. But don't worry, nothing here could likely pierce his Majesty's hide, given your descriptions," the assassin explained.

Otto watched in total bafflement as Georgiy ran through the entire history of eating etiquette and safety when dining with others.

"The key kill points of course are the throat, eyes, and heart. The knife is held by the right hand; most people's dominant, so be wary of those who would sit next to you on your left. That will always be your greatest threat at a dinner since they could strike and kill before you'd be prepared to defend or fight back," Georgiy explained.

"I see. Any additional rules of thumb to ensure His Majesty's safety?" Norne asked.

"Well for starters, make sure there is *no* Adamant in the room at all. Dinners on your turf are ideal but when in the house of others, formality be damned, you *must* have soldiers scan the room first. Poison testers during the dinner would also be nice," the assassin advised.

"No need to worry about poison. I've tested him and Chaos has immunity to all poisons known to man, so he is good for regular eating." Norne hand waved.

"Still, a literal spike in the food could cause a problem, even for him. You can never be too safe." Georgiy warned.

"I see." Norne nodded and leaned back in her chair. Suddenly Georgiy smirked. When she leaned back, her head was sliced off by a saw that was concealed in the back of her chair. It fell out the bottom through the hole the assassin cut to hide it in there before Norne took her seat.

Otto and Heidi were shocked.

"What have you done! You've ruined us! What do I tell Chaos now?" Otto panicked, in a very telling way.

The assassin was laughing ecstatically. "I did it!" he laughed while jumping up and down.

To all of their surprise though, Norne was clapping for him as she entered the door.

"What?" the assassin asked in a panic, looking at the beheaded Norne in the chair.

"You did well. This was all staged to test your abilities and confirm you were as good as you say. I'll admit, I'm impressed. I was on my guard and had an eye out for everything but still, if that was me, I'd be dead. You're hired. We'll speak more when I return to Tartarus. And don't worry, the cheque is in the mail." Norne laughed, before waving at the decapitated Norne which turned into a puddle of water.

"Of course. Pleasure doing business with you." The assassin bowed before leaving.

"Norne! What is happening!" Otto cried.

Norne noticed her family's shock at seeing her at work.

"Forgive me for bringing work during this stay." She sighed.

So, as it was it continued for a week—Chaos was out at war, but Norne stayed home to help Heidi with the baby. In reality, Norne was kept busy preparing Arcosia for Chaos' impending takeover. Everyone was getting ready for his return and poor Otto was just slowly realizing how screwed he was.

Though there was the matter of the Church. The Empire of Tartarus had no room for the worship of anyone but its Emperor, so naturally, the priesthood would want some guarantees.

"The Head Priestess will be out to meet with you shortly. I beg your patience; she is very busy with her divine duties," one of the temple's Nornes told the princess of the same name.

"Sure." Norne rolled her eyes.

She sat alone on one of the pews of the empty cathedral, looking up at the stained-glass windows and statues of Arcos, the god of the moon. She couldn't wait to tear it all down and replace it with the draconic imagery of Chaos' own state religion. She was in charge now and she was going to make the replacement process as painful as possible for the religion she hated so much.

That of course begged the question of why she felt so compelled to report to her mother on this matter at all. Left to her thoughts, Norne began to consider the idea that it would be fun if Beatrix would have to come on bent legs to beg her daughter to keep her high status. But she was already here, being disrespected as usual by the fashionably late priestess.

Norne grew impatient waiting alone, before taking note of the young Nornes in training being taught by their senior. She remembered those days and she almost thanked god they were over.

"And we pray that Arcos raises a hedge of protection around his children and protects us from evil spirits and bad omens." The priestess led the children in their rehearsed chant.

Norne snickered at the inane practice. A 'hedge of protection' had always puzzled her, but it was probably out-of-date imagery regarding herding communities protecting livestock. It didn't scale up to the supposed world ending the evil of the demon king Bolverk being repelled by a mere shrub.

As Norne watched the group, some of the kids took note of her and excitedly waved, wearing innocent smiles. Norne just looked away, annoyed by the little flesh creatures which in turn made them sad.

"Sister, why do we pray for a mere hedge? Arcos is lord of the world. Couldn't he give us a castle instead?" one of the children dared to ask.

"Here we go." Norne rolled her eyes, knowing the canned answer.

"We ask as the heroes of old did. Those prayers in the holy texts are special. Those traditions keep us close to Arcos and are beyond questioning for both you and me," the sister Norne helpfully responded.

The child wasn't suitably convinced but knew to just agree with it. It had never satisfied Norne back when she would be smart with the teachers. At times it really felt like she knew their own religion better than they. If she wasn't the princess, they would have beaten her for such insolence. So many questions those pretentious clergywomen could never properly answer.

"If Arcos created everything, what created Arcos?"

"Can Arcos create something so heavy he cannot move it?"

"If Arcos can do anything, why can't he make my family love me."

Norne paused. She didn't remember that last one. As a child, she had visited the head Norne crying that very question. It all came back to her. Otto had destroyed the gift she had given him—an ecclesiastical commentary on all the holy texts. He claimed to love them so much that Norne was certain it was the way into her father's heart. But the contradictions and illogical tidbits her commentary highlighted, though in the least accusing way, were declared blasphemous. Her years' worth of work was destroyed publicly, and she was once again made to apologize to all the leaders of the church as well as to the whole of the nation.

Nobody liked it when she asked questions, or even when she gave answers.

"Apologies for the delay, Lady Norne. We can discuss the issues regarding the transition now." A high-ranking priest approached Norne with a smile and snapped her out of her reminiscing.

Norne took note that the priest had come alone.

"And where is the head priestess? My appointment was with her." Norne stood up.

"The Head Priestess is very busy with her divine duties. I hope I will suffice for you." The priest smiled robotically. Norne glared at him. Beatrix's power plays were always so irritating.

After several more days of rinsing and repeating (with far more success), Norne had met with many of Arcosia's most power-ful people in the army, church, and bureaucracy to grant guarantees and negotiate loyalty. Now, Norne went and sat in the above-ground hallway with a beautiful window view of the palace's winter gar-den, a garden of sorts filled with evergreens and other plants that endured winter climates year-round.

As she had requested, several high-ranking members of the castle staff came to meet with her.

"Lady Norne! We have been loyal to you and served you since you were a child! In our time of need, please do not abandon us. We serve you and Arcosia. We shall serve His Majesty Chaos as well!" They prostrated themselves before the smug princess and begged her.

"I am a merciful woman—let's discuss your place in the new administration." She grinned.

So, they discussed in secret, negotiating their future positions under Tartarus. Norne didn't mind keeping them around since it would save on retraining staff and having to wait to get over the learning curve. However, just as the verbal contracts could be final-ized, Norne paused.

"Hey there, guys. Looking at the garden?" Otto awkwardly entered and inserted himself into the conversation.

The servants quickly became silent and stood at attention, finding it awkward to have him still milling about.

"Cute garden, yeah? It was a fun way to use up the remaining building funds from the castle. Now the trees are as tall as the building. Heh heh…probably should've just used the money to start paying off the debts since Beatrix won't let me take any more out of the church treasury." Otto awkwardly laughed.

As he continued to laugh, the servants quietly made their way out, leaving Norne there to hold the bag.

"Where are they going? You notice everyone acting weird lately?" Otto nervously asked.

"They have much work to do Your Majesty. Pay them no mind," Norne robotically answered.

"No, no. Not Your Majesty. Hey Norne, we're family. Just call me, dad." Otto walked over and stood next to her.

Norne froze. A couple of years earlier, and she may have been happy to hear that.

"Well…if you're done looking at the garden, remember what day it is?" Otto excitedly asked.

"Wednesday?" Norne asked in confusion.

"That's right! As mandated, it is time for Wednesday prayers." Otto was excited to observe the Arcosian day of religion, Woden's day!

"Oh right." Norne sighed.

"Come on Norne. It'll be just like when you were a little girl!" Otto excitedly suggested since this was his idea of fun.

"I—" Norne began to protest.

"Listen, as happy as I am for Heidi—having a baby out of wedlock is bound to put her in need of another redemption and really, I can't afford it if you keep this up and I need you redeemed too! You're still a virgin, right? Arcos knows what sins you've accrued that I'd need to pay off! Please, if you come to the temple, I can at least rest easy knowing that Arcos will regard you better!" Otto admitted to Norne worriedly.

She sighed. In Arcosia, people sufficiently overcome with sin would need to be 'redeemed.' They were bound to lose their divine luck and favor as well as their place in the afterlife with Arcos lest they pay a sufficient price of redemption to the church. When Otto meant he could not afford it, he meant it literally.

Arcos would declare those up for redemption through his divine mouthpiece, the head priestess Beatrix von Arcosia of course. She would extract the required sum needed to return to Arcos' good graces, as it was defined in the scrolls.

Arcos had standardized these prices (mostly to prevent priests from taking the grift too far and straight-up extorting those in need of 'redemption').

The prices of those in Arcos' sight were equivalent to what they had to pay to redeem themselves and they were constituted thusly:

"And thy estimation shall be of the male from twenty years old even unto sixty years old, even thy estimation shall be fifty coins of silver, after the standard of the church's treasury. And if it be a female, then thy estimation shall be thirty silvers. And if it be from five years old even unto twenty years old, then thy estimation shall be of the male twenty silvers, and for the female ten. And if it be from a month old even unto five years old, then thy estimation shall be of the male five silvers, and for the female, thy estimation shall be three coins of silver. And if it be from sixty years old and above; if they be a male, then thy estimation shall be fifteen, and for the female ten silvers. But if he be poor of spirit or of silver as to not be worth the above standard, extract from him all that he has and from his wife also. May his empty wallet fill his spirit. And if it be female, she should be alone, do not punish the man for his wife's sins. Should that be insufficient, toiling in servitude shall pay back to the church what coinage could not. Finally, to those of Arcos' chosen, the priesthood and the royals. If any of this superior class shall fall from their grace before Arcos' sight and does not love the eternal light of Arcosia, may they be accursed in his sight!

For those of royal blood and of the cloth may their price be half of what they are worth may they be male and all their worth if they are female! Though they may not be enslaved," the corresponding Arcosian passage declared.

Only the ending of the passage was necessary, but Norne had memorized the whole thing, so here it was. It was tradition for the father to redeem his children if he was alive. Though he didn't even dare ask how wealthy Norne had become as shadow leader of Tartarus.

Norne gave in, she had time to waste. After all, she hadn't slept since she got back so a nap was in order.

They passed through the hall connecting Otto's rinky-dink, low-budget, McMansion castle, into the pristine and immaculate church of Arcos. In Italia, Tartarus, and Mesos there was some variation of the saying, "there are spiderwebs even in the King's castle." In Arcosia it was a fact.

The cathedral palace on the other hand was spotless as always and sparkling with immaculate silver decorations. A division as clear as night and day. The Nornes, priests, and nobles had gathered for the service. Norne and Otto took their seat in the royal section in the front row. Whispers among the crowd annoyed Norne, since they had all taken notice of her return to the chapel.

"Remember dear, we're in church now. No scowling, remember you'd look much prettier if you smiled more," Otto patronizingly whispered to her. Her entire childhood she'd heard that and had to comply but for today, she couldn't be bothered. Otto prepared to chastise her again, but the sermon was about to start.

As the upper-class rumor mill got up and running instantly in the cathedral, the speaker took to the stage and was annoyed that they cared more about her. This was the Head of the Arcosian Temple, a position under Beatrix that handled this specific planet while she oversaw his jurisdiction *and* all other churches of Arcos in the Universe.

Even more in her shadow than Otto, he insisted on making his impact in his fiery and iconic sermons.

He would decide what he wanted to talk about that week and then search the scriptures for it. Failing that, just make it up! Not that it mattered, the Arcosian literacy rate was abysmal, and even those who could read the holy texts couldn't be bothered, since once they returned to their own homes and could take off their zealot facades.

Ironically Norne, the evangelizing atheist actually knew the scrolls better than any of the most passionate Arcosian clergymen. She was not amused by the irony. Her mother made her memorize them all. Norne made the talking heads sound like amateurs on the subject.

The Arcos religion was far less prescriptive on moral actions in day-to-day life and more focused on taxation, holidays, the fabrics one could wear, foods they could or could not eat, and the animals they could and could not boil in their own mother's milk. This was a relief; it would have been tragic if people focused on arcane rules and missed a religion's doctrine on how to be a decent human being.

Norne's mind was wandering.

The priest had taken so unbearably long to prepare, that her mind had gone to weird places.

For this holy Wed-nes-day, he had a speech about the importance of never changing like Arcos. It was filled as usual, with obvious pandering to the king. Constant praise of Otto for his long reign, his military victories as inspired by Arcos, and of course his unmatchable piety as a true adherent to Arcos in a Universe of heathens.

Norne figured he had missed the memo, but perhaps it was just a force of habit to keep Otto happy like a child being infantilized by constant praise.

Norne didn't speak the whole time, but she did pay attention. She made a game of counting contradictions in his assertions cross-referenced with her memories of his ramblings from her youth.

The thralls cheered for the head priest, though Norne knew he had no idea what he was talking about.

Finally, mercifully, it ended and Norne left.

"Pretty good, huh?" Otto excitedly asked.

"Of course, Your Majesty. What was your favorite part?" Norne asked.

Otto paused, "Um—I liked the uh—part about Arcos." He nodded.

"I see." Norne did her best to avoid any obvious sign of mockery. His mind had been emotionally stimulated but as per usual, his brain remained at a perpetual flatline. As to be expected.

Finally, after that, she managed to get away from her father's desperate attempts at bonding. That night, Norne was lying down in bed but was too bored to sleep.

"I barely got… anything done today because of him. I hope Chaos makes his death painful," Norne growled as she lay there and looked up at the ceiling. She was still deciding what to do with her mother and sister, but despite his constant attempts to get closer to her, he might as well have been six feet under already.

And she lay there, back home and bored. For over an hour, she continued looking up at the ceiling. This was ridiculous! Norne had tons of work to do, so she sat up and decided to continue juggling the tasks of ruling, even remotely.

Retrieving her paper notes on tablets she had confiscated from the princess of Mesos, Norne continued studying them. The letters she was unable to access before, despite now being in her possession were written in some strange language she'd never encountered before.

The closest match was the ancient Italic language families, so Norne restlessly poured over both Italic and Etruscan dialects to try and understand what some said. Others seemed to be yet other languages and those weren't even worth bothering to solve with how different they were.

When attempting to track down the messenger, Norne had interrogated the mailman but only learned that the princess' contact within the Committee would come to him with the correspondences. She was a blue-haired woman, a feature rare even in Immortals so Norne had people looking constantly for anyone who matched the description.

However, for now, Norne was on her own. Endlessly trying to translate the language, all she'd managed to do was possibly identify this language's version of periods which at least gave her an idea as to sentence length assuming her hypothesis was correct.

It was useless. However, the gifts and gadgets stored with the letters were of great interest as well. A device for capturing light to create images like a painting, a device telling exactly how hot or cold it was in a room, a giant wheeled device for transport or combat to replace slave drawn carriages, etc. All things Norne remembered playing with alongside the princess. But now was not the time to think of all that, they could be put to work, benefiting the Empire.

Norne had hoped to read the matching letters sent by these inventors with their prototypes however, even remembering what she was told by the princess, she failed to make any matches.

"Forget it! I have other things to do!" Norne gave up on cryptography and went to another pressing issue.

She had paperwork on her desk pretending to do official business instead of researching the Immortality of the Typhon cultist, which was, of course, what she was actually doing. As the night dragged on, though she made no progress, she kept herself busy getting nothing done. She went over things over and over, cursing the wall she had hit on her research.

"Damned Grak, completely destroyed my prime sample. Unless he would've become useless like the others," she remarked, while theorizing why the corpses of Leona, Sofia, and the general whose name she couldn't remember lost all their Power after Chaos destroyed Typhon's brain.

Shaking around a vial of the general's now normal blood in frustration she continued jotting down observations as to the permanent changes to the biology even after the Power had left.

She was deep in thought, thinking of an undead army at her command. However, eventually...this too bored her. She *really* hated being home.

"Might as well check up on things to pass the time." Norne thought.

So, when she closed her eyes, she activated Norne-2, an ice double she could remotely control. This experimental ability was left on Tartarus. Less powerful than her ice doubles made for combat it more fully resembled her body, even upon close inspection (though its only attack was a quick pulse of ice).

Norne used her other body on Italia to see what is happening in the new territory. In Italia, Norne walked around the Palace. The guards all stood at attention in her presence. They were no longer Centurions of Italia but instead Imperial Knights of Tartarus. The conqueror had been conquered.

Norne made her way to the banquet hall where the windows and doors were open, letting the cool air into the reformatted castle. There, she saw Aurelia sitting with Magnus on the porch and looking up at the moon.

It wasn't exactly a romantic scene. Despite the fact that the two had been forced into a marriage to legitimize Tartarus' occupation things remained completely platonic between them. After all, that was just for political purposes.

Aurelia had survived the bloody battle of that day. When Norne found out Chaos had spared her, she was furious and prepared to finish the job herself before Magnus of all people stood up to defend her.

After all, to better control the people a beloved legitimate ruler serving as a puppet was indispensable. If she were killed the revolt would be unparalleled and the integration of the province delayed by decades. Norne couldn't let emotion foil such a perfect opportunity.

"Fine. Then she's your problem." Norne had told Magnus before storming out.

And so now she was. Magnus married into the Italic royal family and came to live in the palace which wasn't such a big deal since a new Imperial Knight headquarters was to be built in Reme anyways, so it just meant he had less of a distance to travel into work.

Back when Magnus had first moved in, the newlyweds were a bit awkward. They personally brought his things in themselves and barely said a word between them.

Finally, after Magnus set down his dresser with changes of clothes and Aurelia put down the wall sized bookshelf the two had decided to take a break.

"You can take off your armor and get comfortable. This is your home too now." Aurelia sat down on the couch with a sigh.

"If you attacked me without my armor, I would stand significantly less of a chance than with it." Magnus coldly responded.

"Come on, you can stop worrying about me. I won't try anything. I know when I'm beat." Aurelia shrugged.

"Forgive me, Aurelia… but I don't believe that for a second." Magnus plainly said.

"Fair enough." Aurelia glared.

The room was silent again.

"Significantly less of a chance? I'm sure you've read the reports. What do you say your chances are of defeating me now?" Aurelia asked with a grim expression.

"You have been deprived of your power enhancing armor, had your power sealed to be less than my own and are surrounded by hundreds of hostile guards at my command. In short, I would not have a chance of defeating you." Magnus explained.

"Wow. You're smarter than you look." Aurelia laughed at the misdirect. She figured it was his yearly attempt at a joke.

"It would be more manageable if we sealed your Power completely... but then you would be completely defenseless. I repeat that the guards posted here to prevent your escape have many hostile members among their midst. Yet a dead hostage does not make a good one, you understand." Magnus explained.

"Right. If I die, your little occupation falls apart." Aurelia followed along.

"So, though you have been weakened, you have enough power to defend yourself, even if it places myself at risk. The assimilation of Italia is just that important. Besides, you would surely kill me, but you would stand no chance escaping the entire base full of Imperial knights that would be upon you right after." Magnus explained while looking out the palace windows to the base that was under construction.

"You don't have to reassure me that you're being cautious. After all, I wear constant reminders of that." Aurelia pointed to the primitive tracker chained around her neck. It contained an Adamant charge that would blow her head off if she ever left the planet.

"And yet you still don't trust me?" Aurelia asked.

"No." Magnus plainly responded.

He then began continuing to unpack as Aurelia sat there and watched him.

"Fine. You saved me back there... from both of them. So, thanks. I hate you the least." Aurelia admitted.

"Please don't." Magnus solemnly said.

Aurelia was surprised.

"Oh yeah. Sorry for almost getting you killed back at that party. I was just trying to mess with Norne, but remaining acquaintances all this time without ever addressing this just felt wrong." Aurelia sighed.

"Don't apologize." Magnus stopped her.

"Magnus... if you feel you've betrayed our friendship then save it. I'm still alive at least, so I'm grateful that you've stood up for me as much as you have." Aurelia said.

"Aurelia... it is not personal. At every stage your survival and comfort were only considered insofar as it secured the efficient assimilation of a militarily powerful province for the Empire. You have not received any special treatment: my loyalty is only to Tartarus." Magnus declared.

"I see." Aurelia raised an eyebrow.

She stood up from her seat and walked over to him.

"Listen, we need to set the ground rules." Aurelia explained.

"Of course. As a guest in your house, I will obey what you outline." Magnus responded.

"Yeah. First of all, if we're forced to live together, you need to drop the formalities. You have to treat me like you used to before all this marriage crap. I'm going to be miserable enough already, and I don't need any other headaches on top of that." Aurelia pointed at him.

"I will keep that in mind." Magnus awkwardly responded.

"That means no mushy, romantic stuff. It was funny the first time you tried your best to be romantic, but I would throw myself off the roof if you tried it again." Aurelia said.

"Duly noted." Magnus nodded.

"And no children. You can adopt or whatever if you want, but my policy towards the gorilla extends to you. Separate beds and hands off." Aurelia sighed.

"Oh, of course!" Magnus cried in a panic even at the thought.

Aurelia couldn't help but laugh at his exasperated response. Magnus was impressed. It almost felt like he felt worse about her situation than she did.

"Come on, stop packing, the palace has a view that's to die for." Aurelia took him by the hand and led him to a nice spot by the banquet hall where they could look at the stars.

She couldn't let it get her down. Aurelia remained strong and acted as if not much had happened. She really did enjoy Magnus' company. There were worse people to be forced to marry in their archaic court culture.

She kept back her despair because she had to be vigilant. She had to be at 100% so she could avenge her fallen loved ones. She had to save her silent rage for the two she really hated.

And at that moment, their story and Norne's intersected. Norne-2 stepped into view after arriving on Italia.

"Am I interrupting?" Norne approached.

"My Lady!" Magnus quickly bowed before Norne as soon as he heard her.

Norne smiled at his reverence but turned to Aurelia who didn't even move. Her casual attitude with Magnus vanished as she became as cold as the nighttime air.

"If you were going to kill me for insolence there wasn't much I could do anyways." Aurelia said while taking in the beauty of the night's sky.

"Show Lady Norne the proper-" Magnus furiously began but with the wave of her hand, Norne had him standing silently at attention.

"I don't see why you're so upset Aurelia. I've made your dream a reality: you will get to rule Italia as it evolves into a state beyond what your father could've ever imagined." Norne mocked Aurelia while walking over and sitting next to her instead.

"The dictator means 'the one who speaks, and others follow'. Just pray you and Magnus can keep me on script." Aurelia refused to even look at Norne.

Aurelia's new living conditions were less than ideal. Since she had used her Power the Dictator on almost the entire government, Norne decided it was more efficient to simply relay orders to her so she would be forced to parrot her orders. So, she was condemned to an ignominious fate of receiving orders to dictate to her mind slaves for Norne. She kept Italia in line and loyal to the

Empire, while Magnus kept her in line and loyal to the Empire. All the while, her hatred burned against her oppressors and even Norne knew she was plotting some kind of revenge. And whenever she laid eyes on that accursed ice witch, she could barely hold herself back.

This shame, this complete and total failure, this agonizing loss: this was what her fascismo had wrought. Now her imagined idyllic past, her glorious prelapsarian paradise was a nostalgic dream of the bargain bin, tin pot farce that got her here in the first place. Ready to start the mad murdering menagerie again. This was their fascism.

"I can tell this will be one killer of a honeymoon. Make sure her explosive restraints are properly fastened if you take the puppet off world." Norne stood up and walked past Magnus with the confident gait once shared by the Dictator.

"Oh wait... for morale, I'm supposed to ask how you are doing." Norne paused as she remembered.

"Exceptional, my lady. The New Province is being integrated as planned. The old guard have already sworn fealty to the Emperor and those who were worthy have been added to our ranks of the Imperial Knights. As the location of the new Imperial Knight headquarters, it has proven indispensable in bringing future glory to the Empire!" Magnus saluted as a report.

Aurelia was disgusted. This was the one part of him she couldn't stand. She hated whenever he'd prostrate himself before those she hated.

"Excellent work. I believe your wedding gift will arrive soon for you and your family." Norne smiled.

"I am honored. My sister was nervous about bringing the baby here to Italia so a housewarming gift would do her especially well." Magnus thanked her.

"Good. Keep up the good work Magnus." Norne saluted.

"I shall milady! In Justice!" Magnus saluted her back.

Norne content in soaking up Aurelia's impotent misery at her presence took her leave. Once Norne had left them, Magnus sighed.

"...I know it is difficult. But if you wish to survive, you're going to have to get used to working under her." Magnus warned his wife.

"Magnus... I will not rest until that witch dies the most painful death imaginable. That is all there is to it." Aurelia menacingly warned him instead.

Norne returned to her body on Arcosia.

She was back, but she still couldn't sleep. She had been completely unable to fall asleep since that day. So Norne went to her desk to try and do more paperwork.

While she was doing paperwork in her childhood room, Otto knocked before entering without a response.

"Hey Norne," Otto whispered.

"Yes, Your Majesty?" Norne immediately got in character.

"Want to uh...talk about something?" Otto randomly asked.

Norne didn't know how to respond.

"This is the first time that all four of us have been together again and...well, I don't know what to do," Otto said.

"I'm sorry, I cannot. I have very important work to do," Norne lied.

"I see. It's fine, Heidi and Beatrix said the same thing, so it would've just been us anyways." Otto's face was downcast as he slowly closed the door.

Norne rolled her eyes, but Otto opened the door again nervously.

"Norne...have you noticed your mother acting strange?" Otto asked.

"I don't think so. It's useless trying to read her though." Norne sighed, becoming annoyed.

"Okay. Good—good. Because—" Otto continued rambling, clearly as bored and uncomfortable as Norne. She began quietly tapping her finger impatiently. It was clear to her that everyone distancing themselves from Otto was getting to the king, but she really preferred that he mentally unravel elsewhere.

"Norne, your mother and I weren't very close. I let the 'trophy' part of trophy wife overtake the real position but…ever since Drakon Jr. was born she's seemed even more distant. Not the same as you or Heidi more like she—she—I'm not stupid you know—she didn't really love me, but at least she bothered pretending before," Otto confided in his daughter.

"She is a good actor. I wish I didn't know but she told me you weren't any good." Norne grinned.

"I knew—Norne I knew she had needs, but before I thought the money and power was enough. Before at night she'd at least sleep in the royal bed as distant as she was on her side. With me I mean—I'm just. She did it before—but Norne—you don't think—you don't think—no one else will talk to me, but it's been eating at the back of my mind! Heidi and Chaos were an item without my knowing and Beatrix—Norne—you don't think she and—and he—" Otto looked his daughter in the eyes and began tearing up despite his best efforts.

Norne paused and dropped her pen.

A few minutes later, Norne furiously stomped towards her mother's door. The four Holy Knights that guarded the true ruler of Arcosia stepped up confrontationally. With a stomp of her foot, she froze them all solid and walked past without issue. She flung the door open to her mother's room. The Queen was humming to herself carefreely putting makeup on in front of her massive mirror.

"Before you ask, he likes perfumes from Uruk best." Beatrix didn't even turn around but kept applying the makeup Chaos liked.

"How long? Were you doing it before Heidi or just copying her shtick?" Norne asked furiously.

"Does it matter either way? Your monopoly on the beast has never existed. The best way to control him is with the one thing you won't do. It's only natural someone else would come from that angle," Beatrix explained after putting her makeup kit away.

"Heidi has the right idea, even if she's too stupid to appreciate what she's stumbled upon. Chaos is poised to swallow the Universe in his conquest. Korova knew what to do when Typhon took over. Any good Queen does. In this society that is how you survive and thrive but you're too much of a child, even now. You lack the skill to pursue things to their natural conclusion so forgive me for stepping up to that," Beatrix coldly said.

Norne was furious and matched icy death glares with her mother.

"I'll be taking your puppet. Sorry not sorry." Beatrix patronizingly patted her on the head before walking out.

"Why you!" Norne began.

"Always dealing with Chaos directly can get a bit exhausting so forgive me for opting to hold the strings of a puppeteer for convenience. You turned out far more useful than Heidi so be proud, parents do have favorites after all." Beatrix maneuvered her fingers as if she were literally pulling Norne's strings.

"You—those letters about removing distractions—about Cy—and those guards who somehow knew where I would be after killing Sargon. All of that was you, wasn't it? You planned even that?" Norne confronted her.

"When it was taking you so long to finish off that old fart, I worried you were holding off for her sake. There I'll admit I underestimated you. But either way...she was just a distraction. You don't need 'friends' to do what I have planned for you. You're better off without her." Beatrix grinned patronizingly.

Norne's surprise turned to fury, but Beatrix just smiled in her phony motherly way. "There's the door. I have some final prep to do if you don't mind my little puppet." She grinned at Norne.

CHAPTER 23

After speaking with her mother, Norne lay in bed looking up at the ceiling, thinking about everything.

"This is all such a pain. I need to sleep and then think about this later. Chaos will be back soon and—" Norne's thoughts raced.

Suddenly two soldiers broke into her room and yelled, "Princess Norne! His Majesty, the king has summoned you for an immediate audience!" the soldiers ordered.

A tired and ticked Norne sat up and gave them the look of death. Shortly after, she entered the throne room where her father Otto sat on the throne.

Norne was still angry, but her mother and sister were passive and bored despite Otto's continued instability.

"Otto, can we hurry this up, dear? I have much prayer and meditation to attend to as head priestess so I must retire as well." The Queen phonily smiled.

"Yeah, dad and the baby is finally asleep… I need the night off." Heidi waved while turning to leave.

"I have no excuse. I'm just tired." Norne pushed her irritation down enough but in its absence, her boredom and contempt showed through as she coldly turned to leave as well.

Otto was furious.

JAIDEN BAYNES

"I am the patriarch of this household, and you will respect me!" he shrieked. His flaccid demand fell on deaf ears.

The room was filled with silence.

"I am the *King* of Arcosia, but no one is talking to me! When Chaos returns later today his celebration is done by *my* charity. Your neglect of the respect of the host is contemptible! Remember who is in charge here!" Otto screamed.

None of the women responded and Otto saw Heidi roll her eyes. Otto became furious.

"Heidi! You rebellious child, *come here!*" he screamed.

"I'm really not in the mood. How about this, we can talk after Chaos' return party." Heidi smirked slyly.

"Oh, dear there is no need to be so cruel. Go talk with your father." Beatrix smiled.

"Beatrix...why don't we talk as well. What do you say you forgo work and take the night off with me, like the old days?" Otto grinned.

Beatrix lost her grin. Norne took notice—she *never* dropped her guise around Otto.

"My beloved wife...you have been lacking in your marital duties and as your king...and as your *husband*, I request your services. What possible reason could you have to object?" Otto was visibly shaking now.

Beatrix sighed audibly before turning to Norne.

"Norne, wasn't there anything you wanted to tell your father? It has been a great many years since—" she began to try and pivot.

"Answer me, girl! No more dancing around it or playing games! Let's talk!" Otto stood up.

Beatrix gave him an icy glare of death that was easily a match for Norne's. Anyone who thought Norne got it from her father would be set straight by the sudden chill Otto felt down his spine when facing Beatrix.

"Stop talking around me—all of you. Out with it, what is going on? Have you forgotten that I am your King and not that foreign ape-man!?" Otto yelled, trying to maintain control of the conversation.

"Right…right…of course, dad. You're in charge now can we please go back to—" Heidi yawned until her mother interrupted.

"No dear, don't bother. He's far too stupid to be worth it anyway," she plainly said out loud to everyone's shock.

"Would you care to repeat yourself, woman?" Otto asked.

"Fine. You wanted to talk openly so here it is, and I'll use small words so you can follow along. Otto, your tenure as king is over. It is done. Finished. When Chaos returns today, he will kill you where you stand, assume the throne, and perform *your* marital duties infinitely better than you've ever been able to. Everyone will be glad that you are gone, the three of us included." Beatrix dropped her normal façade for a blunt, vulgar reality check for the emasculated king.

Norne and Heidi didn't even know what to say to that one.

"How long have you been planning this?" Otto asked.

"Since Typhon, the Destroyer appeared in Tartarus. I made preparations in case a superior force appeared here as well. Don't worry, all the setup is complete so your replacement will be orderly and painless. Those two were glorified thirst traps to lead the inevitable superman to me. Honestly, I was worried when the second turned out to be a girl as well, but it turned out fine enough and I couldn't bear any more, to be honest." Beatrix was uncharacteristically chatty in this situation.

"You were my wife for so long…did you ever love me?" Otto asked.

"Gods no. No offense but you are you. I have a couple of hours to go before I can finally be rid of you forever and I hope you know that I can't *wait*." Beatrix smiled ear to ear.

"How dare you! I am your king and—" Otto began to yell but Beatrix fearlessly interrupted him.

"If you lay a hand on me, the guards will seize you and kill you where you stand. The church? The crown? They're *mine*. So don't you forget it you useless, impotent, effete, manlet. Do I make myself clear? The punishment for harming the Queen of Arcosia is death," Beatrix warned him as her voice chilled his spine.

"I loved you. Beatrix, I don't understand—" Otto tried to earn some sympathy with tears starting to appear on the shattered man's face.

"Alright, let me use smaller words, pin brain. Ahem…why in Arcos' name would I waste my time with an imbecile when I am already queen? By god do you really think that you were the one running this disaster of a country while running around for your stupid wars? 'Your country.' The nerve! You couldn't lead children to a picnic, so sit down and be glad I didn't have you killed sooner." Beatrix's unfiltered shrieks at Otto shocked everyone, even Norne.

This very un-priestesslike priestess might as well have screamed, 'I killed Baldr' for good measure in this bridge burning of epic proportions.

"I could have you executed, you unfaithful *swine!*" Otto screamed back.

"Someone needs to work on his listening skills. Nobody respects you, especially since we all know you will be a red stain on the wall by the end of the day. Besides this entire castle's staff has worked for me long before Chaos even entered the picture, you impotent simpleton! Now shut up and let me get back to my private time in peace!" Beatrix shrieked to the point that she began losing her voice. Her vitriolic hatred came out after decades of masks and suppression.

Otto couldn't respond. As Beatrix massaged her throat and regained her voice, she concluded.

"Consider this our divorce. It was a long time coming— goodbye Otto." Beatrix coldly said.

"But—" Otto squeaked. Beatrix looked at him, wondering what he would say for himself.

"But divorce is a sin in Arcosianism. Arcos wouldn't allow his high priestess to sin," Otto said in almost a whisper.

"You're such an idiot." Beatrix sighed, almost in pain from talking to her own husband.

"I do love these family chats." Heidi tried to be funny with a quip.

"Shut up dear, the adults are talking. I've been waiting to do this since before you were born. Don't ruin this like you do everything else." Beatrix scowled at her daughter.

The room fell silent.

"What the Hel mom!" Heidi got defensive.

"Oh, save it. Anything you did well you got from me, and you are by far a failed protégé. But what can you expect when you have a brain as slow as your father's? Honestly, you proved more useless than Otto, so don't cross me." Beatrix continued her sharp-tongued outbursts. She sounded a lot like Norne.

"Oh yeah! I bet you used to say that about Norne until she fished in your newest in a long line of boyfriends!" Heidi yelled.

"From her infancy, she was smarter than you. Don't cross me or remember I can have you killed too. Chaos' devotion is to me but even without that, as stupid as he is, even he hates you," Beatrix snarled.

"Pfft. Just remember that Drakon Junior is upstairs." Heidi tried to give a comeback, but Beatrix just rolled her eyes.

"Gods I hate this family," Norne finally spoke and cursed them all out loud.

The room became silent. Everyone turned to face Norne.

"Hey Norne, did you hear mom? I think she said she was going to kill us off! We can't just sleep on that—those two old farts have been against us from the start! Come on, we're sisters, forever, right?" a worried Heidi had the gaul to say.

"Heidi, step off. I was in a mood at the time. Don't cross me and you get to live." Beatrix was calming down from her cathartic outburst.

"Oh! Because threatening to kill someone is just something that you do when you're in a mood?" Heidi cried.

Suddenly it clicked for Norne.

"I wish you were all dead," Norne said out loud as if she had a clarifying realization.

The room fell silent.

"What? You say the most random things Norne." Heidi nervously laughed.

"How cute, the puppet thinks she's still in control. That's my girl." Beatrix laughed, notably less nervously.

"Norne, come on…this is just a family argument. We get a little heated from time to time but—you love us—you love *me*, right? And you're close to Chaos, so in fact, you could probably convince him to spare your dear father, couldn't you?" Otto weaseled out a request.

"No. Since we're all taking the time to 'share,' I think I'll rather enjoy watching him kill you actually," Norne bluntly said.

Otto panicked! His emotions immediately turned to an outburst of fury, resuming the yelling.

"I never raised a hand to you!" Otto yelled.

"Congratulations for meeting the bare minimum!" Norne yelled back.

"Your mother is crafty, but your raw Power comes from me! The strength you wield in battle is inherited from a long line of Arcosian kings!" Otto reminded her.

"Thanks. But your Power is all I needed. You, I can live without, just how I lived without you until I was suddenly a useful pawn for you," Norne coldly said.

"Norne! It was harsh, but my raising you made you strong! Look where you are today!" Otto tried to turn things around. Beatrix scoffed.

"I guess you're right. All of you made me who I am. So, thanks all around. *You* have served your *purposes*." Norne stared Otto down.

"You would abandon your father to *die* at Chaos' hand!?" Otto yelled.

There was a long and tense silence. Heidi just played with her hair, having lost interest in the conversation while the Queen sadistically giggled to herself. Norne, completely stone-faced, simply pointed at the ground and said, "bow," in a demanding tone.

"I beg your pardon!" Otto cried.

Beatrix began audibly laughing.

"Stop beating around the bush for the sake of your inane pride. Do you want to be spared from Chaos' wrath? Bow before me and beg." Norne grinned.

Otto was hesitant, but surprisingly quickly, descended to the ground and bowed before Norne. "You can control that monster… please don't let him kill me," Otto begged through clenched teeth.

"I dunno, you don't sound grateful enough. If you truly want me to save you—renounce your god, to my face," Norne demanded coldly.

"What!" Otto cried.

"You came to me for help so it's all but said out loud. Tell me plainly that the giant chunk of rock in the sky is just that. A moon is a moon, not a deity. You want to live, you pray to *me* not the rock." Norne looked down on her father.

"I—forgive me Ar—" Otto began.

"Do not call its name. Space rocks cannot forgive you. Know it, you know it—now say it." Norne became impatient.

"I…renounce Arcos god of the moon. He can't protect me from Chaos—but you can—so do it!" Otto angrily said.

"Good. Chaos will not lay a hand on you." Norne grinned. In a flash though, she grabbed her father by the throat and held him to the ground.

Heidi and the Queen gasped.

"I will kill you all before he even returns." Norne insanely grinned. Otto's eyes widened; he was going to die.

With a vicious jolt, Norne palm struck the base of the blade to force the knife through King Otto's skull, killing him instantly. The other two women froze in disbelief.

"It is surprisingly easy to kill Immortals. After all, none of you are gods either." Norne stood up, retrieved the knife from her father's corpse and stared at Heidi next.

"Get back! She can freeze you if she makes contact!" Beatrix grabbed Heidi by the arm and jumped back to put some distance between them and Norne.

Norne threw her knife but instead of blocking it, Beatrix leaned out of the way, making sure to not even touch it!

"Mother! That's right—you're the only one I ever told the secret of my ability. However, in exchange remember you had also taught me Charles' Law!" Norne grinned.

"Ha! Charles' Law? What a lame attack name—" Heidi childishly began to mock her, but her mother angrily stopped her.

"Shut up Heidi! We need to focus on surviving!" Beatrix showed her true side while dashing for the exit of the throne room with Heidi in tow.

Suddenly, Norne's Power began emanating from her in a large sphere. Beatrix knew she couldn't freeze anything at a distance, so she initially thought this freeze attack spread was a bluff.

However, she had a sudden realization. "Charles' Law?" she asked out loud.

Norne's icy Power suddenly cooled the area around her and created a powerful suction towards her, not just of air and things in the room but also the Power in the air.

Beatrix was horrified, first her escape slowed down but suddenly she began flying back towards Norne at an even faster speed.

"Mom what are we going to do!" Heidi shrieked.

Without a word, Beatrix immediately threw Heidi at Norne to save herself, making her daughter shriek even louder. Heidi screamed bloody murder as if she had food on her face at a public event. But all the screaming in the world couldn't save her as she quickly made her way to Norne.

Norne caught her sister, grabbing around her mouth with one hand and covering her own with the other before freezing Heidi solid.

Unphased, Beatrix desperately looked for a way out. While she was distracted though, the knife that Norne threw past her before stabbed Beatrix in the back making her lose balance. Norne grinned, increasing the suction inwards which drew her mother in.

Beatrix panicked as the knife and suction brought her right to Norne who floated in the air and grabbed her by the throat.

"So, mother—how am I so 'predictable' and 'childish' now? I'm about to kill you!" Norne cackled like a madwoman.

"Do not conflate…a deviation from my programming with autonomy. My teachings are embedded into you deeper than you'll ever know. Anything you ever think or do is something I put in that skull of yours!" the Queen screamed at Norne.

Norne didn't react and only coldly stared at her. And that glare was Norne's response. The Queen grew fearful as Norne grinned. "If you're quite done," she said before instantly freezing her solid.

Norne dropped the statue onto the ground but as she stared at the frozen queen's face, she couldn't help but think, "what if this too is only something she wanted me to do." Norne's eyes widened.

Incensed by her inability to escape them even in death, Norne waved her hand and froze the entire throne room solid.

"See that…for the record, I have significantly improved the distance of my ability. I did that! My genius and practice let me cover further distance than I ever reported to you! I could have killed you the second you stepped into this room! You don't know me!" Norne shrieked while stomping her frozen mother into pieces.

After panting for breath after the emotional outburst, Norne couldn't help but smile and look up at the empty throne.

Walking up to it with a cackle, Norne grinned. "Chaos was right…that did feel good." She sat on the Arcosian throne.

Blame the mother. That was the go-to conclusion many would arrive at. It was easy and societally accepted to do so. Especially since stepping back and critiquing what kind of society could produce such outcomes was far more uncomfortable. But the fact that Norne's parents treated her as theirs had treated them and so on certainly begged the question as to if all societal woes could so easily be pinned on single bad individuals.

No matter the cause, this was the result—Queen Norne von Arcosia now stood alone as supreme ruler of Eurasia; she had cannibalized her peers and allies to gain dominion over the entire known Universe. If given the chance, any of them would have done the same. That was the nature of Empires.

Shortly after things cooled down in the throne room, the knights of Arcosia entered and bowed before Norne.

"Clearly you weren't all that attached to my mother. It really is just whoever wears the crown, isn't it? First my father, then my mother as well. Will you try to betray me next?" Norne sat upon the throne with her feet resting on the frozen head of her father, his crown ripped now sitting on her own head.

"We live to serve the crown," the Arcosian knights simply replied.

"Fair enough. Prove your loyalty to me. Arcos is dead. From now on anyone who worships that moon god will be put to the sword. Kill any heathens who worship anything in this Universe other than the god Emperor Drakon of Chaos. May your loyalty be drawn in their blood! Go forth now and purge the heathens from *my* country," Norne ordered them.

Chaos was due to arrive a little after noon. By the time daylight was fully overhead, the capital city's population was decimated. Any remainders of the clergy, young and old were put into large heaps and burned in the town square.

As the Norne genocide continued, finally the old Head Priest of Arcosia's temple of the moon revealed himself. He was now the highest authority in the Arcosian religion given Beatrix's death. However, his entrance was quiet and understated, humbly groveling before the new Queen.

Norne for her part still sat upon the throne, reading a favorite Arcosian writer of hers, Nietzsche. A writer whom she would still insist she understood.

"You came out yourself. Oh good." Norne stood up, crushing Otto's frozen head underfoot as she did.

"I do not know what possessed you to do this Lady Norne—but demon witch of ice—I offer myself to you. Please, if there is any goodness in your heart, take my life as a tribute and spare the other children of Arcos." He got on his knees and bowed to her.

"Oh, a martyr complex. That's a new one. Do you think your life will be enough to sate my—my desire for death? *Or* do you think your sacrifice will call upon some miracle? Either way, you arrogant old goat, your pride is worse than my own." She walked over to him.

The priest shook in fear as she approached, however, she walked past him leaving him unharmed. He was shocked and turned around to watch her observing the slaughter.

"Come watch the death with me. If you wish your death to be more meaningful than others then know once you have sufficiently despaired, I may be fully pleased in killing you," Norne heartlessly said.

He walked over and asked, "then…will your great wrath subside?"

"No," Norne said, devoid of emotion in her voice. It hadn't been long, but even if she didn't want to admit it, she already found that the violence inflicted on her family did not make her truly happy. It seemed that nothing did.

At this point, she had long lost any purpose in the killing. It was purely just to fill the time till Chaos arrived, fill her emptiness, whatever.

Right on schedule, Chaos arrived only to find Norne alone on the throne.

"Hey so…this time I was only gone a week and it looks like a tornado flew through here," Chaos said when he saw her.

Norne only smiled.

Shortly thereafter, the survivors of the culling were being assembled in the town square. As they were shuffled into place for the address, they saw the desolation and destruction around them, doing their best not to see it.

The Head Arcos priest was hung in the square, the Nornes and lesser priests both young and old with him. Those who did not renounce the moon in this snap inquisition were cut to pieces and the blood of children who clutched their familial religious ornaments ran through the streets. Statues and monuments to Otto and his family were obliterated and the holy relics were smashed and destroyed.

In Arcosia, there were paintings and art depicting all manners of Hels. As she waited for the gathering to finish, Norne looked up at one while Chaos sat on the ground, bored out of his mind. Holdovers from the old pagan worship that the immigrants had sung on their way to Arcosia mixed with the new ideas of Arcosianism to form the modern concept of Hel; people suffering all kinds of torture for their degeneracy. In the texts, it was always so surreal and nonspecific—otherworldly and unimaginable. But when people cast their mind to an idea of Hel to put it on a canvas, they could only ever depict something like real life. The catch was that after all the suffering, they were forced to live through it. That was the only way Norne imagined human suffering could ever be compounded, to make it drag on longer than was the limit of any form of cruelty.

In older tales, Hel the place had a mistress of the same name. Hel, the goddess of death in her frozen prison ensured everyone around her was just as miserable as she was. If she had to exist in such a miserable place, then as their ruler everyone else did as well.

Now, all that was left was to seize this world and remake it in her own image. Norne smiled as she heard the metallic footsteps of a soldier approaching.

"Is everything ready?" she asked without turning around.

"The people are assembled, my Queen." An Arcosian knight bowed to her.

"It's about time." Chaos stood up excitedly.

Chaos and Norne dramatically walked onto a makeshift stage that loomed above the assembled survivors. Soldiers of both Arcosia and Tartarus manned the perimeter, standing attention in a coordinated salute. Chaos on the left had his Imperial Knights saluting him on the left stage and Norne strode forth on the right with her Arcosian soldiers allocated accordingly.

"I am Queen Norne of Arcosia," Norne began her declaration. The people were silent.

"But I am also, an agent of the glorious Tartarian Empire. To ease in the administration of two separate nations, a marriage is in order. The Holy Arcosian Kingdom shall be reorganized into a territory of the Tartarian Empire. As peers—as friends and allies we are joining with them all today," Norne continued.

The crowd was silent. They didn't care who was calling the shots, they just wanted to survive this.

"Arcosia is now under my decree, a Province of the Tartarus Empire. The old is dead. The only god Arcosia needs is...your new Emperor! Drakon of Chaos!" Norne presented him.

He leaped into the air, no into space!

The crowd was awed by his unreasonable feat of strength. Norne grinned as the spectacle was going as planned, but Chaos just kept flying up.

"Wh—what is he doing!" Norne began to panic.

Chaos excitedly whooped in the air before rearing his fist back and at ludicrous speed, punched Arcosia's moon, shattering it into pieces.

The crowd assembled in the capital cheered. Norne's eyes widened at the dazzling spectacle. She couldn't explain why but she was left speechless and felt liberated by the destruction of that oppressive symbol. It too would fade, but at this moment, having tied up all loose ends, Norne was the happiest she had ever been in her life. Finally, the sun shone on Arcosia, and the crowd's applause grew even louder.

Chaos dramatically landed in a ball of fire that shook the city. When the dust cleared, he confidently stood on the stage, holding Norne close to him with one arm.

"I'm the one and only god you'll ever need!" he thunderously announced while triumphantly raising his fist in the air.

And so, Chaos was Emperor of all nations in the known Universe.

At the end of the day, outside the Arcosian royal palace, Norne and Chaos stood by the swing facing the planet's beautiful first sunset as Norne pushed the infant, Drakon Junior. Chaos was completely bored and busy looking up at the clouds.

"Do you want to take a turn pushing him, Chaos?" Norne asked, trying to role-play as a family now.

"Are we done yet?" Chaos impatiently asked.

"We can be…you're not interested at all?" Norne asked.

"Meh, not really. Kind of just figured Heidi would take care of it. All the fun parts are over so it's not important," Chaos said.

"Oh." Norne realized and immediately dropped the act, not bothering to catch the baby's swing.

"Well…y'know the offer still stands for…us to try some of the fu—" Norne began propositioning only for an Imperial Knight to run out.

"Lady Norne! It's an emergency, revolt in Arcosia from the zealots hidden within our own ranks there! Just as you feared, they've almost captured the outskirts to trap us here in the capital! The zealots have placed us under siege," the knight cried.

"Of course. I'll be back late. Don't forget the kid in the swing." Norne got up and followed the guard to deal with the problem.

"Kay." Chaos said without listening.

Chaos sat on the hill for a few seconds, looking at the sunset before spying a group of young noble ladies passing through the winter garden.

"Score!" Chaos cheered and excitedly stood up and ran over to say hello.

Drakon Junior was left in the swing alone all night. Neither had time for useless things.

Norne personally led the suppression of the rebels and slew them all without restraint. They were not going to ruin her day.

Only a few hours later, out in the Arcosian wastes, as a blizzard fell from the insanely frosty weather, Norne and Chaos were in the same field they had first sparred in when they came to Arcosia.

After being thrown back, Chaos lay in the snow, coughing up blood as four ice copies of Norne held down each of his limbs. Too tired to sit up, he just focused on getting his breathing under control after exhaustion. As he stopped coughing though, Chaos noticed each of the ice copies melting into more compact ice blocks before freezing solid again and pinning Chaos to the ground.

Now, even when he scrambled in a panic, Chaos couldn't move even if he wanted to. Then Norne's foot came down on his throat. Ice began spreading from her heel as he gagged.! Norne looked down with a sadistic grin at the panicked Emperor.

"What's wrong Chaos? I thought you enjoyed fights with my ice puppets?" She grinned as she pressed her foot down harder.

"I—I thought you were happy to see me!" Chaos managed to squeak out through the pain.

"I am. I'm having a *very* good day. And us getting to fight like the old days…really gets my blood pumping." Norne smiled at him with deceptively warm and genuine happiness.

"Fight's over! You won! Now breathing please!" Chaos desperately tried to free his arms so he could get her off his neck.

"What was that? I couldn't hear you?" Norne mockingly said.

"You won! Uncle! You're killing me here!" Chaos cried as loud as he could, given the circumstance.

"Alright." Norne took her foot off him and with the wave of her hand melted the ice off his limbs. He sat up, gagging and holding his throat in pain. As he did, Norne rather inappropriately snuggled up next to him as if this were some sort of romantic engagement.

"You're a crazy woman!" Chaos turned to her as the soreness subsided.

"I know." Norne kissed his neck to 'make it better.'

"What happened while I was gone?" Chaos asked after a stunned silence, confused by her behavior.

"Killed my family earlier. Then I got bored. But now that you're back... I'm feeling better again," Norne said as she leaned on his arm.

"Neat. That always cheers me up too." Chaos laughed.

"Tied up all loose ends, secured our Empire, and beat the pants off the strongest man in the Universe...things are looking up for me now." She smiled.

"No need to keep rubbing it in! You're just on a high horse because you won this time. I remember last time when I broke your arm you were crying like a little baby! You just dish it out but can never take it." Chaos puffed his cheeks out in embarrassment from Norne's teasing.

"That's different. I am a refined lady. In a fight, I kill my opponent before they have the chance to even hit me. You're the one who needs to take it and dish it out." Norne scoffed, deflecting the insult.

"Whatever. You don't need to laugh though... I mean, whenever I beat you up in a fight, afterward I get this weird feeling like... like I feel like *I'm* hurt. Not physically but like one of my favorite things broke or when my feelings get hurt. I can't explain it," Chaos stumbled his way through trying to understand sympathy.

"Who knows. You're a weirdo." Norne shrugged.

"I'm gonna go Monster hunting. You're mean." Chaos huffed and stood up.

Norne panicked, she'd just gotten him back and she wanted to spend time with him. After all that work, this was what it was leading to. Now she could get her man, just like her mother wanted—wait.

"Damnit!" Norne screamed.

Chaos was startled by Norne's sudden outburst.

"Are you okay?" Chaos hesitantly approached her.

"I'm fine." Norne calmed herself down.

Looking up at the worried Chaos, Norne hesitated. All the books said this was where a dramatic confession would come in but...her mother was the one insistent on that. Now Norne was second-guessing herself, was that what she wanted too? Would the rest of her life simply see her as the next avatar of her mother's will—nay Imperialism's will?

"Chaos!" Norne stood up dramatically which startled him again. "No time to waste! We have a Universe to conquer, remember?" she declared.

"Yeah!" Chaos cheered.

"We will go out and conquer yet unknown lands! We will take all we desire and subjugate everything for ourselves! We will grow infinitely and seize the riches of this world only for the two of us!" Norne cried.

"Yeah!" Chaos applauded.

"We will have it all and then we will finally, *finally* grasp happiness!" Norne announced.

That was the nature of Empire.

CPSIA information can be obtained
at www.ICGtesting.com
Printed in the USA
BVHW041502131122
651758BV00038B/250